Praise for National Bestselling Author L. A. Chandlar's
Art Deco Mystery series

"Engaging, vivid, and intriguing, this historical mystery is
not only a fascinating behind-the-scenes of Fiorello La
Guardia's New York, but an action-packed adventure with
quirky characters, snappy dialogue, a hint of romance—and
starring one of the pluckiest, most entertaining heroines ever."
—Hank Phillippi Ryan, national bestselling
author of *Trust Me,* on *The Gold Pawn*

"Chandlar does a good job of evoking the period."
—*Publishers Weekly* on *The Silver Gun*

"Dangerous villains and gangsters in 1930s NYC, with humor,
history, vintage cocktails, and art as a backbone . . ."
—Jen J. Danna

"*The Silver Gun* has humor, excitement, mystery, danger,
romance, lots of great characters, and more! I highly
recommend *The Silver Gun,* especially to those who live,
work, or vacation in the Big Apple, and to cozy readers
who like their mystery mixed with history."
—*Jane Reads,* 5 Stars

"[*The Silver Gun*] was just phenomenal . . . I
absolutely loved this book and HIGHLY recommend
it to anyone who is a mystery lover."
—*Valerie's Musings,* 5 stars

Also by L. A. Chandlar

The Gold Pawn

The Silver Gun

Published by Kensington Publishing Corporation

THE
PEARL
DAGGER

L. A. CHANDLAR

KENSINGTON BOOKS
www.kensingtonbooks.com

KENSINGTON BOOKS are published by

Kensington Publishing Corp.
119 West 40th Street
New York, NY 10018

All Kensington titles, imprints, and distributed lines are available at special quantity discounts for bulk purchases for sales promotion, premiums, fund-raising, educational, or institutional use.

Special book excerpts or customized printings can also be created to fit specific needs. For details, write or phone the office of the Kensington Sales Manager: Kensington Publishing Corp., 119 West 40th Street, New York, NY 10018. Attn. Sales Department. Phone: 1-800-221-2647.

Kensington and the K logo Reg. U.S. Pat. & TM Off.

ISBN-13: 978-1-4967-1346-9 (ebook)
ISBN-10: 1-4967-1346-X (ebook)
Kensington Electronic Edition: September 2019

ISBN-13: 978-1-4967-1345-2
ISBN-10: 1-4967-1345-1
First Kensington Trade Paperback Edition: September 2019

10 9 8 7 6 5 4 3 2 1

Printed in the United States of America

For the artists
Who make the world a bigger and better place.
Especially for you, Destinee and Kellye

For the artists
Who make the world a bigger and better place.
Especially for you, Destinee and Kellye

ACKNOWLEDGMENTS

The mystery reader and writer community is unbelievably encouraging and generous. I want to say a special thank you to my editor, Esi Sogah, for your endless enthusiasm and wisdom. The marketing team with Vida Engstrand and Larissa Ackerman has been such a joy to work with. My production and editing team of Paula Reedy and Carly Sommerstein make editing actually enjoyable—I know: amazing! And the cover art director Kristine Noble has done just sublime work making the Art Deco Mystery Series truly beautiful. Thank you to Jill Grosjean for working through this wonderful book deal with me. And there are countless authors who have taken the time to be interested and kind to a newbie. You have no idea how your acts of generosity have impacted me and I'll never forget it. Special thanks to Jen Danna, James Ziskin, Adam Hamdy, Alyssa Maxwell, Eric Bishop, Mariah Fredericks, Kellye Garrett, Charles Todd, and Hank Phillippi Ryan.

A big thank you to my husband and Number One research assistant and tech guru. I love that you know just how important my characters are to me and how you search high and low for the coolest books and photos! You're amazing, Bryan, thank you. And for Jack and Logan, my biggest fans and very, very tall sons. I am so grateful to get to be your mom.

I also want to give special thanks to Jamie Tulenko for finding an incredible signed book and letters from Fiorello! And to Don Wilson for lending me (and I really gave it back!) his amazing book on Winston Churchill that helped immensely for this novel.

Thank you so much to my agent, Paula Munier, with Talcott Notch, for believing in me, sharing my love of martinis, and, most of all, for sharing your wisdom and your love of art and life with me.

Lastly, dear reader, I can't thank you enough for caring about this era, for loving these incredible real people as well as my fictional friends, and for enjoying the adventure with me. I am so grateful to get to share this different side to the thirties that is often overshadowed by the Depression. I hope the vitality, the humor, the artfulness (the cocktails!), and the joie de vivre that Fiorello La Guardia truly exemplified helps you soak up and enjoy life even more. Cheers!

By the pricking of my thumbs, something wicked this way comes . . .
—the second witch, *Macbeth*

PROLOGUE

The day was full of changes. The light from the sun alternating from bright gold with a brilliance that hurt your eyes, to a dull gray as the thick white clouds raced across the azure sky.

Chunk. He started with a jolt. "Charlotte! I taught you better than that," he said with his usual gruff demeanor.

Charlie flicked her long auburn hair over her shoulder in a care-free motion. She turned her dazzling green eyes to him and said, "I wondered what would get your attention."

"Why—You did that on purpose," he groused as he walked over to the large wooden target, gathering the knives and, lastly, the dagger from much higher up. It had lodged in a branch almost six feet to the left of the trunk, *much closer* to where he'd been standing, in fact.

"What's on your mind, Kirkland?" she asked, looking closely at him. He could feel her scrutiny and tried to look insouciant. She was really good at reading him.

Didn't work, damn it. He looked at her and her eyebrow cocked skeptically as she put her hand on her hip, basically telling him that he didn't come close to fooling her.

"Grrrrr."

She laughed. "Spit it out, Kirkland. And hand me those knives. You can talk while I practice."

He shook his head as he watched her capable hands carefully

take the knives and that one special dagger, Matthew's mother-of-pearl and ebony knife, and begin to throw with uncanny precision.

Chunk. The first knife hit about an inch above the bull's-eye.

"Well. Here goes. I'm glad you, Matthew, and Laney have come here to Rochester, safe and sound. And I am even more glad that we finally got Rex. But . . ."

Chunk. The next knife hit at three o'clock, about an inch outside the bull's-eye.

Putting his hands in his pockets and shaking his head pensively, he said, "I just can't help but feel that we might not be done. It feels like the Red Scroll Network will keep on going, despite Rex. I know it sounds ridiculous."

Chunk. Six o'clock.

Charlotte turned to him, weighing the remaining knives in her hand. "No. It doesn't sound ridiculous. I've had similar thoughts."

"You have?"

Chunk. Nine o'clock.

"Yes. Matthew and I have talked about it, too. But we've done the best we can. When we changed our plans . . ." She had been about to say something, but then petered out, like she'd caught herself. He, too, was a keen observer and her eyes shot to him trying to assess if he'd caught that misstep.

Chunk. She missed. Her last throwing knife missed the mark.

"Damn it."

"What do you mean, Charlotte? Changed plans?" he asked.

She quickly recovered even though the accuracy of her throw had suffered. "You know. Moving here instead of continuing on in our work."

He wasn't completely convinced, but sure, he'd go with it. "Well, yeah, it will be hard to find you here. I'm sure we'll be okay."

Chunk. The final throw—the pearl dagger—and it hit right in the middle of the bull's-eye.

"Show-off."

Charlotte chuckled her low laugh as she slowly sauntered to the tree. She started to methodically dislodge the knives, her petal pink feminine dress in complete juxtaposition to her knife-throwing talent. She took a deep breath and he watched her shoulders rise and then settle as she turned to him with a contemplative look on her beautiful face.

"You feel pretty certain the Network might continue on?" she asked.

"I just think that Rex would go to great lengths to have his legacy continue beyond the grave. The bastard loved toying with everyone. The ultimate game would be to have it go on. Even when he didn't."

She put her hand on her hip and nodded slowly. "Hmm. Yes, you may be right." She put her hand on the ebony handle of the dagger, its mother-of-pearl scrollwork glistening in the sunshine. She pulled hard on the handle, dislodging it from its perfect landing place. Something made her shiver despite the warmth of the day.

Charlotte walked toward him weighing the satisfying handle in her hand, feeling its worth, weighing its mettle. She nodded, having come to some sort of decision.

"Kirkland." She nodded curtly to the dagger. She deftly threw it with a light hand and a good arc, so he could catch it easily as they'd practiced a hundred times.

"Here. You're gonna need this."

She turned smartly around and walked into the house.

CHAPTER 1

Who knew pinball machines could set off such an explosive development?

"Lane, I've got a lead for us," said Roarke.

Roarke Channing was a top-notch investigative reporter and he also happened to be my sleuthing partner. When possible threats or the odd piece of curious information came through the grapevine at work—New York City's 1937 mayoral offices—Roarke and I would investigate.

He continued after a quick sip of his espresso, "I think that given the nature of the rumblings on the street, we need to follow up on it."

He sat across from me in a little French café off York Avenue. Roarke wore his signature wide pinstripe suit with his crisp white shirt, wide red tie, and fedora with a matching red ribbon. I grasped a cup of cappuccino in my cold hands as I soaked in the warmth of a glowing fireplace. The café was a little slice of Europe, with the kind of casual elegance that only the French seemed to achieve effortlessly. A little ripple of joy went through me as I breathed in the scent of coffee and cream.

"I agree. If only for the fact that those gangs are notorious for following through on their threats," I said.

"Exactly. When Fiorello got rid of thousands of those slot machines from the delis, he also targeted the pinball machines. They fell through the cracks at first, but now he's set his sights on them to finish the purge. And as we've already seen, that makes Fio a target."

Mayor Fiorello La Guardia, New York's ninety-ninth mayor, was my boss and dear family friend. The little dynamo was fearless against the criminal gangs that had taken shape during Prohibition. When Fio took office just after Prohibition ended, he went to work. Ousting corruption, bringing health care and low-income housing to a desperate city, a whole fleet of public pools and parks, the first public arts high school . . . all accomplished with the panache and joie de vivre of the finest ringmaster.

I set my cup down and rested my chin in my hand. "So, to sum it up, you and our sources at the NYPD have intercepted increased agitation against the mayor. What about Uncle Louie Venetti? He hasn't been as active on that scene, having most of his slot machines thrown onto barges and dumped. He's been working in other arenas, right? So do you think that these rumblings are other gangs vying for control?"

"I think that's definitely possible and I can't tell who's working with who. It's all been vaguely threatening, like bar talk and an occasional intimidating note. But you know, Fio gets those all the time. So it's hard to decipher what's an actual threat," said Roarke, thinking it through.

"Absolutely. He gets that kind of mail a couple of times a week. But he gets ten times more notes that are encouraging and grateful. I think it's all those petitioners he listens to every single day. Fio really does take note of their concerns and they never forget it." I finished my cappuccino and set my napkin on the table. "So what's this lead you have?"

"Okay. So, an informant of mine has been running messages for different groups of, let's just say, a less than savory type of crowd. He doesn't ever look at the messages, not because of any moral high ground, but because the less he knows, the safer he is." I nodded. Made sense to me.

Roarke went on, warming to the subject. "The way it works is he receives a note by messenger that it's time. He has a pickup place where he gets the message and directions on where to take it, so he's never seen the person who is sending the messages. This morning, he caught a glimpse of a note when he dropped it inadvertently. He quickly grabbed it up off the sidewalk but the words *mayor* and *get him out of the way* definitely got his attention."

"I bet," I said, eyes wide with appreciation.

"Yeah. So he read the whole thing and started sweatin' bullets and sent me word right away. Usually he does a dead drop for the messages, so he never sees the recipient. But today, I guess there were too many ways for the message to get into the wrong hands because he has direct orders to hand it to a particular person. He gave me the time and place. I want to see just who this message is for."

"Yeah, we definitely need to see who it is. But, uh . . . where exactly is it all going down?" I asked a bit warily since we had gotten into many debacles on our past sleuthing sprees.

"Oh, don't worry about it, Lane." Roarke chuckled. "It's an easy one. It's smack in the middle of Grand Central Station."

I breathed a sigh of relief. For once it wasn't in an unsavory, dark, and dangerous location. "Great! I'll meet you after work and let's check it out."

Eight hours later I was running away from bad guys down a busy thoroughfare in my high-heeled, red Mary Janes. Again.

"Roarke! Honestly. This must stop," I said between gasps of air.

He chuckled.

"You're *laughing?*" My sides hurt. I twisted my ankle a ways back, scuffing the side of my left shoe. My blouse had begun to untuck itself from my vigorous running. Roarke looked impeccable. *Bastard.*

We were in pursuit of information, and we found it. But we also found trouble. As usual. Roarke's informant did in fact make a drop at the exact time and place he'd given us. He stood by the famous brass clock in Grand Central and I assumed he wore some kind of identifying article of clothing because the guy came directly to him without hesitation.

We recognized the recipient right away, a notorious gangster with the appellation the Crusher. Unfortunately, he had looked over at *us* right at that moment and started toward us. Which led to the running and the panting. We darted up a stairway to the walkways behind the large windows in the Great Hall. From below, you could always see the forms of people walking to and fro. We went right to the top, as far as we could go.

Roarke dashed around a corner and I could still hear our pursuer's footsteps clacking down the marble hallway, but at least they weren't right behind us.

"Roarke, here! I have an idea." His dimples came out as his golden-brown eyes darted to the doors I was trying one at a time.

The third door finally opened. We quickly went in and softly closed the door behind us, but the lock wouldn't slide. We looked around at the small room as I tucked my blouse back in. I stared daggers at Roarke; he hadn't even broken a sweat. I was probably red as a beet.

"What?" he whispered.

"Nothing," I whispered back with an annoyed grunt.

Steps click-clacked down the hall. We both stepped backward, then turned around. There just wasn't anywhere to hide and nothing to use as a weapon. The oval window was about six feet tall. I noticed that it tipped out from the bottom as the steps sounded just outside our door.

"Oh no," whispered Roarke.

I shook my head disgustedly; I couldn't believe it was coming to this. *Of course it's coming to this.* I grasped the pearl dagger I had in the wide belt of my black skirt and used the point to tip out the window.

"I didn't think it'd get this far," said Roarke.

"It always gets this far," I groused as I carefully put the dagger back in my scabbard and crawled out the window onto the carved ledge, shifting to the far side. I curled up in a tight knot, bringing my knees to my chest. Roarke mirrored my cautious motions, shuffling to the opposite side to get out of the view of the window. I tipped the window back down as far as it would go, keeping a hand in a small crevice to be able to open it again. We were curled up on a ten-foot-deep, sturdy ledge up against the frigid outside wall of Grand Central Terminal. But when the other side of the deep ledge was over a several-hundred-foot drop to the streets of New York City, it seemed very insubstantial indeed.

"Don't look down," he said.

"I always look down."

Far below us was Vanderbilt Avenue and 42nd Street. The lights of the cars snaked along the busy dark streets. The ever-present horns honked with the occasional siren in the distance and the hum of thousands of conversations were all part of the invigorating sounds of a city that never sleeps. At least in the darkness of that early night in January, no one would see us from below and start a scene. Hopefully. My breath made puffs of air in the cold black night. My teeth started to chatter.

A crack of light pierced the dark room. The door inside opened; neither of us moved, holding our breath. With the camouflage of the night, and the fact that we had both gone as far as possible to the edges on either side of the window, not to mention you'd have to be crazy to crawl outside, I hoped we would be invisible.

A beam of light flashed around the window.

"I think they got away," said Roarke's informant.

"Yeah. They're not in here, we scared them off," said the tinny voice of the Crusher. "We have the plan to get the mitney, let's go."

The bright light moved slowly around the oval, double-checking the window, and then the door closed with a loud click.

We finally let out that breath.

We waited just a few moments longer, but we couldn't take much more of the cold nor the height. I slowly tipped the window back up and scooted over, climbing carefully back into the warm room. Roarke joined me and put a hand on my arm.

He asked softly, "You okay?"

"Yeah. You?"

"Yes, but I could handle an outing with you that didn't end in us dangling from a deadly height."

I was so indignant at his remark that smacked of the pot calling the kettle black that I sputtered indignantly, making his dimples appear.

I finally managed, "Shut up, Roarke."

"That was a close one."

"Ahhh . . . let's keep the dangling out the window part on the down-low to Finn. And Fio. And Valerie," I said as we walked down several flights of stairs then toward a long ramp leading to an exit.

"Definitely." Roarke lit up a cigarette as we cautiously left Grand Central Station at a corner doorway along Vanderbilt and 42nd. I looked up to see if I could view the window we'd just been crouching in, way up near the roofline. I spotted it and shivered.

I sized up that cigarette of Roarke's even though I hardly ever smoke. "Hand me that." I took a small drag. Just seemed necessary. My hand only shook a tiny bit.

As we walked, I ducked my chin down into my coat. The air was frosty, making us pick up the pace, trying to warm ourselves. "So, what did we learn?"

Roarke finished the cigarette and flicked it to the sidewalk. "Well? My informant was right. He gave the message to the one we recognized: the Crusher. On that thought, why do all the gangsters have nicknames? Machine Gun Kelly, Pretty Boy Floyd, Bumpy Johnson . . ."

"Yeah, why's he called the Crusher?" I asked.

"You don't want to know. I asked. I wish I hadn't. Just know that the name suits him, despite the fact that he's teeny tiny."

I shivered again. "Got it. By the way, what's the name of your informant?"

"Punchy."

"You've got to be kidding me," I said.

"Nope. You saw his face," he said with a sardonic laugh.

I gave it some thought. "Yeah. There's something about him that makes you want to punch him right off the bat."

Roarke nodded and said, "Exactly. He confirmed that there are rumblings with considerably dangerous people. And if Crusher is involved, he definitely has the ability to carry out the threat against Fio. And what or who is a mitney? I've never heard that term before."

I shook my head as I answered, "I'm not sure, either. And you're right. Punchy confirmed Crusher is behind it so we have to take it seriously. Which is strange, considering how silly that sentence just sounded." He took my arm and gently pulled me back a few feet at the curb as a car took the corner fast.

"Yeah. He doesn't mess around. But I can't believe what started all this!" he exclaimed exasperatedly.

I grinned as I said, "I know. Pinball. Talk about a deadly game."

CHAPTER 2

The next morning, Fio arrived at our house for his almost-daily breakfast with Aunt Evelyn, Mr. Kirkland, and myself. He never entered anywhere without a lot of hubbub. Ripley, our German shepherd, was sent into delirious barking when one of his favorite people barged in the front door bellowing, "Good morning!"

I quickly ran a red lipstick around my lips and secured a little red pillbox hat into place. It matched my red, Mary Jane high heels and I stopped to admire my ensemble in the long mirror by my bedroom door. I loved the brass buttons that ran up the back of my black dress, and my thin red belt matched my hat, shoes, and lips.

"Laney Lane, my girl!" bellowed my boss, the ninety-ninth mayor of New York City.

Grrrrrr, I thought. I went by Lane, just Lane. But that was our morning ritual, so I yelled happily down the stairs, "Coming!"

I ran to the dining table greeting my aunt, Evelyn Thorne, and our family friend, Mr. Kirkland. I stole a glance at Mr. Kirkland, who looked like a deep-sea fisherman but happened to be our household cook, butler, and gardener. Not to mention resident bodyguard and grandfather figure. He had also been a spy in the war, which made him wonderfully complicated. I shook my head as I thought to myself that he'd never been treated like a servant, really. But in my eccentric home, with my artistic aunt as the head, typical roles and assumptions went out the window. And she didn't care one tiny bit when tongues wagged about the actual relationship between her and Kirkland.

He'd made buttery biscuits this morning that we covered in honey he'd collected last summer from the beehives he kept on our roof. It was divine as it went perfectly with a hot cup of coffee.

Fiorello La Guardia was New York City's firecracker mayor and I was his trusted aide. I had secretarial duties, but I also handled press releases, organized events, and attended meetings that he wanted my thoughts on or needed me to transcribe.

While we ate, I filled them in on our news from Grand Central. I conveniently left out the part about running for our lives.

Fio said, "So you witnessed Roarke's informant—Punchy, you said?"

I nodded as I took a bite of biscuit.

He continued, "Okay. So Punchy had seen the note that said something about getting me out of the way, and he handed it to the Crusher. Then what, you just walked away?"

Aunt Evelyn narrowed her eyes at me. I knew he was going to ask that, so I crammed another large bite of biscuit in my mouth, giving me more time to prevaricate.

Kirkland chuckled, knowing how Roarke and I work, and came to my rescue. "Lane, any other important information about Punchy and Crusher? We need to get this information to Finn."

I quickly answered, hoping to divert more questions about *what happened next*. "I sent a quick message to Finn last night that I have information for him. I'll fill him in when I see him."

Fio nodded and said with a wry smirk, "Oh yeah. You can bet he'll be waiting for you at the office. I'm kind of surprised he's not already here."

Finn was a New York City detective and recent boyfriend. But that title didn't quite do him justice. We'd shared many intense times over the past several months, which brought us closer together, faster than I'd ever expected. He'd been attractive to me right away, with his gray-green eyes and dark brown hair, a smile that pulled to one side. Not to mention arms that had the power to drop a bad guy yet with the grace that spun me effortlessly across the dancefloor.

I chanced a glance at Aunt Evelyn and she had a cocked eyebrow with a look that said she still wasn't convinced that we hadn't
gotten into trouble, and that I'd better divulge everything as soon
as possible.

We quickly ate the last crumbs of the final biscuit and Fio declared, "All right. Let's go, Lane! We've got work to do!"

We gathered our coats and hats, then walked down Lexington
in the chill winter air. The city was coming alive and sparks of
heart-warming sunshine glinted off the windows in pink and orange. I always loved the good scents of the city in the crisp morning air, but in the cold weather, the homey scent of bread baking
when the doors of Butterfield Market opened and closed was even
more cheering. The paperboys and dog walkers and little kids
were all starting their day right alongside the Wall Street men with
their three-piece suits and top hats, and the working men and
women sporting their factory jumpsuits. We all hopped onto the
downtown subway to City Hall with Fiorello greeting many of the
people by name since he was a familiar figure on this route.

Mayor Fiorello La Guardia was five feet, two inches tall, a minority on both sides, his father Italian, his mother Jewish. He *was*
New York. And I suppose all that he'd endured with his rather
small frame, not to mention his years defending his minority sta-
tus, was a significant reason why he'd always fought for the little
guy. He fully understood the plight of the underdog.

We arrived at work. With a cup of coffee in hand, and a wave to
my friends and cohorts Val and Roxy, I dove into my many tasks.
Finn had not, in fact, shown up at work. But with a quick phone
call he let me know he'd catch up with me that night.

As was typical of every day, a long line of petitioners had
queued up. Fio listened to every single person and actually did
something about their problem. A vendor having trouble with the
red tape of renewing his license? Fio got it done. A low-income
housing need? Fio got them in touch with the right person, and so
on. We had our heads down, working hard for about an hour and a
half until every person had been taken care of.

After the lull lasted approximately sixty seconds, Fio yelled out,

"Lane!" I jumped up from my desk to his bark about a hundred times a day. But with this particular tone, I knew something especially vexing had gotten under his skin. "Grab your coat!"

"Right, boss!" We ran out the door, down the staircase, and jumped into his waiting car.

"Ray! Get over to the Lower East Side Relief Station. On the double!"

"What's up with the relief station?" I asked, hanging on to the handle just above the door as Ray the driver took a corner with the speed of a '37 Streamliner.

He growled, "They're not doing their jobs. They're not helping the people. I have a plan." *Oh boy.*

We got to the station, and knowing my boss had a talent for the spectacular, I was a little stunned when he calmly and quietly went to the back of the long line of people. With a flap of his arm, he motioned for me to keep quiet and blend in. He wanted to witness for himself what was really going on at a place meant to serve the citizens. The place was packed with people wholly consumed by their day and the task at hand, fingering little slips of paper between cracked and overworked hands, worrying the rim of a scrubby hat, anticipating rejection yet hoping for the best. . . . With Fio's atypical silence and the fact that the people were so consumed, no one recognized him yet.

I looked around. They were all in deep, deep trouble. No one was working except one stenographer interviewing an applicant, despite the long line of people in need. Everyone was lounging about; even the policeman on duty was carelessly tipping back in his chair, his cap tipped over his eyes so he could catch a few winks. I could practically feel Fio's blood pressure rising. We waited a few more tenuous moments, still unrecognized.

Then he was done. Fio tipped down his slouch hat like it was his rakish fedora and barged his way to the front.

"Where the hell do you think you're going?" barked a mean-looking worker. Fio always had storm superlatives applied to him, but at the moment he truly was like a cyclone. He took the guy by the shoulders and sent him spinning into the crowd. Another employee rushed up and he, too, was sent careening away. Then an even meaner-looking, cigar-smoking, derby-hatted guy came up, ready to pounce on the Little Flower.

I squeaked in alarm as Fio knocked the cigar right out of the guy's mouth with one hand, and his derby hat with the other. He growled, "Take off your hat when you speak to a citizen!"

The penny dropped. This surly little man was *the mayor.*

The entire room went silent. The slothful policeman uttered, "My wife is gonna kill me."

In a spurt of Olympic-worthy style, Fio suddenly hurdled the railing separating the inner office from the crowd. Fio went right to the director's office and discovered he wasn't even there.

"Lane! Call Welfare Commissioner Hodson. NOW."

I ran to the nearest phone as a stunned secretary sat there wide-eyed. "You better move it, honey," I said, nodding to Fio as I quickly dialed the number. "Commissioner William Hodson, this is Lane Sanders with Mayor La Guardia. You'd better get to the Lower East Side Relief Station on the double. Hello?" The commissioner forgot to hang up the phone; I think he ran right out the door.

During my little phone call I watched Fio scold the policeman as he hurriedly got himself in tip-top shape. Then Fio grabbed a high stool just inside the railing he'd vaulted—I'd never forget that moment of gymnastic exuberance as long as I lived—and said as he took out his pocketwatch, "Let me see how fast you can clear out this crowd of applicants. Go!"

I guarantee that office never worked as fast as they did that morning. The boss had flown into action at 9:16 a.m. and by 9:37 a.m. on the dot, the entire crowd-now-turned-audience had been interviewed and ushered out the door. It was moments like this that reminded me Fio was a product of growing up on the Arizona frontier. I could easily envision him on a white stallion with his cowboy-at-heart swagger.

Fio brushed his hands together and said, "My work here is done." The commissioner arrived and Fio notified him that if the absent director didn't have a good excuse—meaning he was bleeding or comatose—he'd be fired. As we swept past that mean, derby-hatted fellow, Fio said, "And there's another S of a B that has no job!"

We exited the building as I wished with all my being that Roarke had been here so he could write up this story, and then I saw it. The roomful of people that had been treated by the relief station like they didn't matter, didn't deserve respect . . . had not gone home. They had lined up outside and as Fio banged out the door, a collective cheer erupted. Fio shook hands with a few people, listened to their stories, and talked with them in their own language. Fio was fluent in several languages, speaking easily with the people in Yiddish, German, Italian, Croatian, and even Hungarian. I recognized that language, since I lived up in Yorkville in Manhattan where a large group of Hungarians had congregated. After the last woman left, letting go of Fio's hand, which she'd been holding in warm appreciation, we headed back to City Hall in triumphant fashion.

My boss was rude, abrasive, brash . . . and yet his heart was kind and passionate. As we drove back to the office, he gazed at the city he loved as it passed swiftly by. And sure, he manhandled two ruffians, fired a couple of people, and called a guy an S of a B, but I also saw a tender smile grace his lips in that contemplative moment.

Later in the day, it was that same compassionate heart that had us speeding up to Harlem.

Having only gulped down two bites of my sandwich at my desk—we were having quite the busy day—I leaped from my dearly desired lunch and once again flew down the steps after my boss, who was dashing out of the building. This was life in the mayor's office. We zoomed up to the West 100th Street police station. Besides storm superlatives, Fio inspired many action verbs. The press couldn't find enough adjectives that adequately expressed his vigor. I'd never forget during Fio's first week in office, Lowell Limpus wrote, "He had the nation's biggest city dizzy. Brigades of bewildered reporters were unable to keep up with his chameleon mind." *Tell me about it!*

Ever since he became an attorney back before the war, Fiorello was known as the People's Lawyer. Always fighting for the people who were up against corrupt city government and didn't stand a chance on their own, many who were immigrants facing deportation. He had a ten-dollar fee, and if he took the case but they couldn't pay, they still got his best service.

So it was on this bustling day that we ended up at the police station and we were all reminded of Fio's legal background. By law, the mayor can sit as magistrate. The station was suddenly a court and a blur of action. Fio covered several cases, getting to the bottom of them quickly.

I was pooped. It had been a long day of running around. It was stuffy inside our makeshift courthouse and smelled like sweat, old food, and hopes teetering on the edge of redemption and disaster. My back hurt from the hard bench I'd been sitting on for a long time, and I stifled a yawn as the final person came forward.

A middle-aged, rather nondescript man came up. He'd been arrested for running slot machines and pinball machines in his deli. The guy was too skinny and had a weirdly invisible quality. Despite his gauntness, a small paunch pushed out and over his belt, his oily balding head shined from the yellow lights, and his shoulders caved inward, weirdly giving him the same malformed look as the older, persevering rats in the subway. But I couldn't really say what color hair or eyes he had, it was all too vague. He gave me the willies. I watched as he drank a glass of water, dribbling a little out of his mouth. When he spoke up about his case, his voice was whiny, capping off the sleazy persona and bringing Dickens's Uriah Heep to mind.

Fiorello listened to this Mr. Eugene Murk with distaste written all over his face. He found that the pinball machines and slots were mechanical larceny and the players didn't get a gambler's chance.

He topped the day off with a resounding declaration that shook the station: "Only a moron or imbecile could get a thrill out of watching these sure-thing devices take people's money. Let this serve notice to owners, racketeers, and other riffraff who run this racket that they will enjoy no comfort!"

The skinny, greasy Eugene would be held for trial. But as he left the makeshift courtroom sullenly and with a few policemen outright laughing at him, he turned around and gave Fio a look that I'd never be able to erase from my mind. The hair raised on the back of my neck. I got a bad feeling that this would not be the last of Eugene Murk.

CHAPTER 3

Roarke had heard about our busy day and met me at the office after work, dying to hear all that had happened. Needing to breathe, and to be in a place that exuded energy and life, we headed uptown to meet our friends at one of our favorite spots, the Savoy. We quickly ditched our coats in the coat room after we paid our entrance fee of sixty cents.

Roarke and I looked at each other with silly, eager grins. The music was pumping through the massive place, its earthy, rebellious sound making me walk faster into the heart of the fun, looking for our friends who were to meet us here. "Stompin' at the Savoy" just happened to be playing, written a few years ago by Chick Webb; he was leading the band tonight. I pulled Roarke along with me, into the thronging masses.

The room was dazzling with its soaring ceiling and double bandstand that ensured the music never stopped. If one band needed a break, the other one on the opposite side took up where they left off. Large mirrors covered the pink walls, with twinkling colored lights, and a spring-loaded floor that was scrubbed every night and replaced every three years. But the most shining, exhilarating aspect was the people at the Savoy.

We spotted a couple of familiar faces and went by to say hello. Two NYPD officers, Pete, an on-again-off-again boyfriend of Valerie's, and Scott, a constantly amused friend because he had the funny ability of showing up at my most spectacular moments. Such as tackling a would-be purse snatcher and arriving at the police station in high style, perched on the end of a junk cart.

"Hi, Pete! Scott! How are you?" I greeted.

"Great! Boy, this place is hopping tonight," exclaimed Pete, whose head was several inches above everyone else's.

We all took a moment to enjoy the energy, then grabbed the nearest person and joined the dance. The hot music swirled around us, and the camaraderie of the physical art of dance united us all. Ever since the day it opened, the Savoy was consistently near capacity, a staggering four thousand. I swear the place held a kind of magic. Despite the racial tensions outside those doors, inside the ballroom, no one cared one iota if you were poor or rich, black or white, uptown or downtown . . . you just had to dance.

Roarke and I were doing our best with the Lindy hop and I overheard the couple next to us. The guy said to the gal, "Hey! Clark Gable just walked in the house!"

The gal replied loudly over the music, "Oh yeah? Can he dance?"

Roarke and I grinned at each other as we heard this exchange. Just then I felt a heavy-handed tap on my shoulder.

"May I cut in?"

I looked behind me, then had to raise my eyes way up to greet the giant man standing behind me. "Sam! How are ya? Sure! Let's go!"

Roarke nodded to Sam Battle and quickly found another partner. Sam was a close friend, and he and his wife, Florence, frequently went out with Finn and me. Florence was dancing with her brother, and their fancy footwork just about set the floor on fire. The determined set to her jaw as she concentrated on her moves was in complete juxtaposition to her prim pearls and the utter joy that shot sparks through her eyes. Her bobbed hair bounced in time with the music, and she squealed with glee when they executed a perfect Lift Flip up and over his shoulder.

Sam was a very large man and quite the vigorous dancer. I braced myself because dancing with him was like dancing with a thunderstorm. He flung me around and I pretty much just had to hold on for dear life. I enjoyed every second.

This might have been the only place in the country where a white person could dance with a black person and people didn't look at the two opposite-colored hands touching; they looked at the rhythm, the footwork, and the absolute joy of the dance.

Sam and Finn hit it off last summer when we saw *Voodoo Macbeth* together. Usually Irish policemen didn't socialize with black policemen. But Finn had dealt with a lot of discrimination aimed at himself back in England because of his Irish roots. When Finn had firsthand experience of being denied a position with Scotland Yard simply because he was born in the wrong place and had the looks of an Irishman, not to mention signs in store windows saying *No Dogs, No Irish*, it affected him deeply.

Thinking back to our date at the theater, there was just something about that *Voodoo* production of Orson Welles's. At the theater, I kept watching Finn out of the corner of my eye, wanting to see his expressions during the magnificent show. His face had a raw look, completely unveiled, uninhibited. But one scene in particular had hit Finn hard.

> *Double, double, toil and trouble;*
> *Fire burn and cauldron bubble.*
> *Cool it with a baboon's blood,*
> *Then the charm is firm and good.*

I felt a twinge of concern as a curtain of emotion had come over him, filling his eyes with wariness and a kind of fear. *What was the cause of that?* At the end, it was obvious that the play had moved him. He adored Welles's adaptation, its eerie jungle theme and hypnotic drums. It was absolutely spellbinding and thought-provoking.

Just then I was suddenly brought back from those thoughts as Sam lifted me high up and then into a stomach-dropping dip, my hair brushing against the floor, his big grin never quitting. I was right back up again and my muscles were starting to feel flimsy when Sam bellowed, "Finn! Over here!" My rubbery arms were pretty relieved for the pause in the action.

"Sam, thanks for the dance!" I yelled.

Finn shook hands with the six-foot-three-inch-tall, almost three-hundred-pound man and energetically slapped him on the back. Then he laid eyes on me and scooped me up.

"Hi, love," he said as he gently pulled me close and turned to the mellow tune with a smoldering saxophone. I always enjoyed dancing with Finn. And I didn't have to brace myself quite as much as I did with Sam.

I sighed. "This is nice."

I felt his chuckle. "You looked a bit like a rag doll with Sam."

"I *felt* like a rag doll. He's a one-dance-a-night kind of guy."

"And your favorite red shoes are scuffed," he remarked in his British accent tinged with Irish, which I happened to find very attractive.

I had forgotten about that from my escapade with Roarke the day before. I could have easily scratched them while dancing, but something in my eyes must have looked shifty. I was thinking of the sleuthing with Roarke that always ended up with us running away from criminals.

Finn's eyes narrowed as they pierced mine. I tried to look innocent. "Really? I hadn't noticed."

"Oh dear."

I changed the topic. "Come on! Let's go get a drink." I took him by the hand and we threaded our way through the crowd to the long bar. They didn't serve hard liquor, so we ordered two beers instead of a trendy cocktail. The cold, frothy lager hit the spot.

"I have an appointment with Commissioner Valentine and Fio tomorrow afternoon," said Finn as he placed his glass on the counter.

"Oh yeah? New case?" I asked.

"Well, it might be an old one."

"Another Red Scroll mystery?" I asked with a dubious cock to my eyebrow.

"Not sure. As you know, that gangster the Crusher has been making thinly veiled threats against Fiorello because of his penchant for demolishing the whole pinball racket."

Knowing I wasn't good at hiding things from Finn, such as my more dangerous moments from sleuthing around on this exact case, I took a big swig of my beer, hiding my face behind the glass.

He squinted knowingly at me, but kept going. "Well, I'm wondering if they think the leftover crew from Donagan might be behind it."

"And therefore the Red Scroll Network." He nodded. "I don't think so. It doesn't have their panache. Besides, we don't know for sure what happened with Donagan, who killed him, and if there really was some sort of heir to the Network," I said.

"True. But I think Fiorello and Valentine want us to make certain that it's dead."

Just a month or so ago, a few criminals were after the proof of identity to claim the legacy of Rex Ruby, leader of the Red Scroll Network. We'd thought the heir was Donagan Connell, and when we found his dead body, the final gold pawn upon his bloody chest (Rex's last pawn), we knew Donagan's underground crime syndicate had come to an end. But just who killed Donagan? I was guessing that person was the heir. And then what?

I filled him in on most of the details of my sleuthing with Roarke. "Finn, so Roarke has an informant, Punchy, who found a message that he'd been hired to take to someone, but he hadn't known who. That message was about Fio and getting him out of the way."

He ordered another beer, then said to me, "I take it you and Roarke followed him to see whom he was meeting. Yes?"

"Yep. And it was definitely the Crusher."

"Well, that confirms that he's most likely the one behind all these mutterings. Thanks. We'll keep an eye on him. Did you . . . get into any trouble?" he asked warily.

"Nah. Nothing much. Hey, look! Clark Gable really is here!" I stood on tiptoe to get a better look at him.

"I wonder if he can dance," said Finn with a cheeky grin.

CHAPTER 4

The following day, I sat at my white chair in my smoky-blue room, cup of coffee in hand, reading before the beginning of the day. The front door downstairs burst open to a cacophony of Ripley's barking and Fiorello's bellowing. I walked to my dresser and checked my shoulder-length brown hair. I smoothed my navy-blue jacket and cream skirt, and added some rose-pink lipstick. It hadn't snowed in a bit, so I was okay wearing high heels to work without boots. I slipped on a navy pair with little ankle straps and headed downstairs.

Fiorello was already at the table enjoying a coffee and some scrambled eggs and bacon.

"Morning, Mr. Kirkland, Aunt Evelyn, Fio!"

"Laney Lane, my girl!" greeted Fiorello.

"Grrrrrr." Our usual banter brought a smile to my face. "How are you, Fio? How's Jean's cold? Feeling better?"

"Oh, yes, yes. Just needed a bit of a rest." The La Guardias had two children whom they adored. Fortunately, his daughter's bout of sickness was just a small thing. Everyone dreaded pneumonia, and the seasonal outbreaks of scarlet fever. I'd heard of a new drug possibility, they called it penicillin, but it sounded like a miracle medicine, just too good to be true. Something that would stop pneumonia in its tracks? I had two friends die in elementary school from a simple scratch that turned into blood poisoning, and several more that contracted scarlet fever and tuberculosis. Every season it seemed some young child died on the block. I wondered what it would be like to have a drug that stopped that. I feared it would never happen. But one could hope.

Aunt Evelyn retrieved the pot of coffee and patted Fio's shoulder as she walked by. "Good, Fio, I'm so delighted. You need to bring the family over soon! We haven't seen them in quite a while!"

I studied Kirkland's face as he thought about having the La Guardia kids over. Kirkland liked the energetic children, but they *adored* him and showed it in overwhelming displays of affection, which made him turn all red and bluster around a lot. In fact, I think they scared him a bit.

We all chitchatted about our day ahead. Aunt Evelyn was working on a particular painting that must have captured her imagination because she kept sending longing looks over toward the stairs that led up to her studio. She was dressed in her long skirt and peasant top that was her favorite painting uniform, and her black hair with fine gray streaks cascaded down her back.

"You don't have to stay, you can go paint right now, Aunt Evelyn," I said with a sardonic grin.

She blushed and sputtered, "Oh no, no. I'm fine. I just have a good idea. I need to work on it today because tomorrow, Nina and I are going to the Jewish Theological Seminary to see some of the museum pieces."

"Oh? For inspiration on your own work?" I asked.

"Actually, I'm trying to convince Frieda Warburg to donate their family mansion—it's utterly a behemoth for them to keep up—especially since Felix, the chancellor, isn't doing too well. She needs to plan ahead."

Aunt Evelyn—artist, philanthropist, rascal—had friends in all places, high and low, notable and obscure, religious and irreligious. Nina Mittman was a close friend and also a patron of the arts. They were always running around to various institutions telling people what to do.

I chuckled and turned to Fio and said, "Hey, ah, Finn tells me that he has a meeting with you and Commissioner Valentine today."

"No, Lane! *We* have a meeting with Valentine today." I widened my eyes and was about to say something clever but he interrupted me. "No time to talk! We've got work to do!"

With that daily mantra exclaimed, Fio took up his fedora, cocked it at a rakish angle, and saluted Kirkland in farewell. I grabbed my large purse and notebook, said a quick good-bye all around, and raced off after my boss.

We took a different way to work every day. Sometimes the bus, sometimes the elevated trains along Second or Third, or the subway along Lexington, or like today, we hopped into the awaiting car.

"Hi, Ray!" I exclaimed to the driver and self-proclaimed body-guard. Fio set himself down into the car and immediately got to work. First, he arranged his desk that he had outfitted in the backseat. Then he began rattling off directives to me as he simultaneously looked at his calendar and jotted down his own notes. He wrote a little reminder to stop by his art school.

Fio adored music and art. He played a mean horn, sometimes at funny moments including the takedown of the Artichoke King and Daley Joseph, two of New York's infamous criminals. New York audiences often found Fio guest-conducting at the symphony. The High School of Music and Art was his dream, and he made it come true last year. His face lit up every time anyone mentioned the school. Art was life to him. Maybe that's why he and Aunt Evelyn had a special relationship. They understood each other.

We arrived at City Hall and I raced up the steps. Inside, I admired the gorgeous rotunda as I did every day when we climbed toward our offices. I'd never get tired of that view.

"Morning, love." And that view was pretty nice, too.

"Hey, Finn. How are ya?"

We shared a smile in the doorway to our offices.

"Ahem."

I pulled my eyes away from the grin that consistently sent sizzles up and down my spine, and turned to see Valerie and Roxy, my favorite work cohorts, smirking at us with knowing looks in their glittering eyes. They each had a cup of coffee in their hands, ankles crossed, watching us like an entertaining sideshow. I heard Finn's chuckle behind me.

"I'll see you with the police commissioner at five."

"Great. See ya, Finn." I turned my eyes to my friends, Val in her dark green pantsuit with brass buttons with the high-necked blouse she favored, honey-colored hair perfectly complementing her sweetly freckled face. And petite Roxy, with her to-die-for cleavage nicely highlighted in a black sweater with her short, flaxen hair silhouetting her round face.

"Enjoying your coffee?" I said with a mock sneer.

Val's eyes went wide. "Oh bugger. I thought he had a morning meeting today."

"Oh God, he's here! Go! Go!" yelled Roxy, running for her desk.

I cackled as they both bolted back to work as I could just hear Fio's quick footsteps clipping down the hall at the last few feet before the door.

"Good morning!" he boomed, slamming the door open. The office had been in a nice and busy flurry already, but when the Little Flower entered, we doubled our efforts. And Fio didn't believe in coffee breaks. So . . .

I got to my desk and immediately slipped a piece of paper into my typewriter and started typing up the list of items Fiorello discussed on the way in. There was already a line of petitioners waiting. We made our way through the day, the clock utterly not moving. I wanted to get to the meeting with Valentine. I was feeling antsy for some reason.

Maybe it was not knowing the whereabouts of Morgan that was getting to me. She was a new friend who was captain of a gang of street urchins who had come to our aid on several occasions. To my delight, avid reader that I am, we had our own group of Irregulars. Sherlock would be proud indeed.

But Morgan—who had always been known as just "Morgan" since she was a bit touchy with personal details—had been absent the last couple of weeks for our standing ice cream date. She'd been "on business" before, so we'd missed meetings, but never two weeks in a row. Something was up with her, and it ate away at me in the back of my mind. That mixed with the mystery of why the police commissioner was calling in Finn and me; I felt distracted and on edge.

Around four o'clock when twilight was hitting hard, making it seem far later than it was, Fio came bounding up to my desk.

"Lane! I need you to go with me over to Hell's Kitchen. I found more pinball machines!"

I suppressed the need to roll my eyes as I yet again grabbed my coat and hat and purse. We jumped into the sedan, and Ray drove us over to the aptly named area. Since the 1800s the area west of midtown along the Hudson River was home to a hotbed of gangs. At one point, supposedly there were more speakeasies than children. Underground crime was high, but regular crime was low due to the gangs to which people were in service or in debt. It was a weird hierarchy and Fio hated all of it.

We drove up to 46th and all the way over to Eleventh Avenue. It was always a haul to the far west side. Right next to the Landmark Tavern, an Irish bar and restaurant from the 1800s, was a deli with the aptly named if not imaginative sign out front: Deli. It looked like it was a front for something else. I guess you get used to reading between the lines in my kind of work. Whether it was the few shifty-looking people outside, the food that they did indeed sell although it looked dusty and stale, or maybe it was the couple of prostitutes on the corner—it all added up to no good.

"Uh . . . are you sure we should be here and not the police?" I asked, staying in the car.

"Oh, the police are already here, Lane. They've got it under control, that's how I heard about it."

Fio has a police radio in his office, in his home, and in his car. I think it's safe to say that he's obsessed with it. He is often a first responder to all of the big emergencies in the city, especially fires, car accidents, and big crimes. It's one of the reasons he has the press in a frenzy. He's impossible to read and no one has enough energy to actually follow him consistently.

I looked up as I caught the prostitutes backing away, farther down the street. They also must've gotten the notion that something was not quite right. Fio and I eased out of the car. My door slammed loudly, echoing off the buildings. It was very quiet, which was strange in the city.

Inside, I glimpsed a short man edging toward the back. I immediately thought of my romp with Roarke through Grand Central. *Could that be the Crusher?*

"Do either of you know what a mitney is?" I asked on impulse.

Fio said, "No, never heard of it."

Ray said, "It's an old term for a cop. Like, it kind of stood for the shoulder clamp of a cop on a thug's shoulder."

"A cop?" I stuttered, my mind racing. A cold sweat prickled my neck and forehead. My stomach dropped as I realized what this meant. "Fio!" I said urgently. "They're aiming for the cops!"

He and Ray shot their eyes to me. Ray quickly scanned the area and uttered under his breath, "Shit."

The static tension in the air made all of us brace ourselves. Something was going down.

"Lane, back up to the car. Slowly." Fio put out his arm to carefully push me toward the car; he only had eyes for his police radio.

Inside the deli, another flash of movement caught my eye. The windows were cloudy from grime and disregard but there were people inside. Three policemen came out the door; they must've been searching the premises. But whatever tension we'd been experiencing, they hadn't felt inside. Their nonchalance was in direct opposition to the braced stances Fio, Ray, and I had taken.

I immediately recognized two of the policemen, Scott and Peter. Scott nodded at me and smiled at the same moment two men came around the corner, guns in hand, pointing at Fio. Ray was on it first.

"Get down!" yelled Ray.

I hit the ground, scraping my hands on the harsh cement. And without even knowing I'd done it, I had my dagger in hand.

Gunshots fired.

I covered my head. Fio was on the ground right next to me, our faces close, our eyes locked in terror. *Shit.* More shots, glass breaking.

Hands scraped and bleeding, heart thumping, I slowly turned my head, looking under the car toward the store. Two forms on the other side of the car hit the pavement with a sickening sound.

Thud, thud. I instinctively reached out my hand beneath the dirty car, my elbow scraping against the wet street. But he didn't reach back. His eyes were directed at mine, but he was unable to see anything.

Everything went silent.

"Peter!" Someone was screaming as I ran around the car and knelt down next to him. *I think it was me.* Blood was everywhere. I softly stroked his hair from his forehead. "Oh Pete." I felt a weak arm reach out to my shoulder as Scott sat up slowly, also hit, in the leg. He felt for Pete's pulse.

"Lane, he's gone."

CHAPTER 5

The third policeman had nabbed one of the gunmen and quickly handcuffed him as Ray and Fio called in the shooting. The bullet had hit Scott on the outside of the leg, creating a deep gash. I quickly got his belt and my scarf, then tightly wrapped them around his thigh as a makeshift bandage and tourniquet, eliciting a groan of pain from him.

"You okay?" I asked softly, a hand on Scott's shoulder. He just nodded, unable to take his eyes off Peter. I helped him stand up since there was no way he was staying put. The street had cleared like a magician's disappearing act; a movement in the window from someone stealing a furtive glance from inside the store caught my eye.

"You! You did this!" I yelled savagely as I took off toward the store. Despite the shock of everything, I was seething with anger and suddenly, I had the guy by the collar with both fists and smashed him viciously against the wall of the deli, making a few loaves of bread topple off the shelf that rocked with the force of my shove. "Why? Why did you do this? Where is Crusher?"

"Whoa, whoa, whoa! Lane!" I felt two pairs of hands carefully try to pull me back. Fio and—thank God—*Finn*.

"He's behind this! I know it!" I gave him one last shove before I released my death grip on his smashed collar. "He's Eugene Murk," I spat out. "We were up at the West 100th Street station yesterday and Fio sent his pinball case to trial."

Eugene finally found his greasy, thin voice. "No! It's not like that!" My eyes darted to Finn and he couldn't help a grimace of distaste as he looked at Eugene. "I'm the one that called it all in! Who's Crusher?"

"What?" I exclaimed.

He rearranged his paunch a little and tucked in his yellowing shirt, wiping his nose with his sleeve in the process. "Yeah, I got a plea bargain and I'm helping the police with the pinball and slots."

"It's true, Lane," said Fio from behind me.

"And it's because we followed his so-called lead that Peter is dead," I said, still seething.

"I know," growled the mayor. "Murk! Who were those gunmen?"

Eugene Murk's tiny pig eyes grew as wide as they could, as he backed up even farther against the wall, knocking more bread off the shelf. "No, really! Um, a guy named, lemme see . . . it started with a C. Cushman! He got me into the slots, you know, to make ends meet. You can't blame a small business owner such as myself! It's hard these days." He smoothed his almost nonexistent hair against his head, then ran his hand along his pants, a sheen of greasy residue left behind. "I think he might have been one of the gunmen."

Fio looked dubious. Finn said, "What's he look like? Can you describe him?"

"Yeah, I think I can. Of course, I couldn't see very well from the back of the store . . . but he's a little under six feet, a really big nose, kinda like a bird. Scary as hell. Uh . . . walked with a limp . . . is that good?" He looked at Finn like he might be his salvation. I didn't think that would be the case.

"All right, all right. For now, we'll get your testimony and keep looking into it all." Finn turned to me and I'm sure he could feel me fuming. "Lane, we can't hold him on anything." He turned back to Eugene and breathed out through his teeth, "Yet. Get outta here." Eugene slithered away to the back of the store and disappeared behind a curtain.

A flare of white outside the window made Fiorello, Finn, and me turn simultaneously. Scott was hobbling to the back of the ambulance. I exhaled as Finn's hand found mine. A white sheet blew softly in the cold breeze as it gently alighted onto the motionless form of our friend.

Back at the office, Fio informed Valerie and Roxy of Peter's death before informing the office as a whole. It was awful. Val's normally cheery, freckled face had crumpled with the news. She and Peter had been an item for a while. It ended, but they remained friends and Pete had been integrally involved in the last couple of cases. We sent Valerie home and Roxy was going to go with her, but Val stoutly refused. She needed time alone. We all had lost a dear friend and an excellent cop. What I thought was going to be an exciting caper-of-a-mystery was turning out to be anything but. Pinball was indeed becoming a deadly game.

CHAPTER 6

Valerie made her way across town. She hardly knew where she was going, sort of. She stumbled once, reeling from the shock of Peter's death. A stranger asked her if she was okay. Val felt herself blush, embarrassed and a little confused. "Uh, yes. Thank you. Just not feeling quite right." She patted down her hair and kept going. It was like her feet knew the way and she was just along for the ride.

How could he have died? It didn't seem possible. She'd known for a while that she didn't love him, but still . . . they were friends and had been a little more. She felt a tear spill down her face and she swept it away with her white kid-gloved hand, uncaring that it made a smudge on the crisp surface.

Val got on an uptown bus and sat numbly by the window. She glimpsed the Chrysler Building, its triangular windows at the top bringing a smile to her face. It reminded her of a star, and it seemed a hopeful reminder of all they'd come out of the past few years. The art and music and architecture and cocktails of this era were *so beautiful*, so full of life despite the Depression the world was in. Despite the fact that they'd had the world's biggest war and practically lost an entire generation.

Her eyes fluttered toward Grand Central. Lane loved that Grand Concourse, but Penn Station was Val's favorite. It truly was the world's most beautiful train station. Soaring glass ceilings, the sounds of adventure in the air.

A small smile crept over her light pink lips as she remembered that their first meeting had been in that hall. She had met him by random coincidence, and yet it felt like fate had a hand in it.

She got off the bus several blocks away, desiring the cold, fresh air. As she walked, she contemplated everything. Life was feeling very complicated, heavy. Her parents and home life, and now Peter's death. She felt the load on her, more than she ever felt before.

Maybe that's what compelled her to go to him.

She finally got to the six-story apartment building with the address she'd memorized quite a while ago. She buzzed up, then heard the reciprocal buzz and opened the door. She had six stories to climb up.

Every step brought her closer. Her heart was feeling lighter even though her burden was becoming more apparent. She quickened her steps, despite being out of breath.

At the top, she looked right and left to determine which apartment. She walked over to the right and knocked on the door. It opened.

"I . . . I don't know why I'm here," she said.

His smile reached his deep blue eyes, radiating comfort, safety, tenderness. "That's okay. I'm just glad you're here."

Suddenly she felt her face crumple.

"Valerie, are you all right?" Concern rippled through him and he reached out to carefully bring her inside. "Come here."

She had never wanted someone's arms around her more. She numbly walked forward and carefully put her arms around his waist and he brought her head to his shoulder, caressing her soft hair.

"Val, what's wrong?"

"Peter's dead."

"*What?*"

"He was shot today outside a deli Fio was raiding for slots and pinball."

"Oh my God." He pressed her head softly into his chest and kissed the side of her head.

She slowly looked up at him. He took her face into his hands, his thumbs carefully wiping the tears from beneath her eyes. She closed her eyes, not ever having felt that kind of tender care in her life.

Her green eyes opened and locked onto his. "Raff. Thanks," she whispered.

His eyes never left hers. With the sweetest, slowest motion, he carefully brought his soft lips to hers. Her knees buckled the slightest bit, and with an automatic reaction, he picked her up into his arms.

CHAPTER 7

We moved the meeting with Valentine to a couple of hours later, and I completed everything I'd been working on. I used the agitated energy coursing through me to tackle the biggest jobs and finished it all up in record time. Fio was wrapping up, too; he tapped a packet of papers on his desk together, aligning all the pages in a satisfied *tap tap tap*.

The Tammany tiger grinned over at me from the floor. My boss loved to antagonize his opponents; well, actually he loved to antagonize everyone. He goaded his commissioners to all compete against each other for his attention. He felt it would make them work harder. But his hatred for the corrupt Tammany Hall knew no bounds. So he had a tiger skin brought in for his office floor décor. The Tammany mascot was the tiger. *Fio, Fio, Fio.*

Just before seven, Finn came in and after a shared look of understanding, we went to the coffee room to grab a cup before the meeting.

"How's Val?" he asked solemnly.

"Awful. It was such a shock. She and Pete weren't dating anymore, but still . . ."

"I know," he said as he brushed his hair back with his hand in a gesture of disbelief. "I can't wrap my mind around it. The department will have its inspector's funeral next month. We need to give the family time to get here and for the city to prepare for the parade. I can tell you, Pete's death is rocking the whole department. Anyone who hadn't liked the Strong-arm Squad is having second thoughts now."

"I can imagine," I said. "I'm not fond of the judge, jury, and executioner aspect of it. But there are times when I just don't give a damn, you know?"

"Yeah, absolutely."

Commissioner Valentine, harried and concerned, entered into the offices and I headed over to greet him. "Hello, Mr. Valentine. I'll take your coat. How are your officers? And are you doing okay?" I knew he'd had to break the news of Pete's death to all the divisions today.

"Thanks, Miss Sanders. I appreciate you asking. We are all grieving, of course. I just can't believe it was Peter. He seemed so substantial, so untouchable. But none of us are invincible. That's for goddamn sure."

I got him a black coffee, then we all headed into Fio's office. I retrieved my own chair for the meeting.

Fio was always in a rush, always the impetus of frenzied action. The police commissioner was more metered, more introspective. He looked steadily at Finn, then me, then Fiorello. He was a good police commissioner and boy, did he clean house with the Strong-arm Squad as his main thrust of action. Valentine gave his special plainclothes cops the go-ahead to rough up any gangsters. He wanted to make the police so intimidating to the gangsters that they'd tip their hats to the policemen when they walked by. Fio selected him for the police commissioner because he'd heard of a "good cop" in Brooklyn. He searched him out and Valentine knew his plan as police commissioner from day one.

One of his plans involved Finn working undercover as a dirty cop in an effort to root out the corrupt officers who had been rampant since Prohibition. Thank God that mission ended. Now, apparently, Valentine had a whole new project for him to work on. For *us* to work on.

"*London?* You think I should go to London?" asked Finn, a shadow running across his handsome face.

"Yes. Mayor La Guardia and I have been discussing this for a while. Meet up with your latest contact, Miles Havalaar. We need to get a final answer on any remnants of the Red Scroll Network. With Europe heating up all over again, we have a vested interest in our allies. If a known criminal network may be setting up shop again, I'd like us to nip it in the bud while we can. It wouldn't be right to just let it go. We want to extinguish any momentum they could gain here. We don't know who killed Donagan Connell yet and we have to see if there's any word about a possible heir, find out if there's any real threat to this crime network starting up all over again. That is one thing we need to go to great lengths to stop before it even gets started."

Fio nodded. "Yes, I think we have to go back to where it all began. We of course will keep an eye on things here, as well. But London was the Red Scroll's genesis."

Finn shook his head as he contemplated this idea. "I don't know, sir, I just don't know. Are you sure we need to go that far?"

Finn had been born in Ireland, but was raised in England. His family was less than congenial. He'd felt their profound betrayal somehow, and it haunted him. I had a feeling his hesitation to go all the way to London wasn't just about the long distance, it was about his family, too.

Before anyone could answer, Roxy knocked on the doorframe, then said, "Excuse me, you all need to come out here."

Oh boy. She was pale and clearly had some kind of ominous news. We quickly got up and raced out the door to the main offices.

"Oh my God, Morgan! Are you all right?" Roarke was standing over her, watching her drink a cup of tea, his hands on his hips. She had a black eye and Roarke's tie was wound around her wrist.

Storm Fio caught sight of her and erupted. "Good Lord, Morgan! What happened? Roarke, tell me what happened. I can't believe I'm seeing—" I placed a hand on his arm to stop his tirade so that someone could indeed tell us what happened.

Morgan looked exhausted. She rubbed her face as if she had an invisible washcloth.

I said with a rush of air, "I haven't seen you in a couple weeks. I sent word to your lieutenants because I couldn't find you. What happened?" I sank down to my haunches to get close to her. I put my hand on her knee.

A ghost of a smile touched her as I said "lieutenants," but then faded away. *Damn.* She'd been through something horrible.

"I got caught following someone. They held me all this time, I just escaped. Thank God you sent word. The kids were on it, but when they heard from you, they realized they needed a little more help than usual." Her gray eyes raised to look at Roarke. "Not too shabby, Roarke," she said.

His eyes glittered as he bantered with, "Not too shabby? I think I was better than that!"

"Yeah, and I'll never forget the sight of you in a babushka." That raised a lot of eyebrows. Roarke snorted.

"But um . . . really . . ." She tripped a bit over her words, then she tenderly patted her banged-up wrist with Roarke's red tie wrapped around it, then looked at Roarke with her serious, gray eyes. "*Thank you.*"

His dimples disappeared as he felt the moment, too, and replied with a matching tone, "Absolutely. Happy to, Morgan."

Then she seemed to get her strength back in an instant and turned sharply to me and Fio. "Lane. Fio. We have work to do."

Fio mumbled, "That's my line."

"I saw who killed Donagan. And you're not going to believe who it was."

"Lane, you better sit down," interrupted Roarke.

I hate it when people say that. It has the opposite effect. It makes me want to stand up to prepare and brace myself.

My face must have relayed those feelings loud and clear because he countered with, "Or not."

Finn took a step closer to Morgan. "You saw the shooter? Up close enough to identify him?"

She nodded. "Oh yes. For sure. But it wasn't a him. It was a *her.*"

I said, "Eliza? It couldn't be her, she'd been holed up since the big shooting." Eliza had been Donagan's lover and mastermind at deception. But Donagan had used her just as he'd used everyone. To get her out of the way, he'd set up an elaborate plan that he hoped would get all of his competition for the legacy of Rex Ruby out of the way. Eliza thought she'd gunned down Finn and myself in a rickety old shack on the Lower East Side. But in the shack had been someone she hadn't expected: her own brother, Tucker Henslowe. She finally knew what side Donagan was on: his own.

Morgan shook her head and slowly said, "No, Lane. It wasn't Eliza. It was her mother. *Daphne.*"

"I think I better sit down."

CHAPTER 8

Since the tender young age of ten years old, when my parents had been killed, I had recurring dreams of things my parents taught me, things they wanted me to remember. Survival skills, reading people and their body language, even throwing a knife with deadly accuracy. I could never decide if they did all that because they suspected their early demise or they were just built that way since they were both spies. I also had bits of memories flit in and out of my mind. Memories that would come back to the surface bit by bit, sometimes in dreams.

Daphne with her long white-blond mane of hair had been in those dreams from the beginning. Right after I fell into the frozen lake when my parents had been killed while we were ice skating, I remembered her leering over me at the hospital in an emerald green hat. I think she planned on killing me but had been interrupted.

Her husband, Rutherford Marco, had been Rex Ruby's son, and apparently, he'd been a big disappointment to his father because he lacked the ruthless nature that Rex hoped he'd have. I guess Daphne made the cut.

A gold pawn had been left on the blood-soaked chest of Donagan, along with several hundred-dollar bills. The pawn was Rex's final game piece, proving *everyone* was his pawn. It was only and always about *his* choice, his plan, his game.

So Daphne is the heir?

"I can't get over that, Morgan. You saw her up close?"

"Oh yeah," she said with big eyes. "I wish I hadn't. She was brutal. And *so* creepy. Didn't you say she was locked up at Metropolitan Hospital? The lunatic asylum? She looked like she could summon her sanity at will. Sheesh, Lane, no wonder you had bad dreams about her all these years."

I locked eyes with Roarke. "I don't want to go back to Metropolitan, but I think we should."

"I know. We need to find out what's really going on," he said. "Do you think maybe her insanity was just an act?"

"Oh, I don't think it was wholly an act," said Morgan.

"It's not an act," I said definitively. "But that doesn't mean she's not brilliant, cunning, and extremely dangerous."

Roarke and I had gone sleuthing to the infamous lunatic asylum on Blackwell's Island, called Welfare Island now, with its prison, workhouse, smallpox hospital, and lunatic asylum all on one narrow slip of land between Manhattan and Queens. That was the day I recognized Daphne as the woman from my dreams, and boy, did she recognize me. She'd had a Hollywood-style flair, and at first was excited to do an interview with Roarke, our setup for the appointment with her. But then the veneer on her face, holding in the sanity, slipped and crashed to the ground. It was like a different person under there. One that terrified me.

Finn abruptly said, "I'm going with you two this time."

"*That's fine,*" said Roarke, as I said simultaneously and with gusto, "Good!"

"You should go check out her room at the asylum, but she's not there now," said Morgan.

"She's not?" I asked.

"No, just before I got caught by her goons, I saw her buying passage to London."

"*London?*" asked Finn incredulously.

Morgan nodded and Commissioner Valentine grinned triumphantly as he said, "Well, that settles that."

We got Morgan into a car with Roxy as her chaperone. She agreed to go up to my place to recuperate. I phoned ahead to Kirkland and

Evelyn; they'd be sure to take good care of her. We needed a council of war. But first, Finn and I had to finish our meeting with Valentine. Roarke joined us.

Fio pounded his desk with a fist. "So! We need to get you to England right away."

Valentine nodded, taking a deep drag on his cigarette. He was a thoughtful man, and I could practically see the cogs in his mind working. "Yes, I have a couple contacts there, too. I'll get them word that you're coming. Make an introduction with them and your own contact, Miles Havalaar. If Daphne Franco is heading back to where Rex's syndicate began, it can't be good."

"Lane, you look like you're thinking hard. Have an idea?" asked Fio.

"Well . . . the gunmen that killed Peter, they made a threat to you, Fio. But then they ended up nabbing Peter, which sounded like the plan all along from when we overheard Crusher talk about getting the mitney. Add to the mix that Rex's network was about stealing art and whatnot. But all of it, the whole thing, the bottom line was always making money and creating chaos while he played his games. Do you think it's possible that *Daphne* and the Red Scroll were behind the shooting? That she has a hand in the pinball and slots racket?"

Fio took a deep breath. "Sure, it's possible. But we don't have enough information yet on who works for who. There are a lot of other gangs who would be just as keen to get me out of the picture."

"You shouldn't be grinning, Fio," I said, shaking my head. He loved making the bad guys mad; it meant he was doing the right stuff.

But with all this talk, I was getting fidgety. I agreed with the need for Finn to go to London; it had been President Roosevelt himself who had sent him there last time to check on the rumblings of the Red Scroll. But it was *my parents* who seemed to be the cornerstone of it all. They had been the ones to figure out the complexity of the Red Scroll Network in the war, and then my father and Kirkland were the ones who at last took out Rex Ruby, the masterful leader. And most importantly, it was Rex's followers who murdered my parents. Why was I getting worked up and fidgety? Because I started to get the feeling I wasn't going to be "allowed" to work on this case and go to London, too.

"I can hear you, Lane," said Fio, rather omnisciently. "Stop fidgeting."

"But I am not going to let—" I started to sputter.

He cut me off before I could continue. "Oh, Lane, please. You're going, too."

That shut me up. My eyes darted to Finn. He said, "*Pfft.* Of course. Like anyone had a choice. You have your own money; you'd be on the next ship anyway, right?"

"Well . . . yes. I would."

Valentine wasn't flummoxed in the least. In fact, he looked like Roarke when we get onto a good sleuthing scheme. His eyes were gleaming with excitement topped with a devilish grin. "Besides," continued the police commissioner, "we need someone with a set of skills that you have readily exhibited, Lane. I rather look forward to your escapades."

Finn closed his eyes and murmured, "Oh dear God. *Escapades.*"

I had a special knack for doing the spectacular and gathering a pretty good audience to witness it, including an amused NYPD. Finn and I were the talk of the town, let's just say. And the cause of more than a few friendly wagers.

Fio spoke up. "Lane, you really shouldn't be quite so dramatic, though." My eyebrow shot up.

"You mean such as, not bringing my trumpet and shooting down the criminal right as he's about to blow up a bridge?" Fio had done that. With pizzazz. He turned a little red as I pointed out his own dramatic tendency, yet at the same time he looked quite pleased with himself.

He couldn't figure out a good comeback, so he left it with, "Mmm, yes."

Valentine was enjoying the banter, his eyes going back and forth like watching a tennis match. But I also had my eye on Finn. I had recently faced the ghosts of my past in Rochester, Michigan, and they were nothing to sneeze at. I came out unscathed, but it had been a deadly game. And I still had a lot of questions about what exactly my parents were involved in while they were in the war working with intelligence. They were invaluable in stopping Rex Ruby. But there were still questions of how they infiltrated the Red Scroll Network. And there were a couple of moments where I was not one hundred percent sure of their trustworthiness. They at one point had to look like they were part of the crime syndicate, and there were dark parts to undercover work. I loved my parents. But I wasn't sure I trusted them.

So, London held possible secrets for me and my parents. But London also held dangerous ghosts for Finn. Those were the questions I was searching for in his face and those dark gray-green eyes of his. Finn had both psychological and physical scars from some sort of accident that I believe his devious younger brother orchestrated. But he hadn't told me the whole story yet. He would. When it was the right time.

I caught his eye at that moment, and we shared a knowing look. I loved the idea of a trip with Finn. But there was something else there, in the belly of this mystery. Something that sent icy tentacles of apprehension right through me.

CHAPTER 9

Ray drove Finn, Roarke, Fio, and myself up to my place. Ripley, our giant German shepherd, was uncharacteristically not on guard at the side window of our red front door. I loved the half-moon shapes of the uppermost windows, Aunt Evelyn's studio. And the sight of the copper-topped, bumped-out window of the parlor in our townhouse warmed my heart. This place. It was a welcoming and joyful home, and it made me feel better, the mere vision of it easing out the tension of the idea of going back to Metropolitan Hospital and all that we faced with losing Peter.

We came in and I yelled out, "Hello!"

"Back here!" answered Aunt Evelyn. We trooped to the back room, a little area off the enchanting patio, with its charming lanterns and lights strung on the branches of the maple that created a natural canopy. Even with some of the more sensitive lights taken down for the winter months, the sturdier ones glistened and twinkled as the breeze caught the branches.

"There you are, buddy," I said, grinning at Ripley, who lay completely covering Morgan's lap on the comfy small couch next to the fireplace.

Morgan looked clean and peaceful. Aunt Evelyn was sure to get her into tip-top shape, and Ripley had an uncanny way of comforting those who needed his kind of furry reassurance. Morgan softly rubbed his head and his big ears. Ripley looked rather delirious laying his head to the side, letting his tongue loll out of his mouth. Morgan laughed a sweet, genuine little chuckle. She still had Roarke's red tie around her wrist, but I glimpsed a clean bandage underneath.

My stomach rumbled as I smelled beef stew brewing on the stove.

Mr. Kirkland gruffly laughed when he heard it—it wasn't a quiet rumble—always proud of his cooking. And who didn't like to cook for those who truly appreciated it? Like me. I was always starving.

Aunt Evelyn came over and helped me get the dishes ready. Roarke went and sat with Morgan while Finn opened a bottle of red wine. Because of her European upbringing, Evelyn always had a lot of wine on hand, God love her. Fio and Kirkland stood at the stove discussing the finer points of beef stew.

I said softly to Evelyn, "She seems okay?"

She nodded seriously. "Yes. She's a bit bruised and banged up. But nothing *else* happened to her," she said knowingly as she pierced my eyes with her flinty glare.

I blew out a grateful breath. "It sounds like she had a narrow escape. I sent word to her lieutenants. Plan on them showing up later."

"I figured," she said with a smirk. "That's why Kirkland made *two* pots of stew. And brownies. He loves those little devils."

I chuckled. "I know. I wish we could get them to live in regular homes."

"Well, I think some of them do. I believe some just work with Morgan. But yes, I want to keep trying to get them into safer situations." She turned to me then and put a hand on my cheek.

"I'm so sorry about Peter, Lane. Are you all right?" Even with all the commotion of hearing about Daphne and then Morgan's narrow escape, Peter's death hung heavy on all our shoulders. I felt the prickle of tears and she pulled me in for a hug. She must have been painting, because she still wore her Gypsy garb and her long black hair fell past her shoulders. She was soft, heartening, and smelled of lavender and oil paint.

"I got in more Sanders hot fudge," she said consolingly.

"You know me so well. Thank you."

We all ate companionably. The thick, dark gravy and big chunks of beef and vegetables tasted substantial and comforting. It had been a long, long day, but we still weren't done. With the plates cleared, we got down to business.

"Okay, Morgan. You ready to tell your story, dear?" asked Aunt Evelyn.

She quickly looked at Roarke and then began. "Yeah. Well, it started the night I followed Mr. Hambro, who had been tailing Donagan. I don't know why I did it. Your friend, Fio, Mr. Hambro, is quite capable. But I had this feeling that I wanted to see what was going down. So I followed Donagan and his shadowy partner to Putnam and Paulsen's downtown. Donagan went inside, swaggering all the while, talking about Rex's games sending taunting messages in red envelopes, planting clues around the town on architecture, and playing with people while he twirled that gold pawn in his fingers like a cat toys with a mouse. . . . He said all of that was exhausting and childish to him.

"After about twenty minutes, I heard a savage scream and then Donagan stumbled out. He wasn't holding anything but a little piece of paper. He obviously had not received the legacy he'd been hoping for. Mr. Hambro skulked away after that, but I was rooted to the spot. I couldn't move; it was like I had to watch the entire thing play out."

Morgan took a sip of hot tea then went on. "Up ahead—it was a really foggy night—I spotted a hooded figure. Donagan did, too, and went toward it like he wanted to talk to the person. But as he got close, the figure pulled out the silver gun, Lane. And shot him."

I couldn't help myself, I gasped. "She *did* have the silver gun! It was the same silver gun?"

"Oh yeah. She came closer to Donagan and I saw the bloody scroll on the handle and everything. That was when she pulled her hood down and I saw her long, almost-white hair. Donagan was just as shocked."

"I bet," muttered Kirkland.

I was sitting on the floor, up against Finn's knees. His hand came down and brushed my hair lightly with his fingertips. "What did she say to him? Could you hear?" I asked.

"Yes. I kinda wish I hadn't. She's really creepy."

"I know," I agreed.

"She said something about everyone being kings or pawns of men," said Morgan with her fingertips massaging Ripley's ear.

Finn said, "That was the quote from Napoleon that Rex left for Donagan. Everyone was a pawn to Rex. Even Donagan himself, his hand-picked apprentice."

Morgan nodded. "Yeah. Then Daphne said she had demonstrated to Rex, from the beginning, that she was his most trusted partner. And that she was the rightful heir. Then she said she would give him what he deserved for messing with her children. That's Tucker and Eliza, right?" she asked.

Kirkland nodded. "Then what did she do?"

Morgan gulped. "She unloaded the gun into him. Then she sprinkled money over him and placed a gold pawn on his bloody chest. Then she just walked away. *Whistling*."

"*Jesus*," whispered Kirkland.

At that, Evelyn popped up and began to pour restoring tots for all of us. Even Morgan got a little taste.

Fio was rubbing his chin thoughtfully. "But she didn't see you at that point, right?"

Morgan shook her head. "No. I waited there. The whistling in the fog lasted so long. I stayed put until I couldn't hear her anymore. Then I was about to get up and I had planned on just running full-out all the way up here. I had to tell you who was behind everything! And I was scared, I don't mind telling you."

Ripley must have understood her desperate tone, because he raised his big head and put a giant paw on her shoulder while he gave one big lick up the side of her face.

"Aw, Ripley! Yuck!" She laughed. "Thanks, buddy. I'm okay." He put his head back down and she resumed petting his silky ears.

Kirkland's chest shook as he silently chuckled. "Good boy, Rip."

Morgan took up her story again. "Well, I started to walk away. I went along the side of the building, hiding among the shadows. Then I caught sight of her hooded figure and she looked like she was walking with a purpose, on a mission to do something, so I decided to follow her. Nearby is the shipping terminal where you can buy tickets. It was dark, but it wasn't that late and it was still open. She walked up to the counter and bought a ticket. After she left, I went up there and asked where she was going."

Roarke asked, "They told you?"

She grinned. "Well, it was a young guy and I asked really nicely."

Roarke laughed. "You should become a reporter."

She replied, "I'm thinking police officer."

"Nice," said Finn. "You'd be a good one."

"Well . . . maybe not," she said ruefully. "After the guy told me she booked a passage to London, that's when I got caught. It was her goons. Had to be, because I didn't recognize them. I know the look of a lot of Venetti's gang now, and Donagan's. But these guys weren't familiar. They spotted me following her and then followed me. *Damn*, I can't believe I got caught!"

"But you were gone for almost two weeks. What happened?" asked Evelyn.

"Not much. Thankfully, they couldn't decide what to do with me. Daphne didn't want to see me. Or maybe let me see her. So she'd give the goons messages. They questioned me, but I didn't say why I was following her." Morgan subconsciously rubbed the side of her face that had the black eye. I ached for her.

"I made up a story about following people who might have money on them, that I'm a good pickpocket so I find wealthy marks. And I *am* a good pickpocket," she said with a smirk, but then darted her eyes to Fio, who was looking at her through half-closed eyes.

She squeaked, "I mean! *Used* to be a pickpocket. I'm still good at it, but I don't do it. I was able to demonstrate on them how I do it, so it lent credibility to my story." She sounded like she was forty, not about sixteen.

Kirkland was rubbing the bridge of his nose between his thumb and forefinger like this all might just be too much for him. Finn patted him on the shoulder in solidarity.

"They kept moving me to new locations and I was getting desperate. I tried to escape twice, and that's why they tied the ropes so tight," she said, rubbing that bandaged wrist. "I was able to pry an old nail from the floor and had just started to try to cut the cords when Roarke found me." She darted a look at my sleuthing partner and said, "How'd you find me, anyway, Roarke?"

"One of my informants—shut up, Lane—got word to me that he saw a girl that fits your description at an old, dilapidated school." I always teased Roarke about his legions of contacts. He's incredibly connected, so I took his *shut up* in the playful way that he intended. "He knew the school had been abandoned, so he figured it was likely that it was the girl I was looking for. When he got word to me, we were near the place, so we ran up there and she was alone. We finished cutting the ropes and got the hell out of there."

"Morgan, didn't you say he was wearing a babushka?" asked Aunt Evelyn with an amused look on her face.

"Ah, well," replied Roarke. "I didn't have much time to disguise myself to go unnoticed in that area. So I grabbed an old tablecloth drying on a line and wrapped it around me, then a little scarf around my head. I hunched over trying to look like an old lady. *Why* are you laughing, Morgan?"

She snorted, "Aw, Roarke! That pink scarf around your head. I'll never forget it!"

Just then, a loud ruckus attacked the front door. Ripley and Kirkland went running.

"Morgan, I think your lieutenants have arrived," I said as the loud noises got closer and louder as they trooped back.

The first in line was the tall boy, Eric Spry, her second in command. "Morgan," he said in a rough whisper. She stood up and carefully made her way over to him.

"I'm okay," she whispered back. He was usually a wary, always-watching and always-aware-of-people-watching-him kind of guy. But today he looked more vulnerable than I'd ever seen him as he held out his arms to her and encompassed her in a hug that spoke volumes. They must have had quite an interesting history together.

The rest of the crowd had gone silent watching all this, then Connor, the little rascal with the freckles, frank smile, and tooth missing in front, started giggling. Then he couldn't take it any longer and yelled, "We missed you!" He ran over and hugged her with a mighty squeeze that must have hit a bit of a bruise somewhere because Eric and I both saw her grimace. Eric's face went dark with that knowledge, and then Morgan laughed, fiercely hugging the little guy back, which eased a bit of the darkness on Eric's face.

There were five more of her crew who had piled in and they all cheered along with Fio. With a backdrop of happy chattering, slaps on the backs, and general merrymaking, we set up the rascals' scrumptious dinner with enough stew, drinks, and brownies to feed an army.

I set the living room Victrola with a favorite album by Benny Goodman. Our home was full, friends had been reunited, and we all received sustenance from both the food and the camaraderie.

Roarke and Finn and I drew to the side for a moment watching Fio and Evelyn trying to wrangle the crew to their seats. Kirkland laughed to himself, enjoying his appreciative crowd that kept asking how much they could have, could they have seconds, thirds, fourths. . . . When Connor stood next to him, hands on his hips imitating Kirkland's every move, I spotted Aunt Evelyn eyeing them with a sweet smile. Kirkland was giving a robust lecture on seasoning the meat and vegetables properly while Connor nodded with solemn understanding.

Finn said, "So, tomorrow we'll hit the Metropolitan."

"Yeah. We have work to do. We need to find any scrap of information on Daphne that we can," I said.

"I'll drive," said Roarke. "I'll pick you two up here at eight. Morgan's doing great, she'll recover just fine, I think. But she was lucky we got her out, Lane. She was quickly losing her value.

They'd have had to come to a decision soon on what to do with her," he said darkly.

Finn nodded. "Great work, Roarke. Tomorrow we'll start the investigation. Pinball games, a dead cop, and now the lunatic asylum. We've really gotten ourselves into some deep water this time."

Roarke and I just nodded, then I poured us a little more wine.

CHAPTER 10

We convinced Morgan to stay the next few nights with us so she could recover. She started to refuse, but the stormy look on Eric's face made her stutter to a halt and acquiesce. We even talked her into staying in the guest room instead of the front room couch. That's the thing, above the bruises and the stress of her being missing for two weeks, that convinced me her trials had been far worse than she was letting on. I wondered if we'd ever really know the whole story.

I awoke bright and early. We had a mission to accomplish.

As was the case the last and only time I had visited the infamous lunatic asylum, I felt the need to brace myself by preparing mentally and physically. I wore my favorite black trouser suit, the one that Marlene Dietrich would tip her hat to, a white silk blouse, and of course my trusty pearl dagger in its slim scabbard that always fit perfectly in the wide belts I preferred. Deep red lipstick for courage and I was ready to go.

Roarke and Finn met up with each other earlier and I heard the honk of Roarke's Packard as I raced through the kitchen, grabbing a piece of toast as I downed a quick cup of tea. I threw on my red sweater coat with the matching red fur collar and ran out the door. I hopped in the back and greeted the guys.

"Hey, Lane, we decided not to notify the hospital ahead of time. If Daphne was allowed out of there, treating it as an undercover office or home base, she must have some people in her employ," said Roarke.

"Definitely. Better to surprise them. But how do we get them to let us into her room to snoop around?" asked Finn.

I remembered Roarke's dimples coming in real handy last time. I smirked at Roarke in the rearview mirror.

"Shut up, Lane," he snickered.

"Let's just say that the attending nurse was easily swayed by Dimples here," I said, patting him on the shoulder.

Finn chuckled. "Last time, I was sitting outside there just down the street for quite some time, wondering what on earth you could be doing in there," he said.

I recalled that day, that first meeting with Daphne Franco. Her theatrical posture, draped across her bed, long white-blond hair cascading down her back, all topped off with a dramatic trans-Atlantic accent taken right out of *Mutiny on the Bounty*. When Roarke and I had the mock interview, we were digging around for clues to see if she was linked with the current crime syndicate. At the time, we had no idea she was Eliza and Tucker's mother. But what made my skin crawl was when she swiveled her gaze to me, recognizing me as the daughter of her enemies. The thin veneer hiding *something* lurking behind there came crashing down. Her eyes dilated, thin veins popped to the surface of her pale face, and she let herself be racked with a maniacal laughter that bordered on the hysterical. I couldn't get out of there fast enough.

My eyes locked with Roarke's in the mirror. "I know," he said, reading my look of wariness and nodding. "I remember that first meeting all too well."

"That good, huh?" asked Finn.

I leaned forward and clasped my hands along the back of the front seat, resting my elbows on it. "So, fellas, what's our plan this time? I'm thinking Roarke can get us access, but what's a good cover story?"

"We don't need a cover. We have me this time," said Finn with a determined half-smirk. "My badge will get us in. She's wanted, don't forget, now that we have Morgan's eyewitness account."

"Hmmm," I said. "I wonder if we should follow a subtler course, though. If there are people working with her or for her, I wonder if we might be able to uncover more if they didn't know that we're involved in police matters."

"True," said Finn.

"I have an idea," I said.

"Oh boy," said Roarke just as Finn said, "Oh no."

I patted their shoulders and said, "Leave it to me."

We took the Queensboro into Queens, past the factory with the tall white and red smokestacks, then circled around to the only bridge onto Blackwell's Island. The morning light reflected off the shining buildings of Manhattan in amber and rose, the East River sparkled with its vivid blue in the cold sunshine. Despite the beauty of the surroundings, the island had its own special brand of sinister atmosphere. It was a land of the lost; nothing healthy and thriving was here. Every person was imprisoned and isolated either from illness, poverty, or a criminal mind. As we crossed the bridge onto the island, I felt an ache like we were leaving something dear behind and I missed it already.

Main Street ran right down the middle of the island, the only street on the slim strip of land. Metropolitan was near the north end, closer to the lighthouse. As we drove, I got my story straight in my mind.

We all got out of the car and I said, "Okay, just follow my lead and use your dimples, Roarke."

As we walked up to the front door, the octagonal tower looking down upon us with distaste, Finn pointed to a strange-looking circle behind the bushes. "That's ominous."

"What is it?" I asked, unable to see it fully from where I was standing.

Roarke said, "It's a life net. The fire department uses it to catch people jumping out of buildings."

I could easily imagine wanting to jump out of those threatening windows above us. We got to the front desk, and as luck would have it, the same receptionist was there. By the look of the blush on her cheeks, she remembered Roarke. *Perfect.*

Finn chuckled low as he caught the pink on her cheeks and Roarke's.

In a good, thick Southern accent that seems to appear when I'm trying to be covert, I greeted her. "Hello, my name is Sissy McGraw and these are my colleagues Bobby Drake and Neville Darling." Finn started to laugh, then turned it into a snort-cough. "We were here just a couple of months ago to interview Daphne Franco, as our readers are keen to hear about the lives of the famous actors here in New York City. Would she be available for a follow-up interview?"

The nurse receptionist had a moment of indecision. She said, "Well, this is most uncommon, but Mrs. Franco is one of our, uh . . . *special* patients." *I bet.* "She's actually not . . . available . . . at the moment." She busied herself with looking at clipboards, flipping pages up and down.

"Well, you do think she would like another interview, wouldn't she?" I asked, knowing Daphne ate up that kind of attention, insane and criminally minded or not. "And I can't imagine she'd be happy that we left."

The nurse's eyes grew wider, knowing she'd probably be in trouble if she didn't handle this properly. "I have an idea," I said. "How about this. How about you take us on a tour of her abode. We could give the story an angle on how this Hollywood honey lives and the people around her. We could feature you a bit, too, sweetie. You have great bones and those eyes! Like Dorothy Lamour . . ." She clearly liked that idea and was enjoying the flattery.

"Well, let's see," she said, consulting the clock. "I think I can make that work. But let's be quick about it, I don't think Dr. Davis would like me taking you up there. But he's never interested in magazines and papers anyway. What he doesn't know won't hurt him, right?"

"Right."

"Okay, he's with patients for the next thirty minutes. That should give us a good fifteen minutes just to be safe."

We made a big show of getting all her pertinent information and the spelling of her name. Roarke brought his camera, so Finn took the notes while Roarke took a photo of her and I conducted an interview. Then we began the journey to Daphne's room.

Just like last time, despite the rather scary myth of the lunatic asylum, it really just looked like another hospital. Except for the rounded staircase that went along the inside edges of the octagonal tower. We went up those and I spotted a picture on the wall. I don't know why it gave me the heebie-jeebies, but it was a photo of the nurses all standing along the staircase, in circular rows, looking stoically at the camera. It was supposed to be cheery, I suppose, since you could see the top of a Christmas tree in the middle. But it was not cheery in the least. There was something sad and sinister about the stoic looks surrounding the holiday tree. We kept going up and up. My anxiety was growing and I jumped as I heard a random scream echo from somewhere. Finn put his hand on the small of my back and said softly, "It's pretty eerie in here, isn't it, love?"

"Yeah, I know. I've read some books about these places. There isn't a lot of science behind their methods yet. And it doesn't take much to get someone committed. I wonder how many people here really need to be here," I said with a shudder. As I recently learned from our last case and from facing the ghosts of my past, the one thing that I feared most was loss of control. And there was nothing that scared me more than being incarcerated in a place like this against my will.

People truly feared mental illness, and that's what made it easy to commit someone. It was this very institution that the famous female reporter, a hero of mine, Nellie Bly, infiltrated to report what was going on. She was in here for ten days and received torturous ice baths; all the women were forced to sit silently in a row on hard benches over twelve hours a day; there were abuse at the hands of the nurses, filthy rooms, raging illnesses spreading around, and rotting food. Once Nellie got herself in, she no longer pretended to be insane. But the saner she spoke and acted, the more they thought her unstable. It became impossible to convince anyone of her sanity. After her newspaper's lawyer arrived to get her out of there after her predetermined ten days ended, she wrote the big story and became a major player in investigative journalism. No one had gone to such lengths before.

After that, this particular place became better appointed. I still feared for the people here, but I hoped that they received better treatment after the article and the state awarded a significant amount of money to help the mentally ill in their care.

We got to the top of the stairs and the nurse looked back at us. I caught something that raced across her face. Had she heard us? What did that look mean? It meant something; the hackles on my neck were rising. Daphne obviously came to realize who we were last time after recognizing me at the end of our interview. Did she caution the staff about us? But then the nurse turned on an easy smile and started in with a rehearsed tour guide voice.

She pointed out rooms of interest as we went. We made our way down the long, tiled hall, our footsteps clipping along. The doors had a staunch, heavy look to them. There was no doubt that they were all locked. We passed several patients here and there; one was in a straitjacket.

"Something feels weird, Finn," I whispered, turning my head to the side.

"Yeah. But is it just the place?" he whispered back.

"I don't know." Roarke was doing a great job talking up the nurse and he did indeed use those dimples of his. He even increased his flirting with an occasional small gesture of touching her arm, or putting a solicitous hand on the small of her back.

We turned down a narrow hallway that contained only one door. It was the room that I remembered, and I certainly had memorized the way back out again. The nurse opened the door and ushered us in. Daphne was definitely not there, but her personal effects were placed around like I remembered, giving the room an unnatural feel of a normal apartment. Frames upon the dresser, a frilly robe tossed artfully across an armchair, a pink coverlet on the bed with lace trimmings. I turned back to the nurse, about to ask a question.

And the door slammed behind her, the lock banging into place. We were trapped.

CHAPTER 11

"I knew it!" I said, exasperated. I broke out in a cold sweat; in a place like this, it was easy to make people just disappear. Fio knew we were coming here, but I'm sure he figured Finn could keep us out of trouble, so he may not have thought about backup. But he'd get us out sooner or later. In here, however, later could be deadly.

"All right," said Finn. "Let's look around before anyone else gets here. We'll have to come up with an escape plan, but maybe we can find something here to help."

"You guys look around, I'll keep watch," said Roarke, looking out the small square window in the door. "I can see down the hallway. The nurse is running for help."

Finn and I raced around looking at everything. We were on the third floor, and there was a window without any bars on it. I walked over to a dresser and a few framed photos decorated the top. One definitely caught my eye, a photograph of her in a hat with little dyed feathers adorning the band. It was the hat that she wore when she hovered over me when I was recuperating from the accident, the very vision that tormented me in my nightmares. And she was sitting next to someone very interesting . . .

I opened a drawer and said, "Figures."

"What'd you find?" asked Finn, running over.

"I knew she'd have a feather boa," I said disgustedly as I pulled out a light pink boa, just the thing I'd imagined her donning the last time as she had lain dramatically across the bed.

"That's it?" asked Finn.

"Actually, no. Look at this."

Underneath the boa, and two pairs of extremely frilly underpants, was a slick black box.

"You know what that is, don't you?" said Finn ominously.

I nodded as I took the box into my hands. "I can't believe it." I flicked the lock and opened it to find the duplicate silver gun, with the deep red scroll on the handle. The gun that had been part of my dreams for years, the one that my dad found on Rex Ruby when he killed him. And the gun Daphne used to kill Donagan. Now I had both of them, the evil yin and yang guns. I slipped the box into my purse. "Let's keep looking."

In the closet we found many sets of clothes, certainly not the wardrobe of an inmate. We found the typical items in any woman's bedroom: perfume, many pairs of shoes, coats, and purses. Roarke took a minute to get some pictures of the room. We wouldn't have enough time to scour every inch.

"Hmm . . ." I said, tapping my lips with my fist as I took a good overall look at the room. "So this is clearly not a typical patient's room. She's made a special arrangement. If this is her residence—and it's definitely a great place to hide, I'll give her that—then she has to have a way out of here."

Roarke said, "Unless she just has her own key and uses the door. It's not like these places are regulated yet, and this door is the only one on this hallway. So there could be a separate entrance or stairway. Knowing her as we do now, she's probably the queen bee around here."

"True," said Finn. "But let's look for any secret doors or anything. We need all the help we can get."

I pushed and knocked on all the walls, all the doorways, both in the room and the bathroom that was attached. We were running out of time. All I knew was we needed to get out. If they had orderlies come at us with drugs to knock us out, they'd need an army of them to take all three of us down, but I'm sure they could manage even if Finn did have a gun.

"Guys! They're coming!" yelled Roarke.

Finn was in the bathroom. "Stand back," he said. He used his gun to bash out the glass in a small window. Then he took a towel and wrapped it around his gun to break out the remnants of the glass. The only piece of furniture that I could move was a chair, and I wedged that under the handle of the main door to slow them down a bit.

I ran into the bathroom as Roarke climbed out the window. Finn turned to me. "There's a tree just outside. We can grab onto a drain right there to reach a heavier branch. I know you're good at climbing trees, love," he said with a wink. I did like climbing trees. And I'd take *any* way of exit at the moment; they almost had the door open.

"Let's go!" I said, grabbing his hand. He helped me up to the window and, sure enough, there was a tree nearby. We were far off the ground, but quite honestly, compared to the ledge of Grand Central and dangling off the Queensboro, like I did not too long ago, this was a piece of cake.

Roarke was almost down and I grabbed the drain in my right hand, then eased a leg outward toward the tree. I got a foot on the branch and pushed off to the tree. "Come on, Finn!" I climbed toward the trunk, then headed down. Finn followed suit, and just as he pushed off to the tree, the door inside crashed open. We raced down the tree and started running to the car. I looked back to see two orderlies and the nurse looking out the window at us.

"See, Finn?" I said.

"See what?" he asked.

"It's not just Roarke and me that this stuff happens to."

"Oh, it's definitely you and Roarke," Finn said with a sarcastic snigger. "It was silly of me to think my presence could stop the absurdity."

"You got me there," I said resignedly. "Hey, Roarke, we need to get that film developed on the double."

"Will do," he said as he slammed his door shut and started up the car. "Did you see anything of interest?"

"Well, the whole affair was certainly of interest, Dudley and Neville. But one photo on her dresser was definitely fascinating. Not only did she have that hat on that I remember her wearing from all those years ago, but she was sitting next to Rex Ruby. And despite her being his daughter-in-law, it did not look like that was their only relationship . . ."

"Well, now, that makes his reason for choosing her as the heir a little clearer, doesn't it? I got a few close-up shots of the other photos, too, and the room overall," said Roarke.

Finn nodded as he lit a cigarette, took a drag, and handed it to me.

"I can't believe I got the other silver gun. I knew it wasn't gone; I wasn't even that surprised when Morgan said Daphne killed Donagan with it. It's like they have a life of their own." I took a couple thoughtful puffs, my hand shaking just a bit, then handed the cigarette back to Finn. That woman got under my skin like no one else. "I have to decide what to do with them now. Feels like they're cursed. What's a good way to get rid of a cursed gun?"

"That's a fine question," said Roarke. "It was already resurrected from the East River once."

"It just keeps coming back," said Finn, flicking the butt of his cigarette out the window.

I would have to keep the guns for the time being; I couldn't really dispose of them. A solid safe deposit box was where I'd stash them. We were all bantering, that's just how we operated, but I couldn't help but feel uneasy. Daphne must have retrieved the gun when Eliza dropped it over the bridge. The only way that could have been done is if she had been watching and waiting. The gun had dropped off onto a shallow area near the banks of the large pillar. It would have disappeared forever, sinking into the muck of the East River, unless someone had been right there, right on site. And if she'd been watching us, just *how long* had she been in the shadows, observing our every move, patiently waiting to strike?

CHAPTER 12

Going back across that wonderful, beautiful bridge into Manhattan was like going home after a long and arduous journey. All our shoulders began to lose the tension and we breathed deeply like we'd been holding our breath for a long time.

"I'll get the film developed right away," reiterated Roarke.

"Great. So we know she's been a partner with Rex all this time. And it looks like this has been her hideout, at least *a* hideout. But the other thing we *didn't* find was any evidence that she's been involved with the pinball and gambling racket. Plus, from Morgan's description, Daphne's goons don't seem to be the ones from the deli, the ones who . . ." My voice slowly ebbed as it was so hard to talk about Peter being killed. Those words were like poison, making me not want to utter them.

Both Roarke and Finn grew still. Finn's jaw set in grim determination.

"Right," said Finn. "But it's not definitive, so when we head to London, we can search for Daphne herself, for any other clues about her possible involvement with the pinball case, and then any rumblings about a resurgence in the Red Scroll."

"Plus, I need to see if I can find out more about my parents' involvement with them. Maybe Miles will have more information now. And then . . ." I looked at Finn a bit warily, knowing he'd also be facing shadows from his past.

"Yeah, *and then* is right," he said as he shook his head minutely.

He looked out the window, at the skyline of Manhattan. His home now. I knew only too well what it was like to head into the unknown, wondering what I would find. I put my hand on his shoulder, remembering that the scariest part of that was not what I discovered about my past and my parents, but what I'd discovered in myself. The fear and the anger that I didn't realize I'd been carrying.

I looked out at the East River, heading into the sea. I could just glimpse a large ship going out toward the wild waters of the frigid Atlantic. The ocean that led to Europe, to Finn's past. I wondered what we would find, and how it would impact us all.

The *Queen Mary*, or one of the other Cunard Line ships, left New York Harbor and Southampton every single Wednesday. As luck would have it, it was the *Queen Mary* herself that we would be taking across the Atlantic. Fiorello was able to secure us two tickets and Aunt Evelyn upgraded us to two first-class cabins.

The *Hindenburg* would have been faster—only about two to three days, versus the five or six days on the *Queen Mary*—but it was on its winter schedule currently, only flying to Buenos Aires this time of year. Besides, Finn wasn't too pleased about taking something like that again. His last flight had been on a military dirigible when he was hurrying back to the States to, well, to find me in a rather tricky predicament. He preferred not to relive that again for quite some time.

Those five days on the *Queen Mary* were something I'd never forget. Ocean liners were built for speed. They made them gorgeous and had the best amenities, but still, speed was the key. It was chilly outside, being that it was January, but we spent our days eating and meeting new friends, swimming in the indoor pool, and reading for hours by one of the many fireplaces and cozy spots. In the evenings we saw shows, danced for hours, walked the glorious deck under a glittering blanket of stars, and enjoyed a sweet time of just the two of us.

One night, Finn and I were dancing to a song by Cole Porter, the large band in their black and white suits, playing their hearts out for the appreciative and more-than-slightly tipsy crowd. I looked up at Finn and despite our lively dancing, his eyes held a closed, far-off look with a touch of brooding.

When the music slowed to a more sultry number and he drew me in close, I tilted my head to the side and asked, "Are you worried about seeing your family?"

His eyes shifted to mine and that closed look immediately left, warming and coming to life in the sparkling lights of the effervescent ballroom. In this lighting, his eyes looked like melting chocolate as he smiled at me.

"Yes, love, I am. They're an unpredictable lot, to be sure. I think that's what has me the most cautious. I was never able to understand how they work or why I'm so different," he said with a contemplative sigh.

"How are you different?"

"Well . . . you'll understand as soon as you meet my mother." He gave a little eye roll. "And Sean and my dad, well . . . Sean and I used to get along as young boys. But then he became . . . *hmm* . . . manipulative and he had a merciless quality that always had me on edge. I could never grasp what he was all about and it made me feel off balance, somehow. Out of control. I didn't feel good about life, about myself, back then. I wasn't happy. I'd put all my hopes and aspirations into making a life for myself in America. Lane, I'm just not sure what we're walking into. Some things are just left dead and buried. And I don't want to go back to that time that was so bleak."

I nodded, scrutinizing his face, guessing what was behind his eyes. "So, you aren't hoping for a reconciliation with any of them?"

"No." He paused, a stab of concern hitting his earnest face. "Why, do you think I should?"

"Hell no!" I blurted. He laughed outright, the pang of unease slipping from his countenance. "No, Finn. I get it. You'll know what to do when you get there. There are some relationships that are just poisonous. Knowing you like I do, I know beyond a doubt that you've given them multiple opportunities to reconcile. And if they've remained closed and cold . . . then that's their loss. You did make a life for yourself in America. A very successful one. It's sad that they chose to miss out on being a part of your life."

He smiled in earnest as he sent me on a vigorous spin, the music swelling and practically lifting us both off the floor as we soaked in the joy of the moment.

When he pulled me in close again, he said in his gravelly whisper, "You know, love, my grandma Viv told me pretty much the exact same thing. I can't wait for you to meet her. You two are cut from the same cloth," he said, eyes sparking with amusement.

"Well, at least someone in your family has some sense! Come on. Come with me. I have an idea."

"Ooh."

I nodded to a waiter and we followed him to the bar where he gave me a bottle of champagne. I took Finn by the hand and led him up the stairs toward the bow of the ship to a little find that I'd been hoping to show him.

We opened the door that led to the deck of the ship, a blast of cold almost knocking us over. I felt my hair slipping from its clips, so I took it down and let it blow wildly about. I snagged two of the heavy blankets that were kept by the door for just such a moment as this, then guided Finn toward the front right, where there was a little inset just big enough for two deck chairs, close together. Because of the way the inset was cut into the ship, it provided a bit of shelter from the wind, but we still had a direct view of the resplendent sky, full of countless stars that were usually hidden from us in New York with all the lights of the city.

We both sat in the long chairs, tucking in the blankets around our legs. Finn opened the champagne and we drank straight from the bottle. We sat back, side by side, gazing at the heavens, Finn's hand in mine.

CHAPTER 13

As they came into view of his home country, the major shipping port of Southampton rising out of the misty harbor, the old sounds and scents came back to Finn like long-lost friends—at first familiar and welcome, but then fraught with crushed dreams and misunderstanding. The very air felt different from his new home, New York City. It was both comforting and disturbing in equal parts. He already missed his city. He'd fallen in love with it the moment his ship pulled past the Statue of Liberty for the first time. Then came the job he loved, then Lane. He ached to go back. New York was now more a part of him than the country where he was born. His childhood home represented haunting memories. Betrayal. Dismissal. Pain.

It was in that moment that the dream from the night before came back to him in full force: his bloody hands, the eerie drumbeats, the heavy, clutching guilt. He knew these strange emotions were tied up in tackling the ghosts of his past, mixed together with the thoughts and fears that were brought out from Orson Welles's *Voodoo Macbeth.*

The play had a strange pull on Finn, dragging out old memories and old stories, ones that he'd rather keep buried. He took another drag on his cigarette and flicked the butt into the sea as he came to a decision. Just like Lane, he had to face his past. All of it. And then decide how to forge ahead. He nodded smartly and put his hands on the cold railing, feeling the wind and small crystals of mist on his face. Then he let the memories of that aptly named voodoo, of that special night, come back to him. Seeing *Voodoo Macbeth* for the first time.

He hadn't been too sure about it.

They walked over to the theater, its lights blazing. Lane and Florence were chatting away, he and Sam tended to be a bit less talkative, but companionable. Big Sam was most definitely the strong, silent type. That is, until he was dancing or something struck him as funny. Then he laughed a great, booming laugh that shocked those around him and then became contagious, spreading to everyone else. Finn admired him deeply, and they discovered a good working relationship in the NYPD and a solid friendship.

Shakespeare just wasn't something Finn was into. Lane loved all things theater, film, and book related. But Shakespeare often felt like it was another language. And a bit boring, truth be told. But Lane said this was a special version of *Macbeth* and because of her genuine enthusiasm, Finn was game. She said she knew the director; he guessed that it was probably a friend of Aunt Evelyn's. She had friends in all places, high and low.

He and Sam talked about work, both of them on the police force for quite a while, so they knew each other's routines well. When they reached the theater, Lane waved and ran up ahead, receiving a big hug from a young, good-looking guy with dark hair and a vivid smile.

She flagged Finn over. "Orson. I'd like you to meet Finn Brodie and Sam and Florence Battle. Everyone? Meet Orson Welles, our illustrious director."

That was the director? He'd pictured an elderly kind of guy. Finn was pretty sure this kid had to be under twenty-five years old. Welles held out an enthusiastic hand, his eyes lighting up from within. Florence got all bashful, her grin speaking volumes. Sam chuckled his deep laugh and mightily shook Orson's hand, like a bear shaking a puppy's paw. Finn shook Orson's hand and bit back a smile when Orson had flexed his hand first, presumably getting the feeling back after the bear's firm grip.

Lane's eyes sparkled as she watched her friends meet. Her zeal for life never ceased to amaze Finn. She extracted joy and pleasure as much as humanly possible. She wasn't an extravagant beauty, not like those formal models who looked like ice ran in their veins even though the external beauty might be staggering. But Lane was *alive*. And that kind of beauty lasts, making you want to just be around it, lingering and enjoying it.

Orson was clearly excited and said to Lane, "I just think . . . I think this will be the greatest success of my life, Lane. I mean, opening night traffic was stopped for five blocks, you couldn't even get near Harlem. Everybody who was anybody was there and there were so many curtain calls at the end, we finally left the curtain open! Just let the audience come up onstage to congratulate the actors. And that was . . . that was *magical*."

Orson leaned closer to Lane, looking at Finn with a secretive look, and said, "Did you keep it secret? Or did you tell him?"

Lane gave a wolfish smile, her eyes glinting with mischief. "Oh, he knows it's *Macbeth*. But that's all."

That's all?

Orson rubbed his hands together, enjoying the anticipation. "Ooh, this will be fun. Are you all ready? Let's go!"

Lane grasped Finn's hand and came in close. She whispered in his ear, "Are you ready, Finn?" God, she was sexy. Yes. He was ready. She kissed his neck and he felt desire heat through.

"Let's go, love."

They walked in and took their seats. He enjoyed the preshow static in the air, feeling the anticipation running through the theater. The sound of the instruments being tuned, the low rumble of conversations, the scent of a mixture of perfumes from the patrons dressing up for the night. He knew the basic story of the play. The man Macbeth wrestling with wanting power, murdering the king to get it, and the backlash of guilt. But it was so much more than that.

When the curtain opened, Finn's breath whooshed out of him. *Macbeth* was supposed to take place in Scotland. But when the red velvet swept back, it revealed a massive, dark jungle with heavy greenery, the suggestion of skeletons, and a captivating yet eerie drumbeat. It instantly drew him in and made his heart pump faster.

The entire theater sat forward just a little bit more. This was *Voodoo Macbeth*.

The first all-black theater cast in the country was perfection. The cool blue lighting shined on the actors' bodies, creating a moonlit glow that gave them an ethereal quality. There was a primal nature to the iambic pentameter of the words. And Shakespeare. God, *his words*. After a few minutes of listening to this older English, it became like watching a film with subtitles where after a while, the words at the bottom blended with the action on the screen and it was as if the words melted into your consciousness instead of actually being aware of reading them. He felt the very essence of the passion, the poetry, and the struggle.

The lilting and beautiful words spoke to Finn's soul. Welles had created a whole world with the music, the artistry of the set, and the talent of the actors who knew this was more than just a play. They were making history. The intensity, beauty, and danger made the words come alive. The evil and avarice became a living thing in the theater. The guilt heavier than anything he'd known. The fear of the inability to control something that began with a single, horrific decision was claustrophobic. The blood on their hands . . . it was magnificent.

And it was personal. The plight between friends and comrades, family struggling for power, murderous decisions that backlashed with potent consequences. So much of it mirrored how he felt about his family and their own murderous desires. And it filled him with dread.

Finn was struck anew with fear at the second witch's line: "Cool it with a baboon's blood, then the charm is firm and good."

The charm. There was a legend that the play *Macbeth* was cursed. Actors were often superstitious to even utter the word *Macbeth* at the playhouse. They called it the Scottish Play instead. He had to admit, there were more injuries and deaths in the play than any other he'd heard about. Maybe that's what worried him most. Maybe . . . *he* was charmed. His family certainly seemed cursed.

Finn grasped the cold deck railing even firmer. He had to tell Lane. He hadn't told her the whole story about his brother. He could have, the night they spent hours on deck, gazing at the stars, finishing off a bottle of champagne. Why was he holding back? It hadn't been his fault, so why not share it with her? But then it occurred to him, he did know why. Finn's brother Sean had caused enough misery. He would be damned if he'd let it affect Lane, too. But he also felt guilt. It was something he'd wrestled with since he left England. That play sent a prickle of fear down to the very core of him.

"By the pricking of my thumbs, something wicked this way comes." He felt it. Something was indeed coming. It was coming for him.

CHAPTER 14

For a charm of powerful trouble,
like a hell-broth boil and bubble.

—the second witch, *Macbeth*

The final day, as we neared the shores of Southampton, I sensed a coolness in Finn. He was distracted and looked like he was steeling himself against something. I found him at the railing that afternoon, looking out toward his old life, his old memories.

"Finn, are you okay?" I asked, slipping my arm around his waist, under his suitcoat, his arm automatically coming around me and pulling me in.

"Yeah. Just looking ahead." He paused as we both looked at the gray sky, the dark green water rolling beneath us. I had to admit, it wasn't too inviting. A nice bit of sunshine would have been quite welcome. "I think . . . I think that I need to tell you the whole story. About Sean."

"You sure you're ready?" I asked.

He took a contemplative breath. "I feel like we don't know all that we could be facing when we arrive. I can't help but feel the old ghosts. Like we were safe in the States, but not here. And . . . I want you to know. It's not that I've been hiding anything from you, I just . . ." He shook his head in indecision.

"Oh, I know all about needing the right timing to figure out old secrets and old ghosts, Finn. You tell me when you're ready. And perhaps when I have a whiskey sour in my hand."

He chuckled softly. "That's not a bad idea at all. Come on. Let's go inside."

We headed in and found a spot at a cozy bar; we only had an hour before we'd dock and disembark. But between bantering with the bartender and running into a charming little old couple we'd met earlier, we never went over his story. I didn't push; Finn had to tell it when it was the right time. But part of me feared that he would wait too long.

Hours later, we were all set in our quaint train, ready to head to London. We enjoyed a cup of tea and some buttery crumpets. I could've eaten about ten.

"Well, that was quite the adventure, love!" said Finn as he set his tea down.

"The *Queen Mary* was gorgeous, I could hardly believe it," I said, dabbing my lips with my napkin.

Both of us felt the heavy weight of fatigue settle onto us. So we leaned back, getting comfortable, and I rested my head upon his shoulder for a little nap.

After a train ride of just under two hours, we arrived in London. I tried not to look like a tourist, certain I was failing miserably, because my eyes were drinking in every little detail.

"What are those red fire-hydrant-looking things?" I asked.

"Pillar boxes."

"What's a pillar box?"

"It's a postal box."

"Mailbox?" I clarified.

"Yes."

"But . . . it's red. Don't the dogs . . ." I sputtered.

"They seem to leave them alone. But if an American dog came by, it'd be a problem."

"I like the red phone booths!"

"Phone *boxes*."

"Okay. Londoners love their boxes. Let's go to the restaurant box. I'm starving."

We headed to the pub where Finn first met his London informant and former spy, Miles Havalaar. I had a soft spot for the guy as we worked closely with him on our last case. He had known my parents and was instrumental in getting us information about Rex

Ruby's heir and revealing the true identity of Tucker Henslowe, a friend who turned out to be anything but.

As we walked, I got a better feel for London, how it was different from New York and Detroit. It was quirky and colorful with odd bits of superstition and ghosts scattered over the city. Mixed in with patriotic monuments to war heroes of old and strange little stores smashed between two bigger buildings with crooked chimneys poking out. It was like a bohemian quilt full of textures, colors, and stories, then coated with a frosting of elegance from famous hotels like Claridges, stores like Selfridges and Harrods, and of course museums aplenty.

We walked into a quintessential London pub complete with sprinkles of hay on the floor, tall pub tables, dark booths, the scent of Guinness in the air, and low, murmuring conversations all against the backdrop of a fireplace glowing with warmth and the feeling of camaraderie.

"I *love* this place," I said with passion.

"I knew you would."

I spotted Miles at the corner pub table near the fireplace. I noticed it was the perfect situation to keep an eye on all the patrons, yet near a back door for a quick exit. He saw us and raised his already half-empty glass, beckoning us over with a lopsided grin.

"Miles! So good to see you!" I exclaimed as I gave him a big hug, making him turn bright red and bashful.

Finn slapped him on the back and waved to the bartender for two more pints of Guinness. Miles was not one for small talk, so we quickly filled him in on the last couple of weeks and talked about our mission here.

Finn began, "So, Miles. There are some questions arising about just what Lane's parents—Matthew and Charlotte Lorian—were involved in as they worked undercover infiltrating the Red Scroll Network. And now that we know who the heir is to Rex's legacy we need to see if the new leader will be starting things up again over here. Police Commissioner Valentine sent us here, in the hope that we can shed light on the possibilities of future gang activity as well as finding out more about the Lorians for Lane's sake."

Miles cast a beady eye on me, digesting this information. My parents and I had always had the last name of Sanders, until I found out recently that our original last name was Lorian. They changed our names to be thorough in hiding out in Rochester, Michigan, when they were trying to extricate themselves from their intelligence work. It had felt strange knowing that I'd been born with a completely and utterly foreign last name. But Sanders was a part of me now. I'd always be Lane Sanders.

Miles hadn't said more than a few words since we arrived, and we let him simmer as we watched his mind work. He looked good. Finn had told me that when he'd first located Miles, he'd been running scared and paranoid for years, running from Rex and the network. But Finn had given him a chance to turn things around and work against that crime syndicate. There was power against fear when you had a mission.

I turned to Miles and said, "So, any suggestions on where we should start?"

"So you discovered the heir, ay?" said Miles with a glint in his eye. "Well, well, well. Let me give it a guess."

Finn ordered us all fish 'n' chips as Miles gave it some deep thought. "Yeah. Yeah," Miles said, ruminating. "I get it. I think Commissioner Valentine was right to send you here. Whoever is the heir has been working all along. It's not someone new, that's for sure, which means they've built up power over all this time."

"Why do you say that?" I asked.

"Rex would've hand-picked someone. He was too controlling to allow it to chance. For certain, yeah. I'm sure Rex would've rather had his own son, Rutherford, be the one to carry on the business. Rex loved the idea of family. But his son wasn't cut out for it, so I thought for sure it was that Donagan fella. He fit what I would think Rex would choose. Yet . . ." His accent grew more and more Cockney as he thought more deeply, his fingers drumming on the table.

Finn prompted him, "Yet . . . ?"

"Yeah. Let me think a moment. Actually, I can see Rex having someone not so visible, not so predictable, let's say, in the wings waiting. Rex was patient. That's what made him so deadly. He played chess when everyone else was playing checkers. My guess is that it's someone invisible. Someone who might not look the lead, but will be that much more lethal."

The waitress quickly set the delightfully homey meal before us in baskets lined with newspaper.

"Hmm," I said, taking a swig of my creamy Guinness. "You're absolutely right. It's been someone on the sidelines, someone whom we never considered being even involved in the game, let alone future leader."

Miles squinted in thought. "Yeah, that sounds like Rex's perfect candidate. Who was it? One of his two grandchildren? Tucker or Eliza?"

I shook my head as Finn answered him. "No. Try their mother. It was Daphne."

"Good Lord," gasped Miles. "God damn, she's perfect," he said in admiration. "So the insanity? Was it just an act?"

I answered, "That's debatable. Let's just say it didn't get in her way. It may have even helped her get farther. We found out that her room at the lunatic asylum was really just a front. Talk about a perfect hiding place. She's definitely the one who killed Donagan. We have an eyewitness."

"That's just bloody unbelievable," said Miles.

"We heard that she booked a passage to London recently, so it clinched the idea that we should get over here," said Finn. "Can you get the word out to your people? See if anyone's seen her?"

"Yeah, but you might have to be patient," said Miles.

"What do you mean?" I asked rather sharply, making Miles jump. I wasn't known for my patience.

Miles eyed me carefully, righting the glass he'd knocked askew. "Like I said, Rex and his whole crew were imperturbable, willing to wait. If things got too hot, they'd cool everything way down. Let people think they'd disappeared or gotten tired or whatever. I'm just saying that they might be working on a new deal, or they might be waiting for us to relax. Let the trail go cold. I'd say he trained Daphne well. If she was able to hide out in an insane asylum, she's got the patience of Job, as my mum would say."

By the disgruntled look on his face, Finn didn't like that idea one bit, either. I'd gotten it into my head that we could finish this. Soon.

"Well," I declared, "what we *can* do is dig around here and find out two things. One, if the Network is still kicking. And two, we can try to find out more about my parents and, for my own sake, close the door on what they'd been involved in."

"Are you sure you want to do that, love?" asked Finn, also eyeing me carefully, his British accent more pronounced here in London than the Irish brogue that crept out at times. "You might find out things you don't want to know."

I thought about it for a moment, my middle finger circling the top of my glass. "Actually, I don't feel a deep need to know for the sake of curiosity, but so that I know what I'm walking into. What's that saying? If there's a spider in the room, I want to know where it is?"

"I think it's a wasp," said Finn with a chuckle. I was famous among my friends for not getting song lyrics correct and now I could add aphorisms.

"Well, either way, I want to *know* if there's anything creepy and poisonous in the dark," I said.

There had been too many times lately where I felt that I was being hunted. I was in the crosshairs because of my job and my proximity to the mayor. But I was also involved because of my parents. I'd love to clear up one side of the issue if at all possible.

"Well . . ." said Miles, setting down his napkin, marking the end of his meal. "I have an idea, a John fellow . . . I think he should tell us a bit of his story. He knew your folks, Lane. He worked on a small bit of a case with them. He's out of the city, but maybe he can help."

"Okay! Let's set something up with this John. We can take a drive tomorrow," I said, taking one last chip.

Just then the door to the pub opened. It had been opening and closing the entire time we'd been meeting, but something was different. A colder wind came in and something made the hairs on my neck stand on end.

My back was to the door and just as I was about to turn, Finn uttered, "Oh no."

I quickly turned around and two women entered with the cold

breeze. They looked like they might go over to the bar, but something made both of them as one turn their heads in our direction.

They delightedly yelled and flapped their arms, waving and making a big fuss. "Finn!" I had a sinking feeling that this wasn't going to go well. I heard him groan the tiniest bit. Miles chuckled. They ran over to Finn and he inched toward me for protection. The women were loud and still flapping a lot as I scrutinized them. They were funny little replicas of each other. They had varying shades of brown hair, but cut almost identically. Their dresses were shades of blue, and they each took off their little kid gloves at the same time. It was like one of those puzzles for kids where the pictures are almost identical and you have to study each picture to see where there were differences. One had bigger eyes and was slightly taller, and the other had a tiny space between her two front teeth. I think it was mainly their mannerisms that were striking. They must've spent a lot of time together to perfect such mimicry.

"Hello, ladies. Agnes, Eunice." Finn introduced Miles and me. They turned to Miles and they shook his hand. Then they turned to me and smiled. Neither of the smiles reached their eyes. They shook my hand, both of their hands feeling limp and lifeless.

Then the taller one took a calculated look at me, then Finn, and said to him, "Have you seen Gwen yet? She'd so love to see you!" She placed a little hand on his arm while I tried hard not to punch her in the face.

I turned to Miles. "This is fun, isn't it?"

Poor Finn was the color of a chili pepper. "No, I haven't seen Gwen. I'm on a work assignment."

Agnes, the one who had put her hand on his arm, now patted it like he was a little puppy. A puppy who wasn't quite right in the head. "Oh right. Of course. You're on *assignment.*"

He got up. "All right. That's enough. Nice to see you ladies. We'll be on our way." With that, Miles and I quickly grabbed our coats and scooted along with Finn.

"What was that all about?" I asked, still buttoning up my coat as we briskly walked down the block.

"That was Gwen's little . . . entourage."

"They looked like mannequins," I blurted.

Finn abruptly stopped and slowly turned his face to me. He blew out the smoke from his cigarette and tilted his hat up on his head, just looking at me.

"What?" I asked.

His face cleared and suddenly he started to laugh. I smiled as Miles caught Finn's laughter. "My God, they really do," Finn uttered as he rubbed his forehead, chuckling, easing his obvious headache and clearing his mind. "Leave it to you." We started walking again.

"What did Agnes mean, with the comment about you being on assignment? It was like she didn't believe you," I said.

I noticed Miles squinting at Finn, trying to assess him as Finn replied, "She definitely didn't believe me. Let's just say when I moved to the States, I didn't leave here on an auspicious note. To say the least."

Just then a beggar in a particularly dire situation, with his pants ripped and his face almost unrecognizable from grime, came into our view. Finn saw him, and I watched as he walked over to the man, said a few words, and gave him a rather large bill. Finn's kindness was one of his finest attributes. Once when I had stalked—I mean, *followed*—him, I saw him reach out to a young street urchin when others had just swatted him away. Kindness to those who have no hope of giving something in return is just about the most admirably telling thing you can witness in another person.

Finn walked back over to us as we continued on. "Did you know that man, Finn?" I asked.

"No."

"What did you tell him?"

"Oh, I just told him about a little church up ahead. They give meals and a safe place to stay when there's room."

"Damn, you're sexy," I said.

Miles barked out a laugh.

"You're not so bad yourself, love," replied Finn.

I took his arm. "All right! Shall we reconvene tomorrow, Miles?" We made plans to meet and he'd look into where we could find his friend John.

As Finn and I walked along, I admired the quaint townhouses and the streetlights that were still gas lit. London had its own personality. Even the sounds were different from New York. You could feel its age in the cobblestones in the crooked lanes, the old buildings darkened by a century of soot, and places like Westminster Abbey and the Tower of London that had been standing centuries before America even gained independence. New York was an older city in America, but still young compared to London, of course. I loved it immediately, but there was a little piece of me that missed my city.

I thought through our goals for our trip. We went on this adventure to unravel any lingering mystery about my parents and to make certain that the Red Scroll Network didn't have a presence here. Europe had enough trouble going on and we wanted to stop any momentum they might gain in their old stomping grounds.

On top of that, I was quickly realizing Finn not only had to face his past, but we had another mystery to handle. Those two women had a profound effect on Finn. And I'd wager a hefty bet that they were up to no good.

CHAPTER 15

There's no art to find the mind's construction in the face.

—King Duncan, *Macbeth*

Miles went back to his place, Finn and I went to our hotel and freshened up. I worried about the right time to ask about Sean. I wanted to know sooner rather than later. But before dinner, we had an important appointment to keep.

The sun was down, and London became a city of gold and black. Gold gaslights that shined in the foggy darkness, top hats making coal black silhouettes on the honey-colored buildings as their wearers walked by. Cars were prominent, but the *clip clop* of horse hooves on cobblestones immortalized Dickens and his characters that trod these same streets.

Back at the hotel, I changed into a new favorite dress that was cranberry red. It had long flowing sleeves with a fitted sheath that flared at the knees, to which I added a wide black belt. Finn decided on a jet-black suit with a fine pinstripe, black shirt, white tie, and his favorite black fedora. We joined up and decided on martinis at the bar for luck.

We clinked glasses and as I took a hearty sip, I sized him up, trying to read him. Trying to see any telltale signs of how London was making him feel, and if those two weirdos had any lingering effects. How could they not? There was something off about them.

"What are you thinking about, Finn?"

"Actually, I'm thinking of *Voodoo Macbeth*."

"Mmm." I nodded. That play had deeply affected him and I

thought it intriguing that the memory cropped up in his thoughts at this particular moment. "What about exactly?"

"I liked how Welles made the jungle background so dark. So tangled. That struggle with power and how far to go . . . it needed a backdrop that was tricky to get through. Genius, really."

"Seems like that's been on your mind a lot lately," I commented as I ate my third olive.

"Yeah. Yeah, it has. The power. The desire. The curse."

"Do you want to tell me about Sean?"

He looked at me, his gray-green eyes serious, sparking with intelligence and a love of adventure. But before he could answer, Finn suddenly became perfectly still. Like a lion on the hunt. Or perhaps a gazelle that suddenly spots the lion lying in wait . . . his eyes looked over my shoulder and I followed his gaze, turning around on my stool.

A strawberry blond, petite woman in a perfectly neat navy-blue suit and matching overcoat was at the door, looking at Finn. My eyes scoured her from head to toe, knowing it could only be one person. Gwen.

When Finn had lived here, before Sean's betrayal, he'd been friends with Gwen and at one point had more significant feelings for her. When Sean proposed to her, Finn had tried to talk with her about Sean's devious nature, but Gwen didn't believe him and went along with the wedding. I'd wrestled with jealousy when he'd been in London a few months ago, but I knew beyond a doubt where his heart really was. That didn't mean I had to like her.

I motioned to the bartender for another martini.

Before she made her way over, I caught Finn's eye and smiled. "You got this, Finn? You okay?"

He leveled his eyes at me and smiled that crooked smile that reached his eyes and my heart. "Definitely, love."

"Cheers, buddy. This is gonna be fun."

He almost spit out his martini as he'd tipped back to get the last drops. He laughed as Gwen approached.

"Finn! I heard from Vivian that you were staying here, I hoped I'd find you. Sorry to interrupt," she said, nodding to me. Her urgent tone precluded us from making official introductions.

"What's wrong, Gwen?" said Finn, his face clouding over.

She exhaled. "It's your father. He's very ill. If you want to see him, before . . ." She stumbled on her words, then stopped. "You'd better come now."

Finn nodded. "Gwen Brodie, this is Lane Sanders; Lane, this is Gwen. Can you give us a moment, Gwen?"

"Of course." She walked back toward the door and paused, her tiny hands on the purse that matched her coat. And hat. And shoes.

"What do you think?" I asked Finn.

Finn blew out a breath. "I haven't seen my parents since the . . . accident. I don't know. They disowned me and I haven't looked back." He looked at his empty glass, memories flooding through his mind. Both good and bad, I'm sure. I laid my hand on his.

"Whatever you want to do, I'll do it with you."

Finn nodded and we walked out with Gwen. But my senses were on alert; there was something fishy about her. When she said that Finn's father was ill, her eyes darted back and forth like she was thinking of what word to use. I didn't trust her as far as I could throw her. Well, actually, even less than that, because I was pretty sure I could toss her ass pretty darn far.

Finn was savvy, intelligent, thoughtful. But I worried that he'd walk right into a trap of sorts. I learned the hard way that sometimes we could have blind spots when family was concerned. I was definitely wishing we'd had a chance to go over his entire story about Sean. I felt that I was going to need to know every single detail so that I'd truly understand just what this family of his was capable of.

We took a cab to a local hospital near the home of Polly and Richard Brodie, Finn's parents. The drive was awkward with me being sandwiched between Finn and Gwen. I leaned into Finn, trying to not touch Gwen and her perfectly matching ensemble. For now, we'd have to put our previous plans for the evening on hold.

As we walked into the bustling hospital, Finn asked Gwen, "Is Sean here?" That's what I was certainly wondering.

She looked at the delicate silver watch on her slim wrist. "Uh . . .

let's see. Not right now. He'll be coming by around eight o'clock."
Finn exhaled in relief. I was still holding mine.

We went up to his father's room after checking in with a nurse. He'd been having heart trouble and was losing weight rapidly. There was nothing to be done other than make him comfortable. We arrived at his room when a tall, slender woman in her late fifties walked out. It had to be Finn's mother, she had his coloring to a tee with her dark brown hair, fair skin, and greenish eyes. But where they differed was that indescribable quality that makes someone's eyes sparkle. With all the possible responses I imagined a mother could make in seeing her long-lost son, I didn't expect this: indifference.

"Hello, Finn. I wondered if you'd show up. He's in there." *Yikes.* Finn had more imagination and friendliness in his little finger than what she showed in her entire countenance. She was a woman who blended in; everything was just one shade too dark or too light to be of notice. Her suit was gray, or was it blue? Her eyes were lighter than Finn's, a watery gray-green. Her mousy brown hair was a faded brown, with no shine, no luster.

I shot my eyes to Finn. I might have growled a little, because his eyes gave me a sort of warning look, but there was amusement right behind it, too.

He didn't even have time to introduce me to Polly before she shuffled off down the hall. Even her gait was lukewarm, neither striding with deliberate confidence nor slowly ambling with contemplation. I looked at Finn quizzically.

He said decisively, in complete contrast to her blandness, "Let's go in."

"Are you sure you want me to come, too?" I asked.

"Absolutely." He took my hand and in we went.

His father was lying flat on his back, his eyes glassed over and looking at nothing. He had the look of someone formerly robust, but weight loss and pain had left him shrunken. Though his eyes looked somewhere I couldn't see, his jaw was set with belligerence and his face pinched with many years practicing disappointment. Finn glanced at me with an *are you okay?* expression and I realized I'd been crinkling my nose in distaste. I cleared my face and nodded.

"Hello, Father."

A blink was the only expression that told us he might have heard Finn. And I didn't think it was from the illness. This was deliberate.

Finn took a breath, and said, "I just wanted to come to see you. I'm sorry you're ill." He let the silence fill the room, giving his father time to decide if he was going to respond. He chose not to. He didn't so much as clench his jaw.

After a pregnant pause, Finn said, "All right, Father. I'll let you be. Good-bye."

I stole a glance toward the door, where Gwen had stepped into the room. Just as she caught my eye, she quickly covered over the small smile that had been plastered over her face. I tried to look like I hadn't caught that oddly timed smile, thinking that it might be better to not let the little viper see anything that might threaten her. I gave her a little *oh well, I guess we tried* kind of look and shrug. Then I mouthed to her, *Maybe we should go.* She nodded.

I took Finn's hand and we left.

We parted ways with Gwen outside the hospital. *Oh darn.* I was starving, so I suggested we go grab something to eat. Finn wasn't always extremely talkative, but he was understandably quieter than usual as we located a little restaurant nearby.

After a few bites of bread as well as a few sips of dark red wine, he was ready to talk.

"Well, that went well," he said dryly.

"Splendid. Both your parents were a *little* too exuberant. Polly and Richard really need to learn to quench their enthusiasm a bit," I said, eyes rolling.

"It's pretty much what I expected. And you know what? Let's order. Then it's high time I tell you everything about Sean."

I took another big swig of my wine and replenished our glasses while Finn ordered our choices. Then he began a careful account of that terrible day when his own brother betrayed him and cut him to the core.

CHAPTER 16

There's daggers in men's smiles.

—Donalbain, King Duncan's son, *Macbeth*

The sun had been high in the sky that Saturday afternoon, the temperature surprisingly warm for a spring day in Kiernan, a small town about an hour outside of Dublin. The manor house was filled with guests and merriment was in the air. Multiple fireplaces were burning inside for the atmosphere they created and white tables with deep blue runners dotted the lawn, laden with drinks and delicious food. People spilled all over the place inside and out, chatting, happily bickering, telling jokes, and shaking hands in greeting.

All were cheerful and jubilant except the two men upstairs, the two brothers, the last of the family to come down and join in. Sean, the slightly taller, younger one, was tying his tie at the long mirror; his smile broad, his dark hair shining, and every single hair perfectly placed. But his broad smile belied something dark and ugly. The tilt of his brow made him look like nothing surprised him, his lips were red and easily told charming lies. His bright green eyes restless and on the hunt for opportunity. He was a hungry man with an appetite that was never satiated.

Finn, also dark-haired and tall, just an inch or so shorter, was standing at the window looking out at the festive crowd. Concern etched a dark crease upon his forehead. He said, "Sean, are . . . are you sure you want to go through with this?"

Sean's face twisted and he flung himself around, growling, "What the *hell* do you mean by that, Finn?" His fists were flexing, ever-ready for a fight. "You always doubt me. Are you really going to do this on *this* day?" he snapped through gritted teeth. His countenance would have inspired fear from a lesser man, but Finn had seen this face a thousand times.

"No, Sean. I don't doubt your abilities, I never have. This is just a very important day, a life-changing decision. I want you to be happy. I'm just asking." And he meant it. But Sean would never truly understand that. Sean was never wrong and always envious. He looked at people through distant eyes that only saw utility, valuable only if personal gain was possible.

His brother shook his head and with half-closed eyes said, "I don't believe you. You're filled with jealousy that it's me and not you. You can't get over that fact. Well, after tonight you'll just have to, now won't you?"

"What do you mean, Sean?" Sean blinked a couple of times and looked like maybe he'd misspoken. If only Finn had caught that look flashing across his face and done something—anything—things could have turned out so differently. But how could he have ever guessed?

"Bah. Never mind. Are you going to come down with me or not?" he growled.

"Of course. You look wonderful, Sean. Let's go."

The two brothers went downstairs, found their parents, and filed out to the lawn. The guests were settled into their seats and the brothers walked down the aisle to the front where the priest stood, looking staunch and ancient. The bagpipes began the traditional bridal march and Gwen came down the aisle shining.

Perhaps Sean had been partially right, Finn thought. Maybe he was a little jealous. He stole a glance at his brother. Maybe he'd been harsh asking him if he really wanted to go through with it. But then, there it was again. That *look*, a smile when the bride looked away. That smile was . . . treacherous. It was the same smile when Sean would knowingly lie to their parents or blame Finn for his own escapades. But he had done all he could, right? Talked with both of them as much as he dared. They were two grown adults, the parents all approved of the marriage . . .

The ceremony moved quickly along and before he knew it,

Sean and Gwen were married. It was a done deal for better or worse. The pictures afterward were a nightmare, pretending to be happy when he had a clenching pit in his stomach. The worst was the photograph of him shaking his brother's hand. Luckily, Finn was always able to master his countenance. But damn, it was hard.

The party afterward had its fun moments, but it was far too long for him. He'd tried to talk with his parents, about having to leave the next day for his new job out of the country. They knew he was leaving but they just hadn't had time to talk, to *really* talk in quite a while.

He had been closer with both parents when he was younger. But the last few years, their relationship had grown strained. He had tried to ask them about it, but they both dismissed it as something that all children feel as they pass into adulthood and independence. It was nothing. But he could never shake the feeling that it was most definitely *something*.

After many guests had left, he went to say his farewells and head toward the city, shipping out early the next morning for the States. He hugged his parents, trying to say with his eyes all the things he hadn't been able to say out loud. He even hugged his brother and clapped him on the back, telling him he was a lucky man and that he was very happy for him. He only got a smile in return that resembled a sneer more than something friendly or loving. Gwen, Sean's wife, was the only one he felt had returned his genuine goodwill.

Finn got into his car and headed out toward the city. The cool night was a balm to his troubled spirit. The scent of wood smoke and the earthy, grassy notes of the evening air made him feel grounded. It felt good to be alone, quiet, released from the endless small talk. He loosened his tie. He tried to begin letting go of what lay behind him and look forward to the new adventure ahead.

It had been extremely difficult living for years in the wake of the chaos his brother created in everything he touched. From twisting innocent words in even the most benign conversations, making other people look foolish or guilty, to using people to get higher up the ladder in his company and then tossing them aside when he was done with them. Sean would ruthlessly do whatever it took, no matter the cost, to get what he wanted. *Whatever* he wanted. Why couldn't anyone else see it?

There was something inside of Finn that yearned for justice and was driven mad when his own parents turned a blind eye to Sean's maneuvering. Maybe that was what made it so much easier deciding to leave his family. To do something that would make a difference. He wondered what it would be like living in the States. He had a lot to learn, but he always loved a challenge. A new beginning. *That's* what he had before him and he enjoyed a frisson of excitement at the potential and possibility ahead.

Just as he was passing an old farmhouse on a lonely stretch of road, the engine started clunking. *Damn,* he thought, *what now?* He looked down, astonished to see the gas gauge on empty. He had just filled the tank a day or two ago. Maybe there was a leak, or maybe someone borrowed his car. The family often borrowed each other's cars to do errands. He kicked himself for not checking the gauge before he left the house. He got out of the car, went to the trunk, and pulled out the gas can. Certainly, the farm would have some extra petrol. He closed the trunk with a slam and looked around. The lone screech of an owl pierced through the night and he heard the thump of capture that made a prickle of unease run up his spine. Rubbing the back of his neck while shaking his head at his predicament, he heard a car coming down the lane. Maybe it was someone from the party and he could get a lift.

Surprisingly, the car didn't have its headlights on. As it drew near, Finn waved his arms, trying to flag it down. Then he stopped dead in his tracks. His stomach plummeted. The car was his brother's. A nearby light in the road illuminated the driver for a split second as the car was just about upon him. Sean was at the wheel, smiling his hateful, arrogant sneer. He'd slowed as if he was coming to a stop. Then he hit the gas.

CHAPTER 17

"My God, Finn."

"Can you lighten up on the death grip, love?" I was clenching his hand as the story had gone from bad to worse.

"Sorry," I said as he smiled while he massaged his hand. I had a pretty good grip. "What happened next?"

A look of pain furrowed his brow, making me ache for him. "Well, he could've killed me, but I managed to dodge a little out of the way. But the car hit my left leg and tossed me into the air. I woke up in the hospital. My fractured knee was the worst, but I was pretty beat up."

"How'd you get to the hospital?" I asked, cocking my brow. Quite honestly, I was surprised Sean hadn't finished him off.

"Yeah. Wondering why he didn't finish me off?" I almost spilled my wine.

We were enjoying our wordplay, but I was serious. Someone must have intervened; Sean certainly didn't suddenly get a conscience and get Finn some help. "Finn. He could've killed you."

"Most definitely. I owe it all—*everything*—to my grandma Vivian. She had followed Sean, in her own car."

"She had her own car?" I blurted out.

"Yes, she was always independent. *Beyond* independent. She had been widowed when my mother was just a child. But her father had secured her future, so she had her own money. Not a fortune, but she wouldn't have to worry. And she was a writer. She worked for a local paper and wrote and published some work. You'll love her, Lane."

"I can't wait to meet her. So . . . you left off with her intervening somehow," I urged.

"Yes. She had followed him, thinking it oddly coincidental that I had just left and Sean then quickly following, leaving his own wedding party. She found us at the *accident* but Sean had made up an elaborate lie about coming across the scene. How he had followed me because, and I quote, 'You know how Finn is, I wanted to be sure he was all right.'"

"Whattaya mean, *you know how Finn is*? What did he mean by that?"

"*Shhhh.* You're yelling."

I slowly took my hands off my hips, which had shot there in indignation.

"Well . . . let me start with when I woke up. Grandma Viv was there, holding my hand. As soon as I had opened my eyes, she smiled the most beautiful smile I'd ever seen. Everything hurt. I had been out cold all night and most of the next day, which was good because they had to reset my knee and I had a lot of stitches. I knew I'd missed my ship to America. And when I saw my knee, I worried I might have missed my new life altogether.

"She explained my injuries. They had some doubts that I'd be able to get back to normal, even walking wasn't a given, but she was a fierce cheerleader. She didn't believe that for a second. And she wouldn't let me believe it, either."

"But where were your parents?" I asked.

"They never came."

I don't think I'd ever heard three sadder words. I was at a loss for what to say. *What kind of parents could do that?*

He quickly went on, "Well . . . I learned from Viv, who had put it all together, that Sean had been convincing them for a long time that I had a drinking problem and that perhaps I had some mental incapacities. He'd make up stories that had a kernel of truth to them. He'd even managed to work out a story about that being the reason that I was going to America; that Scotland Yard had dis-

missed me, not that it had anything to do with my Irish background."

"And that's why Gwen and her friends were treating you as if
you weren't the sharpest knife in the drawer," I said.

"Exactly," he said, nodding. "Everyone seemed to buy it. And
as far as my parents were concerned, this was the final straw. That
I could have done this on Sean's wedding day was an outrage.
They believed him hook, line, and sinker.

"There was probably evidence of Sean's intentional deception,
maybe tread marks in the road, Viv remembers seeing a dent in
the hood, that sort of thing. But because Grandma had arrived and
directed Sean to put me into her car so she could race me to the
hospital, he must've had the time to fix it all because his car was in
perfect shape when she took a look at it a day or two later. Vivian
tried to talk to my parents about the fact that she didn't smell alco-
hol on my breath, Sean's lie that I'd been drinking and ran out of
gas and stumbled into the road, getting hit by some passing vehicle, couldn't possibly be true. But it was no use.

"He's dangerous. But she's a genius. She played dumb with
Sean, thank God. She could have been in danger, too. If he did
that to me, he could have hurt her. But she talked up how wonderful it was that he came upon me on the side of the road."

"Smart lady."

"Oh yeah. So while talking with my parents was out of the
question, she did speak with a detective. Detective Marlowe. But
I was worried. Sean is an opportunist; he calculates the worth of
someone or their reach or their political clout and works to manipulate them into a corner. A corner that can serve him well. Even
when we were kids, he'd find people who could be bought or
blackmailed into submission. He liked having a safety net, he'd
say. That you never knew when the local bully, or a weak kid
whose parents were powerful, or the grocer whom he caught short-
changing a customer . . . might come in handy to have on his side.
So I wondered if he had any police in his pocket. I didn't know
who was safe at this point and who was compromised.

"But Marlowe believed my story, and he believed Viv. He came
to see me and we talked further. Sometimes, people don't believe

you about family issues like that, unless they've faced it themselves. Detective Marlowe's face had said it all: He had known someone devious like Sean himself.

"Marlowe followed Sean around for a few days and he was one of the few people who could see right through Sean's charm. They couldn't pin him for running the car into me, but he believed he was capable of that. Lane, it was such a relief to have someone see it. Vivian told me she had always seen through Sean, too. The charm had never worked on her. She tried talking with my mother, but . . . my mother isn't like you and Viv. She's . . ."

"Cold," I said with a don't-take-this-the-wrong-way grimace.

"That's one word for it," he laughed. "She's not . . . it's like she's not engaged in a conversation. She's been dimmed down. I think it's a real mystery—a sad one—for Vivian. She just can't figure out how her own daughter turned out so utterly different."

I added, "Especially one named Polly. I haven't met anyone *less* Pollyanna."

"Don't I know it."

Our dinner arrived, a simple roast chicken with vegetables. It was homey, fragrant, and delicious. Just the simple pleasure we needed. We took a break from the heavy topic and enjoyed the meal for a bit.

When we finished up, I asked him, "So how long did the recovery take?"

"Oh, several months. It was excruciating those first weeks. Then it just took hard work. Grandma Viv was relentless and had me exercising as much as I could endure. My parents had cut me off at that point. So I moved in with her and we worked together all day on my rehabilitation. She never once wavered in her support. I wanted to give up a couple of times. But that was not going to happen. Not with her in charge. And you know," he said, as he thoughtfully poured the last drops of the wine into our glasses, "there was a relief in having the charade over and done with. It was a different way than I had ever imagined to reach my dreams and desires, and I wouldn't wish it on anyone, but it was a better way. A new, honest way."

I tilted my head in thought. "Remember when we were in Michigan, at my family home, and I couldn't climb my old tree anymore? You helped me. Do you remember what you said?"

His eyes crinkled with happiness and he replied, "I said you needed a new way."

"And you helped me figure it out."

"Yes. I did."

"That's why you knew what I needed. You had needed a new way once, too."

"That I did, love." He finished his wine. Then he smiled wolfishly at me. "And I also remember how that night ended."

"Oh, so do I."

CHAPTER 18

The next day, Finn walked along, taking his time on the way to meet Lane after she visited a few shops. He had a lot to think about and appreciated some time alone to walk and ruminate. Seeing his father again after all those years and knowing he was deathly ill . . . it gave him pause. He supposed that even when parents were not healthy or uplifting, there was a bond there. He kept striving to feel more for them. *There should be more, shouldn't there?* But his mother was cold, Lane was right, and his father was his same old disappointed dad. It made his face flush in annoyance just thinking about it.

Gwen was at least the same, genuine and just nice. He still wondered how she could end up with them all. He also wondered when he'd have to face Sean. Finn hadn't seen him since he glimpsed his arrogant face at the wheel just as he was about to plow into him, head-on.

After his talk with Lane about his mother the night before and the fact that his mother seemed *dimmed down* somehow, he couldn't stop thinking about that fact.

Finn walked toward the Thames, just below London Bridge. He and Lane were going to do a few touristy things and she wanted to see the bridge. She also had a list a mile long to see the Art Deco buildings she favored. Big Ben? Sure, she'd love that. But she really wanted to see the Daily Express building with its black and glass front with smooth corners and glossy finishes. The newspaper headquarters was only about four years old.

He loved this walk. Every city had its own personality, and outside of his family issues, he was pleased to discover an old love for London. At one point, he'd hated this city. He'd hated the discrimination against his Irish roots and the fact that London had come to represent Sean and their parents. His father had been boorish, but what he loathed more was his lackluster mother. *What was that word Lane hated?* Oh, yeah, *hapless.* His mother was hapless.

He chuckled at the memory of Lane chatting about hating that word. She was so funny. Maybe that was what attracted him to her the most: she was the opposite of hapless. And endlessly unpredictable.

Which was a timely thought as he approached her. She didn't see him coming; her back was to him as she was facing the river. *What on earth is she doing?* She had her hands on the railing looking out. But then she suddenly slammed her purse to the ground. He was about a hundred feet away now.

She kicked off her shoes and hiked her skirt pretty damn far up her thighs. *Holy shit.* He walked a little faster. And then she unhooked one side, then the other garter and took off her silk stockings right then and there. She had a few curious onlookers. One older gentleman walked into a lamppost and an old nanny made *tsk tsk* noises as she walked past with her perambulator. Then Lane pulled her skirt properly down, balled up the offensive pieces, and with an angry grunt launched them right into the Thames.

He came up to the railing, mirroring her relaxed hands now resting on the railing as she looked serenely at the river traffic.

"*What* are you doing, love?" She looked up at him, a large, unrepentant smile on her face. Her blue-green eyes lit up with the brilliance of the sun shining into them.

"I threw my stockings away."

"Into the Thames."

"Into the Thames," she echoed. "I'd worn them too long and

they'd stretched. I'd been fighting them sliding down all morning. I couldn't take it anymore."

"And you needed to remedy the situation immediately."

"Exactly." Her eyes were sparking with amusement, daring him to disagree.

"Well? With that taken care of, shall we?" She nodded smartly as he aimed her in the right direction for their tour. Arm in arm, they marched off to see the sights.

CHAPTER 19

After the tour of London Bridge we went to a few sites including my favorite Art Deco ones like the zippy, black-and-white Chez-Cup cocktail bar situated in the Regent Palace Hotel. Afterward we headed to the appointment that we had to postpone the night before.

It was a little chilly out, but I looked forward to meeting Finn's grandmother for the first time, which warmed me with anticipation. Vivian sounded like someone I would like. But after meeting his lackluster mother and hearing about Sean's monumental deception, she became exceptionally interesting. I could understand why Vivian was dismayed at how her own daughter, Finn's mother, turned out so bland.

I'd heard that Gwen had been visiting Vivian when Finn last visited London. If Viv could see through Sean's deceptive personality, could she see through Gwen's? I was pretty sure Finn still thought Gwen was an unwilling participant in Sean's affairs. *Maybe*. But I read a lot in her face. To be clueless about Sean, she'd have to be naïve or obtuse. She was neither. I hoped Vivian would be a savvy ally.

We took a cab to Vivian's nursing home. It looked like it could use some updating, but was clean and friendly. We found her out in the wintery garden. London was so rainy, though, that the garden was a bit greener than what we'd left behind in New York. And there was no snow on the ground, so the little walkway around the garden path was clear for the inhabitants. There were little benches scattered all around, climbing rose branches promising luscious blooms, old wisteria trees that held the memory of summer days, and the crunch of old leaves with their earthy scent. It made me think of Frances Hodgson Burnett's *The Secret Garden.*

A spry woman, about my height, leaped off a bench and with a long, lively gait just about sprinted over to us.

"Finn! How lovely." She embraced Finn with a hearty hug, peering at me over his shoulder and winking. Her dark blue eyes radiated with mirth. *Oh, I do like her already,* I thought.

"Mammo. So good to see you! Looking chipper as ever, I see," said Finn, releasing her.

"Oh yes," she replied. "Feeling quite good today. And this must be Lane. Delightful to meet you, my dear."

I took her warm hand in mine and pulled her in for an unexpected hug. I knew Brits didn't hug quite as much as Americans, but she'd just have to put up with it. "Vivian! I'm so happy to meet you."

She might have been surprised, but she embraced me just as fully as she had Finn. "My dear," she said quietly in my ear, "we shall be good friends."

"Absolutely," I whispered back.

She released me and looked at Finn and then at me, brazenly appraising us as only grandmothers can do. Finn had put his arm around my shoulders and we smiled at her.

Satisfied, she exclaimed, "Come! Let's have a spot of tea, shall we? I'd like to warm up. Lane, my dear! Where are your stockings?"

"In the Thames," I replied as Finn held the door for us both.

"I see."

When we got back to her room, I discovered it was a suite of rooms. The building had been an old Victorian mansion that was absolutely sprawling. She had her own rooms with a little living area. A tea service was already set out and she carefully poured for us. I asked for a little milk and one lump of sugar.

After we all got settled, she asked, "So I assume you saw your father, Finn?"

Finn nodded, setting his teacup down on the little table covered in lace next to him. "Yes. He doesn't look well. How long has this been going on?"

"Well, your parents don't tell me too much, but I believe he hasn't been feeling well for about three months. It seems to be heart-related. He has trouble with the feeling in his limbs. The doctors aren't certain."

We chitchatted a while, getting to know each other and catching her up on our lives in New York. We told her about the last case and the gold pawn.

"Oh, that sounds just about as good as Agatha Christie's *Cards on the Table*!" she exclaimed.

"You have that?" I practically shouted. It wasn't slated to come out for a while in the U.S.

"Oh yes, it's delightful! Here, my copy is over there next to the bed. Take it! I'd love to share it."

I ran over and got the book, devouring the back cover as I walked back to them. I smiled at Vivian, one book lover to another. There was nothing as bonding as enjoying a good book with someone.

Just then, a knock came at the door, and a strawberry blond head peeked around the corner. *Oh goody.*

"Come in, Gwen!" said Vivian.

Gwen came in, bedecked in a deep purple ensemble. She truly enjoyed matching things; everything was the same color from her shoes to her hat, pinned neatly to her hair in her tight updo. She wore proper stockings, too.

As she set a large bouquet wrapped in paper on the table by the door, she said, "I just wanted to drop by to say hello and bring you these." She took off her white gloves and hung up her coat on the coat rack, then came over.

"Why, thank you, it's always lovely to see you. Can I pour you a cuppa, dear?" asked Vivian.

"That would be wonderful," said Gwen, sitting on the other side of Finn.

He asked her, "Have you heard anything new about Father?"

"No. Nothing new. His heart is weakening and he is losing the feeling in his hands and feet. His breathing is becoming weaker, too. I'm afraid it doesn't look good."

"Oh dear," said Vivian. She took a sip of her tea, then brightened up. "Is that what I hope it is?" she said, nodding with her head to the bouquet.

Gwen smiled broadly and said, "Yes! I finally got them ready. It will look lovely on your little table by the window." She turned to me and said, "I dried a bunch of bishop's lace for myself and Polly at the end of summer. With all this rain, it's taken quite a while. Vivian has been asking for some and I had quite a lot. It did turn out wonderful." She went to the table and carefully opened the bundle. "Shall I put them in the vase?"

"Yes, please. Oh, they look delightful. Reminds me of summer. Thank you, Gwen."

"I love those, we call them Queen Anne's lace in the States. I love how they're so delicate," I said, pouring another cup of tea for myself and topping off Finn's cup.

Finn was quiet, lost in his thoughts. Gwen stood up and began arranging the dried flowers. She said, "Finn, I think your father would like to see you again. You know you really should see Sean, too. He misses you."

I glanced at Finn as a look of indecision raced across his face, something I rarely witnessed in him. Then my eyes met Vivian's. We shared a knowing look of solidarity. There was danger lurking within Finn's family, but how could he not have a meeting? How could he say no to that?

"Well, I think missing me might be putting too positive a spin on it, but I can arrange to see Father again. If Sean wants to be there, that's fine," he declared.

"Excellent," said Gwen. She busied herself making a quick call to the hospital on the phone set upon Viv's desk, then she efficiently swept up the tea service and took it to the kitchenette.

Everything about her was perfectly manicured. Her strawberry blond hair was neat and orderly, not a single wisp of hair breaking ranks. Every nail was filed to a pointy oval and polished in virginal light pink. Her purple suit dress was immaculate, not a wrinkle, not a fuzzy, not a crease. I self-consciously crossed my stocking-less ankles beneath my chair.

Gwen left shortly after and then Finn and I could exhale a bit. We enjoyed a wonderful time with Vivian. She was a delight, and I had such fun getting to know her. We said our good-byes and arranged to see her again in a day or so. Before we met Finn's family at the hospital, we took a cab to see Miles at his pub. He had sent word that he had some information for us already.

"Yeah, it's a funny thing, Finn," Miles began, taking a quick break to slosh down a gulp of Guinness in midsentence. "There isn't any word about Daphne on the street. Not a one." He raised his eyebrows meaningfully at us.

"Oh, bugger," said Finn, taking his own large gulp of Smith-wick's. I placed one elbow up on the bar, and took a good look at my partners. I was clearly missing something.

"But why is that so suspicious?" I asked. "Wasn't she pretty good at hiding, keeping in the shadows all along?"

"Well," said Finn, "you see, whenever a leader of the Red Scroll was around, at least back in the day, there was a lot of ruckus on the streets. It might not have been about a certain person, or specific actions, but there were rumblings. A *lot* of rumblings. It was like their very presence stirred up trouble. Like when you see a pack of dogs getting a walk and a little tiny mouthy one begins to nip at the heels of a bigger dog. It gets them all going and suddenly they're all barking and nipping. The Red Scroll was like that."

"Yeah, yeah. It's just very odd to have it so utterly quiet," said Miles.

Finn said, "Well, let's go meet with that John friend of yours, and you keep an eye out for anything else. Maybe Daphne's kept her presence on the lowdown just like in the States. But we need to be sure. She had to have a good reason to come all this way."

"In the meantime," said Miles, "I have a guy who has the pulse of the art scene. He'll know if there's anything stirring in that world, as well."

"Do you have any German contacts?" asked Finn, his eyes going dark.

Miles nodded solemnly. "Yeah, I do. I know, we need to keep an eye on them. I have another contact who is well aware, if no one else is here, that Hitler is on the move. I actually told him to meet us here today. In his mind, he's not a mover and shaker in the government. Yet. But he will be, mark my words. His views on the European state of affairs seem spot-on if you ask me. I think he has Hitler's number. Jews are fleeing Germany and most other European cities and by the looks of it, they'd better. There are all sorts of frightening reports coming out of there. *Mein Kampf* was one hell of a scary read."

Right at that moment I heard a rather loud and deep command. "I want that gin ice-cold and neat. One olive. Just glance at the vermouth bottle briefly and give the gin a decent pour."

Miles was smiling freely; I'd never actually seen that look on his face. "Here's my contact now in fact."

Finn and I turned together toward the loud voice. The bartender looked like he was fully aware of the man's strange feelings toward vermouth, a slight grin pulling at one side of his mouth.

"Here you go, Mr. Churchill. Just the way you like it."

"Thank you, my man," he said, taking a good long drink, his face reflecting his absolute enjoyment of the perfectly crafted beverage.

"Mr. Winston Churchill, I'd like you to meet my contacts from the States. Mr. Finn Brodie and Miss Lane Sanders."

"Ah, yes. Mayor La Guardia's aide and the detective who left our shores for those more receptive to his abilities." We must have looked rather astonished as he went on to clarify. "My mother was American-born, you see. So I feel a certain tie to your country. And I like to keep tabs on my more, oh, let's say *interesting* contacts here such as Miles and those he'd like to have me meet." Behind me I heard Miles choking back a laugh. "Next to the president of the United States, the mayor of New York City is always a powerful man indeed."

"That's right. Always a step ahead, right, Mr. Churchill?" said Miles.

"Always," said the large man who had the general appearance of a bulldog. His eyes were deep and held all manner of secrets and intelligence. His receding hairline exposed a large forehead that added to the feeling that he was constantly thinking and mulling over options and opportunities. He was not the blur of activity that Fiorello was, but I was certain his mind never rested. He reminded me of what I envisioned Mycroft Holmes to look like.

"Nice to meet you, Mr. Churchill," Finn and I greeted him in turn. He shook both of our hands, then ordered a second vermouthless martini.

What ensued was one of the most intense and lively discussions I'd ever had. This Mr. Churchill swept us all up like a force of nature. Turns out he was an author but wasn't really an Anybody in the current parliament, yet he seemed to have his hands in everything. *Mycroft Holmes indeed.* He mentioned the recent abdication from the throne of Edward VIII, now Duke of Windsor since he stepped down. Churchill had been an advocate of the abdication. Which made me wonder, because most people thought that an abdication meant a weakened government. That thoughtful, intelligent bulldog face, though . . . he would never be inclined to intentionally weaken his country. So he must see other more positive possibilities in the abdication.

Miles asked him, "So is there any activity from Germany that's reminiscent of the Red Scroll?" Miles turned to us then and added, "I filled Mr. Churchill in on our history with all this."

"Oh, there is definitely activity in seized masterpieces. But that's all the Nazis. I have heard accounts already of old families, mainly Jewish, who disappear overnight and suddenly their estates are in control of the government. But the Red Scroll? Not yet."

I said, "Well, I guess that's a positive note for our investigation."

"I'm not sure it is," said Finn.

"What do you mean?" asked Miles.

"Well, they're not just vacationing. I figure I'd rather know what they're up to," said Finn.

"Yeah. The old wasp in the room, right?" said Miles.

"Mm, yes, yes. You're certainly correct there," said Mr. Churchill. "Well, I best be off. If I hear anything I'll be sure to contact you, Miles. And thank you for the martinis. Mr. Brodie? Miss Sanders? A delight to meet you. I hope we'll meet again. I'd like to hear more about your boss. He seems like a man I'd like to know. Good day."

With that, he turned and left. He'd used the word *wilderness* when he spoke of his own government role at the moment. He'd been turned down for some positions and seen a lot of opposition, especially on his views of Germany. He'd been accused of alarmist speech. But there was something magnetic about him. He would not remain in that political wilderness for long, that's for sure.

He may have thought of himself as a nobody, but as we talked, I remembered a small photograph of him, in the first issue of *Life* magazine that came out last November. I didn't know his name or his face at the time, But I remembered it, because I had laughed outright, for the photograph was of him fingering a tooth that looked like it might have pained him. But toward the camera. And with his middle finger.

"You liked him, didn't you?" asked Finn, searching my face.

"I did. He's an interesting man. I can see why you have him as a contact, Miles. He seems like he has a good feel for what's going on."

"Oh, that he does, Lane, that he does. I saw you trying to reconcile his advocacy for Edward to abdicate. Did you figure it out?" he asked with an impish grin.

"No, not really. I was a bit surprised that he was for it," I replied.

"I have a theory," said Miles with a smug look.

Finn chuckled. "What do you think?"

Miles nodded smartly. "I think he saw a chance to get rid of a feeble leader. I think he's on a campaign to get rid of hapless individuals."

"*Hapless.*" I laughed. "Yes. I can see that. You may just be right about that. Now how about you buy me another pint?"

On the way to meet Finn's family at the hospital, we discussed our next steps.

"I'm still wondering why Daphne came to London now, at this particular moment. And I'm more than a little concerned that we haven't heard a word about her," I said as the taxi driver took a corner with more speed than necessary, Finn bracing himself with a hand on the back of the front seat.

"Oi! Driver! Take it easy," he said in an accent that was torn between Britain and Brooklyn, then turned to me. "Yeah, it's making me nervous. But whether we locate her or not, we have a lot to be doing here regardless. Tomorrow, let's head up to see Miles's contact, John. I'll try to get my family situation straightened out a bit. At least with Mr. Churchill's confirmation, it seems that the Red Scroll is not up and running here. Time will tell if that will remain true. But for now . . ."

We pulled up to the hospital, and my shoulders began clenching as I prepared to see Finn's family again. I wondered when I'd be meeting his infamous brother. The loathing I felt for him from the injustice and injury that he caused made my blood boil.

"Lane. Ah, lighten up on the grip?" said Finn.

"Oh! Sorry. Was caught up in my thoughts," I said, letting go of his hand. I'd been crushing it, I was so entrenched. As we rounded the corridor where we'd head to his father's room, a door suddenly slammed open, crashing against the wall. A blur of a large man with molten green eyes came at us. Before I knew what happened, he and Finn were in a death grip, then Finn slammed the man up against the wall. A fierce growl emitted from the guy as orderlies came running, trying to break up the fight. One large orderly apiece grabbed Finn and the other guy from behind, holding them back as best they could. They were very large men and the fury they were trying to hold back was fearsome.

"Sean!" snarled Finn. "What's gotten into you?"

My head shot back to the green-eyed man with his black hair flopping over his eyes as he still pulled hard to get out of the clutches of the orderly. With a grunt he yelled, "He's been poisoned!"

"Who?" yelled Finn.

"Father! And I know it was you."

CHAPTER 20

*Come what may, time and the hour run through the
roughest day.*

—Macbeth, *Macbeth*

Finn was utterly stunned. *How can this be happening,* he thought to
himself. All of Finn's strength just left him, bare and helpless as a
child. The orderly who had been holding him back suddenly
lurched and smashed Finn's face up against the wall with more
force than he'd intended because of Finn's sudden stop.

"Finn!" yelled Lane, desperation darkening her face as she looked
into his eyes, searching for him. "Let go of him!" she commanded in
her best aide-to-the-mayor voice. Because of the strident command
and the fact that Finn stopped fighting, the orderly carefully released
him.

"You two go at it again, I'll get the bobby in here. You understand?" the orderly said. Finn nodded, but Sean was still raging.
"Take the hot-headed guy in there! Don't let him go until he cools
off." The other orderly got Sean to stumble into the closest room.
The door slammed shut behind them.

Finn was still panting. He turned to the orderly and asked,
"What was he talking about? My father's been poisoned?"

"I dunno what that's all about. But I don't like the sound of it."
He turned and motioned to the bobby that had been keeping his
eyes on us from the front door. The bobby came over and decided
that they all needed an escort.

They trooped down the hall, single file like good little school-
children. As they approached the door to his father's room, Finn's

mother walked out. Even with all the fireworks, her eyes remained dull and uninterested.

She said, "Your father is sleeping. You cannot go in."

"Mother, Sean said something about Father being poisoned. What's going on?" demanded Finn.

"We thought that it had been his heart. But it turns out, poison is in his system. That's what's been causing his illness." Her opaque eyes looked at him. No love, no kindness. She thought this was his doing, too. It was like he was a curse on the family. When he was around, bad things happened.

He felt the blood leave his face as it dawned on him. The haunting line from *Voodoo Macbeth* came to his mind, wrapping its claws into his soul. *Is this a dagger which I see before me, the handle toward my hand?* He hadn't poisoned his father, but he felt the defeat of guilt. Nothing had changed in all the years he'd been gone. The crushing weight of being misunderstood and vilified left him limp.

He uttered softly, "How long has this been going on?"

His mother replied, "We don't know. But I don't need to tell you, Finn, that your timing here for a visit is quite coincidental. Is it not?"

He said, "It is."

Lane gasped and said indignantly, "It is not! Finn, what are you talking about? We just arrived. Don't be ridiculous! Poisoning like this had to have been going on for a long time. He'd been ill before we arrived." Her eyes were sparking from the injustice and when she turned to his mother, he automatically put a hand on Lane's arm to hold her back. She looked like she might punch someone. That thought simultaneously brought a small smile to his lips and cleared his murky thoughts. Lane was right.

He turned to his mother. "Thanks for your support, Mother. As always." She pursed her lips and turned her face away in a huff.

He looked at Lane, her deeply caring eyes, so alive in every way.

"Lane," whispered Finn, close to her ear. "She'll never understand. Let's go." Before they could turn to leave, his mother pivoted and walked away like a mopey child. Lane let out a breath. Finn was close, both of them gathering energy and warmth from each other as the only sense of goodness and kindness around.

Lane slipped her arm around his waist and drew him even closer, careless of who was watching. He, too, just wanted her touch, her closeness. The coldness that emanated from his family drew them toward each other, like a fire on a cold winter's night.

Finn's eyes were locked on hers, like there was no one else in the whole world. Lane slowly rose up on tiptoe and whispered in his ear, "You're right. Let's go. Come on." She took his hand in hers and was about to lead him out the door, but before she could turn, his warm lips were on hers, briefly, but full of intensity.

His mind fully cleared, he had a determined set to his jaw. Whatever fear his parents evoked in him, he hated it with every ounce of his being. It confused him, the unpredictable nature of it all.

When they got to their hotel, they barely got to the door before Lane's lips were on his, her fingers pulling at the buttons on his shirt. Somehow he managed to unlock the door and they stumbled into the room. The coldness and harshness of the whole situation made them crave each other. Their warmth and love was like going home after a long and tiresome journey.

He slipped his hand into her blouse, caressing her soft breast as she softly moaned and found every button and zipper on him. There was an urgency and a tenderness that they needed to give each other. To remind them both of the goodness and trust in the world.

She had his shirt off and her red fingernails stroked his chest as she kissed him lightly on his neck and then his chest. She then drew him to the bathroom and turned on the shower, the heat already steaming up the room. She stepped in and the water glistened off her smooth body. He thought he might just spontaneously combust right then and there.

They held each other through the long night, their bodies perfectly intertwined. He'd never known such softness, such tenderness mixed with her burning desire that made him know beyond a doubt she craved him just as much as he craved her.

In the middle of the night, he woke, his heart racing from a strange dream about Sean and an overwhelming sense that he was being sucked down into something like quicksand. In the dream, he'd looked over at Lane on the other side. She'd grabbed his hand to help, but instead, to his horror, he pulled her in with him. Now, not quite fully awake, with the remnants of the awful dream still pulling at him, he felt Lane's hand gently smoothing the hair from his forehead. His breathing slowed and he focused on slowing his heartbeat. The nightmare began to dissolve. She kissed the side of his head as he nuzzled closer. She whispered, "It's okay. I'm here. Go back to sleep. It's all okay."

He was tired, but his desire rose and her softness pulled him to her, compelling and sensuous. They melded together both half-asleep, fully loving, fully enjoying, his nightmarish fears dissipating like a wisp of smoke.

CHAPTER 21

The next morning, we had a quick, early breakfast, then jumped into the car. The bumpy road jolted me as I hung on to the door handle, leaning into the turn. Oxford was about a two-hour drive. We decided on the car instead of the train, so we could get around on our own schedule.

The drive took us out of bustling London and into countryside with rolling green hills, stark brown trees dotting the landscape with picturesque cows and sheep lazily walking about, tails twitching and grazing with contentment. England was much greener than New York during these winter months. It felt nice to see the green, grassy land, despite the fact that the trees had lost their leaves. There was something sprawling about this countryside that felt different from the open country around New York and even Michigan. The roads were so long, curving and empty in the midst of miles and miles of gently rolling green hills.

Neither of us spoke much. There certainly was a lot going through my mind so I could only imagine what Finn was going through. There was the pinball affair in New York, Daphne was nowhere to be found, and we had to deal with Finn's horrible family. It was a wonder that such a kind, generous, and healthy human being such as Finn could come from that crew.

The doctors confirmed that Finn's father had been poisoned, perhaps for some time, long before we arrived. But even with that empirical evidence, his stubborn mother remained convinced that Finn was at fault. For now, though, we had to put that on hold.

As we entered into Oxford proper, I was looking forward to stretching my legs. Finn pulled over and parked. Miles gave us rather vague directions to meet his contact, who regularly had a meeting with a group of his cohorts on Tuesdays. Of course his contact was meeting us in a pub. I wondered if Miles ever frequented a place of business that *wasn't* a pub. Finn held my hand as we walked down the street.

"I don't see any place called the Bird," I said to Finn as my stomach growled.

"Hungry, love?" he asked with a chuckle.

"Always. Hey, let's just ask at this little store."

We walked in and Finn asked the harried man behind the counter full of a hodgepodge of treats, medicines, and a variety of kitchenware.

"Oh, you mean the Bird and the Baby!" I was about to interrupt that no, we were looking for just the Bird, but he quickly added, "See? It's right there, mate. Across the street." He directed us with a long finger pointing out the window.

"Ah," I said. "We should've known. The Eagle and Child Pub."

"Naturally," said Finn with a wry grin. "The Bird."

We walked across the street to the cream-colored, three-story building with its sky-blue sign featuring an eagle carrying a baby wrapped in a blanket within its clutches. We walked in the dark wooden door and over in the back corner were several gentlemen in deep discussion. The place was surely like thousands of pubs around England, yet it also reminded me of my home in Rochester, Michigan. Warm brown paneling crept up the walls to about eye level, above that was more of the cream color from the outside, and a fire in the fireplace cast heat and friendliness around the little pub.

The only thing out of place here . . . was me. I was the sole woman, and I happened to be wearing my red sweater coat with the fluffy fur collar. I definitely stood out. Everyone stopped and took a good look at me, making a blush creep up my face. Everyone, that is, except the group of gentlemen that we were meeting.

Whatever that group was discussing, it had captured their imagination completely.

As we walked up, one of them was in a friendly argument about a story one of them had shared with the group. "But I'm not sure you should use your Aunt Jane's farm as that reference. Don't you think it's a rather tame moniker?"

"Nonsense. It's perfect. Aunt Jane always loved her Bag End, and I'm keeping it that way."

They suddenly noticed our appearance and the entire group swiveled their heads in our direction. A man probably in his mid-forties, with a thin face, broad forehead, and a full mustache, the one who wanted his aunt Jane's farm in his story, stood up and said, "You must be my meeting. Mr. Finn Brodie and Miss Lane Sanders."

Finn held out his hand and said, "Indeed. It's wonderful to meet you, Mr. Tolkien."

"John!" he interrupted. "Please, with this company and Lane here especially, you *must* call me John." He looked at me with an intense stare, piercing my eyes with his. *Am I supposed to know him?*

"Lane and Finn, let me introduce Mr. Lewis," said John.

"Call me Jack."

I shook his hand warmly, instantly liking this group. "Hello, Jack."

John continued around the circle. "Okay! Assume we are all on a first-name basis. We are a small group today. This is Jack's brother, Warren Lewis, call him Warnie. And here we have Mr. Adam Fox and Mr. Owen Barfield." It may have been a smaller group than usual, but the spark of intellect and something like potential mischief made the group very interesting indeed.

Jack spoke up, "Lane, John here was filling us in a bit on your visit. Have a seat, let me order you a pint, and we'd love to hear more of your story." I always liked the name Jack. And with this particular man, I now loved it even more. There was a glint of fire and humor in his eyes. I knew that Miles's contact was a fellow at Oxford, but I was surprised at the energizing feeling of being in their presence. Their very essence seemed to have an abundance of imagination and creativity.

We sat down and I gave them a quick outline of my story involving an old crime network, my parents, and then Daphne heading to London. "Miles told us that you might have some information on my parents and what they were involved in during the war."

"*This* is the lady you were telling us about? Her parents?" asked Adam incredulously.

John nodded and a small smile tugged at the corner of his mouth. "Hmmm," he said as he thought about how to share his information. "All right, then. Let me tell you a story."

Finn and I exchanged a glance and then sat back, eager for this story we had come so far to hear. John had the countenance of a masterful storyteller. He sat back in his chair and crossed his legs. The rest of the group eased themselves into more comfortable positions, all of us readying ourselves for a good tale.

"My family is from Saxony. We emigrated here in the eighteenth century. My grandfather, John Benjamin, was born in Birmingham and he had a small painting that had always been dear to him. It was a Baroque floral painting. I liked it, too. Anna Katharina Block. I remember loving it because it was of a beautiful flower, fresh like the spring. And so many paintings then were of fearsome, sad faces and very dark. Plus, this was by a woman. A bit of a rarity, you see.

"One day, a professional group of art dealers came to our village and held a persuasive meeting about any art or jewelry we might have in our possession. It centered around finding treasure right beneath our own rooftops. It was thrilling. The potential of treasure, hidden in plain sight.

"The group ran a professional meeting and they were extremely pleasant with cordial manners. Everyone came, brought their valuables. They appraised everything, then bought a few, but most people took their newfound treasures home, excited to have something to leave as a legacy or to keep for a rainy day.

"The following morning, we discovered that almost everything of value that the villagers had brought to the group was stolen during the night. No one had realized that the professional, copious notes that the dealers had been taking so carefully, so politely, were to make note of who had what and where they lived. They also small-talked the unsuspecting people, so they knew who had a guard dog, who might be well armed, who might have well-muscled sons at home . . . in short, we were taken for a ride."

John drank the last of his pint with a quick toss and ordered another, slamming his glass down with a touch of fury.

I nodded, impressed by the thoroughness of the con artists. "What was the name of the group? And when did that all occur?" I asked, having an inkling.

"Well, this is where it starts to get interesting," said John, making us lean forward in anticipation.

Finn muttered, "*Starts* to get interesting?"

"It was near the end of the war. Actually, a little after, I'm thinking early spring of 1919. I was fighting in the war, so I didn't arrive home until quite some weeks had passed since the thefts. My grandparents were a little vague on exact dates."

"Okay," I said, tracking with him. "And the name?"

"When the few of us survivors came home, we heard about the con artists and of course were enraged. So we tried to track down the dealers. It turns out, their con on our village is what led to them being taken down. Up until then, from what we could find, every time they went to a village or town, they were careful to use a different title for the company, even different names and faces for the leaders, trading off in each region. But at our town, they called themselves Richthofen Art."

His eyes sparked, looking at us expectantly, waiting for us to get the significance.

Finn took a sudden breath in and said, "Manfred von Richthofen."

"Cheers, mate," said John, clinking Finn's glass.

"Who's Manfred?" I asked.

John replied, "The Red Baron. The famous German fighter pilot in the war."

"The Red Baron," I echoed. "*Red.* That was their mistake."

John nodded sagely. "Miles and his crew were hunting down any group interested in art with the smallest ties to the Red Scroll, anything remotely with the moniker containing red, any possible clue to nail them. I'd heard about Miles Havalaar from another junior officer. Miles had contacts in all places."

"Sounds like Roarke," I said with a smirk aimed at Finn.

John continued, "So I finally found a way to get him the information and I guess it helped in their investigation."

"So how were my parents involved?" I asked, half afraid.

"Well, Lane, I hate to say it, but they were definitely part of the con. At least in our village. But what I have to tell you about them actually happened a few years after all that."

"I'm going to need another pint," I said just above a whisper. Adam jumped up muttering that he did, too.

Finn looked at me, shaking his head. "Just when I thought *my* family was outrageous."

"Oh, they are . . ." I said.

The barkeep brought an entire tray of fresh pints for us all. We grasped the handles and clinked all around. Our expressions were far from jovial, yet full of genuine companionship.

"As I was saying," said John, "I was contacted after the war. A friend of mine who had a note for me. It was pretty cryptic, but basically it came down to the fact that he made contact with someone who had our family's painting by Anna Block. And they wanted to return it."

"Return it?" I said breathlessly, hopefully.

John nodded. "Yes. I wish I had more details, but one day, I received a letter to set up a meeting. I soon met with your parents, Lane. And they had the painting!" He wasn't an excitable man, but his expression turned eager, like a little child retelling the story of a great quest.

"I just . . . I can't tell you how much it meant to my family. It wasn't that the painting was priceless, but it was valuable to us. And after the war had torn apart so much, to have something remain true. Unharmed. And . . . *beautiful*. It just meant so much." His eyes grew glossy with emotion and of course mine did, too. Thinking of my family home in Rochester, I knew exactly what he meant.

Jack, sitting next to me, also wiped at his eyes, whispering to himself, "Very beautiful indeed."

I cleared my throat and asked, "What did they say? How did they get it, to return it to you?"

"We had a wonderful night regaling each other with stories.

They apologized for being part of the con and they divulged that they'd been undercover and working to stop these thefts. Matthew said they wished they could return everything, but it was impossible. They said they decided it was time to get out. And that they could try to return at least one thing."

John stopped and fingered his mustache in thought. "Our painting had captured their imagination, I think. Charlotte said they were hoping to make things right, that this was the step that would redeem the darker parts of what they'd done. Yes, indeed. Matthew and Charlotte Lorian will definitely be friends whom I will never, ever forget."

Jack, Adam, and Owen as one spun their heads to look directly at John. Jack sputtered, "*Lorian?* In your book?"

John got a sly look on his face with a one-sided smile and replied, "Yes. Lorian."

I didn't know what that was all about, but I asked, "Do you have the name and whereabouts of your friend that was the liaison between you and my parents? I'd like to thank him, and I'd also like to ask a few questions about the whole thing."

"Sure, Lane. I haven't spoken to him in years, he was more of an acquaintance. But his name is Alistair Huxbury. It's not too far, maybe a forty-five-minute drive. But, um, a bit of advice. I'm going to send you to the only public house of the village . . ."

"Another pub," I said, shaking my head.

"Of course, my friend was the owner and barkeep. Finn, mate, you, um . . . you fairly radiate Scotland Yard or bobby, at the least. I'd suggest going to the pub separately, at least not as a couple. I think Lane will have more luck questioning without making anyone nervous. Especially since it's about her parents, and she looks like Charlotte. So that helps. Just a suggestion."

Finn said, "Well, Lane specializes in disguises and such . . ."

I gave him a disgusted look and turned to John. "Thank you so much. Could I see the painting sometime?" I wanted to see the piece that my parents went to such great lengths to return.

"Actually, I brought it today. I thought you'd like to see it," he said as he leaned over the edge of his chair to his beat-up, brown satchel briefcase. He unclipped the two clasps and pulled out a small paper-wrapped parcel. John's long fingers lovingly, carefully unfolded the paper. He held out the small square frame to me.

I took the little square in my hands. The painting was of a single flower, its soft pink petals curved upward, the stamen a bright yellow, its lower petals a gentle spring green. It looked fresh, full of the promise of spring and goodness. "Is it a lily?" I asked.

"A lotus," said John.

"It's lovely," I whispered. "I feel like I've seen it before."

"Lane, you have," said Finn, putting his hand on my knee. "It's the flower that outlines that portrait of you at your parents' house in Rochester." I took a deep breath. He was right. It was the flower that created a beautiful frame around an old portrait of me, and the very same flower that was etched into the molding of my father's study.

"Right then," said John. "You'd better get going to that pub. Before it gets too late."

"Yes, thank you," I said. "I'd love to get there today. Really, John, I can't thank you enough."

"Well, truly, Lane, I can't thank your parents enough. And I can tell you right now, you don't even know half the story of what they did for me."

CHAPTER 22

"I don't know *half?*" I exclaimed to Finn as we bumped and jostled our way across the country roads a few towns over.

Finn had no answer, so he just put his arm out and drew me to him, across the seat. "Come here."

I smiled and happily laid my head on his shoulder as we drove. I put on my sunglasses and enjoyed the early evening, that special golden time before twilight, at the threshold of goodness. The hills turned amber as the sun set, the scent of grass and juniper floating through the wind.

Just as twilight began in earnest, we pulled into the small village. Sure enough, it was the only pub in town. We parked a bit down the road and made our plan. John assured us of the safety of the place and the fact that there were plenty of women about because of the live music that was in abundance, so we decided I'd go in first.

I sat at the back corner table, alone. Enjoying the firelight, the cheerful din of an evening of laughing and drinking with friends. My dark beer was warm, which I had grown accustomed to although I still preferred a cold brew. The richness of the smooth taste mingled with the shadowy but enjoyable atmosphere. I finally spotted my contact from John, sitting at the bar contemplating life. He was hard to miss: at least six foot four with a bright shock of flaming red hair and beard.

I went over and joined him at the bar as he softly set his elbows down. His appearance was loud, but his demeanor was soft. As I took a stool, I said, "So you're the famous Alistair Huxbury who helped my parents."

He quickly turned to me, studying my face. I smiled and said to the barkeep, "He'll have what I'm having." Alistair chuffed a whispery, scratchy sort of laugh.

"Well, you must be Lane, the daughter of Charlotte Lorian beyond a doubt. Eh, lass?"

I raised my glass and an eyebrow. "Indeed. *Slainte*, Alistair." We clinked our glasses and each took a long draught.

"So you've been to see John, yes?" he asked.

"Yes, and I got to see the painting of the lotus." He was a deliberate, cautious sort of man. He was as solid as an oak tree, and the look on his face made me feel that his mind was just as immovable. There was no cajoling or manipulating this man. He'd speak when he was good and ready. And only if he was good and ready.

He turned to his pint, looking into the glass intently, gathering his thoughts. I stayed silent and let him ponder. I gestured to the barkeep to refill us both. Alistair at last drained his glass and set it down with a deliberate clunk. When he turned to me, his eyes held something both wonderful and terrible.

I took a deep breath, bracing myself for whatever he was about to say. He said in an awed tone, "They saved my life, Lane."

"What?" I whispered.

"Yes. I owe them everything."

"So you worked with them?"

"No. No, I didn't. Y'see, they happened to come across me when I was not at my best, to say the least. I had survived the war when none of my brothers had. I'm the only one left. All five of them, just gone. It just about killed my mother, she was so heartbroken. The Lorians were here in my village and a group of robbers had set upon me when I was drunk. They'd beaten me bloody well. Your folks showed up, guns blazing, eyes like fire. The ruffians ran away. Then I passed out. The next morning, I found myself in their care, a cold cloth on my head, bandaged up. Sore all over. A complete mess. But they'd taken care of me, gotten me to a little house and over the next couple of days helped me to heal."

It was always touching to find out something new and tender or interesting about someone. I loved finding out aspects of people that might be hidden, or difficult to see. Finding it out about my own parents was incredibly moving.

"Your parents didn't know me from Adam. But they still cared. We got to know each other and they told me about their move to a place called Rochester. And I agreed to help them return that flower painting to John. I was a stranger, and perhaps that's what helped them confide in me. I always hoped you'd find me, Lane."

"Why is that?" I asked.

"They didn't tell me about what they were doing exactly, although I figured it must be some sort of government work. But they did say that they'd made some wrong choices, trying to do the best overall. But they'd let themselves . . . oh, how did they say it?" He brought a big, beefy hand to his chin as he thought about their exact wording. "Yes, they said they'd made a bad choice. No, that's not it. A *dark* choice, yes. I thought that was a strange turn of phrase. But they said that the lotus flower in that painting meant new beginnings. It meant purity and enlightenment. Rebirth, even. To them it was a sign that they could make a new beginning. That's why returning this piece was so important to them."

I let all that sink in. They were *just* like me. Human, capable of choosing darkness. Yet realizing it and making a change. Choosing light in the end. No wonder they liked the lotus flower. But all that was wonderful. There was still something terrible behind Alistair's eyes.

Just then, a band of energetic older gentlemen got up to play, their flutes in hand, a fiddle and drums. They began to warm up and I turned to Alistair. He'd backed off down the bar, a bleak look had come over his face, and he scowled with some kind of inner turmoil. I decided to let him think, so I stayed put as I watched the band tune up.

Then the song began. It was like a switch had been turned on. The atmosphere was at once electric. Their music had a way of lifting the soul, making all of us patrons look around, wondering if we all felt the same. We did.

They began a boisterous and yet genteel song that required dancing. Oh yes, with the strains of that music one *had* to dance. I was by myself, but with the energy of the place, that didn't seem to be a problem. It was assumed that everyone must dance, stranger or not. Big, burly men swept the little tables dotted about the place to the edges of the room.

The pipes, the drums, the fiddle . . . all of them came together and suddenly the room seemed to know just what to do. I finished off my beer in a big gulp and set down my glass just as I was swept up in a big reel. I decided that the only way to not get a foot trod upon or run into someone was to jump in as vigorously as everyone else, hoping my enthusiasm would overcome any missteps.

I was turned round and round. It was so fun, so full of magic in an unexpected way. Which is the best kind.

And then I saw him.

He stepped in the dark doorway and I caught his eyes, with a gleam in them that greeted me and made my heart flutter with anticipation.

I turned and swirled to the violin, with every turn keeping my eye on his form. He slowly made his way over to the dancers. Even through my spins and jumps and friendly embraces that the dance required, I could feel his eyes watching me, my eyes always catching his.

He joined the dance.

I turned this way, he turned that way. The women were lifted in a big twirl and placed down in a different spot. I was six feet closer to him now. We swept past each other in a turn and my shoulder brushed his, sending shocks down my spine. I barely saw the eyes of my many partners. My hair fell past my eyes and I looked over at him, with a small lift to the corner of my mouth.

CHAPTER 23

He saw her just as he entered the doorway. He watched her being lifted and spun about with the energy of the music, the violin and the pipes making every soul in that room feel a need to dance. He needed to be with her. And here they were, wonderfully separated from the worry of his family, the curse, and the feeling that he was in over his head. He couldn't shake the anxiety that he'd pull Lane in the muck and mire with him. Here he felt free.

The reel was like one he learned as a young boy, his limbs knowing what to do instinctively. He lifted his partner up and turned her about, setting her down in a different place.

Six feet closer to Lane.

Her shoulder brushed past his, sending out a flame of desire through his body. Her hair fell down past her gorgeous eyes as she turned her face to him and he saw in her the same longing.

He willed the song not to end; they would be partners soon. One more lift, turn, set the gal down, and . . .

"Finn," she breathed.

He smiled his greeting; her body was close, he felt her familiar form against his own. Her hand clasped his; they turned in time to the music, clapped three times, joined again and made their way around the circle with the music, hands clasped. Turn, her body closer, pressing up against him for a quick moment of unspoken desire and closeness. Then she was spun to another partner.

Three more spins, the song picked up rhythm and the clapping grew with fervor, the speed of the song almost too much for all of them. Big smiles launched all around in the great romp. Take the other girl's hand, keep Lane's eye, spin, *clap clap clap,* pick the girl up, set her down. Lane's hair swirled out with the motion of the energetic spin, her face shining toward him with a smile, her eyes flashing.

Faster tempo, the pipes and violin playing louder, the drummer playing with all his heart. This song was the best damn thing he ever heard. Faster. With a *whoosh* she was suddenly in his arms again.

"Hi, love," he breathed. Her secret smile. Just for him.

The song was almost at its end. He took her by the waist, hoisting her up in the air, spun her, and down. His arm around the front of her waist, hers around his, the many partners spinning around the room like various cogs in a clock. Their eyes never separating. Pipes, drums, violin, faster. One last hoist in the air, feeling her body against his as he lifted, spun her, and *down* in a great last *whoosh* of sound and spent energy. Everyone loudly applauded and cheered the great dance.

He and Lane stood amidst the small throng of merrymakers facing each other. Inches apart. The distance between them like a physical barrier almost visible to the eye, both breathing heavily from the rigorous dance. Her mysterious smile, and then, finally breaking the spell, she turned her head in the other direction, her hair softly fanning out and cascading down her shoulders. Walking away. One last look, and a slight gesture to tell him to wait just another minute.

She walked over to the large gentleman at the end of the bar, a scowl worthy of Fiorello plastered to his face, the fire in the fireplace shining off his red hair and beard. That must be the contact, Alistair.

Chapter 24

That was the best dance of my life. Except for a particular time that Finn and I danced in Little Italy, of course. I walked back to Alistair, still glowering into his glass. I asked for a water from the barkeep and guzzled it down.

"All right, Alistair. Why are you still scowling?" I asked. *Enough is enough.*

He growled, then said, "I just . . . I just wonder, Lane . . . was it something I did that led to them getting killed?"

I gasped, "What do you mean?"

He shook his head as he said, "Helping me and then returning that painting. It was the last effort they did professionally before your parents were killed."

Just then, I felt Finn come up next to me. "Alistair, this is Finn Brodie, New York Police Department detective." They shook hands.

"Yeah, you look like police," Alistair said.

"So I've heard."

I brought Finn up to speed. He said, "Do you really think something about all this gave it away about Matthew and Charlotte's whereabouts?"

Alistair gave a giant shrug. "I don't know. I just know I owed them my life. And I've carried this worry around for years that maybe it was my fault somehow. But tell me, did they ever show you the dagger I gave them?"

"*Your* dagger?" I squeaked.

"Yeah. My family had it for years. I wanted to give them something. Something that was special to me."

"This one?" I said with a smirk and a flourish as I pulled out the dagger from my purse.

"Mother o' God," he murmured. He took the dagger into his powerful hands. He turned it over and over. "My mum told me it was special. It's both black and white. Dangerous and beautiful. It made me think that Matthew would love it because of those qualities."

"He did," I said. "He always loved it. It meant a lot to him. Thank you for all you've done, you helped them more than you know. I came to you because I needed to know if they'd been on the right side, if they were the good guys. Or not. You helped them make a new start and make amends with a family they had harmed. And I can tell you right now, John will be inspiring *generations* of people. Maybe your efforts and my parents were part of that. Whatever happened to reveal where they were and whatever led up to them being killed, you had no intentional part in it. That's what matters. It's time to let go, Alistair."

He looked deeply into my eyes. Searching. Then a slow, earnest smile spread across his face.

"Besides," I said. "They're starting up another dance! Come on!" I grabbed him by the wrist as I heard Finn's appreciative chuckle. I can tell you right now, dancing a reel with Alistair was *very similar* to dancing with Big Sam. I felt and looked like a rag doll.

What seemed like hours later, Finn and I found ourselves back up at the bar and Alistair had taken over for the other barkeep. His jovial nature knew no bounds as he bought several rounds for the place. Next to Finn sat the previous barkeep, Joseph.

Finn said to him, "You know, Joey, it looks as if Alistair is having a fine time!"

Joseph laughed, his thin black mustache curving into a second smile over his lips. "I haven't seen him like this in ages. Did you know our Alistair was quite the hero?"

"Really? What did he do? In the war, you mean?" I asked.

Joseph shook his head. "No. He did his bit in the war, o' course. But right after, I don't know if he told you, but he dove into the drink. He lost all his brothers and it hurt him something fierce. But after he'd hit bottom, he bought this place and turned himself around.

"One night, he up and decided to use the money his brothers and he had saved for many years. He set up a fund for youngsters in the town. To go to university, or in some cases, get some medical attention that was too costly for the family. Gestures like that ripple out and it completely changed the town. After so much loss, there was a little bit of hope. Like I said: hero."

Finn and I shared a knowing look. But before I could say anything, Joseph interrupted my thoughts. "Hey, have you ever heard the Latin term *pulchritudo—*"

"*Ex cinere,*" Finn and I simultaneously supplied.

Joseph grinned. "Beauty out of ashes. It was a saying our town adopted after the war. And let me tell ya, Alistair is living proof of it."

We stayed the night in a room above the pub, having had far too many pints to drive back safely. I woke up with an aching head and a full heart. We made our way back to London, the drive allowing us the time to talk out everything. We'd learned a lot.

"So now we know about the pearl dagger's background," said Finn.

"I never knew where my dad had gotten it. I just knew he dearly loved it. And he definitely showed me how to use it," I said.

"Oh, he did do that," said Finn with a smirk and wide eyes.

"Shut up, Finn," I chuckled.

"Oh, I quite like that talent of yours," he said, eyes simmering as he turned to me.

"Keep your eyes on the road," I teased. Then I contemplated, "So, we finally know what my parents were doing. They did in fact infiltrate the Red Scroll crew. And what a scheme! I thought they were just a gang of thieves, but that group had a perfect way to con people and make it as easy on themselves as possible. It's horrible, but it's brilliant, too."

"Exactly," he said. "People can be easily swayed by a nice face and seemingly kind and professional demeanors. The best con artists don't look like con artists. Plus, everyone is eager to find treasure under their own roofs." I nodded.

"You know . . . Alistair might have been right, I hate to say. Something about this final effort might have led Rex straight to Rochester. *Something* did. Someone had to have let the cat out of the bag on where they'd relocated," I said.

"Yeah. I know. I hope he can truly let it go, though."

"Me, too. He deserves to move on," I said. "All right. So, now we have those bases covered. All we have left for our visit here is to find out if there is still no sign of Daphne. And then deal with your . . . *family*," I said with a nose-crinkled grimace.

Finn laughed. "Yeah. I'm just as excited as you are."

CHAPTER 25

Fair is foul and foul is fair.

—the three witches, *Macbeth*

We walked in the door to the beautiful lobby of the hotel bearing the same name as our favorite dance place in New York: the Savoy. We headed toward the bar for a glass of wine before dinner. Just as we ordered, two hysterical women approached. *Oh no.*

The two friends of Gwen, Eunice and Agnes, once again wore vaguely matching outfits. This time it was a sickly brown. They flapped and squealed as they came to our little table.

"Finn! You're in trouble," said the one on the right.

"What?" he exclaimed irritably.

"They are convinced that you're the culprit who poisoned your father," said the other one. I couldn't remember which was which. But I certainly recalled the third one.

"Finn," said a cold voice. She'd silently crept over to us.

"Hello, Gwen. What's this about?"

"Look, I've tried defending you. But this has gone too far. I've covered up for you in the past, but I can't do it any longer."

"What are you talking about? You've never had to cover for me." The two weird friends huffed an indignant sound as if they knew Finn was lying. Finn and I exchanged a look. The fine lines around his mouth and the strain around his eyes showed the stress he was under. I put my hand on his knee, right next to me under the table, willing him to feel my support.

"I came to warn you. Sean wants to meet. Tomorrow, seven in

the evening at your family home. But don't be surprised if he goes to the authorities."

Before we could make any kind of rebuttal, the threesome turned around and marched out.

I turned wide eyes to Finn. "What the hell?" I exclaimed with my usual grace and subtlety.

Finn slammed his drink back and ran a hand through his hair. He whispered raggedly, "It's happening all over again."

"No. No it's not. Not if I have anything to do about it. Look, we need to go talk with Vivian. We need more details on what happened when you were framed before you moved to the States. They're up to no good, that's for sure."

He shifted his eyes to mine, his mouth tightly compressed. He was breathing through his nose like a bull trying not to charge. I couldn't blame him. I was enraged from the injustice of it all.

"Lane." The way he said it made me sit up straight. It sent chills down my spine. And *not* in a nice way.

"What are you doing, Finn?"

"I've been thinking. Sean is too conniving and powerful. I think I need to face him on my own. When Vivian saved me at the accident, do you know what my worst fear was? That her involvement could've gotten her hurt or killed. I can't pull you in, too. You have to stay away from that meeting tomorrow. It's just too dangerous. It's like I'm cursed, and I can't have you harmed because of it."

"Finn—"

"I'll be back right after the meeting. I promise. But tonight I have to think, and tomorrow I just have to face him on my own." He jumped up, picked up his blazer, and slung it on. He strode away from me, across the bar, and out the door.

Finn was in big trouble. I grabbed my coat and ran to the front desk. I needed to make a few calls.

CHAPTER 26

She woke up in a cold sweat. The dream had been full of blood, full of power, full of . . . darkness. It was disturbing, but she felt like it was a good omen. It meant they were on the right track.

"Gwen, are you all right?" asked the deep and sleepy voice next to her.

She looked over at his tousled black hair and said, "*Shhh*. It's okay, Sean. Just a bad dream." She couldn't help wiping her hands on the warm sheets, subconsciously trying to cleanse her hands of all that invisible blood. She knew she wouldn't fall back asleep, so she got up to get a drink of water.

She walked out to the kitchen and grasped a glass from the cupboard. She ran the water, getting it as cold as possible. She filled the glass and drank it down.

"Can't sleep?" Sean asked, wrapping his arms around her from behind.

"No, too much on my mind, I think," said Gwen.

When he walked in, she knew he admired her lithe form in her nightgown, a lamp highlighting her silhouette. Her mint green nightgown matched her little slippers perfectly. She was always singularly controlled, tightly precise with every movement, never a hair out of place. Even now, her hair wasn't mussed from sleep.

"What are you thinking about?" he asked.

She moved his hands. She preferred nothing touching her. "I'm concerned about Vivian. I'm not sure about her."

"But she's in her old folks' home. She's out of the way," he said.

"It's not a prison or asylum, Sean," she declared waspishly.

A curtain lowered over his eyes as he regarded her. She didn't care, she wasn't afraid of him. They were equals in that way. She'd known fully what Sean was capable of even before they got married. Gwen admired his imaginative efforts, full of cunning patience. A touch of pride pulled at one side of her own mouth. But no one was as patient as she was. No one ever expected the lovely, rather quiet and naïve English lady.

He cocked his head to one side in thought and said, "Well. Perhaps you should make a visit to Vivian and decide once and for all if she'll get in the way or not."

Gwen considered this as she got another glass of water. "Mmm. Yes. That's a good idea. I think I will."

"And if you decide she's too big of a risk, take care of it. We've worked too long for us not to get everything we've wanted."

"I agree." Gwen carefully washed the glass, then dried it with a towel. She opened the door of the cupboard and placed it back in its place with exacting precision. Then she wiped down the sink, getting rid of any water spots. She folded the towel into thirds and slipped it through the towel bar, making sure the ends were even.

She turned to him. He wanted her, his desire heady and strong.

She read that desire, but was determined to keep her cool, keep in control. They couldn't get distracted. Everything depended on them executing this next part of the plan, the one they'd been concocting since before the accident Sean orchestrated. They knew it would come down to this. They could pull it off. They just had to keep focused. Only a few hours until dawn. That night their plan would come to fruition. If they could take down Finn, once and for all, they'd get it all, the whole Brodie estate.

"Good night, Sean." She walked past him and went to bed.

CHAPTER 27

Finn never showed up back at the hotel. I spent most of the night unable to sleep so I went over some plans that were taking shape in my mind while I fairly paced a hole through the Oriental rug in my room. The next morning, when the sun couldn't quite gather enough strength to find its way through the murky sky, I quickly found a cab and made my way over to Vivian's.

I greeted her with a grateful hug.

"Lane, dear, what's wrong? You sounded like something was urgent. Why isn't Finn with you?"

"He didn't call you or come by last night?" I asked.

"No. He didn't. Should he have?" she asked.

"Yes. Something is afoot, Vivian. We need to help him. Gwen and her cronies came by the hotel bar last night and said that Sean wanted to see Finn tonight, and that they're thinking that Finn is the culprit who poisoned their father. How is that possible when the medical report said that he'd been poisoned for quite some time?"

Vivian's face blanched as I told her the news and I noticed a small tremble in her hand. "Oh, Lane. I have no doubt that Sean has officials in his pocket. One time, he must've been only eleven years or so, I caught him talking with the grocer off to the side away from customers. I overheard him insinuating that he'd seen him shortchange a customer and that his father really looked down on folks that did those sorts of things . . . unless of course he had extra boxes of Turkish Delight that were lying around . . ."

"Extortion. At eleven. Lovely. By the way, how on earth did you and Finn end up so normal in this family?" I exclaimed.

"I wonder that all the time. I stepped in of course and yanked Sean out of there. But Lane dear, if he was like that at eleven, there's no telling what he's capable of now," she said with her hands on her hips and a resolute look in her eye.

"Look, let's have some tea and give this some thought," I said. "I know we'll come up with a plan." I went to her little kitchenette and put the pot on to boil. I glanced back at Viv, her eyes focused out the window. A sparrow alighted on a branch, making the small red berries remaining on the bare branch quiver. I found the tea and milk, and a little tin of cookies, then brought the tray over to the table in front of her.

Viv leaned forward and poured for us. She was a steady octogenarian, her mind bright, eyes sparking with determination. She'd been a solid ally for Finn and she would be again. As she plunked two cubes of sugar into her cup, she said, "It has to be a family member or one of the household staff."

"For what?" I asked, pouring a touch of milk into my cup.

"The culprit. The one who's been poisoning Richard. He or she has to have easy access to his food and drink. It's been going on for months, they say."

"And Polly and Richard have no ideas?" I asked.

"They are lacking in imagination, Lane dear," she said with a disgusted look on her face.

"Sean is an obvious choice," I said. "Does he want his inheritance faster?"

"Not faster," said Viv. "To himself. That's why, I believe, he worked on that whole deception on Finn in the first place. He doesn't want to share it."

"But he already has it," I said. "Finn was cut out of the will, right?"

"Well, actually," she declared, "he was cut out of receiving an annual allowance. But he's still in the will. And unless there are criminal charges, or he's found incompetent somehow, Finn will receive the bulk of the estate because he's the eldest. It's English law that the eldest receives the lion's share."

I crossed my legs, noticing I had stockings on for this visit, and said, "Why didn't he just kill him outright? Why did Sean create such an elaborate ruse? He was working on that for years."

"I know. I think he just likes the game of it all. Even as a kid he loved the art of deception. Besides, if he created an entire framework for a black sheep kind of history for Finn, it would be easier to escape any kind of suspicion if Finn had another accident or something. If he just killed him outright, Sean would definitely be a suspect."

I nodded, thinking of the time Finn told me about Sean stealing a bike, then realizing that he'd get a reward for returning it. He'd made quite a show about it, getting all sorts of praise for finding the stolen bike. He pinned it on a local bully and that bully had paid dearly from his abusive father. I wondered if that scheme was the thing that whetted Sean's appetite.

I set my cup down, thinking about Viv's theory. I said, "And that shows that he's patient. Sean could wait. He could work a long-term plan like that. Still. Isn't poison considered a weapon of choice for women?" I asked.

"Hmm. I don't know," she said. "They didn't find out the exact poison yet, either. Not sure if they will. They just know it wasn't arsenic. He didn't exhibit the symptoms of arsenic poisoning, but there are hundreds of poisons available in any household . . ."

My eyes wandered around the room as I thought. "That was nice of Gwen to bring you flowers. Have you seen a lot of her over the years?" I asked, hoping my face didn't betray how much I loathed her.

Viv pierced me with her amused eyes. "So you like her that much, huh?" She shook with a silent chuckle that reminded me of Finn. My heart ached for him suddenly. He was so alone. And hurting.

Her eyes softened as she read my face. "Oh Lane, he'll be all right. We'll find a way to help him."

I cleared my throat and poured more steaming tea. "So. Gwen. Has she always visited you? Did she know about Sean's deception and plan to harm Finn the night of their wedding?" I asked.

"She did visit pretty regularly once Finn left for the States. I never let on that I knew what Sean had done. So I never talked with her about it. I just . . . I *think* she's innocent. But I never felt comfortable letting my guard down completely. Finn and I could see through Sean easily. But he was able to charm so many people. I could never understand how they couldn't see through it. And it made me wonder, if Gwen couldn't see through it, she was either in on it or she wouldn't believe it. Either way, it was a big gamble to trust her."

"I hate her," I blurted out.

"I can tell." Then she snorted. "I don't hate her. Not quite. But I have to say, I'm not fond of how she wears so many matching items. It's a little much."

It was my turn to snort. "You are one in a million, Viv. *Thank you.* For all you've done for Finn. He loves you so much."

"He's my sweet boy. He's more like me than my own daughter. We've always been two peas in a pod. All right, love. We need to come up with a plan. He's supposed to meet Sean tonight?" I nodded. "Then we need to get ahead of Sean's plan. Whatever it is, it'll be dangerous."

Vivian looked about the little room as she gathered her thoughts. She breathed in a little gasp. "Oh dear. I've just had a thought. But I'll need to ask my neighbor about something first, then I'll let you know. Overall, though, Sean has worked for years to get city officials, leading businessmen, and anyone powerful in his back pocket. He may have bribed the police into arresting Finn, or . . ." Her voice petered out. "Oh no," she said, just barely a whisper.

"What, Vivian?" I asked, dread quickening my pulse.

"He might do something worse than go to the police."

"What do you mean? What's worse?" I asked, sitting forward.

"Lane, the whole deception that Sean pulled over on Finn . . . it was all based on trying to show Finn hadn't been in his right mind."

I suddenly realized what was worse. Far, far worse. "Oh my God."

She nodded just a fraction of an inch.

I stood up, adrenaline pulsing through my body. "Over. My. Dead. Body."

I grabbed my coat and ran to the door. I said with grim determination, "Meet me at the hotel at six thirty. I have a plan. Sean thinks *he* has connections? I have better ones."

I banged my way out the door. I needed to act. Finn would confront Sean tonight. I would bet a thousand dollars that he would fall into their trap. He wouldn't see it coming. And something deep down inside had him reeling. His face had looked ragged, as if an ocean of regret had poured over him. I hated that look. Nothing was worse than seeing that in someone you love: despair.

CHAPTER 28

Look like the innocent flower, but be the serpent under it.

—Lady Macbeth, *Macbeth*

The knock came sharp and loud at the door. Vivian's hand immediately found the little beaded purse right next to her. Just in case.

"Come in, Gwen!" she said cheerfully.

"Well, hello, Vivian. Don't you look lovely today. I love that royal blue blouse."

"Thank you, Gwen," she said. Vivian regarded Gwen's perfectly matched, dark peach ensemble. It had to be Vivian's most hated of colors. And there was a lot of it on Gwen, from the tips of her dainty toes to the pillbox hat perched on her pert little head. Viv sucked in her lips as she tried to hide her disgust.

"Would you like a cuppa? I brought Father's special blend, it's so scrummy," said Gwen as she went to the kitchen to get the tea set.

"Oh . . ." said Vivian. "Of course. That'd be delightful. It really is a wonderful blend."

Gwen chattered on a bit about inconsequential things. As she brought the tray over, she said, "You know, I do worry about Father. His heart is still weak. Would you like one lump or two?"

"Two please," said Vivian. "Yes, I know. It's concerning to say the least."

Gwen eased into her discussion; Vivian could see that she was carefully placing her words in the perfect, most useful order. "So,

Vivian, I have to say . . . I'm worried about Finn, as well. He just doesn't seem well, a little confused and off somehow . . ."

Vivian looked at her carefully and she nodded. "Yes, I suppose this all is a bit taxing."

"Oh, I think it's much worse than that. Your tea is getting cold, Viv."

Vivian cocked her head to one side and gave Gwen a long, thoughtful look. "Right, can't let it get cold," she said as she picked up the cup and held it in her hands.

"And really, Viv, I think we might need to get Finn some help. Perhaps professional help. I think it's gone farther than we can handle."

Gwen fastened her eyes onto Vivian's cup as she brought it close to her lips. She sucked in her breath.

Vivian paused. "You know, he does seem tired and a little lackluster lately."

Gwen pulled her eyes from the cup and met Vivian's gaze. "I agree."

Vivian went to take a sip, but then brought the cup back down, "However, I think professional help is overcautious."

"Vivian," said Gwen in a harsher voice. "You can't be serious. This has gone too far. It's just not safe. Don't you think?" she asked rather exasperatedly.

"No, Gwen. I don't," said Vivian firmly, then set her cup down resolutely.

Gwen stood up. "Well, Viv, I'm sorry to hear that. I want to get him help." She casually picked up a throw pillow that was next to her, feeling the velvet, deep in thought, pacing as she gathered her thoughts. "I just . . . I think his childhood was rough on him. And he can't be doing that well in the police department in New York."

"What are you talking about? He's doing quite well."

Gwen took a step closer to Viv. "Well, I think we'd have heard if he'd been successful. I think he's ill and we need to act before he hurts more people." She took one step more, about a foot from Vivian. Vivian's hand rested on her little purse.

"Well, Gwen," she said, her tone changing to something more

sarcastic. "I think I do understand. You've at last made your position quite clear." She smirked, making the blood rise in Gwen's cheeks.

Viv was mocking her, and clearly Gwen could not stand for that. She took one last look at the cup Viv had firmly set down. She raised the pillow up and took one final step closer to Vivian, readying her muscles.

Click.

"I wouldn't do that if I were you," said Viv in a steady voice.

Gwen gasped. The revolver in Vivian's hands glinted in the light, quivering only the slightest little bit.

The door suddenly burst open, the hinges breaking, the molding cracking with small bits of wood flying through the air. "Put your hands in the air!"

CHAPTER 29

Be bloody, bold, and resolute.

—the second apparition, *Macbeth*

Finn spent the night wandering around the city he loved and loathed in equal portions. He stopped at a couple of bars, followed up by restaurants for scalding hot coffee. He had to think. He had to plan. He had to get Lane out of there.

How could he have let her get so close? His family was a curse. *He* was cursed. Why did he think he could change that? Veer off the course his family had set years ago? It was all too heavy. It was like that charm by the witches in *Macbeth*. He'd been a fool to think he could let it all go. That he'd be able to get away, escape. It was impossible to get out from underneath.

Somehow, the rest of the day crept by and the sun set. He made his way to his family home. He stood outside, the warm windows glowing onto the street. The lamplighters had already been by and the halos of light made orange circles on the street. He could see the flickering light of a fireplace in the parlor. The staunch town-house stood imperiously looking down at him. Fittingly, it began to rain a fine, hard mist. He pulled his collar up on his trench coat and his fedora down farther over his face. The warm light from the windows belied what was indescribable coldness within. He dragged on his cigarette, finishing it, then flicking it from his fingers. He took a deep breath. It was time.

What he didn't see was the police wagon just around the corner.

Finn walked up to the door and didn't bother to ring. The door was open a crack, inviting him in. He opened it and immediately the scent of lilies, his mother's favorite, attacked his senses. He'd come to hate that scent, but it was fitting since it was the traditional burial flower. He grunted at his macabre sense of humor at the moment.

"Hello?" he called.

"In the parlor, Finn," answered Sean.

Sean. His brother. *That voice.* That deep, familiar tone made his stomach clench and his knee throbbed with sudden pain, remembering that night all over again, that malicious grin as Sean ran right into him. The searing pain, the disbelief . . . his heart shrank with the fear of being out of control. Finn loved his job because he called the shots. He understood how it all worked, his role and how he fit in with the department as a whole. He was sure-footed. Here, he was anything but. It was like a nightmarish fun house; nothing was as it seemed and everything was out of control.

Finn didn't bother to take off his coat; droplets of water fell to the floor and he imagined the hiss of steam as they hit. He went over to the door of the parlor, so much of this house like a shadow of a dream. Finn had walked these halls many thousands of times, yet it felt like it had been someone else. The lush carpets made his footfalls almost silent. He could hear within the tinkle of a glass with ice in it and the crackle of a fire.

"Hello, Sean," said Finn.

"I'm glad you came," answered Sean, his jet-black hair glinting from the light of a large chandelier looming overhead. He stood with one hand in his suitcoat pocket, calm and nonchalant.

Before Finn could say anything, Sean began a speech that sounded rehearsed. "You see, Finn, I know it was you. You must've hired someone here to initiate the poisoning of Father. And it wasn't a coincidence that it increased so much that he almost died just days after you arrived." A sheen of sweat appeared on Sean's top lip. In a normal person, that would read as nerves. In Sean, it meant he was enjoying himself. To highlight that even more, he smiled. *Smiled,* waiting for Finn's response. Anticipating the pain of Finn having to defend himself.

"Sean, that's ridiculous. What are you talking about?"

"Finn, now relax. Don't get yourself worked up," he said in placating tones.

"Worked up? You're accusing me of planning a murder!"

"Murder? Finn, you're the one that's bringing up murder. Was that your plan? Did you need to get rid of Father permanently? I'd thought you were just getting back at him for removing your annual allowance, but it sounds like you had more of a plan than that."

"You're putting words into my mouth," said Finn. "It's more likely that Gwen was in on it than me, for heaven's sake."

"Now you're accusing Gwen? That's completely irrational and indicative of your mental state. How could you?" he demanded.

This was spiraling out of control. Finn could feel it all slipping out of his grasp. His pulse quickened. Heat rose up his neck, his face. "Sean. You're the one orchestrating all this. You know it!" He walked toward Sean, fists clenched. Ready for a battle.

"Gentlemen, I think you've heard enough," said Sean, sounding smug. Confident.

"What?" said Finn. Three men, two in police uniforms, one plain-clothed, came around the corner.

"Take it easy," said the man in a brown tweed suitcoat with a sickly, limp mustache above his lip. He had his hands raised in a calming gesture. "It's okay. We're going to help you. You're obviously not feeling well. You've made accusations that are unfounded and you seem very ill. We are going to help."

Finn's mind was swirling. The two policemen stepped closer, their postures tensed and ready for a fight. Suddenly, Finn understood the trap. *You seem ill?* They weren't trying to arrest him, they were going to *commit* him. *Dear God.*

He put up a good fight, but the two policemen were enormous. He'd landed a few good punches, but they managed to get his arms in their grasp and they started pushing and pulling him toward the door. They barged out and then he registered the police wagon. The blood drained from his face. When they got to the end of the walkway, he'd have one final chance. If they managed to get him to the lunatic asylum, he might never get out. Worse, he knew the mental specialists these days were happy to "help" an agitated patient get some peace by twirling a small instrument through the nose, up into the frontal cortex. A lobotomy might leave you drooling and vegetative, but you sure were more peaceful and easy to handle. He felt like he might throw up right then and there.

With more work than the policemen had expected, they finally wrestled Finn down the walk. Just as they got to the end, Finn dropped to his knees, surprising his aggressors and making them tilt forward off balance. They'd taken away his gun from his shoulder holster, but they'd made the unwise choice of not handcuffing him.

From the front door, Sean yelled a primal, "No!"

Motivated by a savage fear, in three quick, powerful swings Finn knocked out the two police and turned to whom he'd finally surmised as the "doctor" of the local insane asylum. The doctor had taken off running. Finn was huffing and puffing with the exertion and fear coursing through him.

Sean.

From behind, Finn felt a violent kidney punch that knocked him to the ground.

But it was a mistake on Sean's part. Those two policemen hadn't thought to look for Finn's backup gun. Strapped to his ankle.

In a flash, Finn had drawn his revolver and leveled it at his brother. The rain was now coming down in earnest, blurring his vision, and he felt a trickle of blood issuing from a cut above his eye, but he had no trouble aiming the gun steadily at his lethal enemy.

"You couldn't do it," said Sean, snarling at him.

Finn cocked the trigger. "Wanna bet?"

Just then, two cars careened up and pulled over. His gun didn't waver.

"Finn! Are you okay?" *Lane.* She was here.

Sean registered who the gentlemen were with Lane before Finn did. "Gentlemen! Restrain him! He's not well, he's been making wild accusations and now he's threatening me!"

The two men stood on either side of Lane. Both holding their hands in front of them, in complete control. *Not* making a move to hold Finn back. Then Vivian carefully stepped out of the car, too. *What was happening?*

"Lane! I told you not to find me. I can't protect you. It's too much! I can't stop him."

"Finn," she said softly, moving one step closer. "Yes. You can. Put the gun down."

"No! He'll kill us all. He's capable. He will. And what if I'm just like him? *I'm his brother*," he said with an anguished voice. He turned a quick eye to Lane. The rain was soaking her hair, plastering it to her face. Her bright eyes were set on him. Unflinching and fiery.

"No, Finn. You've already proven that you're nothing like him. Not at all. You proved that years ago. He has no control over you. Put the gun down. Trust me. *We've got it covered*."

Wait. The way she said *we've got it covered*. She was smirking. By God, he did trust her. With everything he had. Okay, he'd give it a go.

He lowered the gun.

"Now's your chance!" yelled Sean. "Get him!"

Lane made a rude sound, then said with a drawl, "Yeah. Now's your chance."

The two men walked toward *Sean*. Not him. "You're under arrest, Sean Brodie, for the attempted murder of Richard Brodie."

"*Game?* Is that you?" stuttered Finn.

"Yes, Sir Philip Game at your service," said the police commissioner, head of Scotland Yard.

"And let's not forget Mr. Stanley Baldwin," said Lane with that secret smile of hers. *Clever girl.*

"Stanley Baldwin," whispered Finn incredulously. "The PM? Bloody hell."

Baldwin just grinned and nodded. "Oh, I wouldn't miss this. Not when I got an urgent telegram from the president of the United States. Seems to me, Sir Philip, perhaps we made a grave error years ago overlooking the talents of Mr. Finn Brodie."

"Indeed it does, sir. Now, c'mon! Let's go, Sean. You've got a long night ahead of you," said the police commissioner.

"Hold on," said Lane. She walked up to Sean and looked him right in the face, scrutinizing every inch. "I just needed to get a good look at him. I imagine we'll never see him again after tonight."

"You did this?" uttered Sean through clenched teeth.

"Oh, you better believe it. Your wife, too. She's already at the jail," she purred.

"You bitch!" growled Sean.

Lane turned her amused and flashing eyes to Finn and in an instant, he knew exactly what she was saying to him without one word. Her eyes said, *Here's your chance.*

Whump!

"Holy hell," uttered Lane.

He'd hauled off and punched Sean a massive blow right in the most tender part of the nose. A hair shy of knocking him out, his eyes rolled around in his head, blood pouring from his nostrils.

"I might've broken a finger," said Finn with a wince, holding his right hand. "But it was worth it."

Lane's glittering eyes said it all, as they always did. She came over and wrapped her arm around his, pressing in close. The rain ran tracks down her face, but was no match for her sublime smile.

Prime Minister Stanley Baldwin, who was holding Sean's arm to keep him upright, said, "Like I always say, I would rather trust a woman's instinct than a man's reason. Any day."

CHAPTER 30

I could finally let go of all the tension, all the fear and worry. I watched as Finn flexed his tender right hand. Perhaps just a sprain or a bruise.

The head of Scotland Yard and the prime minister of England had everything under control. Hands on hips, they both directed the other policemen who came running and driving up to the scene. Vivian was speaking with the PM and looking like an eager, blushing schoolgirl.

A bobby who'd been patrolling the area and was one of the officers to arrive first was giving me a quizzical look as he stood there taking in the scene. He'd witnessed most of it. One side of his mouth pulled up in amusement as he shook his head.

I turned to look at Finn and smiled. "Finn, we may have brought the Lane and Finn spectacle to London." He chuckled softly as he nodded a greeting at the young bobby who was smirking at us.

"We do tend to get a lot of attention wherever we go," he said.

I felt his eyes intently turn to me. I looked at him and brought my hand to his cheek. The stubble from a day without shaving lined his jaw, feeling prickly against my palm. The moment reminded me of when he'd saved me from a shoot-out right on Main Street in my hometown in Michigan, but this time I was the cavalry.

I saw the blood on his face and automatically took a handkerchief out of my purse. The rain was still coming down, but I didn't care. I carefully dabbed at his swollen left eye, then the bloody cut above his eyebrow. I felt the warmth of his hand come around my waist as he pulled me close.

"I tried to push you away, Lane," he said in a raspy voice.

"I know. It takes a lot more than that to get rid of me. I don't quit too easily."

"I love that about you," he said, smoothing a hand around my face and my wet hair.

"You know, Finn . . . there is no charm, no curse." He breathed in a quick breath. I went on, "In *Macbeth* the curse was themselves. Macbeth and Lady Macbeth. The witches just foretold what was going to happen, a dark charm didn't make it happen, or some kind of ultimate destiny. Human avarice did. You already proved beyond a doubt that you were separate from your family's vices. *You already did it.* You just didn't see it yet."

"You did? You saw it?" he asked, sweetly revealing an ounce of the little boy that long ago had lost hope, daring to believe again.

"I did." I put my hand on his chest, feeling the warmth even through the rain and his coat.

Heat from his kiss poured into me as I brought my hand up and around his neck, curling my fingertips into his hair, pulling him even closer.

He pulled his lips away slowly, but staying in the embrace. "You're freezing, Lane. We should get you back to the hotel for a hot bath."

"*That* . . . is a great idea," I whispered as I leaned close to his ear. I felt him shiver as he bent his head down and gently, lingeringly kissed just below my ear.

CHAPTER 31

After a little nap, I changed into a pair of cream-colored wool trousers and a soft, light pink sweater. I didn't put on socks and shoes just yet; the bathroom floor had quite a bit of water sloshed onto it.

"You're smirking," said Finn as I looked into the mirror, brushing on a light coat of raspberry pink lipstick. He was almost ready, lying on the bed with his white dress shirt open wide at the collar, ankles crossed, eyes sparking with mischief as they pierced mine in the reflection.

"I'm sure I am," I said. "C'mon, let's go grab a drink, they'll be waiting for us by now."

We finished getting ready, then headed downstairs, hand in hand. We arrived at the bar and got to witness Vivian clinking her glass with the head of Scotland Yard. In order to not make too big of a scene, the prime minister decided to let us hash out the details with just Sir Philip.

We pulled up chairs as we signaled the waiter. Two martinis, mine with a splash of olive juice and three olives, his neat with a twist of lemon.

"So it looks as if you two have the debrief well under way," said Finn, a teasing grin focused on his grandma. Vivian was glowing with a soft pink tone to her cheeks and the same exact spark of playfulness in her eyes as Finn had just displayed. Honestly, they were more like mother and son than grandmother and grandson.

I took a good swig of the icy, salty martini. As I set my glass down, I said to Sir Philip, "First of all, I have to know, how did you discover that Sean was behind the poisoning?"

"You'd better ask your grandmother," he said with a sardonic salute to Vivian. She turned a deep fuchsia.

"Good Lord," uttered Finn as he signaled the waiter rather desperately for another martini to have on deck.

Vivian cleared her throat, preparing for a good lecture. She would really enjoy Aunt Evelyn. "Right after you left, Lane, I started to give it some thought. And actually, I'm certain Sean is involved, but I think the main culprit in the actual poisoning is Gwen."

"I knew it!" I exclaimed with a victorious kind of punch to Finn's arm.

"Ouch!" he said.

"Oh, sorry," I said.

"You are not."

"No, I'm not," I said, unable to keep the cheeky grin from my face.

Sir Philip cleared his throat, probably trying to get us back in order. *Good luck.*

He began, "So as you know, Prime Minister Baldwin received an urgent telegram from your president. In summary, we got the idea that you, Lane, contacted Mayor La Guardia about Finn's predicament and he immediately flew into action. You have some powerful friends, my dear," he said with a cocked eyebrow.

"Yes, I do," I said. "As does Finn. He'd been under direct orders from President Roosevelt a few months ago, and of course Mayor La Guardia has a vested interest in him. Once I realized Sean wasn't just going for an arrest, but to try to commit Finn, I just about had a heart attack. It would've been a thousand times more difficult getting Finn out of a lunatic asylum than debunking the accusations of poisoning and murder. And they could do absolutely anything they wanted to him in there."

It made my blood run cold. It was shockingly easy to get someone committed. You think your wife might be cheating? A son or daughter not doing what you want? A mother or father too old and difficult to take care of? Get them committed and they just disappeared. . . . And with the web of deceit that Sean had woven over decades, he would've had plenty of evidence. False as it was, it would've been enough.

"And I was not going to let that happen," declared Vivian with a fierce tone. Her fist came down on the table, rattling the glasses.

I turned to Finn and said, "I just *love* her," which made her anger slip away and she laughed delightedly.

"So anyway," she continued, "I got to thinking, and then I spotted the flowers Gwen brought me. The bishop's lace."

I asked, "Oh, that's right. She gardens. Does she plant foxglove, or nightshade or something?" I knew those were poisonous.

"Actually, it's what I *thought* was bishop's lace. I thought it looked a little different than I remembered. It's quite similar, but far more poisonous. Hemlock. They were careful to put small doses over time in Richard's favorite tea that no one touches because he's so picky as to only drink that. So I ran to the hospital with this new knowledge and they tested the hypothesis. Richard started improving right away once they knew how to treat him. He's not out of the woods, but he has a much better chance now. Plus . . . Gwen had brought a tin of his tea to the hospital so he could enjoy it there, too."

With admiration written all over his face, Finn asked her, "So how did you get word to the police?"

She said, "I had the doctors call. I figured it would be taken more seriously if the doctors informed them. Then I was quite taken aback because I got a call right from the top. Sir Philip called, then came over to see the flowers for himself."

We turned our eyes to Sir Philip. He nodded as he said, "Yes, my officers got a call from the doctors not too long after my call from the PM. I decided I wanted to handle this case myself."

I winked at Finn when Sir Philip had said "case." I was always the butt of jokes at home because I was quick to call the intrigues that we got involved in a *case*. Finn chuckled his silent laugh as he shook his head.

"Vivian, why do you think Gwen was at the root of all this? You know I've always thought she was suspicious, but I wasn't sure if that was my own prejudice. I thought that to you she'd always seemed like an unwilling participant," I said, then ate my last olive.

She nodded as she thought about it. "Well . . . Sean is definitely patient enough for a lengthy plan. And I'm certain he knew about it, was part of it. But what got me is that Gwen has been the one visiting me here and there over the years. Not Sean. Like I told you, Lane, I didn't trust her. I thought it was possible that she just enjoyed my company, but when I got to thinking about it, I couldn't help but wonder if she'd been a scout all this time.

"I was Finn's only ally in the family. How else would Sean have known that Finn would be coming here on assignment again? I admit, I did tell her about your trip, Finn. I'm so sorry. If I hadn't, they wouldn't have been able to set up this trap." She reached out and set her hand on Finn's.

"Oh Mammo, it wouldn't have mattered. They would've just come up with a different plan. The fact that I ran into Gwen a few months ago probably got them thinking about how to get me out of the way for good," he said. She nodded a thankful smile at him.

I commented, "But still, all that just shows that she might have been an informant to Sean. What makes you think she had more of a role than that? Maybe he threatened her or she passed on the information unknowingly . . ."

"Today she brought *me* a tin of Richard's tea, too," said Vivian with a droll look.

The penny dropped. Finn's eyes turned a dangerous black as he fiercely whispered, "They tried to poison you?"

Sir Philip and I exchanged glances.

But Vivian was simply smirking as she said, "Don't worry. I knew exactly what they're capable of. I was ready. And no, I did not drink any of her tea. But I have to say it was fun watching her eye my teacup as I kept bringing it to my lips, then not drinking . . ."

Finn made a kind of strangled sound and Vivian absently patted him on the shoulder.

Sir Philip pointedly cleared his throat and continued, "It was a relief we got there in time."

"What?" Finn exclaimed.

"Oh, it's fine, dear, I was prepared. Remember? The hospital had called him, then I decided to call the Yard as well. Besides," she said with a cheeky grin, "I had my revolver."

"You have a revolver?" I gasped.

"Don't get any ideas," said Finn.

Viv was warming to the subject and carried on cheerily. "Oh, don't worry, I took shooting lessons. And besides, Philip was on his way at that point." Finn looked a little peaked.

Sir Philip took up the story again. "So we received the call from the hospital about the poison, and I asked about the origin of this supposition. They had Vivian's name and phone number. I called to make an appointment to chat with her. A little later, I received another call from the Yard that they'd been informed that Gwen was on her way over to have tea. I decided I'd better head on over. Immediately." He gave Vivian a slightly wary look and I had to bite back a laugh.

Vivian blithely went on, "You see, I think Gwen started to suspect that I knew what she'd been up to. Or at the least, that I would have your back, Finn. I believe she came over to see what I knew. Who knows? Maybe she'd try to get me committed, too. I certainly could've thrown a wrench into their plans, that's for sure. And when she came at me with a pillow in her hands, obviously wanting to do me harm, I pulled out my revolver."

"You what?" said Finn.

"Stop yelling, Finn," I said calmly as I sipped my martini. He muttered something indescribable, sounding exactly like Mr. Kirkland, whom I knew would've given *anything* to witness all this going down. I suddenly missed them all: Fio, Evelyn, Kirkland, Val, Roarke, Morgan . . .

"They were used to getting things their way," said Vivian thoughtfully. "And it infuriated them that a little old lady and the man they'd been able to convince everyone was daft and a loose cannon might actually present a difficult problem. I think even years ago, that devious nature is what drew Gwen to Sean. Like I told you, Lane, Finn and I could see through Sean's charm. And Gwen either couldn't see through it, or she *did* and she liked it . . ."

Viv was right; Gwen was too smart not to be able to see through him.

Finn prompted, "Um, yes. Getting back to the story?" She and Sir Philip filled us in on the scene at her apartment, but I don't think it made Finn feel any better at all.

"We arrested Gwen and took her in. We knew it would be going down at Sean's about seven in the evening, which was cutting it close. So I called everything in, even notified the PM, and we all raced to Sean's."

Vivian chimed in, "We picked Lane up on the way."

Sir Philip carried on, "After we got Sean and Gwen back to the station, I personally interviewed those two policemen who'd been working with Sean, the ones who had the misfortune of trying to wrestle you into the police wagon, Finn." He raised his eyebrows appreciatively at Finn.

"They had no idea what they were getting themselves into. Turns out, Sean told them a convincing lie about Finn and they had agreed to the plan, hoping to hear a confession. However, they started to doubt Sean once they overheard your conversation, despite his effort to manipulate your words. Enough was said, though, that they just carried on with their initial mission for the time being. But the final straw was when they saw the PM and me drive up. Let's just say they were completely convinced about which side was the right side.

"Most importantly, Finn, my men overheard a conversation with Sean and Gwen around five o'clock. Sean wanted my men there early in case you arrived ahead of schedule. They hadn't known what it meant at the time, but to sum it up and subtracting some of the more *colorful* language, Sean and Gwen had been arguing about the culmination of their scheme, as it were."

Sir Philip looked pointedly at Finn. "Gwen said they'd been planning it for too long, he'd better not mess things up. Then Sean said that if he'd executed a car accident on their own wedding day, he could manage this." His words had slowly come to a halt, lending importance and solemnity to their weight.

Finn's eyes were wide with vindication. He finally had proof of Sean's deception. His shoulders let go of a tension that he had been holding onto for many, many years.

"My men didn't know what accident Sean meant. But I did," Sir Philip declared. "It had been in the papers; after all, it had been quite the society wedding."

"And . . ." proclaimed Vivian with a determined voice, "I filled in Sir Philip fully and gave him Detective Marlowe's name, the one whom we worked with on the case." She nodded her head smartly. "They'll be launching a full investigation into the entire matter."

Sir Philip sat looking at Vivian with a one-sided smirk, obviously delighted with her spunk. We chatted and wrapped everything up in the next hour. I felt we'd made a great friend in Sir Philip Game, head of Scotland Yard. And I did so enjoy Prime Minister Baldwin's sentiment about trusting a woman's intuition. I liked him indeed.

CHAPTER 32

"Hello, I'd like to place a call to the Savoy Hotel, please." Daphne threw her luxurious fox fur around her neck and over her shoulder as she waited, tapping her toe, looking forward to the call with a cold, satisfied grin of anticipation. "Yes, Lane Sanders, room 407, please."

"Hello?"

"Lane dear, so good to hear your voice."

"Oh my God," whispered Lane.

Daphne's lilting laugh made the clerk turn to her, eyes amused. She gave him a ravishing smile and he happily blushed from his sweat-rimmed collar to his receding hairline.

"Yes, dear, I just wanted to let you know one more little tidbit before I departed. Be sure to ask your friend Alistair if he's spoken with Matthew's sister lately."

Just then the ship's horn blew loudly. "Sorry, darling, I need to rush off. Ta-ta. See you back at home. I have a business venture to attend to."

She casually pulled out her compact and looked at her reflection in the little mirror, making sure every hair was in place. She pressed her lips together, spreading her garnet lipstick evenly, as she heard Lane sputter on the other end.

"Oh, and a funeral to attend," she added.

She quickly handed the receiver back to the clerk. "Thank you ever so much," she said.

"Of course, Mrs. Franco! Any time," he said, his blush resuming with renewed vigor.

"Please, call me Daphne. Ta-ta!"

She opened the door of the little shop at the port and took a deep, bracing breath. With that little phone call, she'd accomplished everything she'd set out to do. It was time to head home.

Daphne adjusted her large, dark gray hat with the elegant ostrich feather. Smacking her lips and getting a firm grasp on her purse, she strode over to the gangplank and boarded the *Queen Mary*.

CHAPTER 33

I replaced the receiver, my heart having sunk down to my feet somewhere.

"Who was that?" yelled Finn from the bathroom.

"It . . . it was Daphne."

I heard a few things drop to the floor in a clatter.

"What?" he exclaimed, rushing to the bathroom doorway, his collar wide open, tucking his shirttails into his pants.

"I think Alistair may have omitted a detail," I said queasily. "Daphne said to ask Alistair if he's heard from Matthew's sister lately."

"Oh no," he said. "Your father was an only child." I nodded.

"My mom, too. I think that made them a good fit for intelligence work. Not many ties, you know?"

I went to the sink to get a glass of water, feeling parched. "And Finn . . . I think she is at least money-wise involved in the pinball affairs. She mentioned that she needed to get back to attend to a business venture. She said that part, 'a business venture,' with a sarcastic tone like I knew what business she meant. The kind of tone that makes you want to kick people in the shins. Then she said she had a funeral to attend."

"Peter's," said Finn with a grim tone.

"Now we know she really was here."

"*Was* here?" he asked.

"Yes, a ship's horn blew just as we were hanging up and she had to rush off."

"Okay, we'd better confirm that, find out where she made the call. Then we need to contact Alistair," he said succinctly, his detective instincts taking over.

"So, Finn . . ." I said, thinking things over. "Something else has been bugging me. Why do you think Daphne had it out for me when I was a kid? She and Rex got my parents out of the way, why me?"

He put his hands on his hips for a moment, thinking. I remembered waking up in the hospital bed after I'd plunged into the freezing water with my parents. I had been the sole survivor. I remembered my eyes fluttering open and seeing Daphne and her green hat looming over me. Then raising a pillow in her delicate hands with the magenta nail polish, about to try to suffocate me. I was so listless, I couldn't react. But she had to put the pillow down and quickly retreat, probably because hospital staff had come in. I'd rehashed those moments for years, but I never was able to recall anything else that might point to *why*.

I looked over to Finn, hands still on his hips. He said, "Well . . . we know Rex always toyed with people. She's definitely like that. But you're right, it does seem like there's something specific with you."

"Yeah, she plays with her victims all right, but she's not wasteful, either. There must be some impetus to wanting a ten-year-old dead. And . . . now we know she knew we were here. Which begs the question, did she intend for us to come? Did she allow Morgan to witness her getting her ticket? Was this part of her plan and it's just been a wild-goose chase?" I stood up, pacing.

"Hmm . . ." said Finn. "I'd say that's definitely a possibility. She's clever enough and patient enough to plan something as elaborate as that. However, even if she intended for us to go to Alistair, it's all new information to us that we needed to know regardless. She can control some of the information dissemination, but she can never control how we will react and how we will use it. She—and Rex—toyed with people for their own amusement, I think, but mainly it's for manipulation. And I know you, Miss Throw My

Stockings in the Thames, you will not let her manipulate you and for cryin' out loud, she won't be able to predict your moves." He walked over to the mirror to finish adjusting his tie, then said, "No one can."

I eyed him, wondering if that was a compliment. Or not. I thought of the older gentleman who had walked right into a lamp-post when I took off my offending stockings. "Well, I have to admit . . . you're probably right on that point."

"All right. Now, let's finish getting ready and then find Miles. We need more coffee and we need to chat."

In half an hour, Miles walked into the hotel restaurant looking dapper in a dove-gray suit with fine pinstripes and a soft periwinkle ascot.

Finn was grinning devilishly at him. "Why, Mr. Havalaar, don't you look glamorous this morning," declared Finn, which made Miles turn red and blustery.

"Well, you said breakfast at the Savoy. How else do you suppose a gentleman should dress?"

"Oh, Miles, he's just teasing. You look perfectly marvelous. Here, let me pour you a cup of coffee." Finn was still silently chuckling at Miles's discomfort, but the coffee and steaming croissant mollified him.

I happily drank the delicious and famous Savoy dark roast. It was the best coffee I'd ever had. I decided to bring some home to New York with me.

Finn filled Miles in on what we learned, then continued, "So I put in a call to Alistair and left a message. He should get back with us soon."

"In the meantime, have there been any other findings about the Red Scroll starting up here?" I asked. I enjoyed his confident demeanor and smiled to myself thinking of the Millionaire's Flight he took on the *Hindenburg*. Miles had changed so much from when Finn first met him. I bet he'd never thought he'd be wearing a genteel ascot at the Savoy, once again in the intelligence arena.

Miles gave a thorough report that there had been no signs about anything starting up again. "But I did find out about one particular meeting that took place, and I have a theory about it."

"We're all ears!" I said, pouring another cup of coffee.

"We haven't seen signs of the Red Scroll starting up again here and quite frankly I'm not surprised because business on American soil is much more lucrative now. We are all still rebuilding from the war. I believe Daphne felt she needed to come here in person to prove that she was in charge now. Something in writing would never do. There are business leaders here, the underground crime sort, who would require proof. I'm certain it would be very wise to make sure they knew she was top dog."

"I would agree with that," said Finn decisively.

"So," I summed up, "Daphne wanted us here, wanted us to find out about Alistair's information, and we have yet to hear about that. But why all that effort? She could have easily gotten us that information without a whole trip across the ocean."

They agreed and I tapped one finger on the table inlaid with an Art Deco design similar to the windows of the Chrysler Building as I contemplated Daphne's motives.

Finn set his cup down with a *thunk* and said, "You're right. The information about Alistair and John, if she wanted us to know about that, she could've easily accomplished that without luring us here. That's the part that suggests she didn't know we were following her, but later learned about our trip, then figured why not have a little fun with us, perhaps."

"Which makes me think of our long history, which brings us back to the beginning. Why did she feel she needed to kill me back then? I was only ten. Why go through such an extraordinary effort?"

CHAPTER 34

On our way to see Alistair, we decided to drop in to visit our eclectic friends at the Bird and the Baby. We walked into the warm pub and asked the barkeep to send another round to our friends over in the corner.

We approached the group just as Owen Barfield was saying to John Tolkien, "So Tollers, do you really think you'll get your book out this coming year? Seems awfully fast."

John replied, "Fast! Seems as long as my little friend's journey, to me. Fast. Bugger." Then he caught sight of us. "Say! Lane and Finn! How are you? Pull up a chair."

Warren Lewis arranged a chair and took my coat for me. He said, "To what do we owe this pleasure? Just dropping in, are we?"

Jack Lewis, a bit of a beefy fellow, had his hands clasped over one knee and a sparkle in his eye. He said, "Oh, by the looks of these two, I'd say they have news."

"I believe you're right, Jacks," said Warren with a gleam in his eye that matched his brother's.

The barkeep came with his full tray and gave us our pints. Finn said, "Cheers, gentlemen! And we do have a tale to tell."

We clinked glasses all around as they pulled their chairs just a bit closer together, readying themselves. Storytelling was, after all, their sole purpose for gathering. I filled them in on Alistair and how he had gotten involved with my parents, how he'd hit bottom after his brothers had all been killed in the war, but the kindness of strangers had reminded him of who he was, and what he had to offer.

"I've had my father's dagger all this time," I said, pulling it out of my purse. "But I didn't know it had been Alistair's." As I thought about the story, I balanced the dagger, blade side up, on my middle finger just as I'd done for as long as I could remember.

John asked, "May I see it?"

"Sure." I flicked it up and over, and handed it to him as Warren gave a chortle of appreciation for my circus trick.

"Your father was very enamored with this dagger," said John with a wistful shake of his head. "He used to practice that very trick, Lane. He loved the story of the dagger that Alistair had relayed."

"There's a story to the dagger? Of course there's a story to the dagger," I uttered, rolling my eyes.

"Well, it's not that incredible. But there had been a tree on the family property, as the story goes, that had been hit by lightning. It burned quite a bit of it, but the wood itself was pretty valuable. They were able to make a few things from it including a long bit that became a mantel. But their favorite was this dagger. A local smith created the blade and the handle with the mother of pearl inlays. Matthew loved the interplay of art combined with danger, black and white, something useful created out of what would have been firewood, beauty that came from literal ashes."

"*Pulchritudo ex cinere,*" I said.

"He told you?" asked John. I nodded as he said, "I told him the Latin for 'beauty out of ashes' and we had a jolly good chat about it."

Jack spoke up. "Well, Matthew and Charlotte's entire story revolved around a journey, of friendships, of mistakes and redemption. Even with that painting of yours, John. The one they wanted to return to your family. The lotus itself stands for rebirth, renewal, a new beginning."

John said, "I do love a good journey."

"Ah," I said, nodding. "No wonder it captivated my parents' imagination. This *journey* was their new beginning." I looked at

Finn and said, "That's why they had the lotus flower interlaced through the paneling in his study and around that painting of me. As a reminder."

John contemplated saying something, then firmly set his glass down as he came to his decision. "You know, Lane, my mother died from diabetes when I was about the same age as you were when Matthew and Charlotte were killed."

"I'm so sorry," I said.

"I only tell you that because I admire people who don't give up. Or turn bitter."

Owen was studying me. I could feel it. I turned to look at him, his piercing, thoughtful eyes. "What's wrong, Lane? You thought of something, I'd say."

"Well . . . let me try to explain. When we first met Alistair, his eyes looked like he was torn. Like he knew something both wonderful and terrible," I said.

"Your parents' story *is* both wonderful and terrible," said Warren.

"True, Warnie," I said.

"You're right, though, Lane. I saw it, too," said Finn. "Maybe it was because of his part of the story. That he felt ashamed for how your parents found him."

"That's what worries me."

"What do you mean?" asked John.

"Even after he told us all about that, we offered him nothing but gratitude and he did look relieved," I said.

"Well, that's good then, right?" asked Owen.

"But it was still in his eyes even then. He was still carrying something terrible."

We made our way to the quaint little village with a solitary pub. This time, there weren't any musicians setting up. It was quiet except for the popping and crackling of the fire in the fireplace and Alistair systematically wiping down the glasses and setting them on the shelf with a muffled *thunk*. I longed for a cheery pipe and fiddle to ease the atmosphere. It was charming, but there was a tightness in the air. Like something held back, taut and ready to release. Maybe it was just me.

"Well, hello there, Finn and Lane! Welcome back, I wasn't expecting ya, was going to call after my shift. Come, have a pint on the house," said Alistair, full of cheer in complete dissonance to my own emotions and expectations. Finn must have been feeling the same way, because he requested a bourbon instead of the pint.

Alistair eyed us with squinted apprehension. "Well, now. Why do you two look all stormy and dark?" I squinted back, hoping to not see anything. But I did.

"Alistair. What haven't you told us?" I asked, cutting to the chase. "And I'll have what he's having."

Alistair's face drained of all color as he plunked down a glass for me and poured in a generous hand of bourbon.

"Oh Gawd," he said, rubbing his forehead. "I've worried all these years that maybe something I'd said or done was the thing that got your parents killed. Do you think that's true, Lane?" he asked, desperation bringing out a sheen of sweat to his brow.

"Alistair, no," I said. "Just tell us what you're not telling us. It will be all right." I shot a wary look at Finn. "Does it have something to do with my father's sister?"

Alistair nodded solemnly. "I'm worried that it does." He pulled himself a pint and sat down on his own stool, across the bar from us.

"Why didn't you tell us anything about her before?" Finn asked.

"Quite honestly, I didn't think it was important."

"But even then you seemed like you were holding something back," I said.

"Well, I have always been plagued by the guilt of it all. To know that your parents' last act had to do with me. But until recently, I hadn't thought anything of the fact of Matthew's sister contacting me all those years ago.

"You see, she found me and told me she'd known that Matthew had been working with me and with John's family. She knew that I'd helped them return the painting. She gave me plenty of information so I didn't have any reason to suspect that she *wasn't* his sister."

"Of course," I whispered. Finn and I exchanged a look.

"She wasn't hunting for information, just had been traveling and dropped in. Wanted to meet me and hear about their story from me. So we chitchatted for a long time. I told her that I thought it was just lovely that Matthew had been looking into a town just outside Detroit, that he'd enjoyed the thought of its woolen mill and a nice little opera house. She said that yes, he was very much looking forward to settling down. And that she'd be sure to get with her husband—Reuben, was it?"

"Rutherford," said Finn.

"Yeah, that's it, Rutherford, to get with Matthew. To suggest that they work together to find a good place where they could all settle down in the same town."

I suddenly had a splitting headache.

"It wasn't until recently that I realized she might not have been who she said she was. Hang on, I have one more thing to give you," said Alistair, heading to the back room.

Finn rubbed the back of his neck and said, "I don't think I can handle one more thing."

"I know," I groaned, slamming back my bourbon.

Alistair came trotting back, a bag in his enormous hands. "Just yesterday, Matthew's sister stopped in again. I was about to call you, but then you called me. She said she had lost track of you, that you had moved out of town with your aunt on your mother's side. She just came in for a pint, but as we talked, she decided that it might be likely that you'd come here sometime."

"I bet she did," I said grimly.

"So she wanted you to have something of hers. I knew at that point that her story was rubbish. It didn't add up. Here you go." He handed me a black velvet bag.

"What on earth?" asked Finn.

"Oh boy," I said.

"Yeah . . . there was something odd in her excitement for you to have this. It was off-putting." He was shaking his head in disgust. "She said it was your favorite."

I felt in the bag and pulled out a diminutive emerald green pill-box hat with little feathers and a small black veil on the side. The one that had haunted me for years. The one Daphne was wearing the day she loomed over me, helpless and vulnerable in the hospital. Right before she tried to kill me.

CHAPTER 35

That night we went dancing.

Both of us needed to get out of our heads, to stop thinking about the case and the Red Scroll Network. We needed to get Finn's family out of our minds, too, and let loose a little.

The hotel concierge told us about a couple of good dance places nearby. We met a few couples who didn't know some of our dance steps, so we taught them a couple of our finer moves of the Lindy hop and they taught us a special little twirl move that we practiced until I was dizzy.

They asked us how the end of Prohibition was going in the States and what it was like living in New York. And they filled us in on how their country was rebuilding, it had been hard, but feeling more normal these days after the war and the economic depression that they termed the Great Slump. But no one dared to speak of the elephant in the room. The one wearing a swastika. We all knew Hitler's Germany was on our minds, but it was a silent, unanimous pact to leave his name unspoken, to not sully the glittering, jolly, companionable night.

On the eighteenth try of the twirl move, I rocked a bit unsteadily in my shoes. "Okay. That's enough Fred Astaire," I said. "I need a drink and to not spin for a moment."

Finn chuckled and placed his hand on the small of my back as he led us to the bar.

"I'll have a White Lady, please," I told the bartender. He nodded smartly as Finn ordered a Pain Killa. My mouth watered thinking of the gin, lemon, and Cointreau in my frothy drink.

"Who are you looking for?" asked Finn, noting my eyes roaming the room.

"It's funny, but being here makes me miss New York more than anything. I miss Val and Roarke."

"We really haven't been here that long, but it feels like it's been ages," he said, sipping his cocktail.

We'd booked our passage back to New York, having secured two tickets on the *Normandie* in just two days. We'd have to take a train and then a ferry across the English Channel to LeHavre, France, where we'd board the famous Art Deco marvel. I'd seen photographs in magazines of the interior of the ship; I could barely wait to look at and touch everything. We had two days to wrap up our time here in London.

"So how are you doing, love? Really," asked Finn softly.

I gave a low whistle of appreciation. "Well, after almost fainting from seeing that god-awful green hat in my hands, I'm not doing too badly."

"You don't faint, Lane," chided Finn.

"I know. I hate it when women faint at random moments in a movie," I said with disgust.

"I know you. You'd only faint to get yourself out of a scrape," he said with a cheeky grin.

"*That* I'd do. Absolutely."

"So . . . again, how are you?" I looked at his eyes, he was standing so close. The place was packed and loud, so we had to pretty much speak right into each other's ear to hear properly. *How was I?*

A tiny bit of moisture rimmed my eyes and gave Finn his answer. He said, "Yeah, me too. I'm so sorry."

I sniffed. "It's just . . . so sad. I feel better knowing my parents went to great lengths to get John's family painting back, to make amends for the darker part of their work. But *damn*, Finn. The very thing that they did to redeem themselves is the thing that led Rex to killing them. Their act of kindness got them murdered. It's cruel."

"It really is, love." He dug around his inner jacket pocket. "Cigarette?" he asked, pulling out his Chesterfields and matches.

"Yes, thanks." He lit my cigarette and I inhaled, pleased to have something to do with my hands while we talked.

"You know, Lane, that piece of intelligence was probably one of the things that clinched Daphne being the heir to the legacy. Plus . . ." He gave a sort of grimace.

"Yeah, got them into bed together. I wonder where Rex and Daphne's story started, how and when Daphne took control of that situation, betraying her husband for her husband's father. She did pay quite a price, though; playing up the insanity role. Could've definitely had its downsides."

Finn raised his eyebrows. "True. You know? I think we should have one more dance, then I want to make another stop before we call it a night. Sound good, Lane?"

"Sure. Sounds great. But I'm not doing that twirl again. I'm still woozy."

We arrived at the pub that started it all.

Miles was still at the corner table, making me wonder if he lived there. He seemed well-established as a permanent fixture. But who I was surprised to see was the bulldog of a man next to him.

"What do we have here, Mr. Churchill?" I greeted. He quickly ordered another vermouth-less martini.

We sat down and filled them both in on all the happenings. Mr. Churchill was a careful listener, squinting his eyes in thoughtful consideration.

Miles said, "Yeah, Finn, yeah. It makes sense that something gave the Lorians' location away."

I said, "It bothers me that their act of kindness led to them being killed."

"Well, Lane, they never gave up, now, did they?" said Mr. Churchill. "One should never, never, never give up fighting for good. Here's the thing. Yes, that act led to someone finding them and their eventual demise." He took his final swig of his drink, then slammed his martini glass down and growled, "However . . . don't believe for an instant that the Network wouldn't have found them regardless. In our day and age, you cannot stay hidden. But, my dear, what they won't be able to control, what they will not be able to contain . . ." His voice grew in resonance and intensity. I found myself sitting forward, hanging on to his every word. "What they are certain to underestimate are the powerful ripples of goodness that radiate out from enormous and selfless acts such as they achieved. It will be Daphne's downfall. Mark my words."

Indeed I would.

CHAPTER 36

Before heading to our ship home, we closed out our time in London with a trip to Scotland Yard to finish up our business between Finn's brother and the police. We made sure they had everything they needed from us for their case against Sean and Gwen. We then headed to Vivian's to say good-bye.

She'd become the talk of the retirement home and had acquired so many fans, she had a full schedule and many dance requests to fulfill for their next little soiree. I felt certain that though we were sad to leave her behind, she would be in good hands and possibly having the time of her life. We promised to come back soon, and that we'd also work to get her to visit us in New York, as well.

The *Normandie* was splendid. Its artful opulence toyed with our imagination and created an atmosphere full of elegance but frosted with the spunk of modern art. I especially loved its rakish clipper-style bow. The luxury had no end, with wide grand staircases, indoor and outdoor pools, and the only ship with an outdoor tennis court. Even the children's dining room had lovely murals of Babar the Elephant and friends. The most stunning room was the first-class dining hall that could seat seven hundred people. Even the bronze medallion doors were breathtaking at twenty feet tall. The room was over three hundred feet long, longer than the Versailles Hall of Mirrors, which was its claim to fame.

I slept in late every morning, enjoying the slow days, feeling the need to rest and recuperate. Finn and I tried to not look at the clocks, to eat when we were hungry, sleep when we were tired. We were at sea, away from any obligations and intrigue. I read books, drank lots of tea, and let the swell of the deep waters lull me into a deep tranquility.

We arrived just five days later in New York Harbor. Evening time in New York was always wondrous. With my hands on the cold railing, overlooking our approach past the Statue of Liberty and Ellis Island, I took in the sight that made my heart race with delight. The air in the harbor was unlike the LeHavre or the English harbors. I think it was the unique blend of both salt and fresh water. It was fresh and uplifting, making you breathe deeper and fostering a sense of eagerness. The thousands of windows in the skyline sparkled like Neverland. My stomach tingled with excitement and I found myself bouncing on my toes like Fio.

Mr. Kirkland and Aunt Evelyn met us just off the gangplank. With a *whoosh*, I was enveloped in Evelyn's arms.

"Oh, Lane! It's so good to see you! I can't wait to hear all about your adventure." She put me at arm's length to take a good look at me with her steely gray eyes.

"Oh, do we have the stories to tell!" I exclaimed.

Finn greeted Mr. Kirkland and I bit back a laugh as I heard Finn say dubiously, "You even brought Ripley, huh?"

Mr. Kirkland gruffly replied, "Well, of course! He missed you, too." Which was a dear thought, and it was indeed so sweet to see my furry defender and comforter. However, it also meant that Finn and I would have to share the backseat of Mr. Kirkland's sedan with the giant German shepherd. Who'd been quite excited and was panting. And drooling.

We made it back to my home and Finn decided to have a late dinner with us and relax before heading to his place. We trooped up the front steps of our brownstone. The warm home, with golden light in the front window to welcome us back, felt just dreamy. It was wonderful traveling, but when you had a safe and sweet home to go back to, it was the best feeling.

We headed back to the kitchen, where all deep conversations happen. Before we could say just a few words—as predictable as all get-out—Roarke and Fiorello showed up, banging through the door like a jolly maelstrom. As Evelyn opened the wine and Kirkland finished up the dinner preparations, we regaled them all with the events of the last few weeks.

Then we sat down to dinner and enjoyed the thinly sliced pork chops with a light apricot jam and soy sauce glaze. Our stories must have really been captivating, because they let us finish the entire tale without so much as one exclamation. I had to admit, our new British friends and the tale as a whole were pretty darn exciting. And Finn and I were getting to be fabulous raconteurs. Miles would be proud.

While we had dessert, my favorite chocolate chip cookies, I asked, "So where's Valerie? I thought she'd come, too. I really missed her."

Fio put his elbows on the table, his fingers steepled together. "Well, I think she hasn't been feeling well lately. She took a couple of days off right after Peter was killed, which was completely expected. But since then, she's just not herself. Frankly, I'm a little worried, Lane. She's been in most days to work, but she's taken the odd day off here and there."

"She never misses work," I said. "Maybe her dad hasn't been doing well. He's never been the same since he lost his job when the stock market crashed in '29. Well, hopefully she'll be in tomorrow. I can find out what's going on."

Finn said to the group, "Can you fill us in on what's been happening with the pinball crew? What's going on with Eugene Murk? Daphne made a cryptic remark at the end of the trip that made us think she knows about or is involved in it all. Said she had some business ventures that needed handling . . . and a funeral to attend."

Aunt Evelyn whispered, "Peter."

Peter had helped us a lot with our last cases. He and Finn had a difficult past to overcome, but they'd come out as allies. His death had seemed surreal when we were in England. Now, the reality of it was hitting us hard all over again.

Fio declared, "Well. Murk is still being watched carefully. We are gathering evidence to make a thorough case. But, ah, well . . ."

He looked shifty and kept adjusting one sleeve. I narrowed my eyes at him.

"What did you do, Fio?" I asked. I darted my eyes to Roarke. He wore his usual wry grin accented with dimples.

Fio was apparently having trouble finding his words, so I prompted him, "Did you antagonize your opponents? Again?"

Fio managed to look guilty and pleased with himself at the same time.

"Well, it's like this. We only had so much evidence, and no one was coming forward. So I made a statement."

"And I got it!" said Roarke. "Really, it wasn't that bad, Lane. Quit looking at me like that. But what it *did* do is give us a clear direction."

Finn said rather menacingly, "What happened?"

Fio's eyebrows shot up; he seemed slightly unnerved by Finn's tone. He said, "I just gave a press release."

"That . . ." Finn prompted.

"That said we would not be threatened by a group of thugs," said Fio.

Roarke added, "Then two days ago, we received a message from an anonymous source. They said that the next time we interfered, they wouldn't take out just one police officer."

"So we got confirmation that they did shoot Pete on purpose, like you and Roarke overheard about getting the mitney, Lane. It wasn't that he got caught in the crossfire," said Mr. Kirkland. "People like that always escalate. Pinball and slots are money. Good money."

It was a particularly insidious threat to target the very people who were supposed to bring order and protection. Fio didn't like that one bit, by the look of his thunderous expression. None of us did.

"Yeah," said Finn, leaning forward and resting his elbows on his knees. "Now we know we don't have an isolated incident on our hands. There's a cop killer on the loose who's promising more to come."

After our illuminating debrief, my sleuthing partner and I pulled to the side while the rest of our group refilled coffee cups.

"Fiorello and Finn have the police department covered and will get the message out to be extra careful and to keep on the lookout for Murk and his crew. But I want to cover all the bases," I said in a low voice.

"Sounds good," said Roarke. "I'll get on my sources, too."

"Great. I want to have a meeting tomorrow morning with the other branch of our investigative effort," I said with a knowing look. "I'll get word to Morgan to meet at our usual spot. You can get in on our weekly appointment at our secret rendezvous."

"Ooh! I like the sound of that."

"You'll love it."

CHAPTER 37

"I can see why you two like meeting here," said Roarke, swallowing a big spoonful of vanilla ice cream topped with hot butterscotch.

We were at our usual meeting place, where Morgan and I had a standing weekly appointment: the Lexington Luncheonette and soda shop.

Morgan looked good. I was searching her eyes, her countenance, for how she was really doing. I heard she'd gotten back "to work" from Evelyn. She was probably like me; getting work done always cleared my mind. I noticed her hair had been washed and brushed neatly. I think she'd even gotten it trimmed. Her clothes, usually nondescript from trying to blend in on the street, were clean and even a bit professional. She wore trousers and a nice pair of navy low-heeled shoes with a small brass band near the toes. She looked more like my office mates at City Hall than the street urchin I used to know. Maybe she was closer to eighteen now. I still wasn't exactly sure how old she was.

"Why are you looking at me like that, Lane? Cut it out," she said, a light blush hitting her cheeks.

"Sorry," I chuckled. I knew not to bring up her looks; she'd kill me. "You know . . . I have a friend I want you to meet. Think you can come down to City Hall later today? It's a professional contact."

"Who is it?" she asked.

"Nope. Not telling. Just come down, you won't be disappointed," I said with a sad look at my diminishing ice cream. I scraped the bottom of my bowl, getting every last drop of chocolate.

"Sure," agreed Morgan. "I'll head down this afternoon."

"You going to lick that?" asked Roarke with an eyebrow cocked at the clinking of my spoon against the bowl.

"I might," I said, scraping the bowl three more times just to irritate Roarke. "All right, let's get the meeting started. The police are on the lookout for that anonymous threat. We can't back down on the whole pinball and slots issue. It will make every criminal out there just shoot a cop and think they can get away with anything they want."

"I agree," said Roarke. "So the NYPD have their avenues covered. What can we do that they can't?"

"I can get my crew on the street to see what they can find out. No one notices if a kid is listening," said Morgan. I wanted their considerable help, but I was also torn, wanting to tell her not to poke around anything too dangerous. But it would be pointless. She'd just argue with me and besides, she really was a valuable partner and she knew it.

Reading my face, she said with a roll to her eyes, "Don't worry, I'll be careful. Besides, Finn and I have an arrangement where I notify him if I hear anything interesting."

On our last case, Finn had indeed figured out a working arrangement with her. She had her cohorts tailing me and even managed to procure a wild escape when I'd gotten in a jam. Despite my feeling a bit chagrined about it, it had to be one of my favorite moments and rescues of all time.

"Why are you grinning?" asked Morgan.

I cleared my throat. "No reason, just remembering something. Okay, have your crew focus on the area around Eugene Murk's store. He's part of this, I just know it."

As she gave it some thought, Morgan looked at me. A small shudder ran through her as she said, "And, um, so you really think Daphne isn't at the helm of all this?"

"Well, until she's locked up, I don't think we can ever rule her out completely." I watched Morgan's face carefully. *Good.* She didn't look too scared. More annoyed, actually. *That's my girl.* "But, as Miles in London surmised, I believe that her trip to London was not to start up business, but to shore up her credibility as Rex's chosen leader. America is more lucrative than Europe these days, so we do need to watch for anything she might be working on here."

"So, your trip wasn't all for nothing?" she asked hopefully. Sometimes she looked so mature, and others, like right now, she looked like a little kid.

"No, we had a few important reasons to go to London. The most important of them was to be sure Daphne wasn't back in business there. We couldn't allow that to happen to our friends in England. Since we knew from your account that she was headed there, we knew for certain that we'd hear about activity if she'd been drumming up business. By the lack of anything stirring, it became clear that she wasn't starting anything."

"Good. I hate to think I'd sent you on a wild-goose chase," she said.

"Oh, it was a very useful trip. We definitely accomplished a lot while we were there." Which was massively understated. "Not a waste of time at all. So, back to business. How about you, Roarke?"

"I've had my contacts on the lookout. Also, the inspector's funeral for Peter is in three days. I'm sure they'll have special coverage over that. And you, Lane? I can hear you thinking."

"Well," I said, holding my coffee in both hands as I took a thoughtful sip. "I need to get with Fiorello. This all goes back to the day he stormed up to the West 100th Street police station and he charged Eugene Murk. Something happened that day that tipped the first domino."

Roarke nodded. "Okay, and we need to look at our first pinball escapade when we were following the aptly named villains through Grand Central."

"Ah yes," I said. "When Punchy helped confirm that Crusher, the known slots and pinball runner, was behind the threats to Fio."

Morgan interrupted, "And why do the gangsters all have those kind of silly descriptive names that end up making them even more creepy because the silly name masks the dangerous part?"

I raised my eyebrows. She'd actually nailed the exact reason why.

"Oh," said Morgan, appreciable understanding dawning on her face.

Roarke declared, "So let's you and me talk with Fiorello tomorrow, Lane."

"Great," I said. "Morgan, get with your crew and let's all report back at our place tomorrow night. But don't forget, meet me at my City Hall office today at three."

"Perfect," said Morgan.

Roarke sealed the deal by buying a black and white cookie for each of us.

Chapter 38

My office was like a second home in a way. I spent so much time there and was devoted to my job. Good jobs could be hard to come by, and to have one that I not only enjoyed, but made me feel that I was making a difference in the world, was something that consistently brought me satisfaction.

I climbed the long set of stairs beneath that incredible rotunda for the thousandth time. And felt solace that it never got old.

"Lane!" exclaimed two dear voices.

I looked up and was delighted to be greeted by my two closest friends, both looking cheerful and expectant.

"Roxy, Val! It's so good to be back!" We all hugged and the length of my trip to London really hit me. It felt like I'd been gone for so long. "We need to catch up. Lunch?"

"Wouldn't miss it!" exclaimed Val as she turned and went to her desk.

Roxy smiled at me and I caught her eye. I asked in a low voice, "So, ah, has Val been feeling okay?"

She casually turned so that Val, back at her desk, wouldn't see her face. Roxy whispered, "Yeah. She's okay, but she did miss work and not just the couple days after Peter died. It's not that big of a deal, but it's *Val*. She never misses work. Fio and I were both a little surprised."

"Has there been anything else going on?" I asked.

"No, just the normal routine. I mean, without you here, we usually hang out just at lunch. But after work we go our separate ways. Come to think of it, the whole time you were gone we didn't go out dancing or to the theater. Maybe she did with other friends, but we didn't together."

"Huh. Yeah, I guess that is odd. Or it might be nothing, maybe she's just dealing with the grief from Pete's death." We made our way to the coffee room after I dropped off my coat at my desk.

Before I could ask her anything else, a blur of activity ran into the coffee room. Ralph, the office flirt, started his onslaught of information at the pace of a racehorse. I winked at Roxy.

"Hiya, gals! How's it going? Boy, you've been gone a while, great to see you, Lane, what . . . what are you doing?" he sputtered.

Roxy and I started our handshake that was a smattering of hand claps and snaps in sync with each other and ended with jazz hands and a clink of our coffee mugs. We both turned to him at the same time to see the look on his face.

"Well, I want in on that!" he exclaimed. Roxy and I were laughing and I pulled her in for a one-armed hug, enjoying our ongoing teasing games with Ralph in the coffee room. She started to teach Ralph the moves. I saluted them, then headed to my desk to dive into the great abundance of work left for me.

I had a busy day and lunch with the gals, and at three o'clock on the dot Morgan arrived. Not only was she wearing her nifty little outfit from this morning, but she'd topped it off with a nice navy-blue three-quarter-length-sleeve jacket. She instantly looked like she was in her twenties. Except for the fact that she looked uncomfortable in the new clothes, pulling at her jacket a bit here and there.

"Hello, Morgan! Come on in." I took her overcoat that she'd had in her hands and motioned to the chair near my desk. "Thanks for coming in. Do you want a coffee?"

"No, thanks. I'm a little nervous. I don't want to spill anything."

"Don't worry, you're going to really, hmm . . . *like* isn't quite right, you'll *appreciate* the friend I want you to meet."

Just then, in walked a middle-aged housewife, with sensible shoes, short dark hair neatly tucked into her hat, wearing a floral dress with a narrow belt around her considerable waist. I shot my eyes to Morgan, whose countenance barely registered the new arrival.

"Hello, Miss Shanley. Thank you so much for coming," I said as I took her coat and added it to the coat rack along with Morgan's, hiding my smirk.

"Morgan, this is my friend Mary Shanley." Morgan was polite and stood to shake her hand, her eyes still not showing any glimmer of recognition.

"Miss Shanley is a wiresplit." I waited for her to figure it out.

Morgan thought a moment. Mary, waiting in expectation, watched her possible new protégée with squinted eyes.

"Wait . . ." said Morgan, eyes wide. "Is she . . . ?"

She got it. I nodded. "Yeah. Mary . . . is one of our first women to make detective in the NYPD. She's part of the pickpocket squad."

"Wait a minute. Mary . . . are you Dead Shot Mary?" she asked incredulously.

Mary lit up and lifted an eyebrow. "You bet your boots I am."

"Wow. I've always wanted to meet you." Her face said that Mary didn't quite look like she'd expected. That, in fact, was one of Mary's best assets.

"You know, Mary here is one of our leading detectives handling pickpockets," I said by way of introduction. Morgan managed to look both interested and sheepish, being an accomplished pickpocket herself.

Mary's eyes narrowed and one corner of her mouth curved upward. "You might be pretty interested in what I do. You wouldn't know much about pickpocketing yourself, now, would you?"

Morgan turned red and said, "Uhhh . . ."

Mary laughed. "Don't worry. Lane says you're reformed. I could tell, though. You carry yourself like a good pickpocket."

Morgan said lowly, almost to herself, "I carry myself . . . but you just walked in." Then she said more loudly, "You were following me?"

"Yep! And here's your wallet back." She handed Morgan a thin brown wallet.

Morgan grasped her purse, pawing through it to be certain. "How'd you do that?" she exclaimed, a bit chagrined yet impressed, since she was usually on the other side of this sort of situation.

Mary tilted her chin upward, considering. "You don't usually carry a purse, do you? You looked a bit awkward with it, so I thought it would be a weak link. Because you weren't accustomed to holding it, what it feels like, how to make sure the opening is secure . . . I just used an Oh Shit and then an Easy Dip."

"Oh my God. The bird doo. I was so concerned about my nice clothes, I didn't even think twice about what else was going on," said Morgan, shaking her head with abundant appreciation for Mary's tactics.

"What's an Oh Shit and an Easy Dip?" I asked.

Morgan replied, "You put something on someone's shoulder that looks like bird doo. Then they're nice and distracted and you can slip your hand into an open pocket or purse and *snap*, easy money. It makes for a good Easy Dip." She snapped her fingers. "Right, Mary?"

"That's the ticket!"

"Okay, you two. I'll leave you to it. Morgan, I think you'll really love Mary's techniques. She blends in, she's patient and cunning, and knows what to look for and how to follow someone while remaining invisible. I'll never forget the time you brought your niece along to Macy's, Mary! Talk about looking harmless. You're a hoot."

"Thank you. My goal is a thousand arrests before I retire."

"And you'll do just that, I have no doubt."

The two new friends decided to talk in an open conference room. I got back to work. A lot had piled up while I was gone, but that morning I'd accomplished quite a bit.

After a while, I looked outside and saw that puffy white clumps of snow were falling from the sky. I had no idea when it started as I'd had my head down, working hard all day. I walked over to Fiorello's door and leaned up on the doorframe, knocking lightly. The Tammany tiger rug grinned up from the floor at me.

"Mr. La Guardia, it's snowing pretty hard out there. You might want to quit a little early tonight," I suggested.

"I never quit!" he said with a smirk.

"You know what I mean. Want me to call Marie for you?"

"Nope! I got it. I'll call her." He looked out the frosty white window. "You're right. It's really coming down. Say, Lane, we need to talk about the pinball case."

"Great. Be right back," I said, trotting to my desk and grabbing the little chair next to it to bring in with me. Recently, in an effort to minimize the length of meetings, Fio arranged to have his office chairs (though not his) *enhanced*. I stayed late one night only to find a handyman in the building sawing off an inch from the front legs of the chairs. So when anyone sat in them, they would constantly be tipping forward just a bit, making it very uncomfortable. Thus shorter meetings. I think Fio knew I'd found out, but we just kept that little secret to ourselves.

I sat down in my chair and got out my notebook. "All right. What do we have? What started it all?"

He shook his head as he thought. "Let's go over the details. I think we need to go back to that really busy day when we were at the West 100th Street police station and the relief station downtown. Maybe it was a person who was there, maybe it was something we did that triggered everything and set it into motion."

"Okay. So we got up to the police station . . ." We carefully went over everything, every step of the way. "But Eugene Murk. How does he fit into this? It just can't be coincidence that he was at the station and then at the shooting."

"I agree, Lane. But I don't see how or why he'd be that motivated to shoot one of us."

A light knock came at the door of Fio's office and we both turned toward it. The door was open; Morgan and Dead Shot Mary were standing there.

Fio said, "Hello, Miss Shanley! Catch any grifters lately?"

"Ah, just a couple. But last week I got four pickpockets," she said with one hand on her hip.

"Excellent. So, you two look like you have something to say."

Morgan stepped forward a bit and said, "When we were just talking, I had been asking Mary about some of her techniques. She told me a few, then there's one you need to hear." She nodded her head toward us and raised her eyebrows, underlining the importance of something Mary was about to reveal.

Mary took a seat and calmly laid her hands in her lap, readying herself to tell the story. "So, I'd been tailing a guy. He wasn't my usual suspect, but I saw him on the street on my way to Herald Square. Didn't seem right. Shifty. He had all the tells of someone who was trying to lay low and doing a bad job of it. I spotted him a mile away. So you know, I did my usual. I followed him nonchalantly all the way over to Hell's Kitchen at 46th and Eleventh."

Fio said knowingly, "Oh."

She nodded ominously. "Mm. I thought he was going to go to the Landmark Tavern. Y'know, all that Irish gang stuff there. But he didn't. He went into the little deli next door."

"Where Peter was killed," I said.

Mary nodded. "Yes, but I had no idea of that until talking with Morgan. In the papers, I hadn't caught that it was *that* deli."

Fio piped in, "So what did you see? Or hear?"

"I felt I was still pretty invisible. No one pays attention to a housewife who's shopping," she said with a smug grin.

"Or a street kid," said Morgan. Mary turned and winked at her.

"So I waited a few minutes, went into a different store, then headed into that deli," explained Mary. "I didn't hear much, but now that we can put this all together, maybe it will shed some light on the whole situation we have here. The guy I tailed was talking with a greasy, smarmy-looking guy who looked like the owner or maybe the manager of the place. He worked the register and hung his keys up after he'd opened a side door that looked like a storage closet. He was kind of skinny and a bit of a hunched stance, had a small paunch. They were getting louder as I entered, oblivious to a couple of us patrons. One lady left on the double, reading between the lines that it might not be too safe to remain in there. I pretended to be enthralled with the selection of bread.

"That's when they started to get even more boisterous and angry. I patted my purse, knowing I could get my revolver easily if

I needed it. Neither of them were packing, but I couldn't be sure if they had a gun stashed behind the counter. And other than yelling at each other, they hadn't done anything wrong."

Fio had his arms folded on his desk, listening intently, nodding once in a while. The sleazy, smarmy guy with the paunch had to be Eugene Murk.

"So the bigger guy who I tailed says he thinks the other guy went too far. It was only going to 'poke the bear' even more. The other guy said that it was fine. He'd gotten pushed around by that—sorry, Mr. La Guardia—that mocky-dago mayor enough. That he'd have the city quaking in their boots. Especially next time."

I was leery that her repetition of those two horrible ethnic slurs about Fio, the fact that he was Jewish and Italian, might cause a C3. I braced myself, already writing a small *C3* on a piece of paper, ready to toss it to Valerie so she could notify the rest of the office to prepare for battle.

But in my preparation for that possible outcome, I hadn't caught what Mary had really said. Fio did.

"Next time . . ." he repeated in a solemn whisper.

CHAPTER 39

Mary nodded. "Yeah. Next time."

"So the owner of the shop, your oily guy, sounds like Eugene Murk. I have a mug shot of him that we can confirm. Can you describe what the other man looked like?" asked Fio. "Maybe it's the Crusher. He's been involved in these pinball scams from the get-go."

"Sure. I don't know what the Crusher looks like, but I can give you a description and if you have a mug shot of him, too, I can confirm it with that. White male, brown short hair, probably in his thirties or early forties . . ."

"Was he teeny tiny?" I interrupted, mimicking Roarke's description of the Crusher back when we were following him.

Mary grunted a laugh. "No, actually. A sort of hefty guy, just under six feet. He was smoking a cigar and wearing a derby hat. Mean-looking son of a gun."

Fio erupted, "A derby hat? Mean? I bet that's my S of a B!"

"What?" asked Mary, confused.

"Yeah, maybe he's the mean guy from the relief station. Do you think he's the guy in charge? Maybe that's Cushman?" I asked.

"You mean like the bread?" asked Mary.

"What do you mean, like the bread?" I asked.

"You know. The big bread company. Cushman. The deli had a shelving unit full of it," said Mary.

"Oh my God. *Cushman*," I said, rubbing my forehead in disbelief.

"Murk made up that name to throw us off the scent," I said exasperatedly. "I'd knocked a bunch of bread off the shelf that night when I shoved him up against the wall."

"Shoved him up against the wall?" asked Mary with a glimmer of approval in her eyes.

"You should see what she can do with a knife," said Morgan with a wry smile.

"All right," said Fio. "So the derby hat guy sounds like a lead we need to follow up on. Lane, call the relief station, get his name. Then I'll notify the police to let them know he's a person of interest. It might not be him, there are a lot of derby hats in the city. But like I always say, I don't believe in coincidences and we ran into him that same day. The day I fired him."

"Got it," I said.

The current and future NYPD female detectives were grinning smugly. "Nice job, you two," I said, impressed. We wrapped up the meeting and I told them to notify the mayor or Finn if they thought of anything else.

The snow was really coming down. As I looked out the window and my fingertips scratched little bits of collected frost from the edges of the cold metal window, I could see a lot of businesses closing up shop early. The sun had set by five. The sky had an orangey-gray glow as the city lights danced with the nighttime light and lit up the falling snow, which gave me a fun idea. I made a quick call, cleaned up my desk, and headed uptown.

I ran up the front steps of our townhouse, threw open the door, and patted Ripley's head. I dashed up to my room and changed into warm trousers, warm socks, and thick snow boots. I clumped back down and over to the kitchen to scavenge some cold chicken from the refrigerator. I went to the front closet and chose my favorite hat and mittens, then set out on my journey.

"Bye, Ripley! Be back later."

I loved walking in falling snow. It was cold but it didn't sting my eyes. I walked down a block to 79th so that I had a better lit path, then walked west. At Lexington I stopped and waited at the corner. I saw Valerie's tall form first.

I waved as she made her way closer.

"It's beautiful, isn't it, Lane?" she said, her eyes glittering from the shine of the nearby lamppost.

"Sure is. I love snow at night."

"I know you do. And last snowstorm, I didn't go out in it at night. I regretted it all year," she said.

"Oh hey, here they come," I said, pointing to the corner. Over tromped Finn and Roarke looking extra-bulky with all their snow gear and wielding two big sleds. "Hey, guys!"

Roarke exclaimed, "Hey, girls! Great night!"

Finn said eagerly, "C'mon! Let's go!"

We walked over toward Fifth Avenue and the best sledding spot: Cedar Hill. During the day, it was utter chaos trying to sled. For some strange reason, New Yorkers didn't care one iota for sledding etiquette. They'd sled straight down the hill. Wherever they stopped, they'd turn around and climb back up. Even in the middle of the hill with hundreds of people careening down at breakneck speed! One time Valerie almost took out a two-year-old and when she yelled toward the parent to tell her kid to walk up the side of the hill, the parent just gave an elaborate shrug like there was nothing that could be done about it.

We walked into Central Park, and it was like walking into a wonderland worthy of Jules Verne. The snow blanketed every surface of every tree, bench, and bridge. The lampposts dotted the walkways with orange halos and the snow muffled the city sounds, making us feel like we were protected and shielded somehow. Something about it made all four of us quiet as we looked around and took it all in. I inhaled the crisp air, settling the moment down in a permanent place to cherish.

The four of us walked down the path to the bottom of the main hill, just a few other sledders were out. The camaraderie of the city never ceased to amaze me. For such a thrilling, energetic, heavily populated city, it had a friendly small-town feel at times.

The funny thing was that all the sledders were adults. One guy finished up a run and came over to us giving a full report on the sledding conditions. Finn and Roarke were taking it in solemnly as if an Olympic medal were at stake. Valerie and I exchanged a grin.

We all huffed up the hill and took a moment to look down the wide expanse, panting a little bit. The whole park was framed by sparkling buildings with windows of orange light blinking down at us. The trees were black and white with their heavy frosting of snow and cars snaked their way down Fifth Avenue, the scent of wood smoke in the air.

"Let's go, Lane!" exclaimed Finn, patting the back of the toboggan. I pushed his back to get us rolling while he paddled his hands against the snow, then I jumped on. We swept down the hill followed by Roarke and Val. The wind stung my face just a bit, the snow kissed my eyelashes, and the thrill of the speed made my stomach tingle.

I heard Valerie laughing and delightedly screaming as I looked over at them where they started to spin near the bottom of the hill. They both were madly paddling the toboggan to turn it the right way, only making things worse because they were laughing so hard. A young couple taking a walk along the path at the end of the main hill dodged them as they waved and yelled like crazy to get out of the way. The couple was clearly enjoying their antics and, in the spirit of the city camaraderie, asked Val and Roarke if they could take a turn on the sled since they didn't have one.

"Sure!" said Val agreeably. There was just something fun and beguiling about sharing a good moment with a stranger. Val needed a minute to get her breath back, so we let the guys use Finn's sled.

I eyed Val in the semidarkness and she looked good. In fact, she looked happy. Happier than I'd seen her in a while. She was generally a cheery person, but the last few months, even before Peter died, she'd been dialed down a bit, subdued. I hadn't really noticed it as the days went by, but looking back at a large chunk of time, I could see it.

"You look great, Val," I said. "You seem . . . really happy."

She looked at me and nodded. "I *am* happy. This is really fun."

"I heard you had to take a few days off of work after Peter died; are you doing okay?"

"Oh yeah. I was just tired and I got a little cold. I figured after all that . . . I should just take a few days off." I narrowed my eyes at her. I *almost* believed her. But before I could ask anything else, she said, "Here come the guys!"

She ran a few yards away, laughing and cheering. The two boys in men's bodies were racing down the hill like professional lugers. It reminded me of our time in Michigan when Finn and I went sledding with a group of young kids in town. When they got to the bottom, Finn quickly pulled his pocketwatch out and exclaimed, "New record!"

I walked over to Val. "I guess everything is more fun if you time it."

Val snorted a laugh. "Naturally."

After several more runs, we were out of breath and my legs were wobbly. We decided to head back to my place for sustenance. The exertion of climbing up the hill a dozen times mixed with the ethereal beauty of the night made all of us quieter than usual as we took the time to just enjoy it.

Back at my place, we shed our gear in the foyer. Ripley was delirious that so many of his friends were over. My cheeks were cold, and the snow on my eyelashes melted, dripping down and tickling my nose. I got us a few towels to dry off the excess water and we made our way to the back of the house to the kitchen.

Mr. Kirkland had left a large pot of vegetable soup simmering on the stove for us. I went to dish some up and Finn got out four beers for us. We all sat down to the simple, delicious meal at our scrubbed pine table. We chitchatted and enjoyed the night. As we relaxed, thoughts about the case started to infiltrate the ease of the night.

I filled them in on Dead Shot Mary's new piece of evidence. That Murk was definitely in on Pete's shooting even though we only had circumstantial evidence, and that he'd planted the Cushman name.

As Finn gave it some thought, he set his elbows on the table and said contemplatively, "You know . . . there's someone who is usually in the middle of all our cases who has been extremely quiet as of late."

Val scrunched her nose and asked, "Who?"

"Uncle Louie," said Finn.

Roarke's eyebrows went up. "Huh. You're right. I wonder why that is."

"Well, he was in the news a few weeks back about a subordinate who'd gotten caught stealing from him," I said as I visibly shivered. "I can't imagine who would cross *him*. That's a dangerous game to be playing."

Val asked, "So when you're in a gang like that, what do you do to get out?"

Roarke said grimly, "You don't."

Finn nodded. "Yeah, sometimes you can pay your way out. But it's not usually money that's required."

"What do you mean?" asked Val.

"Usually it's a finger. Or something awful like that. It's to signify your own sacrifice to get out and to remind you to keep your secrets. If not, they'll come take the rest."

My eyes shifted back to Val; she looked a bit queasy.

Roarke didn't notice and said, "But usually, once you're in, you're in. Forever." He took a last spoonful of his soup, then said, "Why do you ask?"

"Oh. Ah, just thinking of the guy who double-crossed Uncle Louie. I wondered if he'd been stealing money to make a getaway or something."

I said, "Well, it'd be good to check out Venetti's latest activity. It *is* odd that he's been out of the picture. It's possible he was just laying low after that press coverage. But, Finn, he has roots in the slot machines, right? Isn't that where he made his fortune?"

"Yep. Exactly. And Fio's been working against those since he came into office."

"I know. He hasn't done much of his sledgehammer stunts recently. Been too cold." I snickered.

Roarke just shook his head. "Our mayor sure has a good sense for dramatic publicity stunts."

"You can say that again," I exclaimed.

Finn said, "So, I'll check on your derby hat guy from the relief station and see if he has ties with Venetti. He seems to pop up at some pretty interesting moments. If we find out who he works with, we'll know a lot."

I said, "I called the relief station, and he goes by Mr. Wulf. We'd better check on Eugene Murk's ties, too. He's smarter than he looks." My ego still smarted from falling for his fake Cushman name. "Murk and Mr. Wulf are working together, but we really don't know who's leading who or if they're equal partners."

"You know what, Lane?" said Finn. "I'm going to check in with Big Sam. I feel like he recently made a couple of arrests having to do with slots and underground gaming . . . maybe he has information for us."

"Great idea. Plus, we need to go dancing again." I smiled to myself, thinking of a date with Finn.

We wrapped up our meeting. Roarke and Finn walked Val home on their way to the subway station. Finn said he had a plan for our date and that he'd pick me up after work the next day. He had a little surprise first, then we'd meet up with the gang at the Savoy. I looked forward to seeing Sam and Florence. My muscles hadn't had a good dance workout since Finn and I did that energetic reel in England. I'd have to rest up if I was going to dance with Big Sam again.

CHAPTER 40

The snow may have slowed the city down a little bit; Fio had closed the schools for the day, but not the mayor's office. Fio expected us to get to work come hell or high water. This was not of high opinion with his commissioners but we office staff knew to just plan on a longer commute.

I opted to take the Lexington line down to City Hall versus the elevated trains on Second and Third. The snow had stopped for the most part, but had left a thick blanket of about a foot of snow. The streets were quiet, and I enjoyed the clean white snow with the glint of sunshine making it a cheery scene. I walked down Lexington to 77th, passed the Butterfield Bakery, and took the stairs down. It was icy and I wore my knee-high snowproof boots, so I was warm and dry. I clomped down the stairs, threw in my token, and burst through the turnstile with my bulky coat and large bag.

As I stood on the platform, I was surprised to hear a violin suddenly begin a lovely melody. I turned to see a trio with a small drum, an upright bass—I couldn't imagine how they'd managed to get that down here on a day like today—and the violin. It was a strange sensation to be on a dark and dank subway platform, with wintry weather as a backdrop, listening to live music that was simply beautiful. This surprising moment of awareness was what I loved most about the city. Events just happened. I didn't plan on coming across magic, I just stumbled upon it.

Other than the snow, the day was a typical Friday at work. In anticipation of a fun night ahead, it flew by. I asked Fiorello about his thoughts on Venetti's relative silence, and he said he'd get his people on it, too.

Around six, I closed up shop and headed downstairs to meet Finn outside. But instead of him meeting me in person, I heard a quick three honks from a nearby car. I looked over at a green police car with its black fenders and running boards, and the recent idea of a repurposed taillight mounted on the front right fender. Finn waved me over.

I walked toward him as he rolled down the window and I rested my elbows on the windowsill. "Hey there. What are you doing, Finn?"

"I figured with the snow, I'd pick you up in an RMP. It will be a little easier getting around."

"I've never seen you drive one of these," I said, opening the door and getting in. "I really need to learn how to drive. Maybe this summer."

I'd graduated early from high school and jumped right into college. It had been hard finding the time to learn how to drive, and besides, you didn't really need to drive to get around the city just fine. But I knew I'd like to drive. It looked like a lot of fun.

We headed uptown and I asked, "So what's the plan? I know we'll end up at the Savoy, but you said you had a surprise?"

"I do!" he said in a tone that made it clear he would not be sharing that information. I just laughed and sat back to enjoy the ride. The city had gotten back to normal pretty quick. Most of the shop owners had shoveled their walks and more pedestrians were out and about. I saw one young mother slugging it out with her baby carriage, trying to navigate the slushy, slippery sidewalks and street.

Suddenly, a deep blue, fabulous car zipped right by us.

"What on earth was that?" I said.

"He's going way too fast. Hold on, Lane." With a smirk of delight, Finn hit the gas. I noticed he'd also hit the button that lit that red light on the front of his car. We zoomed up Madison, Finn honking the horn to get the racecar driver's attention.

Finally, the guy caught us in the rearview mirror and pulled over. We carefully pulled in behind him. "Be right back," said Finn.

He got out of the car, checking his gun just in case, and walked slowly to the driver. But then I noticed the driver was on the *right* side of the car. "What the hell?" I whispered to myself.

After a few minutes of conversation, Finn at last returned to the car. "What was that all about? Did you give him a citation?" I asked.

"Nah. Turns out he was a British bloke. He and that divine car of his—a Riley Imp—came over on the *Queen Mary*, if you can believe it. I'd noticed the right-hand drive, but was still surprised when I heard the British accent. John Barnard. I let him off with a warning. Couldn't blame him, I'd be driving fast in that beaut, too."

"Me, too," I sighed. Boy, I loved great cars.

We at last arrived at our destination. We pulled over on 81st near Fifth Avenue. I took Finn's hand in mine as we walked over to the steps of the Met. The Metropolitan Museum of Art is one of my favorite places in the world. But at night? It becomes magical.

The front steps and fountains were lit in bright yellow lights, the mist creating shimmering clouds in the frosty air. When we swept in the front doors, I was delighted to hear an unexpected violin for the second time that day. On the upper floor that surrounded the entryway, there was a small band playing classical music with patrons at tiny tables sipping wine and coffee. The enormous flower arrangement at the front desk smelled of roses and lavender. We gave our coats to coat check, bought our tickets, and began to slowly stroll around, enjoying the scenery.

The funny thing about the Met at night is that I always got a whole new appreciation for the art. The many skylights and windows in the museum were not that noticeable during the day. But at night, all of those windows became a glossy black, and the warm lighting made the statues and the paintings come alive.

We ambled through the ancient Greek and Roman statues, a favorite of ours. Then I had to go upstairs to visit Madame X. I loved that painting by John Singer Sargent. He had painted an unconventional beauty in Paris society where originally the right shoulder strap of her elegant black dress was missing, clearly undone, which whispered improper intentions and thoughts. There had been such scandal with the model, who'd been a banker's wife, that Sargent felt he had to redo the painting with the strap securely in place—the version I was currently admiring—and then he moved to another country altogether. His original strapless painting was at the Tate in London. That the portrait was so beautiful and interesting yet only successful after much time had gone by moved me. But I also loved that whole room. There was just something remarkable about the way those large portraits were hung, all of their eyes watching as if they might be interested in *my* story.

I walked toward Madame, the click of my high heels on the floor echoing throughout the long room. I looked at the lift of her chin, her elegance, and the emotion evoked in her posture. I imagined the thoughts that might be running through her mind and felt that in another world, we would be close friends. I had changed at work and I wore my favorite dancing dress, a strapless black satin with sheer black sleeves that hugged my arms and silhouetted my shoulders. The full skirt would twirl nicely. Finn came up behind me; I could smell the woodsy and verbena scent of his aftershave. He came close and gently pulled my hair to the side and kissed just beneath my ear, sending shivers through me.

"We should have visited her at the Tate while we were there," he whispered. That he knew her history, and more than that, he said "visited her," not "gone to see it," made me love him even more.

"Next time," I whispered back. I turned toward him and planted a good kiss on his receptive lips.

He took my hand and led me toward the front of the Met again. We lingered a moment on that second floor, overlooking the entryway. The music, the scent of flowers and perfumes, the rustle of conversation, the energy of people. I fondly remembered a few months ago having leaned up against the very same pillar beside me, watching Finn give me a wolfish smile, then retreat down the steps and out of the museum.

"All right, love. On to the Savoy."

CHAPTER 41

Even outside the place, the Savoy was hopping. The energy of the excited guests mingled with the muffled music that floated out to us through the icy air made me feel alert and alive. I wanted to soak it all in. Since we'd taken Finn's cruiser, we didn't have far to walk. Which was a good thing, because icy sidewalks and high heels don't mix.

We were almost to the door when Finn spotted Big Sam, as well as Florence, a bit farther behind us. Sam was hard to miss.

"Oi! Sam!" yelled Finn over the crowd as he trotted over to them.

Sam waved and took Florence by the hand, walking a few steps closer to Finn as they greeted each other. Then I was abruptly and rudely reminded that the harmony on the inside of the first integrated dance hall did not always mirror the sentiments outside.

A man in a black coat came up to them and sneered as he went by. I was still a ways off, but the guy said something to them and by the thunderous look of all three of them, I was guessing that he didn't approve of our friendship that crossed racial barriers. My eyes darted to Finn, knowing exactly what he was about to do.

He yanked the guy from behind and spun him around, pointing out the police car and presumably clarifying that he'd insulted two police officers. I started to make my way over.

That guy must've been one of the dumbest guys on the planet. Both Finn and Sam loomed over him. But his hatred overcame whatever cranial capacity he'd had as I saw him spit out some final insult.

Whump. Finn leveled him. Then yelled for a couple of passing cops on duty to come and take the guy in to the nearest precinct.

Sam and Finn handed him to the two large black cops who were biting back a grin, hauling in the dumb bastard.

I came up next to Florence and grabbed her hand. I kept holding it as I looked at Sam closely. He was embarrassed.

Sam turned to Finn and said fiercely, "Look, you didn't have to do that, Finn. I can take care of myself."

Finn turned just as fiercely toward him. "I know, Sam! But you're my friend. And just what would you have done if someone called me a WIC?"

That stopped Sam in his tracks. After a long pause, a corner of his mouth twitched, then he said, "Well. That's better than SID."

Finn's face made a funny little quirk from the surprise of Sam's comment. Then he broke down laughing, right along with Sam, who now had tears of mirth running down his large, kind face. I turned to Florence and she must've had the same look on her face as me: one eyebrow raised and a disgusted pull to her lips.

Florence patted my hand, then wrapped her arm around mine and said, "C'mon, Lane. Let me buy you a glass of wine. It's going to take these two idiots a few minutes to pull themselves together."

I snorted and said, "Thanks! I'd love one."

Later on, Finn joined me at the bar, a large smile stretched across his handsome face. "Having fun?" I asked sardonically.

"Oh yeah," he said with relish. Finn didn't mind a bit of a tussle from time to time. I shook my head in amusement. "But get ready for this. You didn't recognize him, did you?"

"No, why? Did you?" I asked.

"Not at first. He cleaned up better than I thought. It was Wulf. Mean derby hat guy, minus the derby hat. I didn't catch his name until we looked at his driver's license."

"You were right, he does keep showing up," I said. "That's very interesting . . ." I took another drink and asked, "So what does 'WIC' mean anyway?"

"White Irish Catholic. And it's not meant to be a kind description."

"What about 'SID'? What does that one mean?"

"Small Irish d—" He cut off that last word, suddenly remembering who he was talking to.

"Oh!" I said, eyes wide in understanding. I nodded with appreciation. "Yeah. I can see why you would not take kindly to that. At least it wasn't 'frotch.'"

"Lane! How do you know that word?"

"It just means 'fire cr—'"

"Don't say it! I know what it means!"

We were joking and laughing, but I could see the anger smoldering beneath both Finn's and Sam's eyes. Certain that the incident reminded Finn of his own dreams of Scotland Yard being snuffed out because of being Irish, I thought about all that Finn had faced over the last month. He'd been through so much, right from the get-go, from envy that rotted into hatred within his own family, then obstacle after obstacle because he was Irish. I knew that was why he was so passionate about standing up for his friends. No one had for him.

After all that, the night went along like any other. The bands were great, sweating up a storm, thoroughly enjoying the exuberant crowd. Tunes by Bing Crosby, Benny Goodman, Fats Waller, and Billie Holiday filled the cavernous place with a bursting love of life. Finn and I were getting a cold beer at the bar when Sam came over and ordered one, too.

"You know, Finn," said Sam. "With all the commotion early on, we didn't get to chat about my contacts for you. I have a couple of names you should check out. Also, I was talking with a buddy of mine who had seen our little scrape we got into earlier with that Wulf guy."

"Oh yeah?" asked Finn, finishing off his beer.

"Yeah. Turns out, that buddy of mine thinks that guy might have some information for us on Murk. My guy has seen him, you know, not a big leader but a lower-management type. He works at the deli where the shooting went down."

That raised Finn's eyebrows and he said decisively, "Well now.

We knew Wulf was working with Murk, but we didn't know he was such a regular presence at the deli. We have him in custody, what do you say you and I just pay him a little visit, Sam?"

Sam clinked Finn's beer glass with his and said, "I'd say that sounds like a lot of fun."

CHAPTER 42

Finn and Sam went to interrogate that unwise individual who kept turning up like a bad penny. Wulf seemed much more intimidated at the police precinct than he had out in public, but he remained reticent to give information. Until, that is, he was neatly threatened with a couple of nights in the Tombs, the nickname for City Prison downtown. The original Tombs had been replaced about thirty-five years ago with an eight-story building complete with a castle and tower design that was reminiscent of the infamous Hall of Justice in Paris and, along with it, the sad and disturbing story of Quasimodo. The Bridge of Sighs was aptly named as it connected the Tombs to the Criminal Courts Building. *Everyone* was nervous about a threat of the Tombs. One time I'd witnessed Fiorello threaten a violent, hardened criminal with a night there. On the spot, he broke out into a sweat and started begging for leniency.

Finn's face had been quite animated at the retelling of the interrogation. I'm certain Mr. Wulf regretted his hateful remarks. In the end, he begrudgingly gave them some information on what they hoped would reveal Murk's efforts and motives. Finn had multiple cops running down the details. What concerned them most was Wulf's apparent loathing of the mayor.

Wulf could only be detained a few more hours, then they'd put a tail on him. Meanwhile, the mayor would have to deal with extra police presence in his life, something he greeted with derision. We decided we needed a council of war.

We set the meeting for the next day, at our usual spot: my place. Everyone was called in, and I had to say, we were a pretty intimidating crew.

Morgan arrived early and brought her second in command, Eric Spry. Roxy and Val came right after and everyone chipped in to help Mr. Kirkland, Evelyn, and me prepare dinner. We decided on one of Fiorello's favorites that was always the perfect crowd pleaser: spaghetti. The aroma of simmering marinara with both beef and Italian pork sausage made my mouth water all day long.

Finn, Big Sam, and Roarke arrived, toting with them several large loaves of fresh bread from the local market. Lastly, in came Storm Fiorello with an excitingly large, white box tied with string.

"Are these what I think they are?" I gasped as I took the box from him. I sniffed the box and grinned from ear to ear.

"Of course, Laney Lane my girl! We can't have spaghetti without some cannoli!" he exclaimed heartily, putting his overcoat in our closet as if he owned the place. He looked at me, then said, "You do know you have to share, right?"

I harrumphed as I took my delicious parcel out to the kitchen.

"I see you trying to hide that, Lane," said Finn. I whipped around to see him, Roarke, and Valerie smirking at me.

"I'm not hiding it . . ." I shifted uncomfortably. "This fern was in the way a bit. It looks better this way." I moved the box from behind the fern and winked at my friends.

Eric and Morgan had just finished up cleaning some of the preparation dishes and Roxy, Sam, and Aunt Evelyn were drinking a little red wine in the corner, chatting up a storm. I took down more wineglasses and another bottle of Chianti. As I poured the velvety red wine, I looked around at my group of favorite people. They were an eclectic mix, which made them all the more enjoyable. I liked how Sam had assimilated into our sarcastic, artful, and boisterous group with ease. I wished Florence could be here, I missed her easy smile, but we had work to do. It was a business meeting, after all.

We gathered around our large dining room table and clasped hands as Fiorello said grace. There were two mounds of spaghetti with meat sauce on oval platters at each end of the table, steam swirling up from the piping-hot meal. There were also two large wooden bowls full of salad and two long baskets filled to the brim with hot garlic bread. I spotted Eric licking his lips in eager antici- pation.

Everyone dished up their plates and we ate the delicious meal with the golden camaraderie of old friends, as if we'd all known each other for years. There was something special about sharing a meal at home that inspired more laughter, more earnest conversa- tion and companionship than at a restaurant.

As we were all soaking up the last drops of marinara with the end pieces of crusty bread, Morgan dove into our business meet- ing with a cheeky grin. "So, Wulf is in the Tombs?"

Finn returned the grin and said, "Nah, we just threatened him with that. We had to let him go. Other than being a horrible human being, he hadn't committed any crime."

"That's a shame. He sounds awful," said Eric with a disgusted look.

"You can say that again, kid," said Sam, clinking glasses with Eric in solidarity.

"So, let's officially bring this meeting to order," declared Aunt Evelyn, clasping her hands together like a professor about to lec- ture. "Let me see if I have it straight.

"The pinball and slot machine racket escalated when they mur- dered Peter. It was an intentional act, not an accidental shooting, and it sounds like Murk is trying to use that to force the city into compliance."

Finn nodded as he took up the thread. "And when Lane and I went to London, we confirmed as much as humanly possible that Daphne and the Red Scroll Network are not up and running in Europe at this time. We could still use proof that she's not behind these crimes here in the U.S., though . . ."

I interjected, "But really, it's not her style. It doesn't have her flair, for cryin' out loud. This is a brute force scare tactic on the NYPD and the mayor."

"We are just talking about pinball and slots, right? Is it really that much money?" asked Roxy.

Fiorello, Finn, and I all responded with wide eyes. Fio said, "Oh yeah. When we started taking down the slots and I had fun with my trusty sledgehammer . . ." He waggled his eyebrows appreciatively. "At the time, I believe Louie Venetti was making tens of millions."

Morgan sputtered, "Tens? Of m-millions?"

Eric whispered, "Holy cow."

"And that was money people should've been using for milk, bread, their rent . . . that's why the machines had to go!" Fio clunked his glass down with resolute determination.

I nodded. "So, yes, Morgan. It's a major racket. And pinball is just as luck-based. You just drop the ball in and hope it hits the slot that pays out the cash. There isn't any challenge or prowess that can get you ahead. Even in poker, it's at least not all luck. You can learn and develop strategy."

"Grrrrr," growled Fio.

I flashed my eyes at him with good humor. "I know! I know you don't like card sharks, Fio. Just an observation."

He harrumphed and carried on. "So. Do we think we need to be on the lookout for a city-wide calamity like we had with Daley Joseph and the bombs on the bridge?"

I caught Sam's eye and shared a knowing look with him. We hadn't met yet at that time, when we'd received threats against the mayor and then a big threat against a major landmark. At one point, it resulted in me dangling off the Queensboro Bridge to clip the wire of a set of bombs that had been strategically placed. When I cut the final one, a burly guy had offered his hand to help haul me back onto the bridge, but Finn took over and grasped my hand to pull me up. Sam had been that burly guy.

Finn shook his head. "I don't think that's their game. We haven't had any threats to other places or city leaders other than the NYPD. But we do have Peter's funeral tomorrow. We need to make sure that's covered, every minute, all hands on deck. What do you think, Sam?"

"I agree. We need to have everyone on it. But we also need to make sure it's not a diversion. That they won't use it as a distraction."

"Good point, Sam," said Fio. "All right. Eric and Morgan? Can you have your crew work the perimeter of the event and listen up for any word on the street of anything going down?"

"Yessir," they replied in unison.

Taking a good look at Morgan, Fio said, "I'll also get Dead Shot Mary to work in the crowd with any other of her rather invisible detectives. In fact, Morgan, let's set up a meeting for you and her to lead your crews together. Sam and Finn? You coordinate your official police units and I think we'll have it covered."

We wound down the evening after I begrudgingly passed around the delicious cannoli. Finn stayed behind after everyone left so we could talk. We finished up the dishes and Mr. Kirkland and Aunt Evelyn went off to their rooms. I dried the last glass and Finn reached up to put it away in the upper cupboard.

Finn looked at me and said, "You know, I'm still wondering about Uncle Louie. He's been too quiet. We need to find a way to check up on him."

"Yes, he bore the brunt of Fio's actions against the slot machines. But he'd had ample time and opportunity to get back at him, yet he remained convinced that Fio was good for the city, and therefore good for his business. But you're right. We need to confirm that."

I put down the towel and looked over at Aunt Evelyn's writing desk with its sweet keepsakes decoratively placed. There was a silver framed photograph of her when she was all of twenty with a handsome young man in Paris, a small palette with old paint colorfully smeared over it, and a little red card that she had been writing on earlier that said *Happy Valentine's Day*. A slow grin spread across my face.

"It's not until the day after tomorrow, but I have an idea," I declared.

"You always do."

"I'll have to talk with Aunt Evelyn first. And let's get through the funeral. I think it's going to be a big day."

CHAPTER 43

The day after what Lane called their council of war, Morgan found herself sitting across from Dead Shot Mary with Eric at her side, the dawn not quite touching the city sky yet.

Mary Shanley looked nice and dowdy in her matronly outfit, uptight hat, and little purse that sat upright like a soldier on her desk. Despite her unassuming attire, Morgan noticed, Mary's eyes were glittering with intelligence and moxie. Morgan had liked her immediately and was impressed with her arrest record, not to mention her cunning, patient methods.

Eric had a skeptical look in his eye when they'd first met Mary. Amused with the situation, Morgan had decided not to fill him in on Mary's looks, so she could fairly see his mind trying to reconcile the frumpy woman with the savvy detective.

Mary clasped her hands on her desk. "All right! So I'll have my people work their way into the crowds, about two people per block, on either side. All along Fifth Avenue, we will have thousands show up. It's going to be a nightmare to keep an eye on the whole thing. But at least we can have our people on the ground listening, watching. We have four relay points where we can send anyone who sees or hears anything and they can get information to me. I'm having those four relays hold a bright pink purse, so our people will see them easily. Again, we're looking for anyone with ill intent, or if we see Mr. Wulf and Eugene Murk, or Daphne Franco. Got it?"

Morgan and Eric looked at each other and nodded grimly. Morgan said, "Okay. We showed all our people copies of their mug shots. I think we got it covered. Should we meet up here about three o'clock to debrief?"

"Perfect. And good luck." Mary stood up and marched them to the door.

Eric and Morgan walked out of the precinct, shrugging into their coats. The night still hadn't made its final farewell to the morning, and their breath made puffs of steam as they discussed their plan of action.

"She's surprising, isn't she," commented Morgan.

"You can say that again. I don't know what I was expecting, but definitely not that. She really will blend in," said Eric, shaking his head in amused appreciation.

"I know. I love that about her," said Morgan solemnly.

"What's on your mind? You look pensive."

"Well," said Morgan, trying to form her thoughts. "I don't like how spread-out everything is. Too much to control." She shivered a little, which didn't escape Eric's notice.

He scrutinized her face, her demeanor. Her mouth was tight, her gray eyes serious. When she was consumed with an idea or a job, this was her usual look. But she had tiny wrinkles at the corners of those beautiful eyes and slightly dark smudges underneath. That was new. Morgan's shoulders looked tense, ready for a fight. He breathed in slowly and released it before he spoke.

"I've had Connor and Diggy keep an eye on Daphne's men. Thought you should know there hasn't been anything new. No sudden moves, no late nights other than going to the bars."

Morgan's eyes shot to him. "Why did you do that?" she accused. "I don't need help or babysitting." She hurled her words at him.

Now her stance was braced even more, her anger aimed at him. He knew she'd react that way. He just kept them walking ahead, letting her vent her pent-up rage.

"I can't believe you did that behind my back. Daphne's crew didn't come after me when I escaped. I knew they didn't want me for anything else. Their message had been received by Lane, they knew I'd tell Lane and the gang about Daphne murdering Donagan. They'd just been waiting for the perfect time. So no big deal. I'm fine."

"I know."

"I mean, everything is under control. I just need to focus on our job now. Right," she said, smoothing her trousers, composing herself.

"Yep."

Eric walked steadily, patiently waiting. Her head was just under his by a couple of inches. She didn't wear a hat, and her dark gold hair was decidedly lighter these days. It was a deep blond, but the old days of dirt making it a grayer blond were long gone. When she was younger, she dressed and walked and talked like a boy. Smart move. These days, she still opted for trousers, but a much more feminine cut. Once, when he came to pick her up for a job, he even caught her with one large hair roller at the back of her head, just turning the ends of her hair into a curl under. He pretended not to have seen it as she whipped it out of her hair, smoothing it down self-consciously.

He would never have laughed at her. He knew she'd be mortified at the thought of someone witnessing her desire to primp. When he saw the roller, Eric had quickly dropped to the ground as if tying his shoe needed immediate attention, so she hadn't even seen him looking her way. Then he'd rambled on about their next work meeting.

In the same way he read her then, he knew she needed to get those thoughts out now. And to see that it didn't make him feel awkward or that he thought less of her.

"So, uh . . . why did you send Connor and Diggy over there?" she asked, her voice now curious and not accusatory.

"I figured it was smart to keep an eye on them. You know, Daphne told Lane that she was going to attend Peter's funeral. At least, she hinted at that. They are up to something." Eric knew she'd love to dig into the mystery and it would change her obvious emotional turmoil into something constructive. That's what he would've wanted. Morgan had to have been terrified when Daphne's men held her captive, and that would most definitely have long-term effects. People like Morgan—and he himself—

needed to have something specific to do. To feel useful. It put things in perspective.

She quickened her pace a bit and took a deep breath, looking suddenly more like herself. Her momentary bout of weakness had come and gone. "I agree. I think Lane and Finn are right, in that Daphne isn't rekindling her European ventures *yet*, but I can't shake the fact that she's up to no good here. The timing is too coincidental."

Amused, Eric said, "And you know how Fio feels about coincidences . . ."

Morgan emitted what he would almost deem as a giggle. He let out a satisfied breath of air. They made their way to get some breakfast, then headed to Fifth Avenue.

There they met up with their crew in an alley on the east side, between 47th and 48th streets. Morgan quickly filled the kids in on their tasks, the relay points holding the pink purses, and ideas of what they might pick up on. Then she got to the point she'd been highly anticipating. She grinned from ear to ear.

"And, Detective Brodie was able to secure us a small budget for our services. I am happy to tell you that we are on official duty with the NYPD. Here's your first payment. The next at the end of the day, after our work has been completed."

Morgan pulled out a slim wallet from her front pocket; she'd never be stupid enough to put a wallet in her back pocket. She handed each of her seven associates a whole dollar bill. Then to Eric she handed two.

She felt so pleased, so satisfied, to give her loyal crew an actual payment that they didn't have to pilfer, steal, or finagle. No one had any words. Not even Connor.

Only Diggy could manage one word in amazement: "Gosh."

Each kid, all different sizes, shapes, and colors, carefully folded then slipped the precious bill into a front pocket. They all looked so in awe, so proud, Morgan wouldn't be surprised if none of them actually spent it. The dollar meant so much more than just one hundred pennies.

Since the funeral was a highly populated event, they decided to split up to cover more ground, and the danger to them individually was lower, so they didn't need to be in pairs like usual. The sun was now up, making the sky brighter, but it was a gray sky. It seemed fitting.

Eric and Morgan looked at each other as their crew walked in different directions and instantly seemed to disappear, their skills at evasion and camouflage so profound. A blue sea of policemen was forming all up and down Fifth Avenue, leading up to St. Patrick's Cathedral. Usually, a parade had a light and colorful atmosphere of expectation. This was a heavier feel. Suddenly, Morgan felt the weight of the day, not just the job.

Her eyes met Eric's. She took a step closer, letting her shoulder touch his as together they watched the police get ready for the procession.

CHAPTER 44

I was up early on that gray day, the sunrise just then reaching the city. I found a note on the kitchen counter from Aunt Evelyn saying that they'd find me later at the reception, and that she knew it was a hard day ahead, but that we'd make it through and it would be a beautiful reminder of the precious nature of life and friends. It was just like her to leave a note of encouragement. And Mr. Kirkland left a loaf of nut bread for me, next to my favorite mug for a good hot tea or cup of coffee.

I threw on my dark heather gray wool coat and walked out the door, a huff of my hot breath steaming up the cold February air. I was glad to have on my knee-high black boots for warmth. I walked over to Lexington and waved as I caught sight of Roarke.

His caramel-colored wool coat was impeccable and the soft scarf at his neck was the color of hot chocolate. "Thanks for coming over to meet me," I said in greeting, giving him a big hug.

"Happy to, Lane. C'mon, we've got a big day ahead."

We walked down to the 77th Street subway station and clanked down the steps. It was warmer there, and I smiled as I heard the strains of that violinist who frequented this stop. Roarke turned in that direction and ambled over, both of us throwing a few coins in the open violin case. I took a step closer to him and wrapped my arm around his for warmth and the comfort of a friend on a tough day.

We took the train down to 51st and then walked east toward St. Patrick's. We strolled companionably along, not bantering like usual. It wasn't that sort of a day. But it was peaceful, and the city was waking up with little signs of life like the scent of fresh bread wafting out of bakeries, newsstand owners piling up papers, children being led to school, cold people holding steaming cups of coffee and sipping them, trying to garner some heat and life from their contents.

"What's Finn's role today at the funeral?" asked Roarke.

"Well, you know the pallbearers are the team that's trained for it, no one that the fallen officer, P-peter, was close to." My tongue stumbled over Peter's name. God, it was hard realizing that this wasn't just a solemn event, it was *my friend's* funeral.

Roarke's arm wrapped around mine as he said quietly, "I know."

I cleared my throat and went on. "He volunteered for the flag duty. God, it's going to be gut-wrenching." Finn would be the one to take the folded department flag out of the casket with Pete's badge, and present it to Pete's parents. The gathering of all the police and fire departments, the mayor's speech, the presentation of the flag, and, with most of the police force being Irish, the bagpipes were all part of the official NYPD inspector's funeral. I'd been a guest at a few of them, and every time, even when the family was leery of a large and public funeral, they'd always felt so blessed to be part of the city in such a way. It was a moment that no one would ever forget. The respect, love, grief, and unity of a city at times like that was stunning.

We arrived at our set place near the cathedral and met up with Fiorello and his family. I looked around at the masses of gathering people, wondering how Morgan and her crew would be able to work in the midst of the thousands. I spotted a matronly woman with a pink purse as she got out a hanky to noisily blow her considerable nose.

The funeral went off without a hitch. I managed to keep it together until I heard Finn's voice as he handed the folded flag to Peter's parents, saying a few consoling words, then Peter's name and badge number 6335 clearly through the silent, cold air. Then the bagpipes played their mournful tones and the tears unabashedly slipped down my face.

CHAPTER 45

Morgan caught a glimpse of Lane in the cathedral, near the front. She and Eric had separated after the procession and she slipped into the service through a side door.

The church service was heavy and mournful, and yet there was something . . . *warm* about it. Morgan couldn't make up her mind about how she felt. She'd been dreading the funeral; she'd never been to one other than a couple of their own who had died. But then it had been a service of their crew's own makings, since most of the time the street urchins were buried in pauper's graves, unmarked except for the signs that they lovingly created with their own hands. But even then, it had been Eric and a few other leaders who had handled that. Morgan would stay at the sidelines, unable to fully join in. Unable to handle that kind of depth of emotion. It made her feel awkward and unsure of herself.

In the service, Morgan admired the interior of the cathedral. The arches reaching skyward, the blues and colorful stained glass windows mixed in with the gray marble columns and walls. It was peaceful inside, again surprising to her. She wiggled her way toward the front, along the sides of the pews, seeing Lane up farther and wanting to keep an eye on her. *Good, she has Roarke right next to her.* Not that he'd be able to keep her out of danger, but it was better than nothing.

As the service neared the end, up at the front of the sanctuary, Finn stood by the casket and took the folded flag, handing it to

Peter's parents. As the bagpipes struck up their song, Morgan glanced at Lane, watching tears flow freely down her face. Lane didn't look self-conscious or embarrassed in the least. She thought that Eric would be the same, not caring what anyone thought about his appearance or his emotions. They just were what they were. She deeply admired that, but always found that kind of confidence out of her reach.

After it all ended, Morgan was surprisingly fatigued and drained. The closest friends and family were gathering at a nearby hall for a luncheon. She met up with her crew and Mary at the set corner. No one had seen anything nefarious and the relays were thankfully not needed. Morgan felt her shoulders unclench a bit. Not only did she not want to see any harm come to her friends, but she wanted the time of mourning to be unsullied. It was a precious time that needed to not be tainted in any way. Now that it was over, a weight lifted.

They decided that she and Eric would follow the crew to the luncheon since they'd been invited, and they let their team depart after giving them the second half of their first official paid job.

The crew dissipated just as the large crowds were slowly walking away. As she and Eric walked uptown a couple of blocks, they quietly talked about the ceremony. Eric knew a lot about the traditions, as if he'd studied up on it. It made her think that maybe they both had a future with the police force.

The masses were melting into the next part of their day, to go to work, to tend to children, to mourn the loss of a son. Morgan and Eric came up to the corner and waited for the light to cross the street. Up ahead, a flash of a bright red hat caught Morgan's eye and it made her take a closer look. Beneath the bright red, a mass of white-blond hair was pinned into an updo. She instinctively grabbed Eric's arm, startling him because she'd never grabbed his arm before.

"What?" he asked urgently.

"There! Can you see? I spotted a bright red hat and the woman has white-blond hair, over by that man carrying the large lamp into the hotel. I think it's Daphne, I'd know that cocky walk of hers anywhere."

He stood on tiptoe to see over the crowds. "Got her! C'mon!"

They raced up the street toward a woman walking fast, her stylish black coat a striking contrast to her light hair and racy red hat. She crossed the avenue at the last second, making Morgan and Eric halt in their tracks as the speeding cars careened by. At that corner, Daphne turned her head, looking uptown as if making up her mind about something. The dashing hat was pulled low over one eye and her lips were a slash of garnet red over her pale face. She was a study in contrasts. She made the decision to walk briskly north again and went to the edge of the curb in anticipation of crossing.

Morgan and Eric raced across the avenue in pursuit. Daphne spotted them and grinned, her white teeth a bright contrast to those dark red lips. She quickly scanned the busy street and darted across. Morgan heard Eric grunt in aggravation. When they reached the corner, the light turned and they, too, ran across the street.

They spotted that bright hat turn and go down the steps into the subway. They quickly clattered down the stairs and even in her dressy outfit, Morgan was able to easily hop the turnstile.

Right when they got to the platform, the doors of the subway car slammed shut and the train started to crawl into motion.

Smack!

Right in front of Morgan stood Daphne, her hand splayed across the glass and with a malicious smile, making Morgan want to strike her.

"Look!" cried Eric as they were walking along with the car, trying to keep up with it for a few seconds.

Just under Daphne's palm, written in red lipstick on a menu, were the words, "See you soon."

Morgan stopped and felt a bit nauseous. After a few moments of silence, Eric casually rested his elbow on Morgan's shoulder and said, "Well, isn't she lovely."

Morgan snorted and Eric allowed one side of his mouth to pull up the slightest bit. He'd aimed to lighten her mood. But *damn*, Daphne was creepy. The scrawled bloodred letters that held the portent of seeing her again filled Morgan with an icy sense of foreboding.

CHAPTER 46

After the funeral, we all headed to the memorial luncheon for the close friends and family. It was a relief to have the ceremony finished. Both emotionally and mentally, it had been a strain on us all. Not only were we mourning our dear friend, but we were anxious about the ceremony going smoothly. On top of it all, we had the profound concern of preventing another cop killing.

I found Roxy and Valerie along the way and we all clasped arms. We needed that touch, that physical reminder of friendship and love. No words could be said to articulate our feelings and that need, but being sandwiched between Val and Roxy, walking together, was enough.

Just then, I caught the scent of a perfume that I hadn't smelled in a long, long time. What was it? It was at the tip of my memories, tantalizing and teasing. It was an overly sweet perfume mixed with an herbal overtone that I'd never have picked for myself. It was from a long time ago, when I was a kid . . . I could feel the memories trying to surface, like a momentarily forgotten word that you almost have. *Let's see* . . . I was at a doctor's office, there was a syringe, and I was afraid. I definitely associated fear with that smell. And the thought of the shot had sent a prickle of sweat and panic right through me.

I couldn't figure it out, then the light turned green and we all crossed the street, abruptly bringing an end to the memory.

"Ooh, look at that fabulous hat! You'd look amazing in that hat,

Lane," said Roxy. Just a couple of people ahead of me was a beautiful bright red hat with a wide brim and I could tell from the angle in the back that it was pulled far down across one eye.

"I love the black trim," I said. "And I have just the lipstick I'd wear with it, too."

Valerie snickered and said, "But she only has black shoes on, you'd certainly wear red shoes."

"Definitely."

At the luncheon we gathered with all of our closest friends, new and old. Sam and Florence were talking with Kirkland and Aunt Evelyn, Roarke was standing with Finn over by the bar, and in the back corner I heard the unmistakable bellowing and screeching that was my boss conversing with a group. It was no wonder that storm superlatives were used for him. I walked over to the little maelstrom.

"Fio, great speech," I said, patting him on the back. "It was perfect and very heartfelt."

"Ah, thank you, my dear," he said in a much softer voice. "That means a lot. It certainly was a tough one. They all are, but this one . . ."

"Yeah. I know."

Something caught Fio's eye and I turned in that direction. Morgan and Eric had arrived and were making a beeline straight for us.

"Uh-oh," uttered Fio.

"Yeah, Eric looks like he's on a mission," I said.

"And Morgan looks incensed," said Fio.

"Yep. Hi, guys! You okay? You look like something's up," I said.

"We saw Daphne," blurted Morgan.

"What?" bellowed Fio.

Luckily the place was already loud with people finally able to talk and enjoy togetherness after the solemn ceremony. I put a calming hand on Fio's arm and Eric shot an exasperated look at Morgan for her outburst.

"Oh, sorry," she said. "It's okay, she's not here and we didn't see her at the ceremony."

Eric took up the story. "We spotted her in the crowds after the services had ended and we followed her. She caught sight of us in pursuit and ducked into the subway. By the time we got there, the doors shut. She wrote a note in red lipstick and smacked it up against the glass for us to read." He'd looked a bit pale when they came in, but at this point he looked positively sick.

"What did it say?" I asked.

Morgan gulped, then said, "See you soon."

"Oh boy," said Fio.

"Um, Eric, you're eighteen, right?"

"Yeah, why?" he asked.

"Come on, I'm getting you a beer. Let's go." I ushered them to the bar and got them a beer.

Finn saw us and came over. He looked at Eric's white face and then at me and Morgan as we both took pretty big swigs of our beer. "Uh-oh. What happened now?"

In spite of ourselves, Morgan and I shared a grimace, then chuckled. Eric rolled his eyes and filled in Finn.

Eric was almost Finn's height and he was wearing a dark brown suit. It was the most dressed up I'd ever seen him. He cleaned up nice. Finn had on his dress blues like the rest of the force. Most of the time he wore plain clothes. My eyes hungrily ran over the dark blue, starched shoulders and the bright white shirt and black tie. He had his hat under his arm.

"Here, Lane, you're drooling," said Roxy, handing me a hanky.

"Thanks!" I sputtered, laughing at myself. "Hey, where did Val go?"

"I'm not sure," said Roxy. "Say, have you noticed that she's still not quite herself lately? I mean, she's good, she's happy. I thought after you got back from London, she'd get back to normal. But she's not around as much and sometimes just disappears like this."

She'd verbalized exactly what I'd been feeling lately. I wasn't extremely worried, because she seemed so happy. But it dawned on me that it had been ages since we had a regular lunch where we talked more deeply about life other than the time when I'd returned home.

"I'd wondered if she'd met someone while I was gone. Has she said anything about a boyfriend to you?"

"No," said Roxy. "But I have caught her looking dreamy once

in a while and writing little notes that she quickly covers with her hand when I come to her desk. So I do think she's got something going on. I wonder why she didn't tell us," she said, fiddling with the crystal button at the bottom of her pretty navy cardigan.

"Well . . . she and Pete hadn't been an item for a while, but so close to his death, maybe she feels awkward about it. I don't know."

We both refreshed our drinks and headed over to say hello to Roarke.

"Hi, girls!" he greeted.

"Hi! Oh hey, I have to fill you in on something," I said, and told them about Morgan seeing Daphne and her rather horrifying note.

"Eeiuw. She *is* creepy," said Roxy.

I looked at Roarke and he looked equal parts horrified and thoughtful. "What's on your mind?" I asked.

He took a drink of his wine and mouthed a few words to himself like he was trying out an idea. "Hmm," he ruminated. "It's winter, I should check that out, yes, I should . . ."

Roxy and I exchanged dubious glances. Roarke pierced me with a look that said he had a sudden brainstorm. "Feel like a late lunch, Lane?"

"Ooh, you're going sleuthing, aren't you?" I purred, liking the idea of sleuthing with Roarke.

"What was that?" inquired Finn, having materialized out of thin air.

Roxy was loudly snickering, not helping at all.

"I have a contact who works at the restaurant at the bottom of Rockefeller Center, you know, where they have that skating rink they're trying out this year. He says he might have new information for me," said Roarke. "He's seen who I think is Murk and maybe even Wulf come into the restaurant."

In a lower voice and moving in a bit, I said, "You know, Roarke, we've been looking for ties between Murk and Wulf with Crusher, who is a much more influential gangster. If he is actually working with them, it would tell us just how big this thing really is."

"We have eyes on them," said Finn. "But we can't get too close because they all know us in the force and can see us coming a mile away. You think you can find out more information, Roarke?"

"I can certainly try. It'd be easier if I had a lunch date," said Roarke.

"I have to stay here with the family," said Finn. Honestly. Sometimes he was so cute.

Roxy patted Finn on the arm and said, "He didn't mean you."

He rolled his eyes. "I know," he said ruefully.

CHAPTER 47

Roarke and I watched the skaters whisking by through the glass. Their colorful coats were a bright contrast against the white ice, the light gray sky, and the muted beige of the buildings surrounding the area. This was right in the area where the huge Christmas tree stood twinkling, reminding us all of hope, goodwill, and cheer. The Rockefellers were trying out the ice skating to see if it was a good tourist draw. Looked like it would be a success to me.

The restaurant smelled of steak, cocktails, and money. It was full of mostly businessmen, just a few women dotted here and there. It made me remember how so many places were still closed to women, which was one of the reasons I frequented a favorite lounge on the Upper East Side, Ophelia's. It used to be only for women and offered a three-sixty view of the city from its gorgeous Art Deco rooftop. Last year it began to include men, as well. I made a mental note to take Finn there.

We only ordered a cup of soup, garnering a dirty look from the waiter, but Roarke and I were personally footing the bill. That was all we could afford. We did manage to order one glass of the cheapest wine we could find, with two glasses to share. We looked around, getting a feel for the crowd. I noticed a couple of policemen still in dress blues who must've attended the services, too.

"What are you thinking about, Lane? You look like something's on your mind," said Roarke.

My fingers made figure eights on the brocade tablecloth as I thought about it. "Well, it's odd. Earlier I caught a scent in the crowd, a perfume that brought back very particular memories. It's right there at the tip of my mind, but I can't quite get it. I can't help it, I keep going back to it. Anyway, do you spot your contact?"

"I did see him, actually. In fact, he just filled a drink order from a waiter. He's a bartender here. Be right back." Roarke got up from the table and went to talk with the guy discreetly. A bartender was an excellent contact. They had a perfect setup to overhear discussions while looking innocuous. They were almost as good as barbers.

I continued to peruse the customers as I took a sip of my wine. We had a lot of moving parts to this mystery. With my trip to England, it made it that much more complicated. I felt a lot of peace that Finn was at last able to face the ghosts of his past, finding justice and vindication. But there was something there. There was a piece to the puzzle that tied together these moving, elusive parts. Daphne and the Red Scroll. The pearl dagger. The pinball murder.

I made a mental list. What were the other pieces that were floating around? Daphne alone had a lot going on. She went to England and made it known to us and to the remnants left there that she was in charge now. She went to Peter's funeral. She told Morgan she'd see her again soon.

Let's see. I took a sip of Roarke's wine. *Hmm*. We had the beginnings of the pinball racket with Punchy and Crusher, way back when I was hiding out on the ledge at Grand Central with Roarke. We had the weasly, greasy Murk, who had been at the precinct when Fio held court. He turned out to be more conniving than I'd thought he was capable of being and was the owner of the deli where Pete had been shot. We also had the derby-hatted mean guy, Mr. Wulf, whom Fio called an S of a B when he ransacked the relief station.

"Hey! Where'd my wine go?" said Roarke as he sat down at the table.

"Oh!" I said, looking at two empty glasses. "Maybe they didn't bring it yet."

"Hah!" said Roarke, exasperatedly shaking out his napkin, getting ready for his sumptuous cup of soup. "That's okay. My guy is bringing us a couple on the house," he said with a grin.

"That's my favorite sleuthing partner. So what did he say?" I asked.

"He said they've all been in a lot lately. In fact, he says they're on the register for today. That's why he'll bring over some extra drinks and coffees, so we can stay longer," he said, nodding to his guy to bring a drink now.

"Who exactly is he talking about?" I asked.

"Well, for sure Eugene Murk, he's pretty memorable when I described him, and he overheard him talking with who I think is Wulf, that they have a big meeting today. I'm hoping the big meeting is with Crusher."

"I can't even imagine Murk in this fancy place," I said, shaking my head.

Then I glimpsed his form and I understood. He didn't come in the front, he'd slithered in the back. He'd oozed over to the end seat at the bar where he could sit, and drink, and melt into the background. Listening, existing, while others engaged, planned, and made deals. He'd be in the corner like a dirty, enduring cockroach waiting underneath the stove.

"Oh, I get it," I whispered meaningfully. "Don't turn around yet, Murk's at the bar. Your contact is giving him a drink. He came in the back. What did you tell your contact to do or say?"

Roarke, unlike most people who would have immediately looked when you told them not to, did not move a muscle in that direction. In fact, he leaned closer and smiled at me as if he were entranced by our conversation, creating the image that he was oblivious to everything else around him. *Damn, he's good.* No wonder I enjoyed our sleuthing so much.

"I just told him to be a good listener. Which he is. I noticed he asks good questions and takes it all in. That's how I got him to be my contact. Of course, I do pay well," he said, shaking his glass as if to demonstrate.

I raised an eyebrow. "How exactly do you pay people, Roarke?"

"Oh, I don't have that much money, but I know a lot of people. So usually I can figure out some kind of barter. Like putting them in contact with someone to help with a housing need, or a lead on a job, that sort of thing."

"Huh," I said, finally having a few questions answered about him. I looked at his great haircut, his dark brown suit with the pencil-thin pinstripes, and his deep brownish black tie. "That's how you have such fabulous clothes, isn't it? You made a deal with a tailor or something."

Roarke gave me a wolfish grin and said, "A good reporter never reveals his sources," then tilted his head back for the final swig of good wine.

"Hey, something's happening over there. Did someone just leave the bar area?" I asked, tipping my head to the side toward Murk. I swear I saw someone leaving quickly out the back.

Murk was clearly agitated with jerky movements as he spoke urgently to the bartender, Roarke's buddy. The bartender was good; although he was getting nervous, with a sheen of sweat marking his brow, he didn't look over at us, breaking his cover. I kept my body language aimed at Roarke, but shifted my eyes to the bar as often as I could.

My view was abruptly obscured by a large, matronly woman who'd arrived at our table.

"Mary?" I asked. "What are you doing here? Did you and Morgan follow us?"

"Oh, most definitely," she said with amusement shining from her eyes. "Listen, Morgan told me she saw Daphne Franco. I'd already had my eyes on your Murk fellow over there. At the very end of the ceremony, after we'd dismissed the crew, I spotted him. I caught him massaging that paunch of his; it's such an odd gesture," she said with disgust. "Anyway, I was tailing him because I just felt like I should, I guess." It's the best quality a detective can have, a gut instinct. No wonder she was so effective.

"So, winding through a lot of back streets, he ended up here. Meanwhile, as I rounded the corner to enter in the front, Morgan came up and said she and Eric had gone back to where Daphne had spotted them hot on her trail. They got the feeling they'd interrupted whatever she was doing. They found her." Mary leaned a fraction closer, eyes wide. "Daphne's here."

CHAPTER 48

"Holy shit," said Roarke.

"Maybe that's what's got Murk so agitated," I whispered.

Roarke looked over, giving up on his cover. "He's gone."

In those split seconds, Murk had disappeared. Mary and I turned our heads and the bartender was looking pale as he motioned with his head to come over. Quickly.

Roarke left money for the bill and we quickly but smoothly went to the bar, trying not to draw too much attention to ourselves. Roarke said, "What's going on?"

The bartender gulped and said, "We'd just been shootin' the breeze, but then a small guy came up to him, he'd come right up to him from the front door. I tried to look busy and disinterested, but giving it my best shot to listen in. They were talking close, almost in each other's ear. The little guy stayed only a few seconds, then left out the back. But I did hear Murk say the name Daphne. I can say he was definitely afraid, he kind of squeaked when he said her name."

"Did he say anything else?" I asked.

He swallowed again, then said, "He called me over and asked me to look toward the door, out in the lobby area, to tell him who I saw. So I did. I went toward the other end of the bar while I shined up a glass and looked out to the line for lunch."

"What did you tell him?" asked Mary.

"I just listed out the three or so people I saw. Two businessmen, one really tall, one average, both with gray hair. And a woman with light blond hair and a red hat."

"A red hat," I whispered. Could it be that red hat that I'd admired earlier? "Was it dipped down over one eye?"

He nodded.

"What did Murk do then?" asked Roarke.

"He looked like he might have a heart attack right then and there. Jerky movements, rubbed his face trying to come to a decision. Then he bolted out the back door, same one the short guy went through."

Roarke and I looked at each other. Mary said, "That's Daphne. Morgan gave me a detailed description."

I felt woozy. It was the same hat. I'd been within a few feet and even admired her goddamn hat. I grabbed Roarke's arm.

"Roarke."

"What, Lane?"

"That perfume, that scent I was telling you about. I smelled it right when I was admiring a lady's hat just in front of us when we were walking to the luncheon," I said.

"So the memory you're still teasing out is from *her* perfume," he concluded.

I nodded sickly.

Mary said, "I'm going to try to tail her."

"Be *very* careful, Mary," I said with a solemn tone. She nodded, then left quickly. For a large woman, she practically floated, just as silent as her looks were invisible.

I looked at Roarke and he patted my hand, which was still gripping his arm. "I think we should follow Murk. Think that little guy must be the Crusher?" I asked.

"Yeah, I do. Let's go."

We wrapped ourselves in our wool coats and made our way cautiously out the back after thanking the bartender. We went through the kitchen, the hustle and bustle of the staff creating enough of a distraction that no one even gave us a passing glance. The only exit was clearly marked. We paused.

"Ready?" he asked.

"Yep," I said decisively as I pushed out the door.

The cold air packed a punch, having dropped in temperature through the day. We had come out the side of the Rockefeller building. It was a kind of alley with several workers loading and unloading a variety of vehicles including a horse-drawn cart. It made me quirk a smile as I remembered a fabulous getaway involving me and Morgan's crew and a large junk cart careening through Manhattan. That thought and the humorous image that would be ingrained in my memory forever of arriving at Finn's precinct in my red gown, disheveled hair, holding my high heels in one hand and dagger in the other, in front of a very amused group of policemen . . . gave me a surge of courage.

For once, Roarke and I weren't being chased, we were the pursuers.

"There!" said Roarke urgently, pointing to the far corner where we glimpsed Murk and Crusher in a heated conversation. Crusher's head barely reached Murk's shoulders, but Murk looked plenty nervous in the presence of a clearly more powerful man. I shivered recalling how Crusher had gotten his apt moniker. I'd disdained Roarke's advice about not finding out the origin of his nickname. He was right, I shouldn't have asked. Suffice it to say, it involved a car door.

We slid up to the side of the building, wanting to overhear and see whatever we could. I leaned into Roarke and said, "So I'm thinking that Daphne is part of this, and maybe one or both of them double-crossed her . . ."

"That's what I'm thinking, too. Otherwise, why have such a scared reaction to her arrival?"

"Yeah, maybe she'd been so far under the radar and the heir to Rex's legacy hadn't been discovered for so many years after his death . . . maybe they'd taken liberties as if she wasn't a threat or at least that the Red Scroll wasn't a threat any longer."

He had a grim set to his lips. "That makes sense. But jeez, they are no match for her. Even with Crusher's history. She's in a different league."

Just then, Crusher saw us. I have no idea what cued him other than a villain's instinct. His eyes went right to mine and the men both took off. In two different directions.

"Damn it!" I yelled. We ran over to where they'd been, looked at each other reading each other's minds, and split up. We weren't apprehending them, we were just chasing. I just wanted to see what happened.

I ended up running after the Crusher. I wasn't in an all-out pursuit, which was a nice change of pace for me. I had on my lovely black boots, which were easier to run in than my usual high heels. I did wish I had on my dove-gray wool trousers instead of my gray dress suit with the wide buttons up the front and on the cuff. But again, I didn't need to tackle the guy, I just wanted to see where he was going.

We were on 49th running west. Crusher took a hard right at Sixth Avenue. I started to get a stitch in my side. You really can run faster and farther when someone is trying to kill *you*.

Up ahead, Radio City Music Hall was on the right, its running lights dazzling even in the daytime. *Born to Dance* was playing with Jimmy Stewart and Eleanor Powell. Crusher ran in through the Art Deco doors. I was gaining on him, so I hit the doors not too far behind.

I'd been here several times, but I still gasped as I ran through the lobby that was a work of art. The gold and red tones created a sizzle in the air, a feeling of anticipation. Whether you were chasing a bad guy or just coming to see a film, I might add. With gold leaf everywhere, tall columns, glamorous Oriental murals that made you dream, and luxurious draping, it was like walking into a golden palace.

The soaring ceiling with the tall, almost skyscraper-style chandelier led my eyes right to the grand staircase up ahead where Crusher was taking the steps one at a time. I took them two at a time. I often said we got to walk through works of art during our wonderful era with its Deco doorways, ceilings, and lights. Today I was running through it.

He kept running up to the very top. I hoped he was heading to the legend, the secret apartment that the music hall designers created for the late Samuel "Roxy" Rothafel, the spectacular producer. I got to the top, sweaty and panting, but he was out of sight. The place was full of employees running about, doing their jobs to prepare for the evening show. I stopped a guy and asked about the secret apartment, it had to be where he was headed because other than the actual theater, there wasn't anywhere else to go. I identified myself as the aide to Mayor La Guardia and that appeased him that I was legitimate. He nodded to a nondescript door. I opened it and quietly went up another flight of steps.

I walked into an apartment out of some kind of jazzy fairy tale. It held the same warm and opulent tones as the lobby, but the ceiling was completely covered in gilt. Floor-to-ceiling windows ran along one wall, with two leather club chairs flanking a gorgeous and glossy brown oval table with drawers. There was another grouping of striped chairs and a davenport in the middle of the room, a cocktail bar on the end. I wished I could spend hours here hosting a party or curling up in a luxurious chair with a favorite book.

The click of a door shutting pulled my attention away. I ran back down the entryway stairs, truly feeling the consequence of running so much. I was dying from heat. I tore off my winter coat, dropping it right on the floor, and opened up my scarf as I kept walking, a trickle of sweat running down my chest.

In the main hall where I'd asked the employee for directions to the apartment, a dark cackle made my head swivel to the grand staircase. Crusher was laughing at me as he ran down those goddamn stairs, looking as if he could run a marathon and not break a sweat.

Bastard. The more I ran, the hotter I got, the more I found myself swearing. I gathered one more burst of strength and ran down the stairs. He bounded across the long lobby and bolted out the door. I wasn't far behind, managing to gain on him. He wasn't laughing now.

I got to the door and burst out. He'd gone up the street about twenty feet or so. He looked back at me and darted out into the frenzied traffic of Sixth Avenue. Cars jerked to a stop and honked their horns.

I was about to cross, when a blur of green came up swerving around the halted cars. A hard arm grabbed me and pulled me back just as the green car swept by, awfully close to where I'd been standing. I gasped and my eyes flashed to Crusher up ahead as he turned to look back. Our eyes locked tight just as the evergreen car rammed right into him.

His body bounced high, up and over the car. The driver stopped with a screech of tires. As the driver exited the car, a bright red hat shone over the roof. Turning to me, Daphne's eyes found mine, sent me an air kiss, then smoothly took her seat again and drove off, not a care in the world.

CHAPTER 49

The man who'd grabbed me abruptly let go, but kept a hand on my shoulder to make sure I was steady. As I spun around, he ducked his head down into his black overcoat and walked away.

"Hey!" I yelled.

He turned slightly back and I shouted, "Thank you!" He curtly nodded. His black fedora had a dark blue band and he cut a dashing figure, tall, and with a good Roman nose. I started to yell, "Who—" but was cut off by a siren. I looked around and Roarke bounded around the corner.

He rushed up and breathlessly asked, "Where's your coat? Are you okay?"

"It's inside. I'm fine, but Crusher . . ." I nodded to the gruesome scene. I quickly filled him in as we went back inside Radio City to retrieve my coat. Now I was chilled, inside and out.

The coat felt secure and warm. We waited outside for the police to arrive, the ambulance drivers already having declared Crusher dead on the scene, a white sheet laid on top of his crumpled, small figure. That diminutive countenance belied a horrid man, but his small form under the sheet still engendered a mournful response in my chest. It was just slightly bigger than a child's.

Roarke said in a low voice, "Did you learn anything? How'd this happen?"

I relayed the whole chase scene and my stomach flip-flopped when I got to the part where Daphne rose out of the car.

He flung his head back and said, "Wait. Who was the guy who pulled you back?"

"I don't know, I think just a stranger. I wasn't going to run into the street, but I'm sure it looked like I might. And she sure wouldn't have bothered to avoid hitting me, either. So I'm glad he did."

"I'm shocked it wasn't Finn," he said, earning a chuckle from me. It felt good.

"I know. Me, too. But I have to say, he did look a little familiar. I never caught his face full on, just the profile. I swear I've seen him before."

The sound of more sirens coming close directed our eyes downtown. A black sedan led the fleet of police cars that charged up Sixth Avenue. The sedan had barely stopped when a short black tornado flew out of the car flapping his arms and bellowing at everyone. Roarke and I stood to the side, his arm around my shoulders.

"Lane! Roarke!" barked Fio. "What in the Sam Hill is going on here? I heard a call on the police radio, thought I'd check it out on the double, then I saw you two on the sideline!"

I think the chase, the heat, and sweat from earlier mixed with the frigid cold, not to mention locking eyes with someone who seconds later would take his final breath, all of a sudden made my teeth start to chatter. I was freezing.

Fio's voice softened. "Lane. Here, you and Roarke take my car back to the office. We'll debrief there. I'll just be a little bit." It was a Saturday, but with Pete's funeral, it was still a working day for the city.

"Okay," I said, my voice sounding funny through the shivers. "Hi, Ray," I greeted as we met Fio's driver. Ray was also Fio's unofficial bodyguard and he read my probably white-as-a-sheet face with quick acumen. As I sat down in the backseat, he reached in and poked a little indent that I hadn't noticed before. A small door popped open and a bottle of whiskey and a glass stood waiting to help.

I looked up at him with a smile. "Th-th-thanks."

Roarke got in the other side and said, "Aw, Lane. Here, let me pour us a restorative tot, as Aunt Evelyn would say."

I would've just taken the bottle, but my hands were shaking, too. After a swig of the burning liquid hit my throat and gut, I felt immediately better. "That stuff really works," I said.

"I know," said Roarke, who had also looked pretty darn white. "Here I'd been thinking that for once we weren't the ones being chased down. It was kind of fun, you know?"

I snorted. "I know! I was thinking the same thing. I still say it's much better chasing instead of being chased. But what a day."

We stayed companionably silent the rest of the way, watching our city flow by us as we rode downtown. The Empire State Building with its staunch and straight sides with impressive height and majesty. The Chrysler Building with the Art Deco windows and style radiating all around it. Both constant reminders of where we'd come from with the Great War and the Depression, yet still creating, building, drinking cocktails, inventing . . . in spite of it. The beauty of life was that much more breathtaking because of the adversity. I found my pearl dagger in my clutch and took a closer look at it again. Beautiful. Dangerous. I liked the combination.

We pulled up to City Hall and both wearily climbed the outside steps, then up the grand staircase to our offices. I paused at the top. I looked down at myself and my blouse had come untucked beneath my suit coat, one boot had a rough scuff up the side, and my hair felt wind-blown. I looked at Roarke. He looked perfect. Not a hair out of place, not mussed, no smudges.

"Bastard," I whispered.

"Heh, heh, heh," he chuckled evilly.

"Shut up, Roarke," I said with a grin, shaking my head.

We walked in and Val was already coming toward me with a bundle in her hands. "I brought you a change of clothes!"

I laughed in earnest as I wrapped an arm around her for a hug and said into her hair, "You always know."

I released her and Roxy was standing there, smirking and shaking her head. "Honestly. You two. Go on, get cleaned up, I'll get you both some coffee."

After I changed clothes and brushed out my hair, I felt like myself again. By that time, I heard Fio make his clamorous entrance even from inside the ladies' room. I went to my desk and looked at it. It was like my room at home. It was the center point, the heart, with my papers, my black fan that I sometimes used even in winter, my favorite pens, and a few loved photographs. It wasn't remarkable, but it was mine. I took a breath and a swig of hot coffee. I was ready.

I went to Fio's office, where Roarke and the girls were already sitting, and I grabbed up my little chair I always brought into meetings. I had to lift my chair up over the head of the tiger skin rug, which brought a grin of delight to Fio.

"So! You've had a big day," said Fio, piercing me and then Roarke with his glaring eyes.

"That's definitely an understatement, sir," said Roarke. Boy, was it.

After Roarke and I filled in everyone on what happened after the luncheon, we all sat silently for a minute, trying to digest it all.

Valerie recrossed her legs for probably the tenth time to keep from slipping forward in her chair and said, "So, that man that pulled you back from the curb? You say you felt like you've seen him before."

"Yeah," I replied. "I don't know him, but maybe I've seen him someplace. I don't know."

She added, "So you think he was following you? Or more like he was in the right place at the right time?"

"I'm not sure. I didn't get a feeling one way or the other. But he seemed very nonchalant, so I guess he just happened to be at the right place."

She nodded slowly, her mind working.

Roxy crossed her legs again and said, "Roarke, what happened with Murk? The guy you were chasing."

He chewed on the inside of his cheek a little, deep in thought. "Yeah, not nearly as eventful as Lane's escapade. But I keep thinking about it. Murk wasn't very fast, but he got across a busy street before me, so I was stalled for a minute. When I rounded a corner, he was leaning back from a car window that he'd been resting his arms on."

"What did the car look like?" asked Fio.

"That's what I keep thinking about. I thought it was black. But knowing what Daphne had been driving, the car that hit Crusher . . . you say it was dark green, Lane?" he asked.

"Yes. Just a sedan, a little sleeker than the police cars, but a similar green. Maybe a little darker," I replied.

"Yeah. It might've been her car. Which, if it was hers, would mean Murk is tight with her. At least, tighter than Crusher had been. Because she had to have raced off to find Crusher right after that meeting. And killed him."

CHAPTER 50

The back room of the deli was hot and sticky. It didn't matter that it was the middle of winter, the room gathered humidity and heat, making armpits and hairlines damp like it was mid-August. The refrigerator needed cleaning and emitted a noxious odor of mold and sour milk.

But they liked the room. It was theirs. Many a meeting was held at the dingy table, plans confirmed, motives questioned, the thirst for dirty business quenched.

"I think that's as good a plan as we've ever come up with," said Wulf.

Murk sat back in the greasy chair, lightly caressing his paunch, clearly pleased with himself. "Yeah. I think so, too. They don't expect that I can do much. Of course I've banked on that for years. They even fell for my red herring of a name. Can you believe they bought 'Cushman'?" He ran a hand through his sparse hair, smearing a smudge of resulting sweat on his shirtfront as he subconsciously circled it some more.

Wulf barked out a laugh. "You mean like the bread? What morons."

"You said it," laughed Murk. He took a breath as a dangerous look came to his eyes. "We have them anxious about our retaliation, taking out more cops. But I wouldn't mind taking out the pipsqueak mayor and that little aide of his. She thinks she's hot stuff.

Takes liberties like she's more important than she should be. Needs to learn her place."

Wulf caught the dark look in his partner's eye and knew enough to shut up and listen. He squinted as he thought about the problem. "You know, boss. You want to get at the mayor and that Miss Sanders . . . you don't get them. You get who they care about."

"I've already been working on plans for our little mayor, but his family is too hard to touch, not to mention I'm not into killing kids," said Murk disdainfully.

"No, no. I mean her boyfriend, that cop. And he's one of La Guardia's right-hand men."

A gleam of understanding hit Murk's eyes as he said, "You know who her boyfriend is?"

Wulf pulled one side of his mouth up in a sly grin. "You do, too. That detective who came in with the mayor the night you had that tall cop killed. They're an item."

"Now you're talkin'. We could get two birds with one stone. Another cop out of the way just as we threatened and teach little Miss Sanders and the mayor a lesson to boot. I like it. I like it a lot," said Murk.

"Okay. Let's put a tail on them and see if we can get an opportunity. If we grab her, he'll come after. Maybe we can even get them both," said Wulf, enjoying the moment of being on the inside of the action. He'd been trying to go up the ranks for a while.

Murk's eyes suddenly zeroed in on Wulf, like a predator sizing up his prey. In a split second, Wulf went from feeling on top of the world to feeling like he might wet himself. He swallowed.

Murk slowly stood up, placing his hands on the table and leaning in to Wulf. "But. If you ever draw attention to yourself again like you did outside the Savoy with that black cop, I'll kill you myself. Go."

CHAPTER 51

That night we all needed a break. We craved music, simplicity, food, drinks, and friends. We headed out to Little Italy.

It had begun to snow again and the narrow streets looked magical, with warm lights blinking out through the dark night that had been softened with a coat of fluffy snow. It felt like it was cleaning the city, cleansing our palates from a rough day. Finn was still busy late in the day, so I called and said I'd meet him at our favorite place, Copioli's.

Roarke, Roxy, and I all went into the sumptuous-smelling restaurant. The scent of garlic, butter, wine, and tomatoes embraced us at the door. The little red candles flickered invitingly on the tables. I waved to Sam and Florence as we pulled a couple of extra tables together. I kept a seat open next to me for Finn.

"Too bad Val couldn't come," said Roxy. "But I imagine it was a rough day for her. She looked really tired."

"Yeah, and she and Peter used to come here with us once in a while," I said.

We went ahead and ordered a few pasta dishes, a few bottles of wine, and a big salad to pass around. I of course ordered the crumb-coated baked green olives that I could eat by the bushel. The waiters brought over steaming fresh bread and all three bottles of wine right away. We dove in, enjoying the easy atmosphere and close friends.

Of course, the real Little Italy was uptown in East Harlem, the largest Italian settlement in the States. But this small area that butted up against Chinatown was special to us, somehow. It was closer to City Hall and all our offices, but it also held a certain charm with its squat buildings pressed up against each other, lights hung back and forth across the street, the friendly waiters that moved fluidly to the rhythm of the place like busy ballerinas.

After we finished off every last bit of the garlic and tomato sauces from each plate with the end caps of the fresh bread, we sat back in our chairs replete and content. I sipped my coffee and started eyeing the dessert menu, when the musicians began setting up. Even just tuning up, the classical guitar and the bass, with the accordionist and bongos player prepping their instruments while laughing and telling stories, the restaurant's very air sparkled with anticipation. In New York, you often just fell into great events. Things you couldn't expect or plan for. Like live music that made the crowd move and share a sudden camaraderie and contagious smiles.

I went over to the bass player and had a few friendly words, then handed him a couple coins and a grin. When the guitarist gave a nod that he was ready, they launched into their first song. The glittering candlelight created sparks on the glassware, the smoky air filled with scents of good Italian cooking and whiffs of perfume, and the smoldering, swing-your-hips music all came together to pull us into action.

The patrons at the middle tables worked together to pull all our tables to the side to create a makeshift dance floor. The owner came out of the kitchen with a pleased gleam in his eye as he dried a platter with a towel. The sultry, rhythmic song made you want to move, it was impossible not to join in. Roarke and Roxy were already dancing and Sam put his giant hand out to Florence.

My partner had impeccable timing, walking in the door with a burst of frosty air. His dark eyes searched for mine and I felt the heat rise through me as we locked eyes. He shook off his snowy coat and hat and came over.

"Come on, Lane," he said in his low voice. He rolled his sleeves up and his arm came automatically around my waist to pull me smoothly into the dance. He smelled like winter and his own particular woodsy aftershave. He'd changed from his dress blues into his favorite black suit with a maroon shirt and black tie underneath a smooth vest.

The muscles of his chest and arms rippled as we danced. I caught the eye of the bass player and winked.

"How was Pete's family doing?" I asked.

"Oh, as good as can be expected," he said. "But I think the large turnout at the ceremony really surprised them, made them feel better that Pete had been loved and successful."

"The whole service was so moving." I set my cheek onto his shoulder, his arm pulling me closer. He felt like home.

"I heard you had a big day," he said with a wry tone.

"*Pfft*. When don't I?" I quipped.

The song ended and the bass player nodded when I looked his way. Years later, Rosemary Clooney would sing a similar song, but I was convinced *this* was the original.

Hey mambo, mambo Italiano . . .

Finn gave me a wolfish grin and we moved into the rhumba kind of rhythm. The place had been alive before, but there was something about this song . . . light conversations ceased, this was serious dancing. Hips swayed lower, smiles grew wider, eyes turned smoldering, the tempo swinging us around the stars. I spotted one waiter swing the hostess onto the floor and another who gathered up a gal standing by the bar. Even the owner came out of the kitchen, pulling his wife along, who happily slid the apron from her waist to fluidly join in.

The band extended the song, none of us wanting it to end. But eventually, they felt the ending. At the final notes, the entire place sang *Mambo! Italiano!*

It was New York's weird magic. We all applauded and even shared a few hugs all around.

We decided to take a quick break and went to the bar for a beer.

"Oh, that was so fun," I said.

"It was! We need to hit another Irish pub, too," said Finn with knowing eyes.

"I'd love that," I said, fondly remembering our reel at the pub in England.

"Love, did you figure out the details to your idea for tomorrow night, Valentine's Day?" he asked.

"I did, in fact." I asked for a water, still parched, then added, "Yes, it's all set. With Crusher out of the picture and Daphne most definitely in the picture . . . we still need to find out more information and specifically if Uncle Louie Venetti is involved in anything. Do I have that right?"

He nodded and said, "Yeah. He's been quiet, but the pinball racket started with him. If he's moved on to other deals, it'd be good to know. If we could find a place where it'd be . . . uh . . . *less deadly* to ask about his whereabouts and activities . . ." He rolled his eyes in emphasis of how difficult that could be. I laughed when he said *less deadly*.

"Exactly. And I have just the thing. Aunt Evelyn set it all up today. Tomorrow night we are going to the Valentine's dance at the Elmo."

CHAPTER 52

Finn looked at his desk. The many layers of green paint kept the two bottom drawers from shutting, giving it the appearance of a dilapidated bulldog. He loved it like a crummy old pair of perfect slippers.

He stacked his finished casework and neatly filed it away. Lane had given him the *Voodoo Macbeth* tickets the night before when they all went to Little Italy. *What a night.* There were fancier and more trendy places, but usually there wasn't enough room to dance. And at Copioli's there was an energy that you couldn't match anywhere else. He supposed it was from the spontaneity. The fact that the crowd made it happen, it wasn't scheduled. There was a magnetism with spontaneous things. He laughed to himself as the image of Lane throwing her stockings into the Thames came skating back to mind. *Talk about spontaneous.* He could only imagine what tonight would hold for them as they went sleuthing at El Morocco.

Finn was delighted to attend *Voodoo* one more time. Plus, they'd seen it the first time at the Lafayette in Harlem. They'd been lucky to get tickets, as it was sold out for ten weeks straight. This time, after touring the country, *Voodoo* came back to New York City and was at the Majestic, in Brooklyn. He not only wanted to experience the whole thing all over again, but to experience it *after* he'd faced his past, what he thought had been a curse.

The delight of a night with Florence and Sam, and meeting that engaging Orson Welles again, filled him with pleasure.

Finn had a busy social schedule with *Voodoo* coming up, on top of the Elmo that night. He grabbed his heavy overcoat and hat and left the station for his quick meeting. He had received a surprising message that just might prove to be a trump card. He opted for his favorite haunt to meet contacts, the English-style pub.

Finn walked in and met with his contact over fish 'n' chips. They carefully chose the back, wanting to stay out of the window. His contact went over the new details he'd located. Things were coming together, but they just needed the place and time.

Finn rubbed his hands together in anticipation. He'd been out-witted when he went to England, unable to foresee all that his de-vious brother had been capable of. Finn still broke out into a sweat at the thought of just how close he'd gotten to being committed.

Despite Lane's positive outlook, she could see the deception when he'd been blind to it. As he and Lane danced late into the night at Copioli's, she'd looked at him with wary eyes when they discussed the fact that as an NYPD detective, he was a target *yet again*. He was certain that images of him being dragged away to the police wagon had been flitting through her mind, because they sure had been filling his own thoughts.

But he assured her he had a plan. She wanted to know the plan, but he needed to keep it even from her. He'd learned that anyone could be deceived when it was the right lie from the right person. No one was impenetrable. So he decided to go on the offense. And with this new contact, he would *not* be taken in again.

CHAPTER 53

I'd been dying for a chance to go to El Morocco, affectionately called the Elmo. If you wanted society to know you? Gaze upon your fashion sense? Get the latest gossip and perhaps be entered into the halls of celebrity by Lucius Beebe at the *Herald Tribune*? You went to the number one rendezvous of café society, the Elmo. However, it cost a pretty penny and you needed to have people in the know to get in. I never had quite a good enough excuse for Aunt Evelyn to pull some considerable strings to get me in. This, however, was just the ticket.

I slid on my new silk stockings that I'd been saving for just such an important event. I clipped on the garters and gently slipped the dress from its hanger. I slunk into the floor-length white satin that gracefully hugged my curves and felt as light as a wisp of air. I had curled my hair into hundreds of twirling chocolate-colored tendrils, then pulled up the back and pinned it artfully into place with curls here and there, and one longer one kissing the side of my face.

I looked at my dresser that held some of my favorite mementos from my mother: her silver brush set and the jewelry I'd wear tonight, along with a sweet little wooden cat with his tail curled around his perfect, stripey legs. She'd always loved little ginger cats, but we'd never managed to get one. I picked up the Art Deco set of silver and diamond earrings and the matching slender bracelet and secured them all into place. Lastly, I took the white mink stole and slipped it around my shoulders, feeling its sumptuous fur that tickled my chin as I snuggled into it.

From upstairs in my room, I heard the ruckus of Finn coming to the door and Ripley and Mr. Kirkland answering, followed by the light steps of Aunt Evelyn quickly tapping down the stairs to join in. I took one last look at my reflection to double-check my deep red lipstick and glittering appearance, then headed down.

"Hello, everyone!" I greeted as I landed on the last step at the foyer. The warm lamp sent glowing shadows throughout the welcoming space. I suddenly remembered a very sweet dance Finn and I shared in that very spot to jazzy piano music floating down the stairs from Aunt Evelyn's studio.

Finn's gray-green eyes connected with mine. Aunt Evelyn gasped a little and said, "Oh, Lane! You look divine!"

Mr. Kirkland was looking between me and Finn, probably sensing the electricity between us because he had a cheeky grin on his face. He said in his gravelly voice, "Lane, you look terrific. Finn? Take care of our girl." That last part he said with just a touch of threat, which made me chuckle.

"I will do my best, sir," said Finn, biting back a smile.

I went to him and kissed him on the cheek, inhaling the scent of the aftershave, which I loved. He turned a quirky smile and a cocked eyebrow to me. I think I might have uttered a hungry *mmmmmm* when I inhaled. I thought that had been to myself.

"Okay! We're off!" I declared.

"Hold the phone!" cried Aunt Evelyn. "I have a little surprise for you that I arranged with a friend. You can't merely walk up to the Elmo or take a cab. The doorman will look down upon you and might not even let you in."

A double honk of a horn sounded from outside and Evelyn remarked, "In fact, it's just on time."

Finn held out his arm to me as we went to the door. He had on a crisp black suit with just a hint of a pinstripe in the fabric, a bright white shirt and tie, and a new black fedora with a white band and tiny white feather on the side. He looked delicious.

Kirkland opened the front door with a flourish. I held the banister as I stepped down the front steps of our brownstone in awe.

"Oh my," I whispered.

A driver stepped out and opened for me the back door of the silver Rolls-Royce Phantom.

"Now that's bloody brilliant," said Finn.

"Take good care of them, Tommy!" said Evelyn.

"Will do, Mrs. Thorne," said the driver, decked out in a matching dove-gray uniform.

The backseat was covered in a soft, buttery leather. Every ounce of this heavenly vehicle was striking.

"New shoes, Lane?" Finn asked, glimpsing the tips sticking out from my gown.

"Yes. They're scrumptious!" I pulled up my dress so he could see them in total. They were white satin with very high heels, a sliver of an ankle strap, and flat beads that had been sewn into a clever Art Deco design on the toes that sparkled in the light.

"Beautiful!" he whispered, not looking at the shoes but at my legs. "Say, Lane, is that your mom's dress that she wore in the photograph with Uncle Louie by the Central Park casino?"

"The very same. I tried it on when we were in Michigan and it fit like a dream. The whole ensemble is hers other than the shoes. Even the little diamond clip in my hair."

"She'd have loved to see you wearing it. You look amazing."

That sentiment filled me with pleasure and reminded me just how much my life and my story were connected with my parents, even though I'd lost them so long ago. It was an odd feeling indeed, to have lived more of my years without my parents than the years with them. It was moments like these that made me feel like they were still all around me.

We wanted to take advantage of the ridiculously dreamy vehicle, so we asked the driver to take us around a bit before heading to East 54th Street and the Elmo. We drove toward downtown and as we neared 42nd, I looked way up to see my favorite building glistening in the moonlight, the Chrysler Building. We cut over to the west side and went through Times Square with all its lights running and blinking with vigorous color and speed. I'd lived here almost fifteen years and it was still a thrill to enjoy the city, to soak it up and jump into the swirling energy that swept you up like a swift river.

We arrived at the Elmo and the driver came around to open my door. There was always a lineup of celebrities and society bigwigs. I glimpsed a Vanderbilt and one of the younger Rockefellers. Was it David? We were the impetus for quite a few head turns.

I looked at Finn and a fleeting look of being in over his head raced across his face.

"How ya doin', big guy?" I asked with more than a hint of teasing in my voice.

The detective who was a professional at working undercover mastered his face and his courage and gave me a wink. "I'm great, love. But, uh . . . let's get a drink on the double." I noticed his Irish brogue that took over when he was preoccupied was nice and pronounced.

We went to the bar and Finn ordered his favorite martini with a twist and I asked for a glass of champagne. Finn turned to me and said, "Shall we nod to France?"

"Absolutely! Here's to Mr. Churchill, a night out in a Rolls, and my fabulous shoes!"

We clinked glasses and after a sip, he said, "That was quite a trip to London, eh? You know I heard from Grandma Vivian, love. They found both Sean and Gwen guilty of attempted murder. Viv hasn't spoken with my parents. They've dropped off the map for a while to avoid the scandal, I assume."

"How does it feel to have faced your ghosts? It's been a long reckoning," I said, putting my hand on his arm.

"I feel . . . lighter, I think. I'd felt separated from it all for quite some time. But I also think I'd carried around the weight of Sean's deception. Thank God Viv believed me. I don't know what I would've done without her."

"She's something else, all right. I miss her."

There was no floor show at the El Morocco, the glittering patrons were the main focus with their furs, jewels, and dazzling dresses. I heard that some of the more famous and flamboyant women had their maids bring them a change of furs to the ladies' room at El Morocco so they could enjoy a costume change. The band started up a new song and it was one I loved.

Before I could say anything, Finn took my hand and said, "Come on! Let's dance."

We walked out to the dance floor. The live music pulsated through the air, bringing people to their feet, forgetting conversations and cares, joining hands and joining in the mass of humanity that were all part of the same song, the same dance.

With long dresses, most of us couldn't do as many steps with fancy footwork, but we swished and swayed across the glossy black floor. The famous zebra-striped material lined every inch of the endless settee that circled the room as well as all the chairs. At a glance in the *Tribune*, you instantly recognized the Elmo from that zebra print. The walls were midnight blue with indirect lighting and skyward reaching palm trees that completed the iconic and exotic feel.

After he twirled me and brought me in close, I asked Finn, "Have you seen any of Venetti's men or Venetti himself?"

"Nope. Not a one. But on Valentine's Day, there is quite a crowd."

I nodded. "I think he'll be here. It may be late, but this is the place to be. He always manages to be at every big Manhattan function, gathering information and meeting people. I think it will be worth a try. But even if he doesn't show, this night is spectacular."

After a couple of hours of delightful fun, tasty appetizers, and cocktails, Finn went to the men's room and I walked toward our little table along the side of the dance floor. The security was tight, so I could keep my fur stole across the back of the chair and my darling little handbag on the seat. Just before I got to the table, someone grabbed my arm and forcefully pulled.

"Charlie? Is that—"

I spun around, ready for a fight. I guess I'd had my arm grabbed one too many times. But before I could deter him, he quickly let go and sputtered, "Oh! Sorry, ma'am. I thought you were someone else. My apologies." He disappeared into the crowd, leaving me mystified.

Finn appeared out of nowhere. "I thought you were going to the men's room," I said.

"Who was that?" he asked gruffly. "I turned around near the door and saw him grab your arm."

I looked at my arm, and although it hadn't hurt, there were red fingerprints. "Grrrrr," Finn growled.

"That's my line. And don't worry, it didn't hurt, he let go really fast. Mistaken identity, I guess. He apologized and ran off."

"*Hmph.*"

"And that's Kirkland's line," I said, coaxing a smile out of him. "Come on, let's go get a Bad Romance—the drink—and you can leave me safely at the bar."

I love a Bad Romance, and it's got some oomph. I sipped at it and inhaled the scent of champagne, cranberry, and a dash of tequila and lime. At the men's room hallway, Finn looked back at me and I waved to him, laughing. I shooed him away and took another sip.

That's when a heavily muscled arm came around my waist and as its owner pulled me gently toward the dance floor he said, "Miss Sanders. We don't have long. Let's have a dance and a chat."

My breath whooshed out of me as I recognized immediately that deep, gravelly voice, the salt 'n' pepper hair and thick eyebrows, the raw power emanating from the man.

I swallowed and, trying not to squeak, I said, "Mr. Venetti. I was hoping to see you tonight."

His eyebrows raised and his lips twitched. He muttered, "Of course."

He gently took my right hand in his and delicately put his other hand on the small of my back. I'd always been aware of his power, and it was a feat of courage to not only be within arm's length of the man, but within his actual grasp. We did a very respectable waltz. For being a brawny, sixty-something-year-old, he was light on his feet. His aftershave smelled spicy and expensive.

"Lane, my dear, there are mysteries afoot, as our Mr. Holmes likes to say."

"You're a reader?" I asked, somehow pleased.

"I am. I read almost anything I can get my hands on. I like to learn. I wanted to know what you found out about the Red Scroll Network and Daphne in England."

This time, my eyebrows shot up. "You knew about that? Never mind. Of course you knew about that."

"Mm, yes. We both have a vested interest in the dealings of that woman."

I darted my eyes around, not knowing what exactly Finn would do if and when he found me dancing with the infamous gangster. *Dancing* with him hadn't exactly been the plan. I knew I didn't have much time.

I filled him in very quickly on everything we learned about Daphne being in London to make sure her newly found leadership was known, but it looked as if her business was focused more in the United States for the time being.

He nodded minutely as I spoke, his black orbs not missing a thing. "And you heard about the Crusher?" I asked, knowing he had. He nodded as I continued, "It was Daphne. She ran her car right into him."

"Now that, I did not know," he rumbled. It was quite clear that he didn't like not knowing important details. My heart skipped a beat.

I cleared my throat, then said, "Yes. My partner—"

"Your partner?" he interrupted.

"Yeah, the investigative reporter I work with, Roarke Channing." I narrowed my eyes as his lips twitched the tiniest bit.

He cleared his face and said, "Go on."

I told him about Roarke catching up to Eugene Murk, and seeing him leaning into the car that might have been Daphne's moments before she crashed into Crusher.

Venetti was watchful, careful, patient, taking it all in. Then before I lost my courage, I asked him my question. "I'm sure you also know that I have a vested interest in the cop killers who took out our friend Peter. They're in the pinball and slots business. I have an inkling that you're not involved, but do you know anything?"

He spun me farther from the side of the dance floor where Finn would be sure to show up. I was surprised he'd been gone as long as he had. "Lane, my dear. As it's Valentine's Day, do you remember what happened on this night eight years ago?"

"I do," I answered. "The Valentine's Day Massacre in Chicago. Between the north side and south side gangs."

"Exactly. Police had been involved, mostly gangsters dressed up as police, but also some crooked cops. Lane, anything to do with cops getting killed means bad business for me. The massacre made the public aware and determined. That kind of public outcry is never good for my dealings. So, no. I do not want that kind of attention."

"I figured business was the bottom line for you, as usual. And besides, it doesn't have your attention to detail. For that matter, it doesn't have Daphne's panache, either. Do you have any leads on who's involved? If they're bad for your business, perhaps you wouldn't mind pointing me in the right direction?"

"Heh, heh, heh," he chuckled. "You know, I wouldn't mind having your kind of leadership on my team someday, Lane. You have excellent instincts."

I was equally pleased and appalled.

"I'll leave you with this: there's more to that little deli by the Landmark Tavern than meets the eye. And more to the owner, as well. That's all for now. Thank you for the lovely dance."

He bowed slightly, and suddenly tilted his head to the side thoughtfully. "You look so much like Charlie, Lane. That's her dress, isn't it?"

"Charlie? Someone else just called me that. Who's Charlie?" I asked.

"Your mother. Charlotte. She loved that stole and if you're not her spitting image . . . you say someone tonight mistook you for

Charlie?" he asked, his eyes narrowing dangerously. I involuntarily took a small step backward.

"Yes. Just before you asked me for the dance, a man grabbed my arm. But he released it quickly when he realized he was mistaken."

He rubbed his chin in thought, then nodded in decision. "Again, thank you for the dance, Lane. I'll be in touch." Louie Venetti walked away, disappearing into the crowd followed by his beefy bodyguards at a discreet distance.

"May I have this dance?"

"Finn!" I yelped. "God, you scared me!"

His arm came around me and pulled me close as a slower song began. A sultry number by Cole Porter.

"You were watching?" I asked as we danced cheek to cheek.

"Absolutely, love. You tend to have *interesting* things happen when I'm not watching. I wasn't gone more than a minute and a half and found you dancing with Uncle Louie. I'd edged closer, but you didn't look too alarmed and you're right. He's all about business. Another Valentine's Day Massacre would not be good," he said.

"He actually brought that up." I filled him in on the information Venetti and I exchanged.

I pulled away to take a good look at Finn's thoughtful countenance as he processed my conversation with the mob boss. He quickly nodded, having come to a conclusion. "Yeah. I can believe that."

"You know, Finn. Something else interesting happened. You know when that guy grabbed my arm earlier? He'd called me Charlie, but I thought it was just a mistaken identity. Just now, when Venetti was leaving, he told me I looked just like Charlie."

"What?" he asked incredulously. "Who's Charlie?"

"*My mom.* Charlotte. I've never heard that nickname used for her."

"Oh my God."

"I know. Odd, isn't it?" I said.

We didn't stay much longer, feeling we'd learned and experienced all we could for the evening. As we made our way to the coat check to retrieve Finn's overcoat, I spotted a tall, blue-green vision. She was all the way on the other side of the place, but I knew beyond a doubt it was Valerie.

Before I could make up my mind to go and say hello, Finn took my hand and led me to the door, as our chariot had arrived. That silver vision of Rolls Phantom loveliness settled my indecision. I left the Elmo feeling just a bit like Cinderella at the ball.

CHAPTER 54

We decided to get a nightcap on the way back to my place. We hit the Ophelia Lounge, the club at the top of the Beekman Tower that I'd wanted to introduce to Finn. The lounge used to be women only, but recently began allowing male patrons. The black-and-white tile floors, rooftop views, raspberry velvet settees, and delicious cocktails made it a favorite haunt of mine. Even in the winter, the tall glass windows allowed for an airy, three-hundred-and-sixty-degree view.

We chose to sit at the bar. It was almost one in the morning, but there were quite a few people sprinkled around enjoying the glittering ambience. It was still early, the night just getting under way. I crossed my legs as I sat upon the stool and admired my white high heels again.

I ordered a red wine, wanting something smooth and mellow. When my glass came and Finn sipped his martini, I said, "Say, Finn, when we were walking out, did you see Valerie? I swear I saw her dancing. I can't believe she was at the Elmo and didn't tell me. I didn't recognize her partner."

"My mind was still on the fact that you had been dancing with Uncle Louie, but yes, I saw her. I've never seen that guy before, either."

Valerie had looked very happy. Happier than I'd seen her look, perhaps ever. She hadn't even glanced in my direction, she'd been so captivated by her partner. Her green eyes simply shone as she looked up at him. I didn't recognize him, but I only had a view of his back and his dark hair. I'd have to ask her about it at work.

Just then, I saw a fabulous red dress go by. "Ooh, Finn! Look at that dress. I'd like that dress."

"You're drooling, love."

"She's about my size, a bit shorter. Similar hair to mine when I'm wearing it down," I said as I contemplatively sipped my drink.

"What, are you considering stealing it right off her back?" he asked with a smirking lilt to his voice.

I snorted. "Maybe."

Just then, as the elevator doors were closing and the girl in the red dress was walking by, someone grabbed her and yanked her into the elevator. I heard a yelp as the doors shut with finality. I also heard some grappling, which made me hopeful she was a fighter.

Finn and I both stood at the same time. We turned to each other and I slid off my fur stole so I wasn't encumbered. "Lane, take the next elevator, it's almost here."

"Got it. You run down the stairs—I won't make it in this dress."

He ran off in a blur and I ran to the elevator. I brought one foot up to set on a chair, the side slit of my dress falling away to reveal my new thigh strap so I could easily retrieve my pearl dagger.

Two men looked at me and grinned. As the elevator door opened I said to them, "Luck favors the prepared, darling."

I turned to the elevator operator and said, "On the double, don't hit any floors. Go to the lobby, a girl's been taken against her will." He looked like he was about to argue, then he saw my knife and the door shut with a slam.

"Okay."

The once-named Panhellenic building, now the Beekman Tower, was twenty-six stories. And even though we went right down, not stopping at any other floors, it felt interminable. I think after glimpsing my dagger and probably from my colorful muttering, the elevator operator looked relieved to have me run out the door as soon as he pulled open the sliding gate.

Finn hadn't made it down yet. I raced to the front door; no doormen in sight. Just outside I glimpsed a flash of red. I ran out and spotted a man hauling the red dress gal down the sidewalk. It was freezing outside, and I spun around getting my bearings, trying to locate anyone who might be a good reinforcement.

No one. I had to do something before he got her into a car. The potential for rescue goes way down once forced into a vehicle.

I opted for a bit of a diversion. "Hey, mister! You dropped your wallet! You there!" I made sure I was nice and loud and noticeable. A few people turned the corner and were walking toward us. No villain liked anyone who was willing to make a fuss. They liked you nice and quiet and compliant. So my obvious gesticulations and noteworthy volume had him grunting with disapproval. Besides, despite our reputation, New Yorkers were very helpful and kind. The people who'd rounded the corner were now avidly looking our way, hoping to help the gentleman retrieve his wallet.

He turned around toward me. I had run a little closer, not daring to get within arm's reach. He was too big to tackle, so I had to use my wits to knock him down. In the same attention-getting voice, I yelled, "Here you go! You dropped it inside the Beekman at Ophelia!"

He suddenly stopped in his tracks, took a good look at the gal in his grasp, then at me, then back at her.

"Uh-oh," I said, not liking the look on his face.

He shoved the girl down to the sidewalk. The people had entered another establishment, and now we were alone on the dark street.

Finn burst out of the door, gun leveled. Despite his speed and what must have been a crazy run down the twenty-six flights, his hand was steady, his dark glare deadly.

"Don't move."

The guy put up his hands with a disgusted look as he spat on the ground. Finn went to him and said to me with a smirk, "Lane, hold this."

He meant the gun. "Don't look so pleased," he muttered, as I took hold of the gun and pointed it nice and steady at the guy.

Finn took off his beautiful tie while he cocked an eyebrow at my sure hand holding the .38 special. The miscreant nodded his head condescendingly and said, "Young lady, do you really know how to use that?"

I cocked the revolver easily. "Yep."

Finn grunted a laugh and wrapped the guy's hands behind his back good and tight. "Kirkland took you shooting, didn't he," he stated. I just flashed a Cheshire grin at him in answer. "I figured."

I gave the gun back to Finn, then went over to the gal and helped her up. "Did you know that guy?" I asked. She looked scared, but mad, too, which was always a good sign that I didn't have a fainter on my hands. I hated fainters.

"No! I was just walking by the elevator on the way to the coat room. He grabbed me and slammed the elevator door shut!"

"Did he say anything? What did he want?" I asked as I put an arm around her shoulders to lead her inside.

"Gosh, I hope he didn't tear my new dress. I saved up for a month to buy it!" she remarked indignantly.

"I love your dress! I was just admiring it when you were grabbed. Here, let me see . . ." I looked at her back and all over to inspect. "Nope! Just a bit wrinkled, no tears."

"He didn't say much. But I kept thinking he'd been looking for someone else, because he said something about the street. No! *The lane.* Something about the lane and that he couldn't wait to get his hands on a guy named Finn. Show him who's boss. What was he talking about? Sounded like gibberish to me."

Stunned and rather speechless, I whispered, "Yeah, gibberish."

She patted her hair and said, "Thanks. I'm so glad you ran out. Say . . . is that a dagger you're holding?"

CHAPTER 55

We decided to call it a night.

Finn arrested the guy and took him in after a quick call to the local precinct. Our driver came by to pick me up and I made my way home. The townhouse looked brilliantly welcoming in the night even though I didn't want to say good-bye to my silver chariot. Aunt Evelyn and Mr. Kirkland must have still been up, because there were a few scattered glowing lights instead of the requisite one left on in the parlor when any of us had a late night. After I patted Ripley a fond hello and stroked his silky German shepherd ears, I walked to the back of the house where my favorite warm room was waiting.

Mr. Kirkland and Aunt Evelyn were reading, caught up in their own literary worlds. Mr. Kirkland had on a thick Irish wool sweater, bringing home the image of a swarthy seaman that I'd always thought of him as. Aunt Evelyn had been painting; her Gypsy garb glowed with its gemstone colors and her long hair trailed down her back. But they were so engrossed in their reading they didn't look up until I was fully in the room.

"Hello! What a Valentine's Day!" I greeted.

Aunt Evelyn looked up at me over her reading glasses. "Oh, Lane dear! You really do look smashing. I bet you and Finn made a glamorous pair. Probably in the society pages tomorrow."

"Well . . ." I said with relish. "I hope that's the one that makes it in the paper, not a photograph of my *other* partner . . ."

"Grrrrr," rumbled Mr. Kirkland. "Other partner?"

"Well, our main goal was to try to pick up on any news on Venetti," I said, sitting down with a *whoosh*. "But a dance with him hadn't been what I was aiming for."

Aunt Evelyn rubbed the space between her eyebrows and murmured, "Oh, good Lord." Mr. Kirkland took that as his cue to pour a little toddy. I declined, opting for a hot tea. I took off my delightfully shimmering shoes and padded over to light the stove for the tea kettle.

"Yes . . . it was surprising. Finn wasn't too pleased."

"I can imagine," said Aunt Evelyn, making me laugh.

"He was nearby the whole time, and I hadn't been giving him the eye or looking nervous, so he kept his distance." I filled them in on what Venetti had told me, both about his aims for business as well as keeping an eye on the deli next to the Landmark Tavern and its owner.

"Also . . . it's very strange. A man grabbed my elbow tonight and called me Charlie. Then later, Venetti remarked that I looked just like Charlie. I had to ask who he meant."

"Your mother!" blurted Kirkland. "Her closer friends and colleagues called her that. And in that outfit that was hers, you really do look so much like her," he said with a sweet smile that reached deep into his eyes. "Charlie. Boy, I haven't heard that nickname in a long time. It fit her fiery personality. She wasn't exactly a demure little flower."

"No, she was not," said Aunt Evelyn appreciatively. "What did that man look like who grabbed your elbow?"

I thought about it and said, "Nothing stood out too much. White, average height, about five eleven or so. Medium brown hair graying at the temples. He looked surprised when he realized I wasn't Charlie; he blinked a few times like he couldn't believe his eyes."

"Hmmm," said Mr. Kirkland, intrigued.

Evelyn and I turned to him and I said, "What do you mean, *hmmm?*"

"There was a guy we used to work with who would fit that description and he had a bit of a tic. Looked like he was always blinking or winking. We called him Sparks because he was a radio guy and with his twitch, it just fit him. Got a couple of slaps, as I recall, from women who thought he was being a little too forward." He chuckled at the memory. "I'll look him up, see what I can find. It'd be interesting to meet up again. Haven't seen him in years. He fell off the face of the earth a long time ago, before Matthew and Charlotte were killed."

I went to fix my tea as the kettle started to boil. I put the tea in a diffuser and poured a little sugar and cream into my cup, then said over my shoulder, "Well, it wasn't the only point of mistaken identity tonight."

I leaned back on the kitchen counter sipping my tea. They both looked at me with a droll expression. I regaled them with the story of the girl in the red dress at Ophelia and our subsequent rescue.

"You really were busy tonight, huh?" rumbled Kirkland.

"Yeah. And I need to buy Finn a new tie because he had to use his beautiful dressy one for makeshift handcuffs. By the way, my shooting lessons came in handy. Finn had me hold the gun on the guy while he tied him up. I think he'd guessed that you and I were in cahoots."

"You took her shooting? I want to go shooting!" exclaimed Aunt Evelyn rather like a sullen teenager. Mr. Kirkland just laughed his raspy chuckle and patted her on the knee.

"And this came in handy once again." I threw my foot up onto the kitchen chair to retrieve my pearl dagger.

Mr. Kirkland choked, then laughed so hard, Evelyn felt compelled to slap him on the back repeatedly.

"Stop it! Stop it! I'm fine," he said gruffly, his laughter ebbing. After he got his breath back, he went and poured himself some tea as I slumped into the comfy moss-green velvet chair.

When he came back to the davenport, he rested his elbows on his knees, cradling the steaming cup between his two hands. "You know, that dagger was Matthew's. But Charlotte was as adept at throwing it as you are, Lane. She wielded that thing better than any street fighter I'd seen. One day, we were talking about life and she was practicing throwing it when we were back in Michigan. Matthew had set up a good wooden target for their practice. We'd taken out Rex, but I couldn't shake the feeling that the Network wasn't finished; even back then I'd had that sense. It was at that conversation that she popped the dagger up into the air, over to me, and said that I should take it. I was going to need it."

"It was my mother who gave it to you?" I asked.

"Yeah. With Matthew's consent, of course. He felt like it was lucky and he wanted me to have it, then one day give it to you."

I took a long sip of tea and rested my elbow on the arm of the velvet chair. "So you were talking with my mom about the fact that maybe Rex's people were still on the prowl. And she specifically tossed you the dagger and said you were going to need it?"

He nodded and said, "Exactly. Just like I said. What about it?"

I gave a knowing look to Aunt Evelyn and said, "There's more to it than that. It's not just lucky." I set down my cup and took the pearl dagger into my hands and closely scrutinized the ebony handle with pearl inlays. "You know the dagger's story, right?" I asked.

Mr. Kirkland had known, but Aunt Evelyn was unaware, so I filled her in on the long story of beauty out of ashes from the outskirts of London. How my parents had seen the diamond in the rough within the drunken Alistair all those years ago, and how the very handle had been loved because of the beauty that was created out of misfortune.

We all headed to bed, full of the thoughts of the last two days and the days ahead. We'd learned a lot, but we needed to debrief and make a plan of action. Finn would look more into the slimy Eugene Murk, the owner of the deli, that seemed to be the impetus of all this. He'd also look into more ties between Murk and the Red Scroll group since he and Daphne seemed to have some sort of relationship.

As I disrobed from my gorgeous gown, I gazed at my wonderful bookshelves full of my favorite books. The colorful bindings added their own texture and depth to the deep blue walls. I caught a glimpse of a favorite red volume of a few of Shakespeare's plays on my shelf. I was so excited to take Finn to *Voodoo Macbeth* one more time, his face absolutely shining when I gave him the tickets the night we went to Copioli's. I knew it couldn't stay in production forever, but I really hoped it would run for a long, long time.

We suffered from so much racism and segregation . . . Aunt Evelyn always said that art helps us heal; maybe *Voodoo* would make a step toward healing. Fio sure believed in art's redemptive powers; it was the very reason he started the public High School of Music and Art.

I was tired. I sat down for a moment in my white chair by the window, my cherished reading spot. Ripley nosed his way into my room and set his big head on the arm of my chair. I smiled and stroked his soft head and big ears. He set himself down with a huff of contentment and I put up my feet on the little ottoman.

I thought about the whole evening full of dances, intrigue, mistaken identity, holding a gun. I thought about that man mistaking me for Charlie. And as my eyes grew heavy, I thought about Valerie and her secrets. She had me worried. It was clear there was a lot more to it all than just a new boyfriend.

CHAPTER 56

Monday morning I was putting on my lipstick and matching raspberry dress with the little ruffles at the sleeve and down the front. The raspberry settees at Ophelia were running through my mind and put me in the mood for pink.

It was still snowy out, so I opted for my tall black boots again and I matched them with a wide black belt and black purse. As I slipped on my second boot, the ruckus that is Fiorello broke into my thoughts. He really was not a quiet man.

His bellows of greeting were matched by Ripley's barking as I bounded down the stairs. He eats fast and was always eager to start the day, so I had to get a move on.

Fio, Kirkland, and Evelyn were just sitting down at the table when I scooted my chair out from the table. Today Mr. Kirkland fixed oatmeal with a little vanilla, a pat of butter on top with a little cream, and a sprinkling of cinnamon and chocolate. It was the best oatmeal I'd ever had in my life.

"So I see you made the society pages, huh, Lane?" said Fiorello with something akin to a sneer.

My stomach dropped. It would not do at all to have the mayor's aide dancing with an infamous gangster. Not at all. "I did?" I asked queasily.

He chuckled and said, "Well, luckily Roarke is close buddies with Mr. Lucius Beebe. They've known each other a while, I think Roarke met him at Yale or something. Anyway, there's a photograph of you, but only you and not your partner, nor his name. There is one woman in the photograph who has a slightly horrified expression as she's looking at your partner, but believe me, no one will be looking anywhere except at those zebra chairs and your lovely countenance, Lane. So it's all right."

I'd gulped a few bites of oatmeal and slammed a bit of coffee down, relieved that there would be no press nightmares for us to deal with. After a little chitchat with Kirkland and Evelyn, Fio suddenly plunked his mug down with good humor and said, "Okay! We've got work to do!"

We quickly assembled ourselves and went out the door to his awaiting car and Ray the driver. When I got to the door, Ray leaned down and said softly, "Don't tell him I told you about the secret whiskey cabinet."

I clicked my tongue and said, "I got you covered, Ray. And thanks."

On the way downtown Fio gave me the usual onslaught of information, to-do lists, and agendas. My pencil flew down the page of my ever-ready notebook. I loved my job. We passed the relief station with its long line of people looking for work. The lines were smaller these days, thank God. I didn't make a ton of money, but I loved making a difference and I could never complain that my job was boring. Tedious at times, sure, like any job. But never truly dull. Of course, dangling off bridges, dancing with gangsters, and defusing bombs hadn't been in the job description . . .

At work we opened up the offices and dove in. The petitioners whom Fio interviewed daily were lined up and ready. I threw my coat up on the hook and dove into the job. From the corner of my eye I spotted Valerie typing away as if she hadn't anything unusual going on at all.

When I had a quick minute's reprieve, I went to the coffee room to get a pick-me-up. Roxy saw me and followed after. She was giving me the eye and then nodded to Ralph, the office flirt and gossip, then nodded to Val, who was still studiously typing. *Aha.* I winked at Roxy. We'd find out from Ralph if he knew anything about Val.

"Say, Ralph, join us for a cup of coffee!" I nodded to Roxy, and poor Ralph, who'd had a hopeless crush on Roxy for months, was incapable of turning down those baby blues of hers. Not to mention her usual style of tight, form-fitting cashmere sweaters. Today she had on baby pink, perfectly highlighting her favored assets and obviously Ralph's favorite assets, as well. He couldn't take his eyes off her.

I beat him to the coffee room and whispered with a wry grin to Roxy, "You wore that on purpose!"

"Absolutely. I had an idea of how we might get a little more information about Val," she said.

"Fantastic idea," I said as I filled my cup. We clinked our coffees together to lend our little operation a bit of luck.

Ralph came trotting in breathlessly. He always spoke a mile a minute and if anyone ever wanted to get a word in edgewise, we had to interrupt him forcefully.

He started right in at about the speed of a Type 75 Atlantic Bugatti. "Hiya, gals! Roxy, you look amazing, Lane, I saw you in the *Tribune*, fabulous dress, who's that guy you were with, you know I've never been to the Elmo, can always spot those zebra prints though, boy, I need a cup of coff—"

"Ralph!" yelled Roxy a little too loudly. "Ha, sorry. Yes, hey, you know, uh, we've been trying to come up with an idea for Valerie's birthday soon, we were wondering if you had any ideas?"

"Me?" he questioned, for which I couldn't blame him as we were her two best friends. I wondered what Roxy would come up with.

I turned to her in expectation. She landed on the not-answering-the-question option. "Uh, yeah. What do you think?"

"Well," he said, putting a fist to his chin in thought. "Let's see, well, besides the usual of little trinkets, hmm. . . . Well, you know, she has that new boyfriend, maybe something that they can do together?"

Roxy and I caught each other's eye. "Great idea, Ralph," said Roxy. She turned to me. "Yeah, great idea. Lane, what was his name again?"

"Raff!" he blurted. *Victory.* "Yeah, I ran into them at the movies last week. They were leaving when I was coming in. Looked like they were in a hurry, couldn't talk long. Seems like a nice guy. That's an idea, maybe movie tickets."

"I don't know much about Raff yet. Do you know what he does?" I asked, pretending to go for more coffee.

"Uh . . . I think he's a policeman or something. At least, I saw a .38 special on him. Well, I gotta run! Good talking with you gals, say, we should go dancing again at the Monaco, that was fun, have a good day!" He pitched his napkin into the trash can and ran out the door.

"Raff," whispered Roxy.

"The movies," I said in hushed tones.

"Seems like a nice guy?" said Roxy, lifting her voice like a question.

"Carrying a gun."

I forced Val to have lunch with me.

I began by asking her out, wanting to get caught up. She'd weakly refused at first, saying she had work to finish up. I pointedly looked at her in-box, which was empty. She laughed a little and gave in after she turned a nice fuchsia color.

We went to our favorite diner and had burgers. Even though she'd been a little deceptive and secretive, it felt nice to be in our regular spot, chatting and laughing. We picked up right where we'd left off without a moment of hesitation.

Until I asked about her new boyfriend.

She turned that fuchsia color again from her neck to the roots of her golden brown hair and almost choked on the pickle she'd just taken a big bite out of. She started to prevaricate and sputtered, "I don't . . ."

I pierced her with the *Please—don't be ridiculous* glare.

She gulped and took a drink of her Coca-Cola. All pretense fell away from her lovely freckled face.

"Yeah, I met him recently. His name's Raff. Rafael Catalano." She sounded completely hooked. I'd never heard her sound like that before.

"You really like him? Tell me about him," I said.

"Yeah," she said a little dreamily. "He's tall, taller than me, which is nice. He's good looking, but just shy of handsome. Which makes him more handsome to me. Weird, huh? And he's kind of rugged on the outside, but he's got an artist's insides. He writes poetry when he's on the subway going in to work every day."

I smiled, enjoying watching her figure out why she felt strongly about him.

"What's he do?" I asked, wondering if the gun would make sense. Maybe he was a security guard or maybe he really was a policeman. But somehow, I doubted that. Those careers didn't allow for a night at the Elmo.

"Oh, he works for some Wall Street bigwig. Crazy hours, good money, he likes the job all right. But I'm not sure it's what he wants forever." She poured more ketchup onto her plate.

"So, he's a businessman? A trader or something?" I asked.

"Oh no. Not like that."

"Oh. Like a bodyguard for the guy?" I was trying my hardest to sound breezy, light, just making casual conversation. But I had the feeling I was walking on thin ice. I wanted more information and yet I got the distinct feeling she didn't want to give it.

"Jeez, Lane, you're asking a lot of questions."

"Well . . . I'm just wondering why you're being so secretive. Why do you want to hide that you're happy? You look happy, Val. I want to share it with you."

Her sweet smile came back and she realized that I really did mean it. I wasn't just foraging for information.

"Oh, Lane. I was just really taken aback by Peter's murder. I met Raff near that time and it just felt like I was being insensitive by suddenly being over the moon about someone."

"I can understand that."

"You can?" she asked hopefully.

"Of course! Look, Val, your friends just want you to be happy. You and Peter hadn't been an item for a while, it had always been on again, off again."

"Yeah, you're right," she said, pulling a long strand of hair behind her ear.

"Wait!" I said, a thought hitting me and making me smirk. "You met Raff not that long ago and he's nice and tall?" I asked.

"Yyyyyes," she said uncertainly.

"Is it the guy who caught you when you tripped and almost fell in Penn Station?" I blurted out at full speed.

She wrinkled her nose in a self-deprecating grimace and set her forehead right onto the table in utter mortification. I heard a muffled, "Yes."

I cracked up. I told her back then that it was actually very romantic. I'd always dreamed of falling, gracefully of course, and having a stranger catch me. I was right. She started to outright giggle and I felt the tension fully leave both of us.

We chatted on about all sorts of fun things. We finished our lunches and I felt that we had made great strides in not letting secrets harm our friendship.

On our way back to work, I prattled on about going to the Elmo. At first I was excited just to share the event. But then I realized she wasn't going to open up about being there, too. She changed the subject quickly as we walked into City Hall and went right to work at her desk.

Despite our good talk, it still bothered me. Why didn't she tell me about going to the Elmo? That's a dream come true for both of us, why not share it? She'd met that mystery man several months ago, which meant she'd been keeping this secret for longer than I thought. And most importantly, the gun. She hadn't given me a good answer about a job where Raff would require a gun. It's possible my office gossip, Ralph, was mistaken. But really, the problem remained that Ralph said he specifically saw a .38 special. Which means he was close enough to actually identify a piece.

There was no mistake.

CHAPTER 57

I called a council of war.

We met at my place and after some wine, cheese, olives, and fresh bread from Mr. Kirkland's own hands, we sat around the fireplace ready to talk.

It was our core group of Finn and me, Roxy, Roarke and Fio, and Aunt Evelyn and Mr. Kirkland. Aunt Evelyn asked the first pointed question. "Why isn't Valerie here?"

Roxy and I exchanged glances. "Well . . . she's part of the reason why I called the meeting," I said. Roarke and Finn caught each other's eye and worry puckered Aunt Evelyn's brow.

"Oh dear," she said.

"But first," I began, "we need to organize and get everything straight. So, to begin with, we have Daphne involved with Murk and the pinball racket. She just took out the last major player, the Crusher. We also have a lot of mistaken identity happening." We had all brought each other up to speed on the rather thrilling last few days, so we could dig right in on what to do next.

Fio said, "I understand why gangsters try to get each other out of the way. So I get why Daphne killed Crusher. But what I'm curious about is why Daphne still has her sights on you, Lane. I mean, she does like to toy with you, but there's something there."

I agreed, but other than Roarke and Finn, I hadn't shared my strange memory of that perfume and a syringe from so long ago. I didn't have any proof that anything untoward happened, just an odd sensation of fear that mingled with that scent.

Mr. Kirkland interjected, "I did find out that that old contact of ours is in town. Sparks had dropped off the face of the earth, he'd moved to California and none of us heard from him in ages. Word on the street is that he's back in the business. I have to see if I can find him myself."

"He did not seem happy to see my mom," I said, eyebrows raised, subconsciously rubbing my arm where he'd left the fingerprints.

"Yeah, which is strange," said Kirkland with a contemplative furrow of his brow. "I'll get on that."

"You know, I think there's something more with Venetti and Daphne," I said.

"Why is that?" asked Finn.

"Well, when we were talking, he asked about what I'd learned in England about Daphne. But he said that he and I both had a vested interest in *that woman*. And his tone when he said it was full of an untold story. I think she had more of a role all along. I used to think she'd waited in the shadows, working with Rex on the sly to become his most trusted partner. But Venetti has something against her. If she was just the next leader of the Red Scroll, Venetti would just take it in stride that she was the next rival in line. No big deal. But his voice says they have a past. And it is most definitely a big deal."

"Ooooh," said Aunt Evelyn. "That makes sense. And with her ability to disguise herself—she had living quarters arranged in a lunatic asylum, for cryin' out loud—she could've been working unseen for ages."

"Exactly," I said.

Finn piped in, "I do have news about that guy we arrested outside Ophelia, Lane." I smiled a little on the inside when he said *we arrested*. "He admitted that he thought the girl in the red dress was you."

"Aw, crap."

In spite of himself Finn laughed. "But I have to say, he'd been aiming for you, but I don't think you were the target." He shook his head like he was trying to make sense of it. "He clammed up after that, but he did rat out Eugene Murk and Wulf. So they were working together, but it doesn't make sense."

"You know, it makes me think of what that girl said when they were in the elevator. She'd mentioned the name Lane, but don't forget she said the guy had been muttering about getting his hands on 'that guy Finn.' Maybe I wasn't the target." I looked at the group carefully. "Maybe I was the bait."

"Oh dear," said Evelyn.

"Why would they be specifically targeting me?" asked Finn, baffled.

"Hmmmm," grumbled Kirkland, making Ripley lay a consoling head in his lap. He patted his big head as he said, "Well, it would be within their plans for another cop as a target, of course."

Roxy spoke up for the first time, having been listening intently. "Well, on top of that, it's well known that you are close to the mayor, Finn. I've heard people say you're his right-hand man right up there with Commissioner Valentine."

I nodded. "True. It'd be a big blow to the department and Fio's administration. It would make it look very weak." I took a sip of my wine. "Oh, wait."

"Oh God," uttered Roarke.

"Shut up, Roarke," I bantered with a smirk. "You say he was working with Murk, right? And Murk is working with Daphne?" I asked Finn.

"Spot-on," he said.

"Murk saw us all together when Peter was shot. You, me, and Fio."

Finn blanched a bit and said, "And you smashed him up against the wall."

Kirkland barked out a laugh, earning a dirty look from Aunt Evelyn.

I said, "I did and I don't regret it. But on top of that, it's pretty common knowledge that you and I are an item, Finn. I definitely got on his bad side, and I am most certainly on Daphne's bad side."

I thought about Finn being a target in England, with his cruel family and just how diabolical they were. A surge of compassion hit me and I looked at Finn, locking eyes. His mouth was set with determination. He'd been a little lost in England, out of his element until things had been righted.

Finn was *not* out of his element now. He wouldn't be fooled again.

Evelyn said, "So that leaves us with Valerie. How and why is she a part of this puzzle?"

Roxy and I shared a look of solidarity.

"Well . . . Valerie's been out of pocket a lot the last few months. She's met someone and has been keeping it a secret for a long time. That's her business and I think it stemmed from her not feeling like she could announce it so close to when Peter was killed."

Mr. Kirkland nodded and rested his elbows on his knees. "But why does it seem like it's part of our case?"

"He might not be. But he's at least his own case to be figured out, because there are a few things that don't add up. She was at El Morocco when Finn and I were there and even when I talked about our evening, she never opened up about being there, too. So she's certainly keeping secrets. But the most worrisome part is that Ralph ran into them once coming out of the movies. Finn, do you know of an officer named Rafael Catalano? Goes by Raff?"

Finn shook his head and said, "No, but I can check around. Why, do you think he's a cop?"

"Actually, I don't. Valerie said he had a job working for a guy on Wall Street but was evasive about exactly what kind of job," I said, curling my legs up onto the cozy chair.

"Then why do you think I should ask around the department?" he asked.

I inhaled and said, "Because. Ralph said he was carrying a .38 special."

CHAPTER 58

"I can't believe you found me, Sparks," said the silky voice.

"After all this time," he said. "It's good to see you again, Daphne. You look amazing, like you haven't aged."

Daphne pulled on her silk stockings, then dropped her deep purple robe and stepped into her black dress. She went to her mirror at the dresser and touched up her lipstick.

She felt his gaze scanning her from head to toe, lingering on her breasts for a moment as she pulled her hair up and placed a gorgeous heather-gray hat upon her head and secured it with a hatpin topped with a large pearl. "Here, can you finish buttoning me up?" she asked, turning her back to him.

"Sure, doll." She looked at his reflection in the mirror as he came over to her, tucking his shirt into his pants. He still had a twitch once in a while after all those years, but his graying temples gave him a more sophisticated air and he still had a tight stomach and nice shoulders. His chest was nicely furred beneath that crisp black shirt.

She watched through the mirror as his capable hands buttoned the pearl buttons up to her neckline. "It's good to have you here again, Sparks."

"I'm glad I found you. I've been looking for years. I thought you might end up back here in New York."

He looked at her pale face, so full of long stories, determination, and . . . sometimes she scared him. When someone made her mad, her face looked like a mask of sorts. You got the feeling that something was lurking behind it. She was a deadly and precise executor of plans. She was beautiful, but also unpredictable. He found that arousing and they'd always been terrific partners.

In the mirror their gaze locked for a moment. Just behind those blue eyes of hers, something flickered.

He blinked, that equally hated and loved twitch of his. That was odd. Why did he twitch just then? He usually felt that twinge when he was agitated. Over the years it became a kind of sixth sense, when there was danger around or something he should brace himself for.

"Oh darling, you're a little twitchy tonight. Can I get you a nightcap?" she asked.

"Yeah, doll, a brandy if you have it."

"I've got everything," she purred. She went to the cabinet with crystal glasses and set them down. She picked up the brandy decanter and poured two fingers into each glass.

Sparks began to relax again. He reached for the brandy snifter she held out to him and enjoyed the rich aroma. He took a sip and then said, "You know, the other day I was looking for you at the Elmo."

"You were?" she asked as she went to the mirror again and checked her mascara, deciding to add a few more strokes.

"I was, I figured you might be there on Valentine's Day."

Her hand stopped in midbrush along her eyelashes. She repeated what he said. "Valentine's Day. No, I wasn't there." She carefully set down the mascara box.

He finished off his brandy and slung on his suit coat while slipping into his shoes.

"Yeah, funny thing. I almost had a heart attack," he chuckled.

"Oh?"

"Yeah, I swear I thought I saw Charlie. *Charlie!* Can you imagine?"

She slowed her breathing and raised her chin to look down her nose. "No, I can't imagine."

"Yeah," he said, warming to his subject. "I grabbed this gal's arm and even said stupidly, *Charlie?*" he said, mimicking his voice.

"She turned around and right away I realized my error. Funny timing, though, huh? It was right after that I found you."

Daphne handed him his hat and he said, "Thanks again, doll. You always did know how to show me a good time."

"Hmm, yes. Take care, Sparks, and I'll see you soon." She gave him a kiss on the cheek and he wavered for just a moment.

"You okay, doll?"

"Oh, I'm fine! You go on, now. Thanks for coming over."

"Okay. See you soon." He placed his hat carefully on his head and turned around.

As he walked to the door, Daphne carefully pulled the long hatpin out of place. Her feet padded along on the floor behind him.

As he reached the door, she whispered, "You shouldn't have gone to the Elmo."

His eye started to violently twitch.

CHAPTER 59

I decided to take a walk and look for books, a favorite pastime of mine. I had an unusually long lunch break because Fiorello was across town at a big meeting with his commissioners. I'd finished up my work and had a bit of time on my hands. I wanted to ruminate on this puzzle. Preferably while browsing for books.

So I headed to Book Row over on Fourth Avenue. I mean, six blocks with forty-eight bookstores, what's not to like? I headed over and saw my favorite book person just coming out of his store. "Hi, Ben! How are you?"

"Great, Lane! Looking for anything in particular today?" he asked pleasantly. Ben was about my age when he opened his first bookstore ten years ago, right before the Depression hit. But he made it, which is what drew me here just as much as the luscious books.

"Anything you think I should read? You know what I like and what I like to keep up on."

"Well . . . I have something that's a bit of a departure from what you usually like. But I promise, no thwarted love." He gave me a wink, knowing I loathed thwarted love more than anything. *Poetic sadness*. Bah!

"Sure! What is it?" I asked, already gazing fondly at three tomes that caught my eye.

"Sinclair Lewis's *It Can't Happen Here*. But come inside, I have to get it."

We walked into the happily messy place full to overflowing with books of all shapes, sizes, and ages.

"Hey there, Fred!" I said to the little guy stacking books pretty artfully. "Did your dad put you to work already?" I asked with a teasing tone.

"Oh, hi, Miss Sanders! No! I wish! I keep asking him, but he says I have to wait until I'm thirteen." He made a rude noise that made me laugh.

I watched his head swivel around the store with pride and under his breath he said, "But we need more books."

"Here you go, Lane!" Ben handed me the book and I flipped through the pages. My favorite thing about Lewis was not just that he was the first American to win the Nobel Prize in Literature, but that he had a gritty way of characterizing strong women in the workforce. I felt a kinship with them that I usually didn't feel with the typical females characterized by simpering, weak ankles, and always asking the lead man, "What should we do?" In real life, at least with the women in my life, I'd never heard a woman ask a man what they should do.

There had been a hubbub about this novel when it came out about a year and a half ago, but I hadn't read it. It didn't really grab my attention at the time.

"It's about a character who ends up winning over FDR as president, with a platform of getting America back to traditional values and patriotism. He makes a lot of promises that speak to all of us who are hurting and wanting a better life," summarized Ben.

"Sounds good, except for the part of beating Roosevelt," I said with a cocked eyebrow. Mrs. Roosevelt was a dear friend of Aunt Evelyn's.

"Well . . . here. I don't want to ruin it for you, so I'll just read the back cover blurb.

> "Vulgar, almost illiterate, a public liar easily detected
> . . . he was an actor of genius.
> A vain, outlandish, anti-immigrant, fear-mongering
> demagogue runs for President of the United States—
> and wins. Sinclair Lewis' chilling 1935 bestseller is

the story of Buzz Windrip, who promises the poor, angry voters that he will make America proud and prosperous once more, but takes the country down a darker path. As the new regime slides into authoritarianism, newspaper editor Doremus Jessop can't believe it will last—but is he right? This cautionary tale of liberal complacency in the face of populist tyranny shows it really can happen here."

I'd seen firsthand how easy it was for desperate people to overlook obvious duplicity if there was something winsome about a candidate, such as Jimmy Walker, New York's favorite wise-cracking mayor. Or if people wanted change at the risk of everything else, including working with organized crime. It sounded an awful lot like the man ruling Germany currently.

I grabbed the book and said, "You got me. I want it."

He laughed and tousled Fred's hair.

"Say, Fred," I asked. "Can you recommend an interesting volume of *Macbeth*?"

The youth rubbed his chin like a professor and replied in the professional voice of a forty-year-old, "I have just the thing. One moment, ma'am."

Ben and I exchanged amused glances as Fred eagerly ran off. He came back quick as a flash and handed me a slim volume in deep burgundy leather. *Macbeth* was embossed in gold across the cover.

"Ooh, that is just the thing. I'll take that, too."

On the way back to the office, I felt a presence sidle up next to me. Then two behind.

"Good day, Lane," growled the baritone voice of Uncle Louie.

I wasn't exactly excited at this friendship that had sprouted. But I was curious about why he found me.

"Hello, Mr. Venetti. Out for a stroll this fine winter day?" I asked, my footsteps clicking on the pavement that had been studiously shoveled.

"I do like a nice walk in the city," he said, his hands clasped behind him like an inspector. "There's no city like ours."

"I agree. I just bought a few new books," I said, wondering why I was chatting him up.

"Oh, which ones—" he started, but then cut himself off. You could always tell a book lover; no matter the nature of the man or woman, a book lover is incapable of tamping down the excitement of a new find. Venetti cleared his throat and said instead, "I have some news for you."

"Not a fan of the phone or messenger, huh?" I noted.

"You never know who might be listening in on the phones, Lane. And I never trust someone more than I trust myself for nuanced or important matters."

Made sense.

"So, remember that man you said mistook you for Charlie at the Elmo?"

"Sure, Mr. Kirkland said he used to work with him. Sparks, they called him."

"Yes, indeed. A radio man. I was aware that he'd worked with your parents and Kirkland. But I believe he may have been a double agent."

I stopped abruptly. "What do you mean?"

"His body was just found at a little hotel on the west side. He was murdered."

"*How?*"

"By hatpin to the base of the skull."

"God damn," I whispered, unconsciously rubbing the back of my neck.

"Yes. He would have died instantly. Whoever killed him knew what they were doing," he said as we started walking again.

"Do you know who killed him? You sound like you know." There was something about his tone. It wasn't a wondering kind of tone; it held a note of surety.

"Mmm," he rumbled. "I think I do. I don't have proof for your boss, Lane. But Daphne was always fond of hatpins. For hats, of course, but one time, she killed someone else like that."

I gave him a sidelong glance. "What's your past with Daphne, Mr. Venetti?" I asked with a cocked eyebrow.

"I'll have to debrief you on that at a later date. Suffice it to say,

I know what I'm talking about. But what I can't guess yet is why she would have killed Sparks."

"Well, let's see. Yes, he would've been a great weapon for her. If he in fact had been a double agent, the authorities were still unaware of that. He had to have done something that made her incensed enough to kill. Did he, uh . . . hmm, how to put this . . . ? Was he in a state of dishabille when he was found?"

Venetti made a funny noise, but said smoothly, "Actually, he was not indecent, but lacked enough thoroughly buttoned clothing that it would be easy to surmise that they'd had a romantic encounter."

I started ticking through the options. "Okay. She's irritated enough to kill. The reason was either personal, which I don't think she would have cared enough. Or it was professional and he made some kind of error. Big enough to cost him his life."

I glanced again at Venetti and he gave me a rare, full smile that made his black eyes dance. "Spot-on, Lane."

CHAPTER 60

"So you killed him?" asked Murk.

"Mm-hm," said Daphne as she wrinkled her nose and looked around at the ugly deli. She did not share Murk's fondness for his place of business, invisible or not.

Wulf's eyes darted back and forth as he tilted his derby hat down a little farther, trying to be invisible.

"Both Crusher and Sparks?" Murk asked, amusement written across his bland, greasy face.

She turned her head smoothly to him, her eyes piercing him with a displeased grimace.

Murk immediately stopped rubbing his stomach and sat up a bit straighter, wiping the grin from his face. Her face had a kind of mask on it that slipped occasionally. Nothing good came of that mask coming down. You wanted to do everything in your power to keep that nice and tight and secured in place. Part of his success was knowing how to do that.

Wulf sat back a little farther, desiring the shadows, not wanting any attention to be brought to himself.

Murk charged into the business at hand, shoulders down and as professional as he could be. "So, now that those two are out of the way, we need to work on the next step. I think we can get Finn Brodie out of the way and if we're lucky, Lane, as well."

"Oh no. Lane's mine. I made the mistake once of not finishing the job. I'm ending it," said Daphne, smiling like the Cheshire cat.

"Excellent. Anything you have in mind? Or will you do the job in conjunction with our mission?" He was pleased that his vocabulary rose to the occasion. Maybe watching some of those Perry Mason movies like his favorite, *The Case of the Velvet Claws*, was rubbing off. *The Case of the Stuttering Bishop* was coming out in June.

"Murk," she said with a bite, abruptly drawing his attention back. She took off her gray hat after slowly pulling out the long hatpin. They all knew where that had been recently. Murk swallowed hard. Wulf stopped breathing altogether, not wanting to move a muscle.

"Pay attention," she purred, pleased that she had him sweating. "I think it would be better to work at the same time as your plan. More diversions that way. Now. Where will this plan take place?" she asked.

"Okay." Murk stood up and walked over to his desk. "I think this will cause the most damage. We can take out Finn, blame it on racial tensions, and cause the most chaos possible. It's feasible. And the public will easily want to blame it on the anti-police sentiment in that community." He circled his paunch, pleased again that he sounded professional.

"Not bad. How?" she drawled.

"Here. We'll handle it here." He pulled out five tickets to the next night's performance. "They have tickets the same night. I had a tail on Lane."

Daphne's eyes glistened with possibility. As she took the tickets into her own hands, red glossy nails folding over the tickets, she whispered, "*Voodoo Macbeth*. Perfect."

CHAPTER 61

I slowly flipped through the family journal that my parents left me. I stopped on the page where my mother was wearing the same white gown and snowy mink stole that I had worn the night we went to the El Morocco. Her hand was flung out to the right, her face alight with imagination and the love of life.

My heart ached a little that her life had been snuffed out so early. That she hadn't been able to fully realize those dreams and desires that were written all over her countenance. Uncle Louie Venetti, infamous mobster, was standing with her, most definitely a member of her party. I could not escape the fact that he knew something.

Because there was definitely something tying together that Sparks character and his subsequent death via Daphne's own hand, and me and my mother. It seemed too coincidental that he was murdered directly after her night at the Elmo. *What else had happened that night besides my dance with Venetti?*

We went to Ophelia and the girl in the red dress had been mistaken for me. We apprehended the guy who tried to kidnap her, devising a way to distract Finn and take out another NYPD officer.

I was nearing the answer. I felt tingly as I leaned over to the side table next to my green velvet chair and took my glass of red wine into my hands. It was on the tip of my tongue, at the tip of memory, elusive and tantalizing.

I looked down at the photograph of my mom, her divine white

dress that fit like a dream. Her face. Her hidden intentions and clever abilities. She knew something.

Charlie.

The night of the Elmo, I had two encounters of mistaken identity. One with the girl in the red dress. The other, Sparks had grabbed my arm. Shortly after, he was murdered. This was about my mom.

He knew Charlie. He let me know that he was acquainted with Charlie.

And Daphne did not want me to know that.

CHAPTER 62

His glossy, behemoth desk was like the altar. Supplicants entered, made their claims, and he either doled out grace or wrath or direction.

Today, his closest, most-favored man entered in.

"Mr. Venetti, you called for me?" he asked, his long legs folding down as he took the low chair before the dais.

"Indeed." Venetti took out a cigar, lit it, and began to puff while keeping an eye on the deep blue orbs watching him intently. "We need to be watchful the next few days. I think Daphne will be making her move soon."

"I agree. I've got people on City Hall, the townhouse, the main precinct, and a couple of other haunts that I've heard they might go to for entertainment."

"Which ones are those?" asked Venetti, hoping to get a feel for any inkling pointing him in the right direction. "We need to get ahead of that woman," he said with a snarl.

"Let's see, for sure that little place in Little Italy, Copioli's. Their favorite movie theater. Can't hurt to keep an eye on Radio City Music Hall given Lane's history with that place. And lastly, *Voodoo Macbeth* at the Majestic Theater in Brooklyn."

"That's it. That's the one."

"What do you mean?"

Venetti leaned back in his chair, reaching out crossed ankles onto his desk and puffing with a sublime look on his face. "Don't worry about the other places. That's where she's aiming. I know it."

"All right, sir. I'll focus our efforts there."

"Good job. We need to end it. She's been a thorn in my side for too long," he growled. "Charlie died knowing we didn't finish her off. And I'm the only one left besides yourself that knows the truth. Everything to stop the Red Scroll from beginning again in earnest depends on us stopping her. At *Voodoo Macbeth*."

His guest stood abruptly with resolution. "I'm on it. You can count on me."

His guest walked out and left Venetti alone, puffing his cigar. He decided to pour himself a bourbon as he ruminated on the days ahead and all that was at stake. Out loud, to no one but himself, he uttered the famous words from *Macbeth* . . .

"Out, out, brief candle! Life's but a walking shadow, a poor player, that struts and frets his hour upon the stage, and then is heard no more."

CHAPTER 63

We arrived at the Majestic Theater. The sky was heavy and gray, snuffing out the stark white glow of the winter moon. The snowy weight of the clouds created a ceiling like a thick blanket over us. The golden windows of nearby buildings surrounded us, but in spite of feeling the excitement of the night, of a time that I had anticipated for Finn and for me and the Battles, I felt a tremor of anxiety.

A string of past moments where I'd felt a strange apprehension flooded my memory. I remembered the static of the air outside of the deli before Peter was killed. Another time when an escaped convict arranged his getaway and Roarke and I came upon the scene with an eerie stillness. The time I walked into Daphne's room at the lunatic asylum for the first time, when her mask came crashing down. I couldn't escape those old ghosts. They were with me like Banquo's ghost was with Macbeth.

Finn, whose arm was linked with mine, must've felt the shiver that went down my spine. He said, "You cold, Lane? Here . . ." He put his arm around me, pulling me close as we walked to the theater with thousands of others, the marquee announcing *Voodoo Macbeth* in rippling lights. Maybe I was feeling these strange emotions because of the realization that Finn would be seeing this after his time facing his parents and his extremely close call in England.

I caught Big Sam's eye and we exchanged a grim smile. He must've felt the charge in the air compared to our last time at the play, too. But in an instant, the spell of anxiety was broken with a ray of sunshine in human form.

"Lane! So good to see you again!" greeted Orson Welles, his face alight with indefatigable energy. "We are nearing the end of our run. I tried to keep it going longer, but it's time to move on, I guess." We all greeted him with handshakes and hugs.

"Say, Lane, come backstage when you can. You're here early enough, I'd love to introduce you to some of the cast," said Orson, eyes ablaze with excitement.

"I'd love that!" I gushed, squeezing Finn's hand in delight.

We joined the masses and headed into the full house. The sounds and sights filled us with the joy that only going to a theater performance can give. Anticipation, art, everyone all dolled up, instruments tuning, programs being handed out, seats taken, waiting for the lights to dim.

"Hey, there's Roarke. He made it," I said, leaning close to Finn. Sam and Florence had an extra ticket and offered it to us. I waved to Roarke as he wound his way over through the crowd. I greeted him with a hug and Finn stood to clasp his hand. He took the seat next to Finn.

I leaned over to Florence next to me and said, "Thanks for the ticket. He'd been dying to come."

"I can tell," she said impishly, looking at Roarke's full dimples, grinning happily to finally be here. I clasped her hand warmly, filled with the pleasure of the whole event and good friends.

The lights flickered and everyone hurried to take their seat. The air grew even more excited, then the house lights went down. The curtain opened to an eerie stage with jungle vines, earthy rhythms of drums being pounded, and a throne with skeletons wrapped around . . .

By the pricking of my thumbs, something wicked this way comes . . .

The witches' speech had always rippled with the delight of spectral thrills and chills. But tonight, I felt an apprehensive tingle through my spine like a cold blast of wind that escaped a door and sent shivers through your entire body. I looked around the dark theater as if I could possibly glimpse anything. It was futile, but I had the distinct impression that someone was watching me.

I took a sidelong glance at Finn, whose face was already fully rapt. I smiled, the odd sensation dissipating quickly against the warmth of his delight. The fact that he got to bring this full circle, after all he'd battled in London and worrying about being charmed, cursed. Dealing with the betrayal of his family and the injustice he'd faced. Then defeating it. *What a night.* I sat back in the velvet chair and allowed my heart and mind to be swept up into the magic of the next few hours.

Welles had changed the witch's role to a male voodoo priest and I'd never, ever forget his closing line. I glanced at Finn, knowing what this line would mean to him. At the very end of the play, as the seconds ticked toward the final moment, the voodoo priest came to the front of the stage, aglow with theater lights that couldn't compare to his own inner light. With bated breath, we awaited that final line, that final curtain. With all-knowing eyes and a radiant countenance, the voodoo priest declared, "The charm's wound up!"

The entire audience leaped to our feet. I'd never known such an ending to a play. The audience shook the theater with applause and cheers. I looked at Florence and Sam, to whom this first all-black and extremely successful production meant the world, their genuine pleasure shining through their glistening eyes. I turned to Finn, who was also completely taken with the whole thing. He clapped with vigor, trying to give back the thanks and appreciation with his clamorous applause. He turned to me and we shared that powerful moment with moisture rimming our eyes and joy filling our hearts. Finn looked valiant.

I took an enormous breath, trying to cement this moment into my mind, forever. All the inspiration, the satisfaction, and the wholeness of excellent art.

Just then, a man came down the aisle and quickly dropped a note into Finn's hand, then left precipitously. Finn read it and turned to me. "Love, the note's from a contact. I need to go have a chat with him. I'll be right back."

He quickly kissed my hand that he'd taken up as he told me about the message. "Okay, I'll meet you out in the lobby."

A motion caught my eye and Orson was waving at me, trying to get my attention. I mouthed to him, *Now?* He nodded happily and I asked Roarke if he'd like to go backstage with me. Florence and Sam declined, having already enjoyed that tour with Orson. We told them we'd all rejoin in the lobby, then Roarke and I went with giddy steps toward our tour guide.

We met Maurice Ellis, Macbeth. And Charles Collins as Macduff, Canada Lee, who played Banquo, and Edna Thomas as Lady Macbeth. I was the most excited to meet Eric Burroughs, the voodoo priest, who had trained at London's Royal Academy. I still got chills thinking of that last line.

Orson took us around to all of the fabulous actors and stage technicians. At last, the ruckus behind the stage began to die down as costumes were changed, makeup was taken off, and the stage cleared and prepped for the next performance.

The backstage was a dark labyrinth full of ropes, curtains, and miscellaneous stage equipment. As we wound our way around, having seen every nook and cranny that Orson wanted to point out to us in detail, he said, "Oh, hold on a second." He quickly disappeared on the hunt for something else interesting to show us.

Roarke said, "Quirky kind of guy, huh?" I chuffed a laugh but there was a long silence. The laughter and mayhem of the stage slowly drew to an eerie stop. Roarke put his hands in his pockets and swayed forward and back on his toes as we waited. The silence grew thicker and I looked askance at Roarke, wondering where the heck our tour guide went. Knowing him, Orson may have just gotten distracted.

Then the lights went out.

CHAPTER 64

F inn got out to the lobby, right on the heels of his contact who had brought the note. "What's going on?" he asked.

"It's going down now. Here."

Finn's eyes shot back to the theater, the crowds were flooding into the lobby. He couldn't make out Lane or Roarke. He waved down Sam, his head a good six inches over the crowd and easily spotted.

"Sam, we've got trouble," said Finn with a nod toward the stage.

"*This* is your contact? How'd that happen?" sputtered Sam incredulously.

"Long story. But he says they're going to go after me here. *Now*."

"Oh, shit," muttered Sam, a hand rubbing his mouth and chin, contemplating the venue and just how hard it would be to keep it all under control.

"Don't worry," said Finn. "I have a plan."

"Actually . . ." said Sam. "So do I. I need to go talk to Jane Bolin. I just spotted her."

CHAPTER 65

"Roarke?" I said in hushed tones. *Nothing.* I slowly walked backward to the wall.

What was going on? I wondered. I immediately recalled the moment at the beginning of the play when I had the distinct feeling we were being watched. *Oh no. What if Murk's crew tracked us down and they're trying to take out Finn here?* My mind raced through the possibilities. The more I thought about it, the more sense it made. They could easily make an incident here look like a racial disturbance which was already a powder keg.

Anger spread heat right through me, ticked off that they could take something so good, so trailblazing, and taint it . . . it made my blood boil. My hands blindly tried to locate a light switch, a closet to get a safer vantage point, anything.

I went around a corner, completely losing my sense of direction. I felt a rope and followed it down to where it held a sand bag. My heart was beating fast and loud; I was certain anyone could hear it. A trickle of sweat broke out on my forehead. I tried to maintain my calm and slowed my breathing. I tried another wall, finding yet another corner, and walked carefully around it, arms out, trying not to crash into something. Still no sign of Roarke. There was something about being in the dark that fed absolute panic. It was the same thing that made you want to race up the stairs from a basement when a light was extinguished. The fear of something behind you that you couldn't see.

I suddenly stilled; something was coming. There wasn't a sound, the air was close with just a slight whisper of a breeze. I waited. The scent of a particular perfume wafted to me.

Daphne was here.

CHAPTER 66

Sam and Finn separated, they'd come back together in the lobby after they'd met with their people. Finn sent his contact to get word to the mayor with their location and the plan, then Fio would get the department on it.

Finn took off his suit coat and rolled his sleeves. He took his gun from his shoulder holster, making sure it was prepped. He hoped he wouldn't need it. Suddenly, a footstep fell not too far away. In a flash, Finn had his gun leveled.

"Who are you?" he growled. It didn't look like any of Murk's guys that he knew of.

The tall, black-haired man with a hawk-like nose had his hands raised, despite the fact that he clearly had a gun. But it remained holstered. He said, "I was sent to lend a hand."

"What?"

"My boss has a vested interest in a common enemy of ours," he said, keeping his hands nice and high.

Finn's mind raced through scenarios and the crews of the criminals he tracked down. *Ah, that's it,* he thought. The guy's mouth twitched a little as he saw Finn's look of recognition. Finn said, "Venetti thinks Daphne might be here." It wasn't a question.

The guy gave a curt nod. Finn lowered his gun a fraction, but said, "How do I know you're his guy?"

"Venetti said you'd need proof. So he said to tell you that he knew you were watching when he danced with Lane at the Elmo.

That he respected that you knew she was safe, that you let them continue their talk."

Finn raised an eyebrow as he considered.

"And I do have this." Some of the higher-up guys with Venetti were given a gold ring with the Venetti crest on it. He waggled his right hand for Finn to see.

"All right," said Finn, lowering his gun completely. He also knew that if the guy had wanted to take him out, he could have from afar already. By the time Finn had seen him, he could have easily shot him if that had been his aim. "What's your name?" he asked, coming closer.

"Rafael Catalano. Call me Raff."

Sweet Jesus.

CHAPTER 67

O, full of scorpions is my mind!

—Macbeth, *Macbeth*

The scent of that perfume didn't bring about just any fear, it was primal. The desire to panic that I'd had before in the dark, alone and lost in the maze that was the backstage, was nothing compared to what I felt now.

I was still holding my breath, my lungs burning. I slowly let it out, my heart thumping, shaky. Everything was silent. The scent grew stronger.

I gingerly bent down, gently feeling around for anything that might help me. I tried not to knock anything over or make a sound. I found some bottles and more sand bags. Then I felt a smooth, metal rectangle that was a hefty weight in my palm. I flipped the lid. I had an idea.

I carefully took off my shoes so my footsteps would be stealthy. I retrieved my dagger from its silken holster in the wide belt of my skirt. I rubbed the pearl handle with my thumb like a lucky rabbit's foot. I held it in my left hand, the heavy rectangle in my right, the cap flipped off and ready.

It was still pitch black, I was unable to see my hand before my face. A whisper of wind came from behind me, which probably meant a door. I faintly heard voices coming from the theater, but most people had already left. The actors were quick in getting their street clothes on, ready to go have some fun after the show. I eased my way toward that door, fighting the frantic notion that I should run screaming.

A voice somewhere nearby echoed all around me. "Hello, Lane."

My heart stopped. I braced myself, raised the Zippo lighter, and lit it, hoping the flare would startle her. I let out a yelp as Daphne's white face lit up within a couple feet of my own. I threw the lighter right at her face. It smashed her nose with a *crunch* as I turned and fled past her, having seen a doorway in the split second of light.

She growled with rage and pain, which spurred me on, reminding me she was just human. Horrifying. But just human.

I gripped my dagger, point down, ready. I'm not sure I could actually stab someone, but I would be very willing to throw it at that damn woman.

I found the doorway. I slipped through, and felt it before I heard it. Searing pain hit the outside of my arm, spinning me around with the force. The bullet hit the wall in front of me, having deeply grazed my arm. Daphne was behind about fifteen feet. I scrambled down the hallway, skittering around corners, holding my arm. The pain could easily make me pass out, but I kept my anger near the surface to keep me moving, forcing myself to think of the people I cared about the most. Here in the building.

CHAPTER 68

A gun went off. Raff and Finn shot their eyes to each other and simultaneously turned and ran in the direction of that sound.

Fear ripped through Finn, knowing Daphne was here, knowing she had it out for Lane. What did Lane know? Why was Daphne desperate to get her out of the way after all these years?

He and Raff stopped at the edge of the stage right entrance. There were hallways like a dark maze leading off into several directions. They went toward the back, the darkest parts. After passing countless curtains and ropes and costume racks, they heard a shuffling sound behind a doorway. He nodded to Raff as they each took one side of the door. Raff kicked it open and they both surged in.

"Roarke!" Finn grabbed the gag from his mouth and quickly unbound him as Raff kept watch.

"Daphne's here. It was Murk who grabbed me. I managed to get a couple of punches in, but he knocked me out." Finn saw a broken lamp in shatters on the ground, Murk's obvious weapon of choice. "Who the hell is that?" asked Roarke, nodding to Raff.

"Long story. On our side. Let's go."

The three of them raced out of the room, but came to a standstill at a corridor that was pitch black, as staunch as a brick wall. Finn lit a match to give them a little vision, in hopes of finding a fuse box or a main switch to get the lights back on.

Raff said, "There! I'll get it." The match went out just as Raff reached the large handle. With a *chunk*, the lights came back on.

"Roarke, I sent word to Fio and the department. Go meet them! We'll find Lane," said Finn urgently. Roarke nodded and raced out.

As Roarke left, Raff came back. He and Finn looked around, getting their bearings. Over to the right, directly behind the main stage, was a door. With blood on it.

CHAPTER 69

False face must hide what the false heart doth know.

—Macbeth, *Macbeth*

The lights came on.

I dodged into a dark closet and closed the door, bolting it shut. *Bam!* Daphne slammed up against the door in total fury. I hit the ground and slithered as far to the side as possible, ready for her gun to shoot up the door. Instead, I heard a frustrated grunt as she hit the door with her fists. Then silence.

After a few moments, I crept over and looked out the bottom slit. There weren't any shadows or feet waiting. I knew her; she'd have shot up the door if she could. She must've had to run off. Either I had reinforcements coming or she had a bigger job to finish.

Finn. He was the main goal; I was probably the frosting on the cake. I put my ear to the slit under the door, trying with all my might to hear anything that gave it away that Daphne might be lying in wait.

If she was there, I didn't want anything to give it away that I was coming out, giving her time to prepare. So I threw the bolt and charged out the door, knife slashing. The hall was empty. I spotted a pile of fabric, waiting to be made into a costume. I ripped a long piece and wrapped it around my throbbing arm, tying a knot and pulling it tight with my teeth. The pain bit through me, but I managed to keep silent, clenching my jaw.

I was on the stage left side. I knew there were more people

around by the sounds I was hearing, but I didn't know who. A bird's-eye view would be helpful. I looked up at the catwalk above me. *That'll do.*

I started up the rickety stairs that were steep enough to be considered a ladder. I made it to the metal catwalk, happy to have just stockings on my feet instead of noisy shoes. I carefully crept along, getting the view behind the stage that I'd craved. Far to the back on the left, I saw two men that I swear were Finn and a stranger. Maybe Finn found another officer in the crowd. They were carefully stepping around stage props and weaving through the numerous curtains.

On the other side, I watched as Murk and the mean derby-hatted guy made their way closer to Finn, guns drawn. But where was Daphne? She couldn't be far. I caught a swish of light blond hair in a spotlight maybe twenty feet from that guy with Finn. Daphne glimpsed something of interest, and bent over. With one hand she grabbed what turned out to be a stage dummy. She threw it down savagely.

That was it. I'd seen her do that very thing once before. I figured it out. *Hot damn.* I took one more look at the three separate parties, all moving around in the semi-dark stage lighting like rats in a maze.

If I yelled out, I could give Finn some warning, but I'd also give away my position.

"Finn! Two at your twelve o'clock, Daphne at six!"

I ducked down as a bullet went whizzing past. *She's such a bitch.* I clambered along and found the stairs farthest from Daphne. I practically slid down them. Daphne's main objective was supposed to get Finn, but from her savage state, I was pretty sure her emotion would override her logic and compel her to do what she wanted most. Finish me off.

I wound my way toward Finn and away from Daphne. I knew the general way, but once again right within the winding passages, it was easy to get lost. I figured it out, increasing speed to try to get to them, but then came to a skittering stop, my stockinged feet slipping on the floor. Despite my best efforts, Murk and that Mr.

Wulf with the derby hat had Finn and his partner cornered with Daphne cackling behind. I hid behind a red settee, hoping the shadows gave me some cover.

Murk was trying to take the lead. "We need to take Finn out back. We have to make sure it looks like one of them did it, but we may as well kill the other one here."

I was seething. Knowing what their wretched plan was, and the fact that Finn was within reach of that woman. Suddenly, several things happened all at once. I viciously threw my dagger as hard as I could, Wulf suddenly turned to *Murk* and backed him into the corner, and a door opened with Sam and two other officers, guns leveled.

My dagger hit Daphne in the shoulder, slamming her to the floor so hard, a hidden trap door opened and she fell through. I got to the hole in the floor and saw her scamper away, holding her arm, the blood on her chest matching the blood on her nose from my lighter.

I couldn't figure out who was working with who, but it seemed like the good guys were winning and all I knew was I needed to get Daphne. Roarke bounded in and yelled, "They're on their way!"

"Who?" barked Finn.

"Everyone."

"She's going toward the front of the building. Come on!" I yelled. We all ran toward the front. The police had the front doors secured, so we raced up the wide theater stairs on either side as if we were going to the balcony seats. Up one more flight. There stood Daphne, bloody, disheveled . . . and smiling. Finn raised his gun, but she ducked to the side and ran up the next set of stairs.

We ran up after her, then a loud crash echoed through the place. When we reached the topmost level, she was waiting for us with her face radiating great expectation. She was standing in the broken-out window.

CHAPTER 70

Here's the smell of the blood still.
All the perfumes of Arabia will not sweeten this little hand.

—Lady Macbeth, *Macbeth*

We all came to an abrupt stop. Daphne had no gun in her hand and one arm was holding the place where she had yanked my dagger out of her shoulder. I spotted it lying underneath the window with a coating of her blood smeared across the smooth blade. The window was at least twelve feet tall with the middle panes able to swing out. She'd smashed the window open with something big like a chair. Now she stood there, glaring at us with a tantalizing smile.

The mask over the face that could be lovely at times had faltered. Now she looked like that time I'd first met her at Metropolitan Hospital Lunatic Asylum. Little veins had popped to the surface of her paper-white skin. The look in her eyes made me wonder again if she could summon both lunacy and lucidity at will.

"Stop, it's over," commanded Finn.

It was like she didn't even hear him; she only had eyes for me. "You remembered, didn't you?" she said silkily.

I nodded. "Yes. You're through. It's done."

She shook her head a little dreamily and looked around like a child in a fanciful dream. She said with a singsong voice, "Tomorrow, and tomorrow, and tomorrow . . . oh, it's not over." Finn and Roarke and I all exchanged dubious glances.

Then she leveled her gaze at me, skewering me with her eyes.

Her voice lowered and she said solemnly, "Oh, I'll be seeing you again, Lane. Soon."

She jumped.

We raced to the broken window and looked below a few stories. There stood four men holding a life net.

"Oh my God," said Roarke. "Like the one we saw outside the asylum against the wall."

Daphne got up from the net and yelled up to us, "I told you. I'll see you soon, darling."

Finn tried shooting down toward them, but he only could get off a couple shots before they scurried away.

All three of us leaned back from the window and looked at each other with wonder.

I said, "I loathe her. But I really admire her contingency plans."

Finn and Roarke barked out a laugh. Finn looked at the bloody bandage around my arm. "We better get you looked at. The bullet must've just grazed you, otherwise you'd be in much worse shape."

"Yeah, I saw the bullet hit the door. My arm's not going to look too good in my sleeveless dresses anymore," I said with a forlorn grimace.

"Oh, I wouldn't worry about that," said Finn as he came up close to me as Roarke descended the stairs. "I think you're the sexiest thing I've ever seen. Inside and out."

Good thing. I was never going to be a dainty flower. I'd dated plenty of guys who wanted a woman to pretty much never use her brain or her courage. I was bored within seconds. Finn was different, which made the air fairly sizzle when I was near him.

We made our way down the stairs in time to catch up with Sam and his officers, not to mention almost the entire cast of *Voodoo*. In front of them all stood a formidable woman with her arms crossed, ready for battle. Sam had the wretched and sweaty Eugene Murk in custody. Just as we made it to the front entrance, in barged all the reinforcements I could ever want.

Fiorello was first in line, bellowing and screeching, followed by about twenty officers. They all came to a staggering halt in front of us. I looked at Sam and shook my head, giving him a wink. Murk looked like a greasy rag doll in the grasp of such a large and competent officer.

"What is going on?" yelled Fio.

Finn and Sam took over and gave them all the rundown, mostly that they needed to get after Daphne. Fio dispatched several of the officers with him to go and set up an APB.

Fio turned to Sam and said, "You've had a hand in yet another fine job, Mr. Battle." He shook Sam's hand and said, "I have some big plans for you, Big Sam. And Mrs. Jane Bolin. Nice to see you, as well. I'd love to have your legal ear on this matter. My office tomorrow?"

That formidable woman gave him a smile and a nod that spoke volumes.

Finn relayed to the very interested, large group the gist of the evening's events. That Murk's crew planned to take out a cop and have it blamed on the black crowd. That when Sam and his men pulled together, it was Jane, a top-notch lawyer, who put two and two together. She figured that a murder of a white cop at the event that showcased the country's first all-black theater cast would be absolutely incendiary to the city and the already tenuous race relations.

The white cops and the black cops and the black theater cast all looked at each other. I could only imagine the depths of all that was going through their minds. Sam put one giant hand on Finn's shoulder and then on Jane's and said, "It's been fun working with you two. Let's all grab a beer." Then he chuckled that deep, rumbling laugh of his that caught like wildfire to the entire group. They all started to meld together, sharing the great story of the night together before they headed out for beers.

Lastly, we took Fio aside and filled him in on Daphne and her acrobatic escape. I took a good look at Fio and said, "You brought your trumpet?"

"It's a cornet, Lane. And yes. Just in case I needed it." Just like he did with the dethroning of the Artichoke King. You couldn't say my boss didn't have style.

Finn waved over a medic to take a look at my arm, which was really painful now that all the adrenaline was wearing off. But before I went in for stitches, I had to find out one more thing.

"Finn, so was derby hat guy—Mr. Wulf—working with you all along? And wait, what is his first name? I just can't keep calling him Mr. Wulf," I said.

"Muldoon."

That's not at all what I expected.

"Muldoon Wulf," I repeated.

Finn pursed his lips, nodding as he said, "Yep. Muldoon."

I shook my head. "I see why he goes by Mr. Wulf. So, again, was Mr. Muldoon Wulf working with you all along?"

With a smug grin, he said, "No, in fact I just recently turned him. I got to thinking about being so utterly hoodwinked in London, I needed to go on the offensive. And when I learned about that Sparks character possibly being a double agent, I began to think through who might be susceptible to a little bit of direction. To maybe change sides."

Fio happily bounced on his toes and responded, "Just goes to show, an S of a B *can* change his spots. Marvelous. Just marvelous." He went over to Mr. Wulf and shook his hand. The mean look that was still resident on his face began to melt away a tiny bit as he and the mayor had a good talk. I expect there was more to Muldoon than met the eye. There's always more to people than what you see on the surface, even the ones you relegated to bad apples.

"Say, Finn, who was that tall guy you were working with in the theater? Where'd he go? Was he one of your cops?" I asked, looking around.

Fio was called away, but Finn obviously remembered a seemingly interesting tidbit about the evening and shot a look to Roarke, who'd joined us. Roarke started to turn around as if not wanting to be part of that conversation.

I said, "Oh, no you don't! Get back here. What's this about?"

Roarke and Finn both took a big breath and put their hands on their hips. "Oh boy," I said, not liking the look of this. "Spit it out."

Finn took one last look at Roarke and said, "He's with Venetti.

Said Venetti had him keeping an eye on us, and that he had a vested interest in Daphne. So he'd work with us to take her down."

"Go on. That's clearly not the punch line," I said.

Finn cleared his throat. "His name is Rafael Catalano. Raff."

"I'm gonna kill her," I said. "Val's gotten herself involved in Venetti's world?" I tried to raise my hands to my hips in indignation, but pain shot through my arm so badly, black spots started to mar my vision.

"Whoa! Take it easy, love," said Finn as he swooped me up into his arms before I completely fell down. "Come on, let's get you to the ambulance. You need some fluids and some stitches."

His face was a mask of concern. I was still coherent enough to enjoy his chest. I think I mumbled *mmmm* again, because he laughed his silent chuckle that shook that nice chest. I rested my head contentedly on him, deciding it was okay to give in to the fatigue just then.

As he made his way to the ambulance, with the sirens blaring in the distance, people milling around, and me in Finn's arms, I was taken right back to the end of our last case where I was in a similar situation. That case tied together with this one, and with Daphne's parting words to us, I was certain there was more to come.

CHAPTER 71

I had to be admitted overnight at the hospital so that they could watch my arm for infection. I tried to talk the doctors out of it, but they wouldn't listen. Finn stayed with me, which made that pill a lot easier to swallow.

Aunt Evelyn and Mr. Kirkland wanted to come, but it was so late, the visiting hours were way past. The only reason Finn was allowed was because he was police. Plus, I did have a maniac on the loose who wanted to kill me. I was perfectly fine with heightened police presence in my life.

The next morning my arm felt much better and the doctors were relieved that there was no redness or swelling. Infections killed an awful lot of people, it was nothing to sneeze at. Finn drove me home to a warm greeting. I swear, Mr. Kirkland looked like he was about to swoop me up and carry me up all those stairs like he did one other time.

"I'm good! Really, don't worry. Just a little tired and my arm is starting to itch."

"Well, that's good, Lane. Means it's healing," said Aunt Evelyn, a relieved arm around my shoulders as I walked up the stairs to our townhouse.

I greeted Ripley and he refused to leave my side the rest of the day, even lying directly on my feet most of the time. I loved that dog.

For dinner, we had a council of war. Mr. Kirkland made a pork roast with pan-browned potatoes and gravy. The seasoning and roasting pork filled the house with good smells and the promise of friends coming to share in it all.

After a meal and a lot of wine, we all sat down in the parlor. Roarke and Finn; Evelyn and Kirkland; Morgan, Sam, Fiorello, and myself. Over coffee we discussed the case and worked out all the kinks.

Fio, fairly bouncing in his seat, said, "So let me summarize." Mr. Kirkland and Aunt Evelyn exchanged amused glances while Finn put an arm around my shoulders and softly toyed with the curls of my hair. I eased farther into him, enjoying his warmth and familiarity.

Fiorello crossed his legs and said in a formal sort of voice, "In order to gain control of the pinball and slots market, forcing the police to leave them alone, Murk and Crusher worked out the cop-killing threat. But their overall boss was Daphne, probably a remnant of Rex's work. She was shoring up her work here, starting to make money again, making that branch of their business profitable."

Morgan spoke up, "So it's confirmed, she really did go to Europe for a reason, not to just lead you on a wild-goose chase."

"Right," said Finn. "We know she was reestablishing contact with underground criminal networks in England, but she wasn't starting up business there. Which is smart, because the money is in the States right now and looks to remain so for a while until everyone figures out Germany's stance and whether Hitler will be sated. If ever."

Sam said, "But what I still don't understand is why Daphne had such a vested interest in Lane after all these years? I know she tried to kill you when you were ten, Lane, but why now?"

I was warming to the subject because I hadn't told anyone what I'd learned yet. *I so enjoy a good reveal.*

"I finally figured it out. In the theater," I said with relish.

Morgan and Fio sat forward eagerly, ready for the story.

"Well, a little while ago, I caught the scent of what turned out to be her perfume. I had smelled it before and that memory stopped me in my tracks. It was a terrifying feeling, and all I remembered was a syringe and being frightened. At the theater, when Daphne was looking for me, I watched her grab a stage dummy lying on the floor, then viciously throw it back down."

I paused, then said meaningfully, "I had seen her do that before." I looked around my rapt audience and continued. "You know how I saw her leering over me with a pillow, that green hat on her head at the hospital after the accident? At the theater I remembered that same day; in fact, right before she came into my room, I had turned my head as I was lying in the bed. I remember my neck had been so sore. I could see Rutherford in his bed in the next room over. I watched as Daphne took a syringe and plunged it into Rutherford. *Her husband.* Then she yanked him up by the collar, just like that dummy, and threw him back down on the bed.

"Before I remembered this, I'd always assumed he died right away in the lake, but he'd survived a while like me, didn't he?" I asked.

Mr. Kirkland was rubbing his chin in thought. "Yeah. Yeah, Lane, he sure did. He died of a heart attack in the hospital. Everyone thought it was just complications from the fall into the lake. My God."

Roarke said, "But after all these years, why does she care? She could've killed you ages ago. Why now the sudden interest?"

"I'm not sure yet. Back then, maybe she thought I'd rat her out. But it was clear right away that I hadn't remembered anything. Besides, who'd trust what a ten-year-old just coming out of a coma would say? But now . . . I don't know. And my mom was involved in that somehow. It's just too much of a coincidence that Sparks called me Charlie by mistake and then she killed him soon after. Daphne's not interested in me bringing her to justice on the murder of Rutherford. It has to do with something that makes her job a lot harder *now.*"

Finn nodded and said thoughtfully, "Back then, she wasn't Rex's heir yet. That could also be a reason for renewed interest in what you could bring to light, Lane. Now she's in charge. Now maybe that memory is damaging to her."

There was one person I could ask.

Fio said suddenly, "Oh, no you don't. You are not going to go have a chat with Uncle Louie, Lane Sanders."

Finn's eyes shot to me. How did Fio know that's what I was thinking?

"Don't even ask how I know. I just do. And no." Fio thumped the arm of his chair as an exclamation point to his statement.

"Well, we can't just invite him to City Hall," I said. "And he has those answers. He'd always known my mother, and I'm not sure how or why, but they had a kind of relationship. And he said he had a vested interest in Daphne, always calls her *that woman* with particular disgust."

"Well . . ." said Morgan with an intriguing air. "Maybe we *can* invite him to City Hall."

"What?" bellowed Fio.

Young Morgan gazed upon us with her forty-year-old smug smile. "We can invite him to meet with us at City Hall subway station."

CHAPTER 72

Two days later, after all the mother hens felt my arm had healed enough, we filed down to the City Hall subway stop. That particular stop is the one I take a few times every week. And there just happen to be gorgeous arches and marble halls, areas that make a fantastic place to pull over and have an unobtrusive meeting with someone.

Everyone was stationed all around, with Mr. Kirkland and I the main ones whom Venetti would meet with. But Morgan and her crew were peppered here and there; Roarke, Fio and Evelyn were not to be left out and were ambling around as if tourists; and of course an agitated detective was on the scene who felt that this was all way out of control.

Right on time, down the steps came a large man with salt 'n' pepper hair and caterpillar eyebrows, followed by two bodyguards, including the guy who was presumably my best friend's boyfriend.

"Good morning, Kirkland. Lane. I do hope your arm is feeling better. Raff filled me in on your rather spectacular night at the theater," he rumbled.

"Thank you, Mr. Venetti. Yes, my arm is feeling better. And thank you for sending Raff along that night." I glanced at Raff and his deep blue eyes held a grateful smile, even though the rest of him was on guard. He was very tall and capable looking and his Roman nose was very attractive.

"Wait a minute," I said abruptly with a raspy voice, trying not to scare all my friends who were on guard. "You're the one who pulled me back from the curb when Daphne hit Crusher outside of Radio City Music Hall."

Kirkland shot his eyes to me and then to Raff. Venetti and Raff exchanged glances. Venetti said, "Let's walk a little. I'll fill you in."

As we slowly strolled, his hands once again behind his back like an inspector, Uncle Louie said, "I've had Raff following you for the same reason that I believe you're here to talk with me. You and I are frequently on the same page, Lane."

"Grrrrrrr," growled Mr. Kirkland quietly.

I dashed a quick look to him, wrinkling my nose and shaking my head. I held up my thumb and forefinger, mouthing the words, *Just a little.* He rolled his eyes.

"So you know why Daphne has had me in her sights . . ." I said.

"Yes. I'm hoping you can fill in some gaps for me, but I figured a little extra help watching you was a good idea. It all goes back to Rex. He started this, and his own avarice is what ended his organization as he saw it."

Kirkland remained quiet, taking it all in. Venetti saw that we were hooked and wanted to know more, so he continued. "As you know, he was constantly toying with people. Making them believe they were highly esteemed, and the next day had them executed on the turn of a dime. It created the fear and mayhem he craved, but over time, it also created a monster."

"Daphne," I whispered. Rex had created a Mr. Hyde, just like in *Jekyll and Hyde.* Someone consumed and enslaved by the darkness.

"Mm," he grunted in acknowledgment. "Rex had been molding and crafting Daphne for years. They'd been in bed together, both literally and figuratively, as he wanted to create the ultimate heir. Someone who demonstrated the most devotion and excellence in the business."

"How do you know all this?" I asked. Venetti and Rex were supposedly archrivals.

"From my own inquiries, and because I received this." He handed me an envelope, old and wrinkled from many readings. It was from Rex.

Mr. Kirkland looked over my shoulder as we read the brief letter together. At the end, our heads popped up at the same time.
Venetti nodded in appreciation of the situation.

I said, "So Rex writes you an antagonizing missive, and his very
plan is what led to his own downfall."

"Exactly. Hubris often does. Long before that, Rex had taunted
me, and every other boss, that he'd been grooming a new leader
for years, that it was a powerful person. But here, in the letter,
when he says that he's decided to choose his own son instead of
that other person, I think he slipped when he wrote 'she.' It had to
be Daphne. I'd known they were sharing a bed, but then I looked
into it further and discovered their partnership."

I tapped my hand with the letter, thinking. Venetti went on, "It
was right after that letter that Rex was killed, then not too long
after that, your parents were killed, Lane."

"So, perhaps Daphne got wind that Rutherford was going to be
Rex's leader; she would not be his choice after all," I suggested.

"Perhaps, but we can't be certain," he said.

"Oh, I think we can." He and Raff both stopped and looked at
me abruptly. "I saw her kill Rutherford."

After a beat of silence, he said, "That'd do it." We continued
walking as I told him about the scene I'd witnessed when I was
ten. After I paused, he said, "Let's see . . . let's see . . . yes, this
makes sense. This is what I believe: Daphne is working quietly
and diabolically behind the scenes, but no one knows her work.
She hasn't been in the spotlight at all, waiting and pining for her
moment to shine. She believes she'll be the chosen leader. But
then she gets word that Rex is not going to choose her after all
she'd sacrificed. Only one person is in her way: Rutherford. So she
gets with Donagan, and maybe suggests that it would be wise to
get Rutherford and the Lorians out of the way once and for all."

"But why come after me? I don't think she cares that there isn't
a statute of limitations with murder," I said.

"No, she doesn't. But she does care if it gets out that Rex never
intended her to be the leader. Her mental abilities were always in
question. Whether her insanity is an act or not, it was a cause for
concern. I think that you were the only witness to that murder,

plus my letter from Rex, not to mention anything else he let out of the bag while he taunted people, could be enough to make her colleagues question her leadership."

I nodded and said, "Right, she went to London to shore up the strength of her leadership there, so she's probably doing the same here. There are plenty of other Red Scroll people still around to claim that throne if she never had Rex's blessing."

Including her children, Tucker and Eliza. *Good Lord.*

"One more thing," I added. "How does my mother fit into all this? Why did Daphne kill Sparks right after he mistook me for Charlie?"

Venetti paused for a long moment, then said quietly, "Charlie . . . was my friend."

Raff and I caught each other's eye. Sadness permeated those four words, his face telling a long story.

Venetti cleared his throat and said, "Charlie and I knew each other from our childhood neighborhood. We ended up on opposite sides of the law most of the time, but she had a way of bringing life to everyone around her. I just . . . I always liked her. I let her down. I should've done a better job protecting her."

I darted my eyes to Kirkland, who had a look of wonder on his face.

"Charlie had been an informant for me. *Only* when I was on the right side of the law, I might add. She was the one who suspected Daphne first. I always wondered if she'd witnessed something that would have revealed who Daphne really was or confirmed Rex's own fears that she wasn't fit."

At this thought, Kirkland gruffly replied, "You know, I think you may be right. Charlie had quite an intuition. Maybe she didn't witness an event as much as Daphne could tell she saw through her ruse. You're like that, Lane. You can see behind the smoke screen that a lot of people put up. See the real person. I like that. Makes me feel like Charlie's still around, know what I mean?"

"I do, Kirkland. I do. Well . . ." said the growly voice of Venetti. "I'm glad we had this meeting. Say hello to all your friends surrounding the place," he said with a wry grin. "I think we'll be getting on this train."

I looked down the track to see an oncoming train, its single white light illuminating the tunnel. Raff nodded curtly and scanned the area as well as each car as it roared past with a *whoosh* of wind.

"Before you go, sir," I yelled over the noise of the train. "Can we assume you'll be spreading the word about Daphne?"

His black eyes focused on me and if I didn't know he was on my side at the moment, I'd have taken a step back to get away from that fierce countenance. "Absolutely. Take care of yourself, Lane. She won't need to silence you anymore, but you've got a scorned and embarrassed enemy now. Be careful."

My stomach dropped at his words, but I held out my hand. "Thank you for being a friend to my mom. And to me."

He took my hand into his, looking into my eyes, searching. He found what he was looking for and a smile lit his eyes.

"You're welcome."

CHAPTER 73

Late that night, after work and after Aunt Evelyn and Mr. Kirkland retired for the night, Finn and I sat in the little room off our kitchen with the fireplace crackling and sending sparks here and there. The snow on the maple tree out back frosted the branches and gave the tree an ethereal glow as it slowly moved in the winter wind.

"Well, at least it makes sense now, why Venetti's been benevolent toward you, Lane," said Finn, resting his elbows on his knees.

"Yeah, my mother and Uncle Louie, childhood friends . . . hard to imagine," I said, shaking my head. "I always knew there was something there. I kept half wondering if he'd turn out to be my real uncle or something. But I confirmed with Evelyn that Charlotte was an only child. For sure."

He grinned at me. "You checked hospital records, didn't you?"

"Yes." I reached over and poured us both more wine. "Oh, hey! I have something for you. I picked it up at the Strand." I ran up to my room and brought down the slim, burgundy volume of *Macbeth*.

"Ooh, it's lovely, Lane. I love it," he said, feeling the embossed leather and appreciating the craftsmanship.

"Look inside," I said with an eager smile.

He carefully opened it and said, "Oh my God. I can't believe you did this." Inside, at the top, I had written, "With all our love and thanks." Then I signed it, and I had the cast of *Voodoo Macbeth*, along with Orson Welles and the Battles, also sign it. Florence even put a little heart next to her name.

"I'll always cherish it, love," he said. "It's meant a lot to me, the whole play as well as Orson's production. What it's stood for both in my life and for my friends . . . *thank you*."

"You're welcome," I said, delighted.

I curled my legs up into my moss-green velvet chair and fingered the pearl dagger that I'd also brought in with me. I sipped my wine, in a thoughtful mood, while Finn looked through Shakespeare's masterpiece.

"You know," I said, "this dagger, and what it stood for, is just what we needed to get through this last case, both here and in London."

"What do you mean?" asked Finn as he came over and perched on the edge of my chair.

"Well, to get through the ugliness of what Sean had planned for you, and all those lies, we had to trust and believe that we could do it, that we could find the beauty in the midst of those ashes."

He nodded as he took the dagger carefully into his hands.

I went on, "Then back here, *Voodoo* was going to be used for evil, but our friends saw through the deception and we believed we could work together. Hell, even Uncle Louie. His business has a dark side, to be sure, but he also was loyal to my mom and therefore me."

"Beauty out of adversity," said Finn softly. "It's actually the meaning of our whole life, Lane. Our era, our jobs, our family life . . ."

I smiled, a feeling of serenity washing over me as I thought of my mother tossing the dagger to Mr. Kirkland, telling him that we'd need it. We did. We needed that perspective above all else.

"I think I'll go get us some coffee," I said, about to get up.

"Hold on," said Finn with an intriguing catch to his voice. "Have you noticed that the end cap on this has a tiny, almost invisible latch?" he asked.

"No. Can you open it? What is it for?"

"Usually, you can store matches in the handle, or sometimes there's a tiny compass in the handle. But that's mostly in hunting knives." His long fingers carefully opened the end. The handle had a small hollow pommel. "There's something in there, but my fingers are too big. Can you use your nails to get it?"

"Sure, let me try." I pulled out a yellowed piece of parchment that looked very old. It was only a couple of inches square and I carefully opened it up. In an old kind of script was written,

We made this dagger to symbolize goodness that
grows in spite of darkness, and the courage that makes it so.

"Oooh, I like that," he said with relish. "Remember when you told me back in London that I wasn't cursed? Like Macbeth?" he asked. I nodded and he quickly went on, "Well, that's exactly what hit me. I'd needed to hear that goodness *could* come out of darkness. And I just needed the courage to believe it."

We spent the rest of the evening talking over coffee and cookies. We thought through the many instances of beauty coming out of darkness, wanting to cement it in our minds and hearts. We thought of Morgan's band of merry men, the cast of *Voodoo* and all they'd been through, team Fiorello, Louie Venetti, and our many new friends here and abroad. I'd have to write to tell John Tolkien and Jack Lewis back in England about the culmination of our mystery and the note we found in the dagger. They did so love a good story.

As Finn and I washed and dried our glasses and cups shoulder to shoulder at the kitchen sink, with playful teases and laughs that warmed my soul, I felt a deep sense of peace and happiness.

I knew Daphne was out there, and I knew she'd come after me. And God only knew where Tucker was and what he was planning. I just knew beyond a doubt that he *was* planning; it wasn't in his nature to quit. He was an enigma, complicated. He was ruthless, yet he had been scared about losing total control, about evil consuming him and losing his ability to choose. Something his mother certainly never worried about. She was the poster child for evil, truly a Mr. Hyde through and through. Tucker, though . . . I wasn't sure. Why care if you'd already fully given yourself over to evil?

No matter what was coming, I believed in the very core of my being that we'd figure it out. That goodness and beauty would triumph over adversity. That in the end, we would have the courage to make it so.

Epilogue

April 1937

His body was still stiff and not at one hundred percent but getting there after a few months of healing and working to regain his strength. He rolled his neck in the morning light shining through the long, slanted windows. He took a deep breath, relishing the feeling of a plan coming together.

It had taken quite a bit of research and networking in the States and abroad, but he had time on his hands. He was letting the other players squabble and fight while he waited in the wings for just the right moment.

The woman he'd cared for had deeply scarred him. It was a wound that remained raw and unable to heal, compared to the rest of his body. But he liked his new plan. He looked around him at the beauty surrounding the lavish appointments in the great room. Lane would've enjoyed this. Too bad it had to be used for his plan. It would be bittersweet, but in the end, a profound reckoning.

"Mr. Tucker Henslowe? The captain is ready for your tour, sir."

"Thank you, I've been looking forward to this for quite some time," he said.

"Excellent, sir, we are very proud of her and we look forward to your article. Welcome aboard the *Hindenburg*!"

> *Where shall we three meet again?*
> *In thunder, lightning, or in rain?*
> *When the hurlyburly's done, when the battle's lost and won.*

—the three witches, *Macbeth*

AUTHOR'S NOTE

You never really know who you're passing on the street, whether someone is destined for greatness, mediocrity, or evil. . . . The most beautiful thing about historical fiction is bringing those wondrous possibilities to light. There are fantastic points of real history threaded through my stories, as well as many cameo appearances. And reader be warned: Always read my Author's Notes. They're really fun and often if there are wild or spectacular parts to my story, especially where Mayor La Guardia is concerned, it probably actually happened in real life.

The flippers in pinball machines weren't developed until 1947. Before then, the ball would be launched and bounce off the pins randomly, landing wherever it might. So the game was definitely a gambling machine versus a game where skill could give the player a fighting chance. Fiorello's words when he talks about pinball were his actual words: "Only a moron or imbecile could get a thrill out of watching these sure-thing devices take people's money. Let this serve notice to owners, racketeers, and other riffraff who run this racket that they will enjoy no comfort!" taken from *The Napoleon of New York*.

The inspector's funeral: the folded flag presentation tradition goes all the way back to Civil War times. The bagpipes weren't officially at every NYPD funeral until 1959 with the Emerald Society, nicknamed the NYPD Irish Brigade, but at most Irish or Scottish funerals, the bagpipes were played even earlier than that. When an officer is fallen, the department retires the badge number forever. In this case, I chose Officer Rafael Ramos's badge number 6335, in memory of the killing of Wenjian Liu and Rafael Ramos, who were targeted in a police hate crime on December 20, 2014.

The Rockefeller Center skating rink was truly just being tried out that year, winter of 1937. And of course you know it was quite successful.

The situation at the Lower East Side relief station had been recorded by an eyewitness journalist and pretty much took place exactly as I wrote it, including Fio calling the mean derby-hatted guy an S of a B (his exact wording), vaulting the railing, timing how quickly the staff could get through their line of customers, and the long line of grateful citizens waiting for him outside. The scene of him taking on the role of magistrate at the Harlem precinct was also true, minus the role of Eugene Murk, as he's completely fictitious.

For my J.R.R. Tolkien and C. S. Lewis fans, you'll already recognize that the group Finn and Lane met with at the Bird and Baby outside of London was a famous writing and storytelling group that did exist in real history at Oxford: the Inklings. I tried to be true to their personalities, but of course the entire scene is fictitious. However, the description of the Bird, the men in the group, and many other tidbits mentioned were true including their debate on whether or not John Tolkien should name his favorite Hobbit home Bag End, from his aunt Jane's farm. His mother did die of diabetes in real life when he was only twelve. The group had several members, but some of the core members were: John (J.R.R.) Tolkien, C. S. (Jack) Lewis, Warren Lewis, Adam Fox, and Owen Barfield.

The Inklings met weekly from the early thirties until late 1949 and from it came such inspiration as *The Hobbit*, which was released later in 1937 (you can be sure it will make an appearance when Lane reads it), The Lord of the Rings trilogy, and C. S. Lewis's *The Chronicles of Narnia*, among a multitude of other works of genius. Any issues of accuracy are my fault entirely or derived from artistic necessity. The mention about the Lorians is because I always wonder about the backstories of what inspires people. I thought it would be fun to play on the Lorians' name for the land of Lórien that Tolkien writes about.

The Savoy Hotel had many firsts as a hotel from their pink tablecloths to flooding the lobby for a party that imitated the streets of Venice. It's a fascinating place and I recommend their cocktail book. Lane loved their coffee, and in 1937 they were the first hotel to offer its own special coffee blend for sale by mail order.

John Barnard—driver of the divine Riley Imp that races by Finn and Lane as they're on their way to a date at the Met—was a mention of a real-life person. He was the uncle of Amber Rose, a lovely friend of mine and a book lover. John did in fact arrive on the *Queen Mary*'s maiden voyage and took his Riley Imp on board. He was pulled over in New Jersey for speeding, but was just given a warning because they were so shocked he was British and driving a right-hand-drive car. And who can really blame the guy for speeding?

Dead Shot Mary was a real person and amazing! She did in fact accrue one thousand arrests before she retired and was the first woman on the force to use her service weapon to apprehend a criminal. She was the first female detective and did in fact use all those methods I talked about with her pickpocket squad, including bringing family members along once in a while to aid in her disguise.

"Mambo Italiano" was written and performed much later, but I've often come across old songs that later make an official appearance by a big performer. I really wanted this song, I wanted people to think of the rhythms and the words, so for the sake of the story, I fictionalized this as the origin story of the song. The mambo began in the late thirties, though didn't officially become a dance craze in the States until the 1940s, but the rhumba started on the East Coast in the 1930s.

Voodoo Macbeth's final performances were at the Majestic in Brooklyn, in October 1936. Here I have taken artistic license to have it end a few months later, in February of 1937. Welles's words when he speaks to Lane at the beginning are actually his own words, abbreviated by me, from a BBC interview in 1982. At the end of his life, he felt *Voodoo* was his greatest contribution.

In 1939, Mayor Fiorello La Guardia appointed Jane Bolin as the first black, female judge in the country. She remained the sole black, female judge for twenty years.

In 1937, Winston Churchill considered himself in a political wilderness and was well known as an author. He really did have a tiny photograph of himself in the first issue of *Time* magazine in November 1936, casually flipping the bird to the camera as he fingered his tooth.

Lane's scene at the Strand bookstore was totally true to history. And little Fred, who took over the store years later for his father, Ben, was always known for saying, "We just need more books."

BIBLIOGRAPHY

Abbott, Berenice, and Elizabeth McCausland. *New York in the Thirties*. New York: Dover Publications, 1939.

Brodsky, Alyn. *The Great Mayor*. New York: St. Martin's Press, 2003.

Browne, Arthur. *One Righteous Man, Samuel Battle and the Shattering of the Color Line in New York*. Boston: Beacon Press, 2015.

Carpenter, Humphrey. *The Letters of J.R.R. Tolkien*. New York: Houghton Mifflin Harcourt, 2000.

Cuneo, Ernest. *Life with Fiorello*. New York: The Macmillan Company, 1955.

Duriez, Colin. *The Oxford Inklings*. Oxford, England: Lion Hudson, 2015.

Footner, Hulbert. *New York: City of Cities*. Philadelphia: J. B. Lippencott, 1937.

France, Richard. *Orson Welles on Shakespeare: The W.P.A. and Mercury Theatre Playscripts*. New York: Greenwood Press, 1990.

Jackson, Kenneth T. *The Encyclopedia of New York City*. New Haven and London: Yale University Press, 1995.

Manchester, William. *The Last Lion, Winston Spencer Churchill, Visions of Glory*. New York: Hachette Book Group, 1983.

Jeffers, H. Paul. *The Napoleon of New York*. New York: John Wiley & Sons, Inc., 2002.

Jennings, Peter, and Todd Brewster. *The Century*. New York: Doubleday, 1998.

Lowe, David Garrard. *Art Deco New York*. New York: Watson-Guptill Publications, a Division of VNU Business Media, Inc., 2004.

Poremba, David Lee. *Detroit: A Motor City History*. Charleston, South Carolina: Arcadia Publishing, 2001.

Schwartz, Ronnie Nelson. *Voices from the Federal Theater*. Wisconsin: The University of Wisconsin Press, 2003.

Stolley, Richard B. *LIFE: Our Century in Pictures*. Boston, New York, London: Bulfinch Press, 1999.

THE PEARL DAGGER

L. A. Chandlar

ABOUT THIS GUIDE

The suggested questions are included
to enhance your group's reading of
L. A. Chandlar's *The Pearl Dagger*.

DISCUSSION QUESTIONS

1. What was your favorite scene and why? Do you have a scene that keeps coming back to mind for any reason, even a minor one? Why was it memorable? (For me, I loved the moment at the hospital when Lane and Finn are assaulted by Sean and Finn is accused of poisoning their father. I loved how it caused Lane and Finn to close ranks, to draw from each other that sanctity in the midst of chaos and injustice. I also LOVED that final scene of *Voodoo Macbeth* and Finn's reactions. "The charm's wound up!" Gives me chills. And of course when Lane realizes backstage, "Daphne's here.")

2. This idea came up in *The Gold Pawn* and will overarch into all of the books in this series, the theme from the Latin phrase that Lane discovers in her father's study: *pulchritudo ex cinere*, "beauty out of ashes." I think it sums up this era and the beauty that I wanted to highlight. What are examples of beauty coming out of ashes in *The Pearl Dagger*? My father-in-law had a large tree hit by lightning once, and his brother made a giant mantel out of it, which is what gave me the idea for the dagger itself. Do you have any specific examples where beauty came out of ashes in your own life?

3. Why do you think Finn found it so hard to see through Sean and Gwen's conniving schemes? Why could Lane see through them? (I think sometimes people have uncanny abilities in seeing truth; they just have excellent intuition. Also, I think that when you've had deception in your own life, or an extremely difficult relationship, you can see it in other people).

4. I love having some characters who are altruistic, some who are absolutely evil, and some who are complicated with the potential for both. How do you feel about the infamous gangster Louie Venetti? What do you think will be developing next for him? How about Tucker?

5. The humorous, lively, and vigorous tones of this entire series stem from all that I've read about Fiorello La Guardia. Is it surprising to you, from what you've come to understand about the 1930s? How so? What scenes or aspects surprised you? (The vitality of this era, especially the tone of the mayor's office, completely surprised me! And that's what gave me the inspiration to write these books. In fact, Lane exhibits many of Fiorello's characteristics herself because I wanted the whole of the book to reflect his kind of spirit. I think, in our time, we've forgotten just who Fiorello was, and I hope to redeem that. We need heroes, especially funny ones who fight for the little guy, who soak up every ounce of life possible.)

Connect with  Us

Visit us online at
KensingtonBooks.com
to read more from your favorite authors, see books
by series, view reading group guides, and more.

Join us on social media

for sneak peeks, chances to win books and prize packs,
and to share your thoughts with other readers.

facebook.com/kensingtonpublishing
twitter.com/kensingtonbooks

Tell us what you think!

To share your thoughts, submit a review,
or sign up for our eNewsletters, please visit:
KensingtonBooks.com/TellUs.